EVOlutioN

Created by   Joe Infurnari . Joseph Keatinge . Christopher Sebela . Joshua Williamson

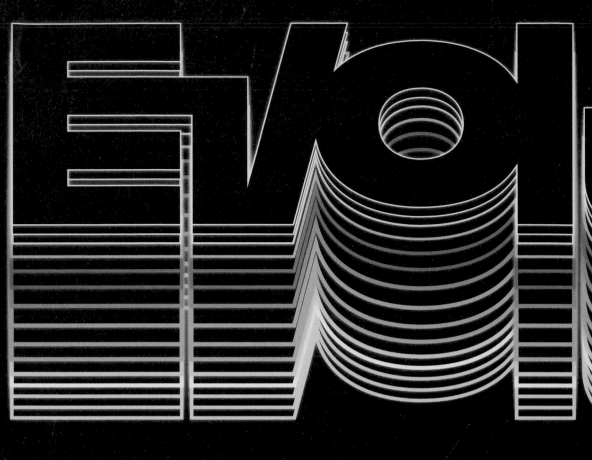

WRITERS
James Asmus
Joseph Keatinge
Christopher Sebela

COLORIST
Jordan Boyd

ARTIST
Joe Infurnari

LETTERER
Pat Brosseau

EVOLUTION VOLUME 3. FIRST PRINTING. OCTOBER 2019. PUBLISHED BY IMAGE COMICS, INC. OFFICE OF PUBLICATION: 2701 NW VAUGHN ST., STE. 780, PORTLAND, OR 97210. ORIGINALLY PUBLISHED IN SINGLE MAGAZINE FORM AS EVOLUTION #13-18. EVOLUTION™ (INCLUDING ALL PROMINENT CHARACTERS FEATURED HEREIN), ITS LOGO AND ALL CHARACTER LIKENESSES ARE TRADEMARKS OF SKYBOUND, LLC, UNLESS OTHERWISE NOTED. IMAGE COMICS® AND ITS LOGOS ARE REGISTERED TRADEMARKS AND COPYRIGHTS OF IMAGE COMICS, INC. ALL RIGHTS RESERVED. NO PART OF THIS PUBLICATION MAY BE REPRODUCED OR TRANSMITTED IN ANY FORM OR BY ANY MEANS (EXCEPT FOR SHORT EXCERPTS FOR REVIEW PURPOSES) WITHOUT THE EXPRESS WRITTEN PERMISSION OF IMAGE COMICS, INC. ALL NAMES, CHARACTERS, EVENTS AND LOCALES IN THIS PUBLICATION ARE ENTIRELY FICTIONAL. ANY RESEMBLANCE TO ACTUAL PERSONS (LIVING OR DEAD), EVENTS OR PLACES, WITHOUT SATIRIC INTENT, IS COINCIDENTAL. PRINTED IN THE U.S.A. FOR INFORMATION REGARDING THE CPSIA ON THIS PRINTED MATERIAL CALL: 203-595-3636
ISBN: 978-1-5343-1246-3

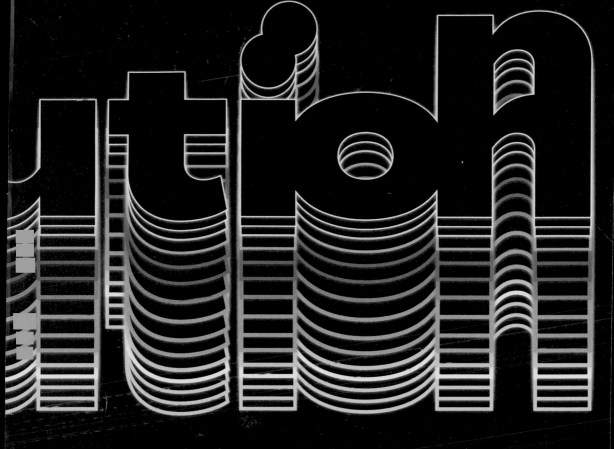

EDITOR	**COVER ART**
Jon Moisan	**Joe Infurnari**
	Jordan Boyd
LOGO DESIGN	**PRODUCTION DESIGN**
Andres Juarez	**Carina Taylor**

SKYBOUND LLC. *ROBERT KIRKMAN* CHAIRMAN *DAVID ALPERT* CEO *SEAN MACKIEWICZ* SVP, EDITOR-IN-CHIEF *SHAWN KIRKHAM* SVP, BUSINESS DEVELOPMENT *BRIAN HUNTINGTON* VP, ONLINE CONTENT *SHAUNA WYNNE* PUBLICITY DIRECTOR *ANDRES JUAREZ* ART DIRECTOR *JON MOISAN* EDITOR *ARIELLE BASICH* ASSOCIATE EDITOR *KATE CAUDILL* ASSISTANT EDITOR *CARINA TAYLOR* GRAPHIC DESIGNER *PAUL SHIN* BUSINESS DEVELOPMENT MANAGER *JOHNNY O'DELL* SOCIAL MEDIA MANAGER *DAN PETERSEN* SR. DIRECTOR OF OPERATIONS & EVENTS FOREIGN RIGHTS INQUIRIES: AG@SEQUENTIALRIGHTS.COM OTHER LICENSING INQUIRIES:CONTACT@SKYBOUND.COM WWW.SKYBOUND.COM

IMAGE COMICS, INC. *ROBERT KIRKMAN* CHIEF OPERATING OFFICER *ERIK LARSEN* CHIEF FINANCIAL OFFICER *TODD MCFARLANE* PRESIDENT *MARC SILVESTRI* CHIEF EXECUTIVE OFFICER *JIM VALENTINO* VICE PRESIDENT *ERIC STEPHENSON* PUBLISHER/CHIEF CREATIVE OFFICER *JEFF BOISON* DIRECTOR OF PUBLISHING PLANNING & BOOK TRADE SALES *CHRIS ROSS* DIRECTOR OF DIGITAL SALES *JEFF STANG* DIRECTOR OF SPECIALTY SALES *KAT SALAZAR* DIRECTOR OF PR & MARKETING *DREW GILL* ART DIRECTOR *HEATHER DOORNINK* PRODUCTION DIRECTOR *NICOLE LAPALME* CONTROLLER WWW.IMAGECOMICS.COM

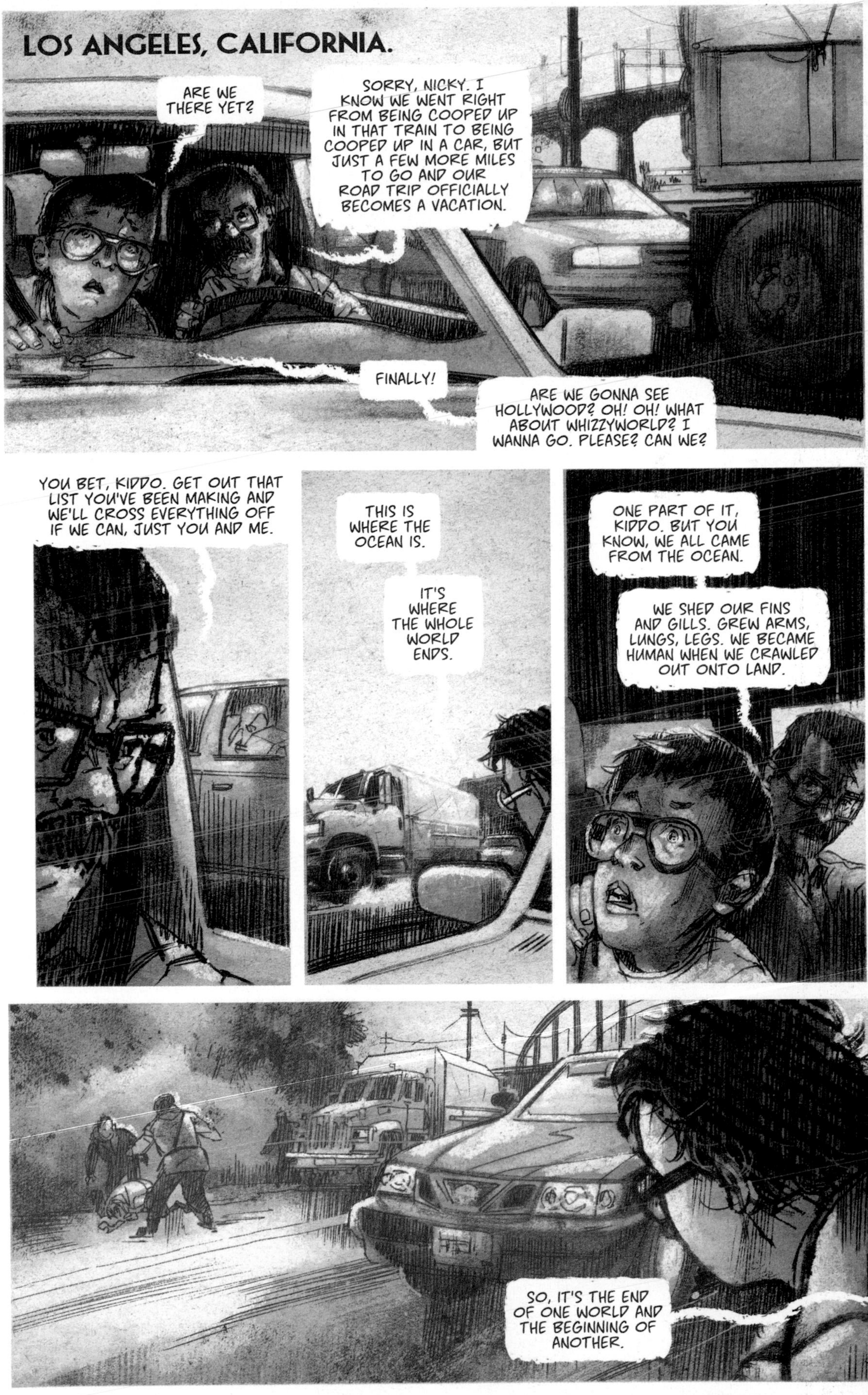
LOS ANGELES, CALIFORNIA.
ARE WE THERE YET?
SORRY, NICKY. I KNOW WE WENT RIGHT FROM BEING COOPED UP IN THAT TRAIN TO BEING COOPED UP IN A CAR, BUT JUST A FEW MORE MILES TO GO AND OUR ROAD TRIP OFFICIALLY BECOMES A VACATION.
FINALLY!
ARE WE GONNA SEE HOLLYWOOD? OH! OH! WHAT ABOUT WHIZZYWORLD? I WANNA GO. PLEASE? CAN WE?
YOU BET, KIDDO. GET OUT THAT LIST YOU'VE BEEN MAKING AND WE'LL CROSS EVERYTHING OFF IF WE CAN, JUST YOU AND ME.
THIS IS WHERE THE OCEAN IS.
IT'S WHERE THE WHOLE WORLD ENDS.
ONE PART OF IT, KIDDO. BUT YOU KNOW, WE ALL CAME FROM THE OCEAN.
WE SHED OUR FINS AND GILLS. GREW ARMS, LUNGS, LEGS. WE BECAME HUMAN WHEN WE CRAWLED OUT ONTO LAND.
SO, IT'S THE END OF ONE WORLD AND THE BEGINNING OF ANOTHER.

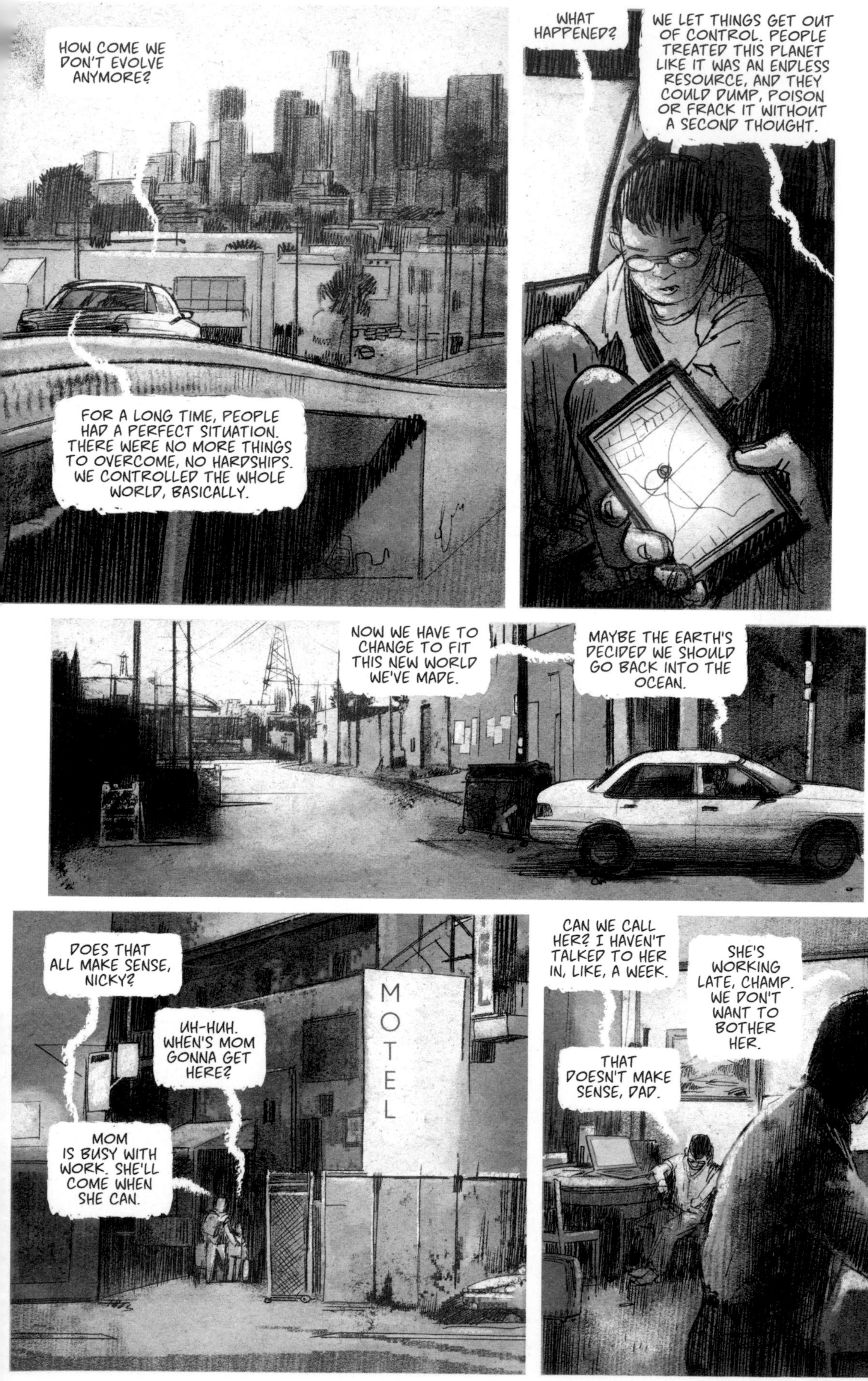
HOW COME WE DON'T EVOLVE ANYMORE?
FOR A LONG TIME, PEOPLE HAD A PERFECT SITUATION. THERE WERE NO MORE THINGS TO OVERCOME, NO HARDSHIPS. WE CONTROLLED THE WHOLE WORLD, BASICALLY.
WHAT HAPPENED?
WE LET THINGS GET OUT OF CONTROL. PEOPLE TREATED THIS PLANET LIKE IT WAS AN ENDLESS RESOURCE, AND THEY COULD DUMP, POISON OR FRACK IT WITHOUT A SECOND THOUGHT.
NOW WE HAVE TO CHANGE TO FIT THIS NEW WORLD WE'VE MADE.
MAYBE THE EARTH'S DECIDED WE SHOULD GO BACK INTO THE OCEAN.
DOES THAT ALL MAKE SENSE, NICKY?
UH-HUH. WHEN'S MOM GONNA GET HERE?
MOM IS BUSY WITH WORK. SHE'LL COME WHEN SHE CAN.
MOTEL
CAN WE CALL HER? I HAVEN'T TALKED TO HER IN, LIKE, A WEEK.
SHE'S WORKING LATE, CHAMP. WE DON'T WANT TO BOTHER HER.
THAT DOESN'T MAKE SENSE, DAD.

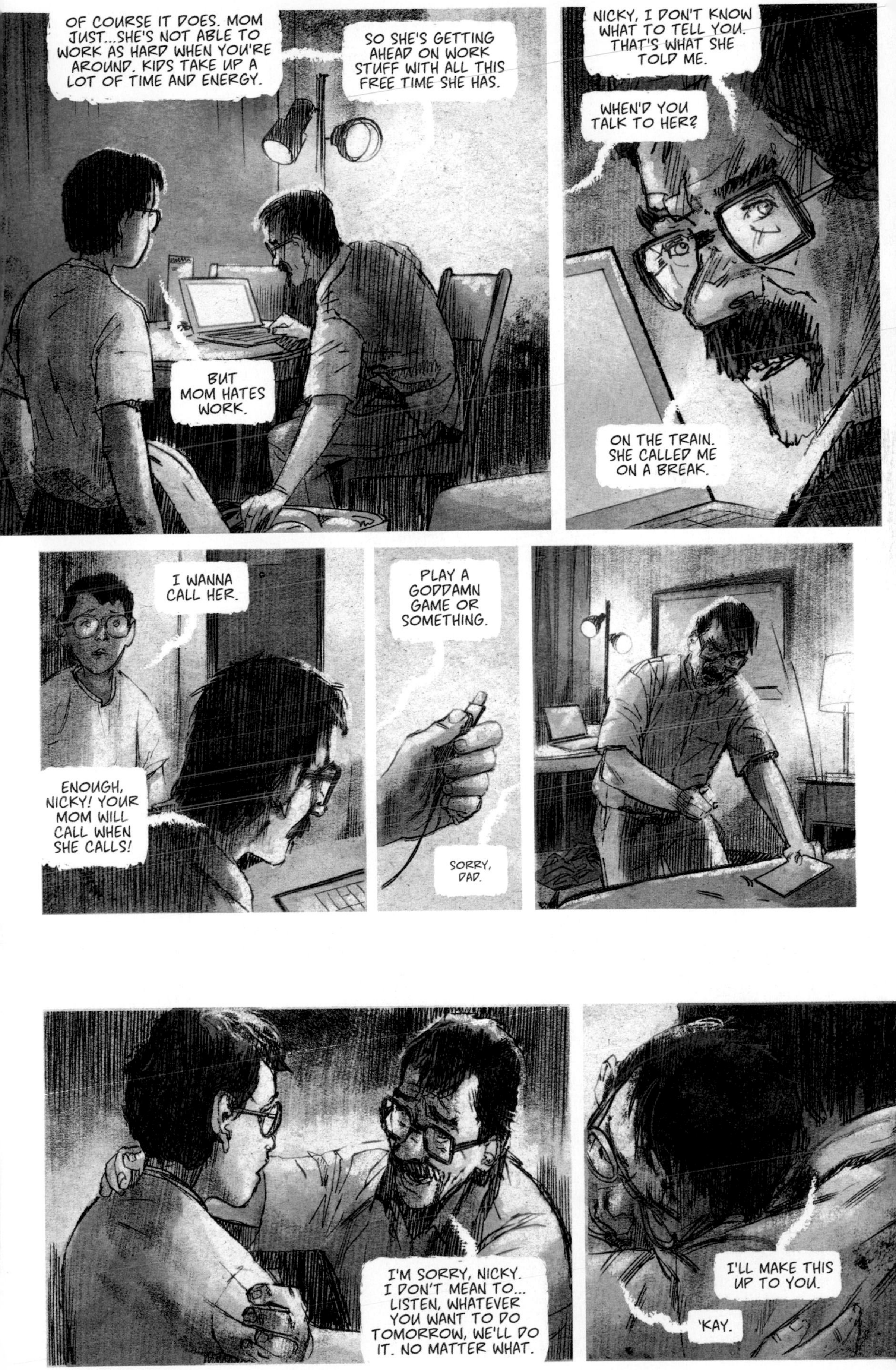
OF COURSE IT DOES. MOM JUST...SHE'S NOT ABLE TO WORK AS HARD WHEN YOU'RE AROUND. KIDS TAKE UP A LOT OF TIME AND ENERGY.
SO SHE'S GETTING AHEAD ON WORK STUFF WITH ALL THIS FREE TIME SHE HAS.
BUT MOM HATES WORK.
NICKY, I DON'T KNOW WHAT TO TELL YOU. THAT'S WHAT SHE TOLD ME.
WHEN'D YOU TALK TO HER?
ON THE TRAIN. SHE CALLED ME ON A BREAK.
I WANNA CALL HER.
ENOUGH, NICKY! YOUR MOM WILL CALL WHEN SHE CALLS!
PLAY A GODDAMN GAME OR SOMETHING.
SORRY, DAD.
I'M SORRY, NICKY. I DON'T MEAN TO... LISTEN, WHATEVER YOU WANT TO DO TOMORROW, WE'LL DO IT. NO MATTER WHAT.
I'LL MAKE THIS UP TO YOU.
'KAY.

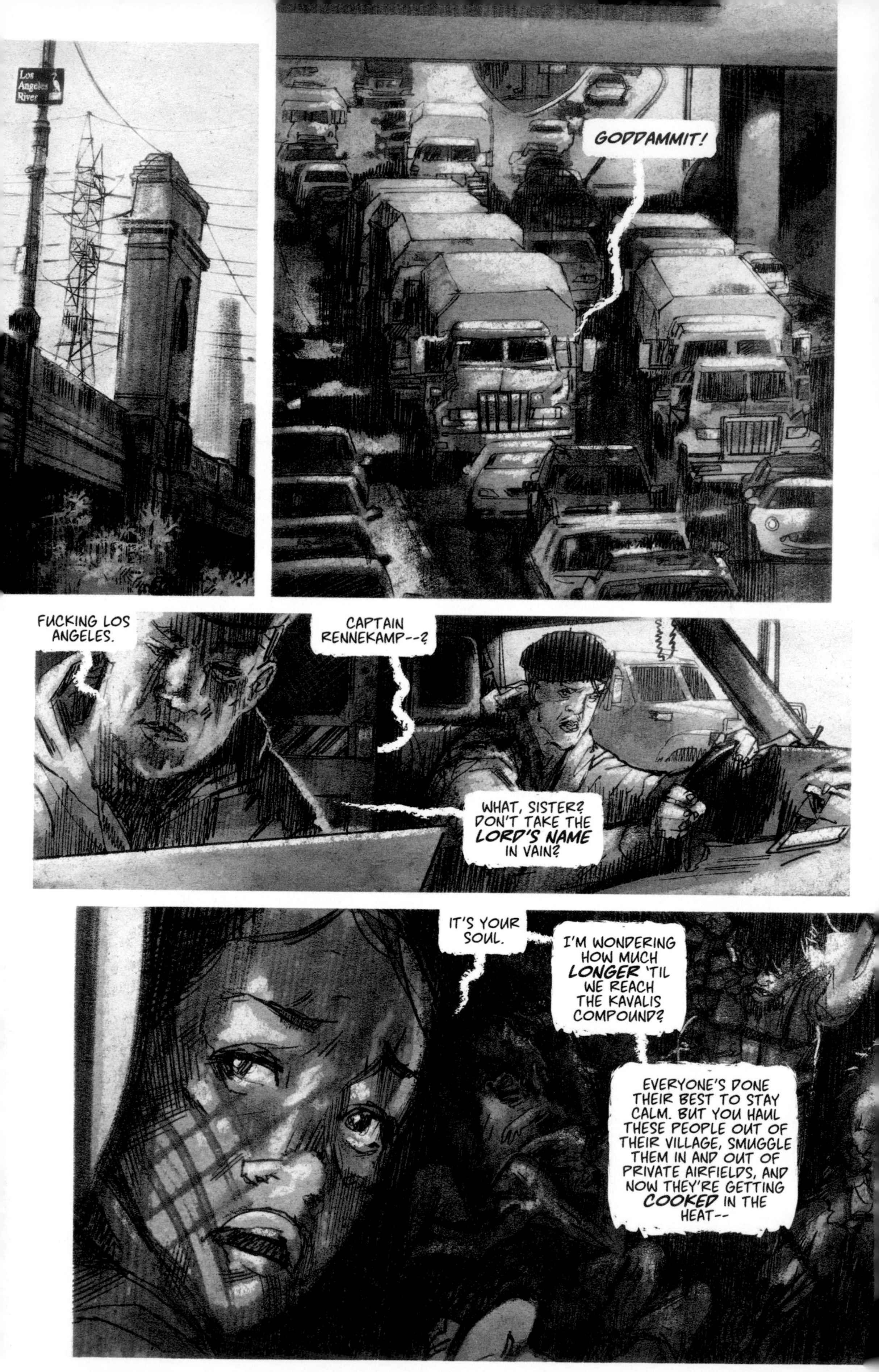
Los Angeles River
GODDAMMIT!
FUCKING LOS ANGELES.
CAPTAIN RENNEKAMP--?
WHAT, SISTER? DON'T TAKE THE LORD'S NAME IN VAIN?
IT'S YOUR SOUL.
I'M WONDERING HOW MUCH LONGER 'TIL WE REACH THE KAVALIS COMPOUND?
EVERYONE'S DONE THEIR BEST TO STAY CALM. BUT YOU HAUL THESE PEOPLE OUT OF THEIR VILLAGE, SMUGGLE THEM IN AND OUT OF PRIVATE AIRFIELDS, AND NOW THEY'RE GETTING COOKED IN THE HEAT--

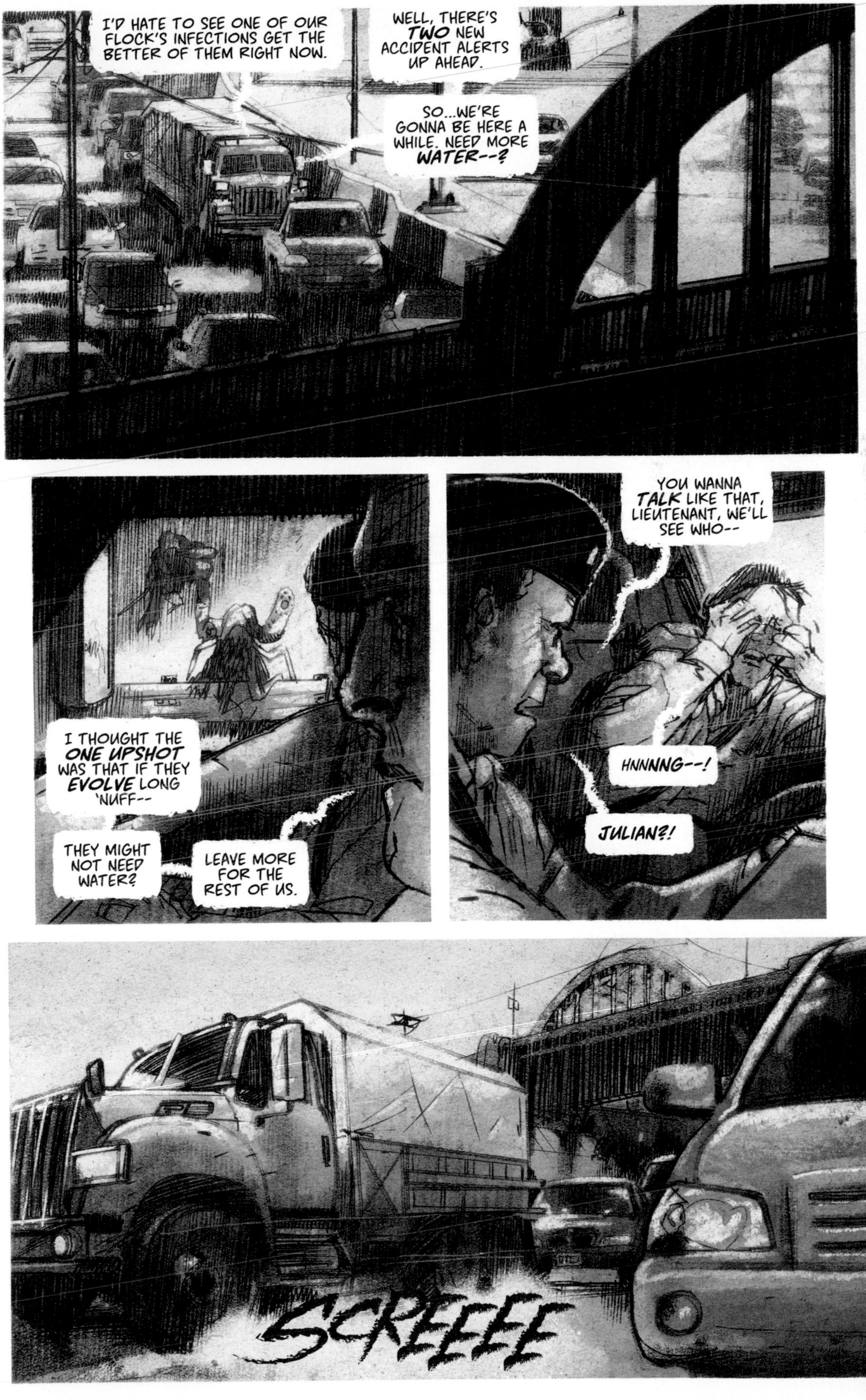

I'D HATE TO SEE ONE OF OUR FLOCK'S INFECTIONS GET THE BETTER OF THEM RIGHT NOW.
WELL, THERE'S TWO NEW ACCIDENT ALERTS UP AHEAD.
SO...WE'RE GONNA BE HERE A WHILE. NEED MORE WATER--?
I THOUGHT THE ONE UPSHOT WAS THAT IF THEY EVOLVE LONG 'NUFF--
THEY MIGHT NOT NEED WATER?
LEAVE MORE FOR THE REST OF US.
YOU WANNA TALK LIKE THAT, LIEUTENANT, WE'LL SEE WHO--
HNNNNG--!
JULIAN?!
SCREEEE

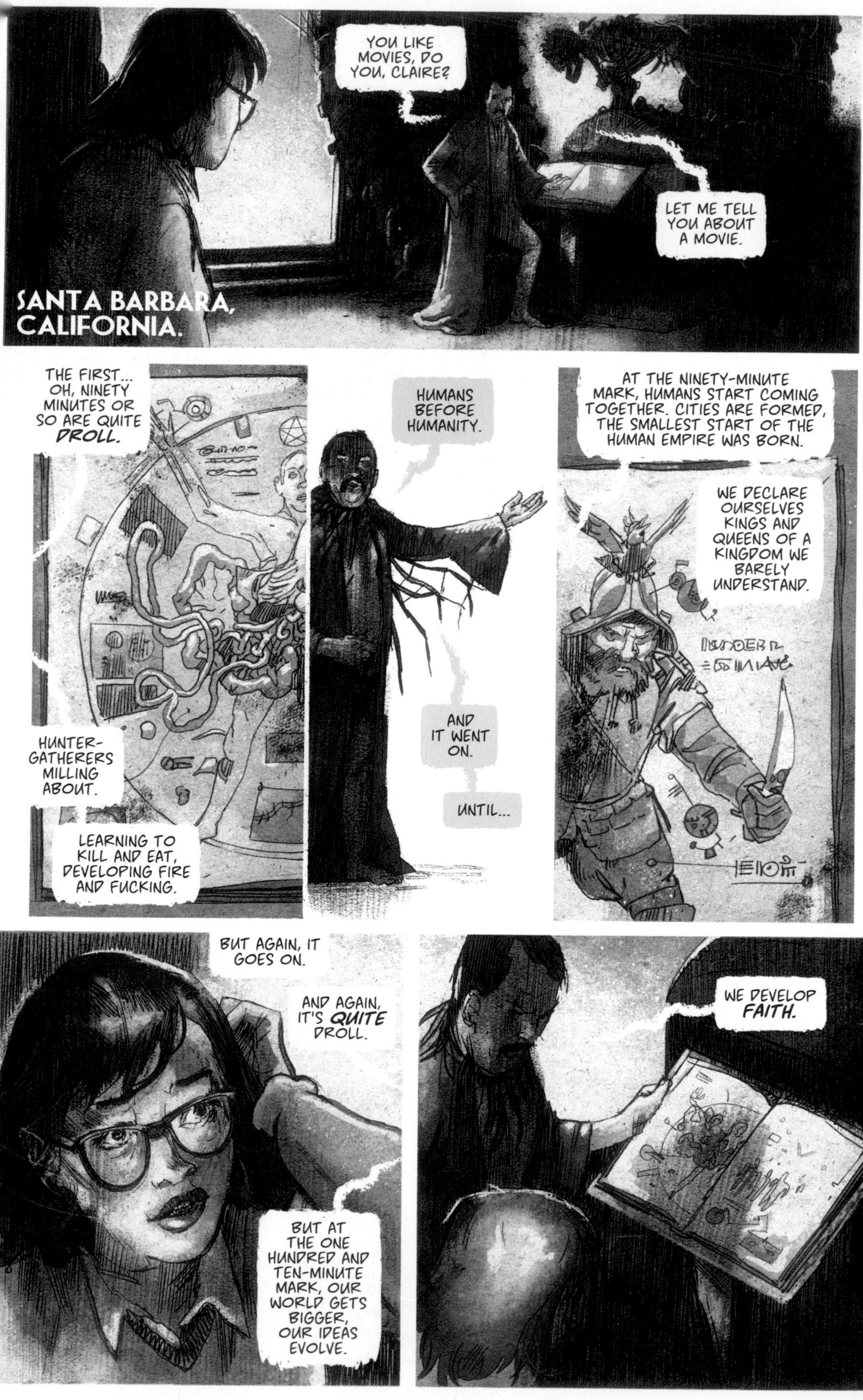
YOU LIKE MOVIES, DO YOU, CLAIRE?
LET ME TELL YOU ABOUT A MOVIE.
SANTA BARBARA, CALIFORNIA.
THE FIRST... OH, NINETY MINUTES OR SO ARE QUITE DROLL.
HUNTER-GATHERERS MILLING ABOUT.
LEARNING TO KILL AND EAT, DEVELOPING FIRE AND FUCKING.
HUMANS BEFORE HUMANITY.
AND IT WENT ON.
UNTIL...
AT THE NINETY-MINUTE MARK, HUMANS START COMING TOGETHER. CITIES ARE FORMED, THE SMALLEST START OF THE HUMAN EMPIRE WAS BORN.
WE DECLARE OURSELVES KINGS AND QUEENS OF A KINGDOM WE BARELY UNDERSTAND.
BUT AGAIN, IT GOES ON.
AND AGAIN, IT'S QUITE DROLL.
BUT AT THE ONE HUNDRED AND TEN-MINUTE MARK, OUR WORLD GETS BIGGER, OUR IDEAS EVOLVE.
WE DEVELOP FAITH.

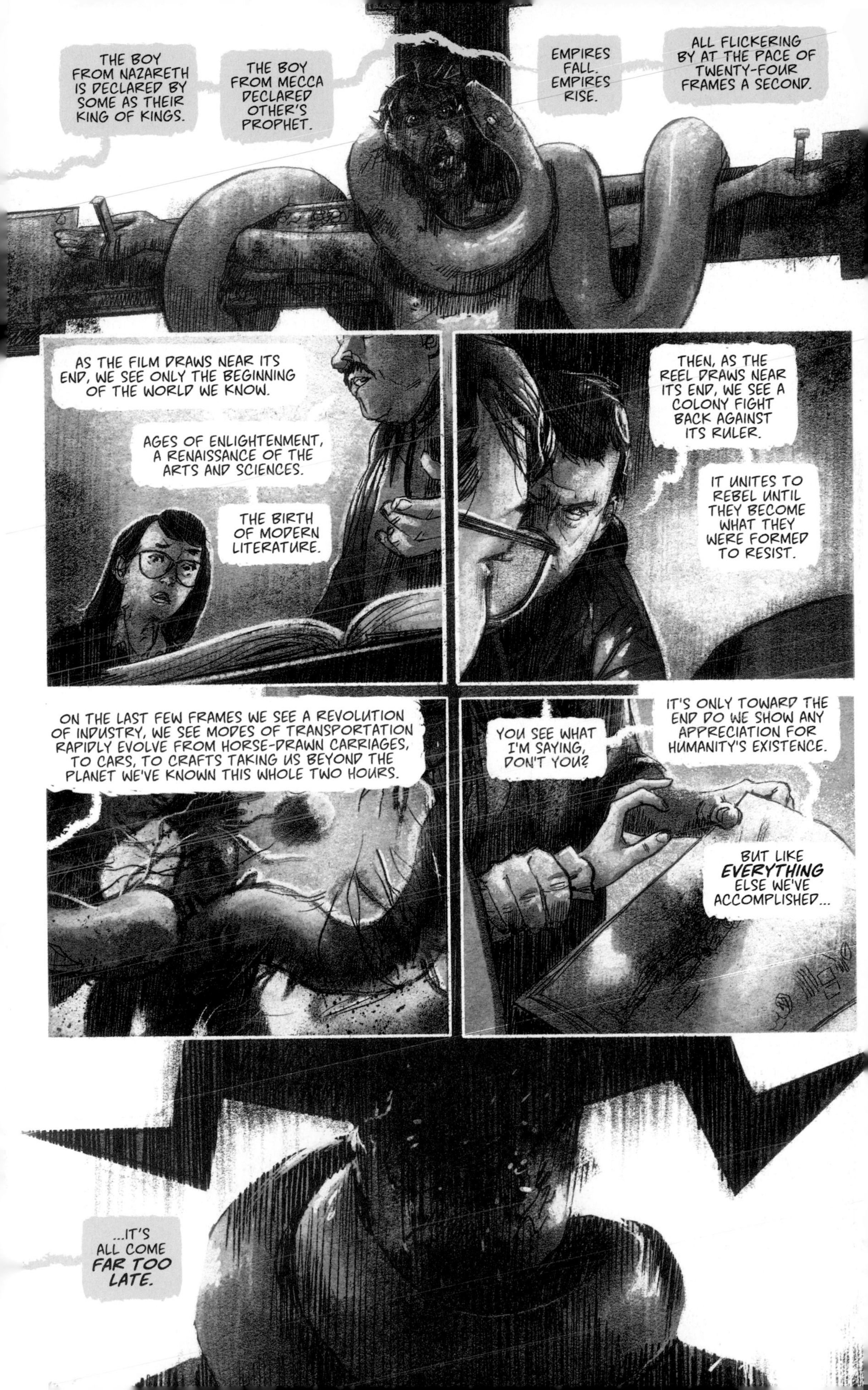
THE BOY FROM NAZARETH IS DECLARED BY SOME AS THEIR KING OF KINGS.
THE BOY FROM MECCA DECLARED OTHER'S PROPHET.
EMPIRES FALL. EMPIRES RISE.
ALL FLICKERING BY AT THE PACE OF TWENTY-FOUR FRAMES A SECOND.
AS THE FILM DRAWS NEAR ITS END, WE SEE ONLY THE BEGINNING OF THE WORLD WE KNOW.
AGES OF ENLIGHTENMENT, A RENAISSANCE OF THE ARTS AND SCIENCES.
THE BIRTH OF MODERN LITERATURE.
THEN, AS THE REEL DRAWS NEAR ITS END, WE SEE A COLONY FIGHT BACK AGAINST ITS RULER.
IT UNITES TO REBEL UNTIL THEY BECOME WHAT THEY WERE FORMED TO RESIST.
ON THE LAST FEW FRAMES WE SEE A REVOLUTION OF INDUSTRY, WE SEE MODES OF TRANSPORTATION RAPIDLY EVOLVE FROM HORSE-DRAWN CARRIAGES, TO CARS, TO CRAFTS TAKING US BEYOND THE PLANET WE'VE KNOWN THIS WHOLE TWO HOURS.
YOU SEE WHAT I'M SAYING, DON'T YOU?
IT'S ONLY TOWARD THE END DO WE SHOW ANY APPRECIATION FOR HUMANITY'S EXISTENCE.
BUT LIKE EVERYTHING ELSE WE'VE ACCOMPLISHED...
...IT'S ALL COME FAR TOO LATE.

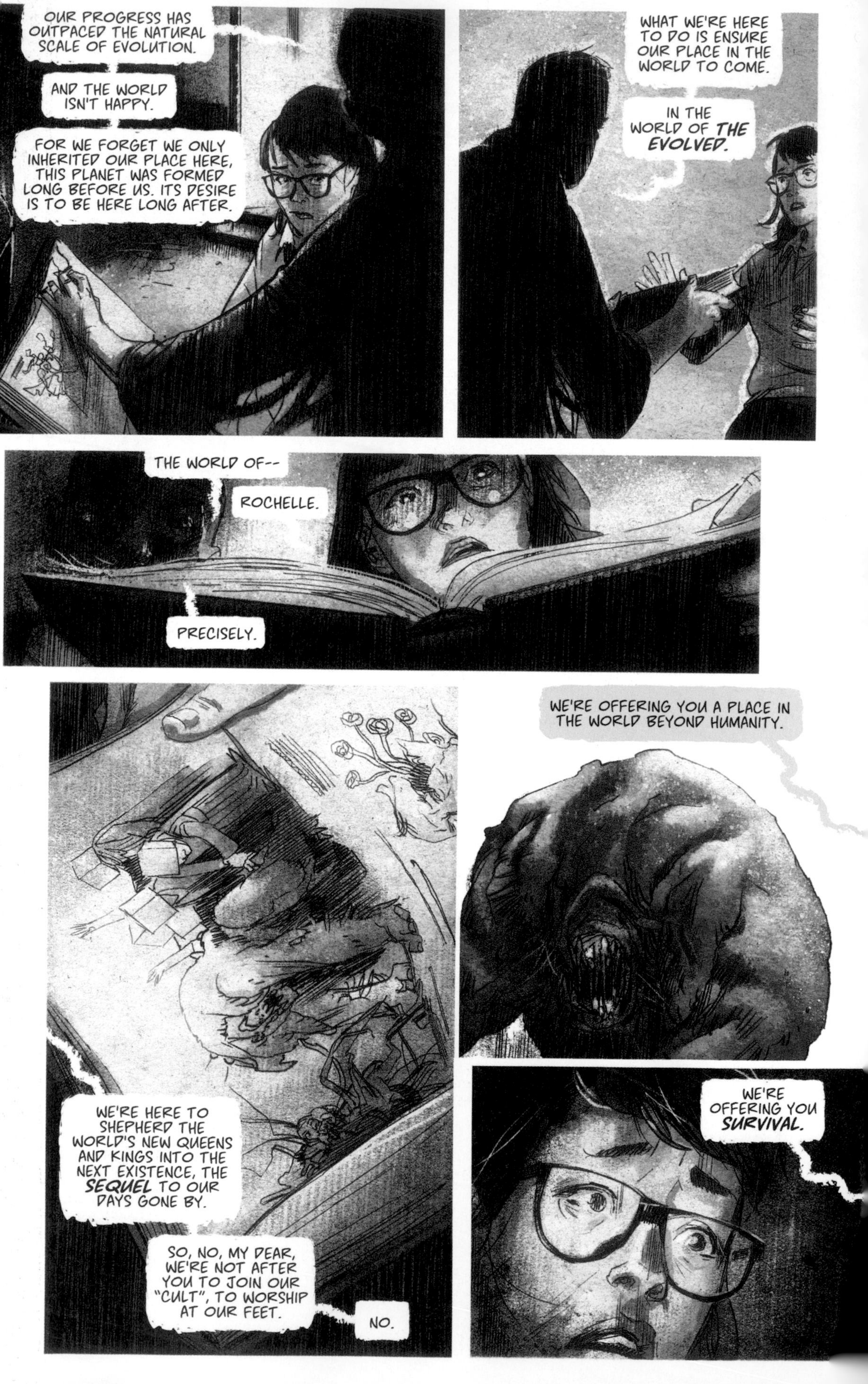
OUR PROGRESS HAS OUTPACED THE NATURAL SCALE OF EVOLUTION.
AND THE WORLD ISN'T HAPPY.
FOR WE FORGET WE ONLY INHERITED OUR PLACE HERE, THIS PLANET WAS FORMED LONG BEFORE US. ITS DESIRE IS TO BE HERE LONG AFTER.
WHAT WE'RE HERE TO DO IS ENSURE OUR PLACE IN THE WORLD TO COME.
IN THE WORLD OF THE EVOLVED.
THE WORLD OF--
ROCHELLE.
PRECISELY.
WE'RE HERE TO SHEPHERD THE WORLD'S NEW QUEENS AND KINGS INTO THE NEXT EXISTENCE, THE SEQUEL TO OUR DAYS GONE BY.
SO, NO, MY DEAR, WE'RE NOT AFTER YOU TO JOIN OUR "CULT", TO WORSHIP AT OUR FEET.
NO.
WE'RE OFFERING YOU A PLACE IN THE WORLD BEYOND HUMANITY.
WE'RE OFFERING YOU SURVIVAL.

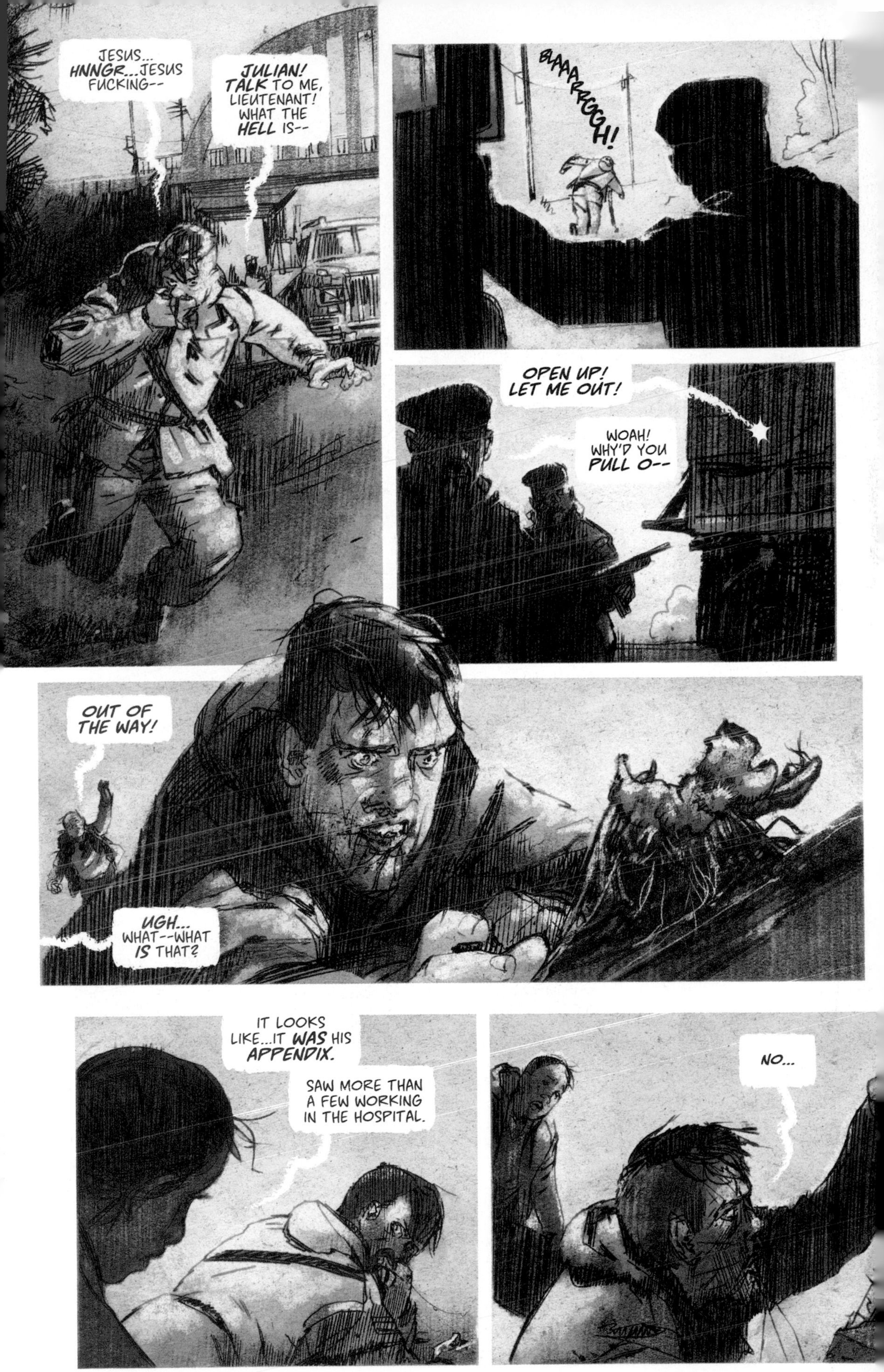

JESUS... HNNGR...JESUS FUCKING--
JULIAN! TALK TO ME, LIEUTENANT! WHAT THE HELL IS--
BLAAARRGGH!
OPEN UP! LET ME OUT!
WOAH! WHY'D YOU PULL O--
OUT OF THE WAY!
UGH... WHAT--WHAT IS THAT?
IT LOOKS LIKE...IT WAS HIS APPENDIX.
SAW MORE THAN A FEW WORKING IN THE HOSPITAL.
NO...

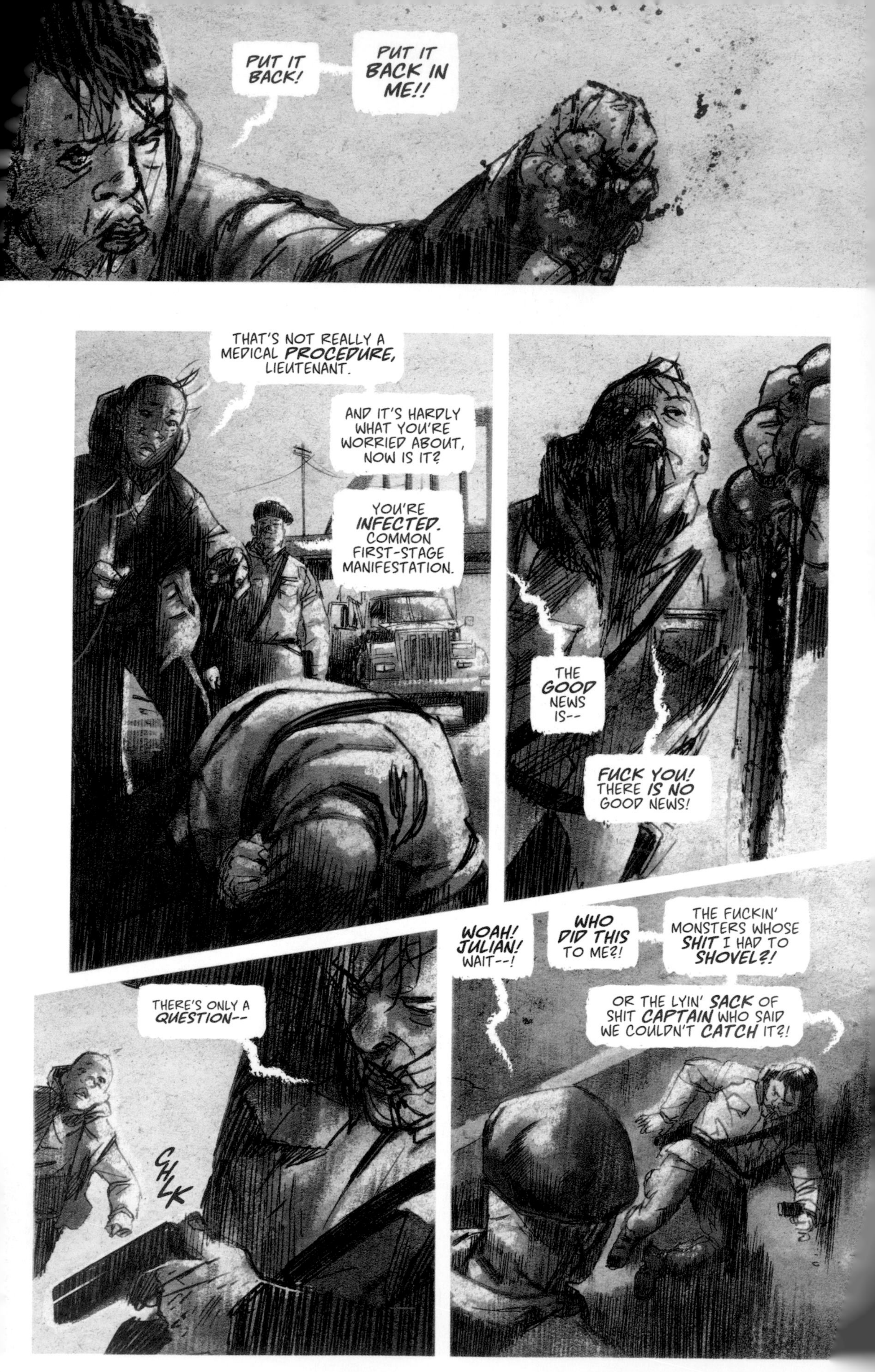
PUT IT BACK!
PUT IT BACK IN ME!!
THAT'S NOT REALLY A MEDICAL PROCEDURE, LIEUTENANT.
AND IT'S HARDLY WHAT YOU'RE WORRIED ABOUT, NOW IS IT?
YOU'RE INFECTED. COMMON FIRST-STAGE MANIFESTATION.
THE GOOD NEWS IS--
FUCK YOU! THERE IS NO GOOD NEWS!
THERE'S ONLY A QUESTION--
CHLK
WOAH! JULIAN! WAIT--!
WHO DID THIS TO ME?!
THE FUCKIN' MONSTERS WHOSE SHIT I HAD TO SHOVEL?!
OR THE LYIN' SACK OF SHIT CAPTAIN WHO SAID WE COULDN'T CATCH IT?!

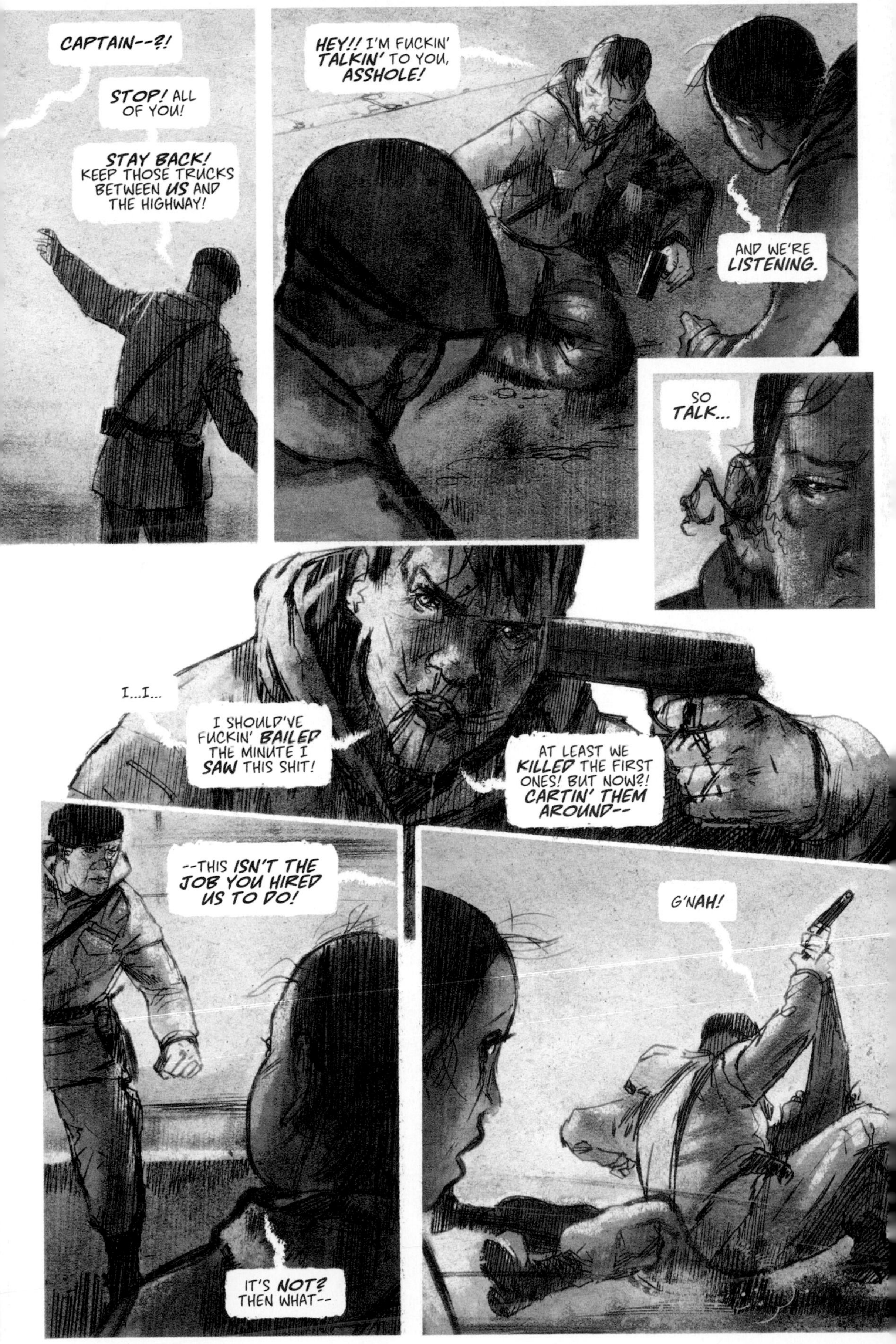
CAPTAIN--?!
STOP! ALL OF YOU!
STAY BACK! KEEP THOSE TRUCKS BETWEEN US AND THE HIGHWAY!
HEY!! I'M FUCKIN' TALKIN' TO YOU, ASSHOLE!
AND WE'RE LISTENING.
SO TALK...
I...I...
I SHOULD'VE FUCKIN' BAILED THE MINUTE I SAW THIS SHIT!
AT LEAST WE KILLED THE FIRST ONES! BUT NOW?! CARTIN' THEM AROUND--
--THIS ISN'T THE JOB YOU HIRED US TO DO!
IT'S NOT? THEN WHAT--
G'NAH!

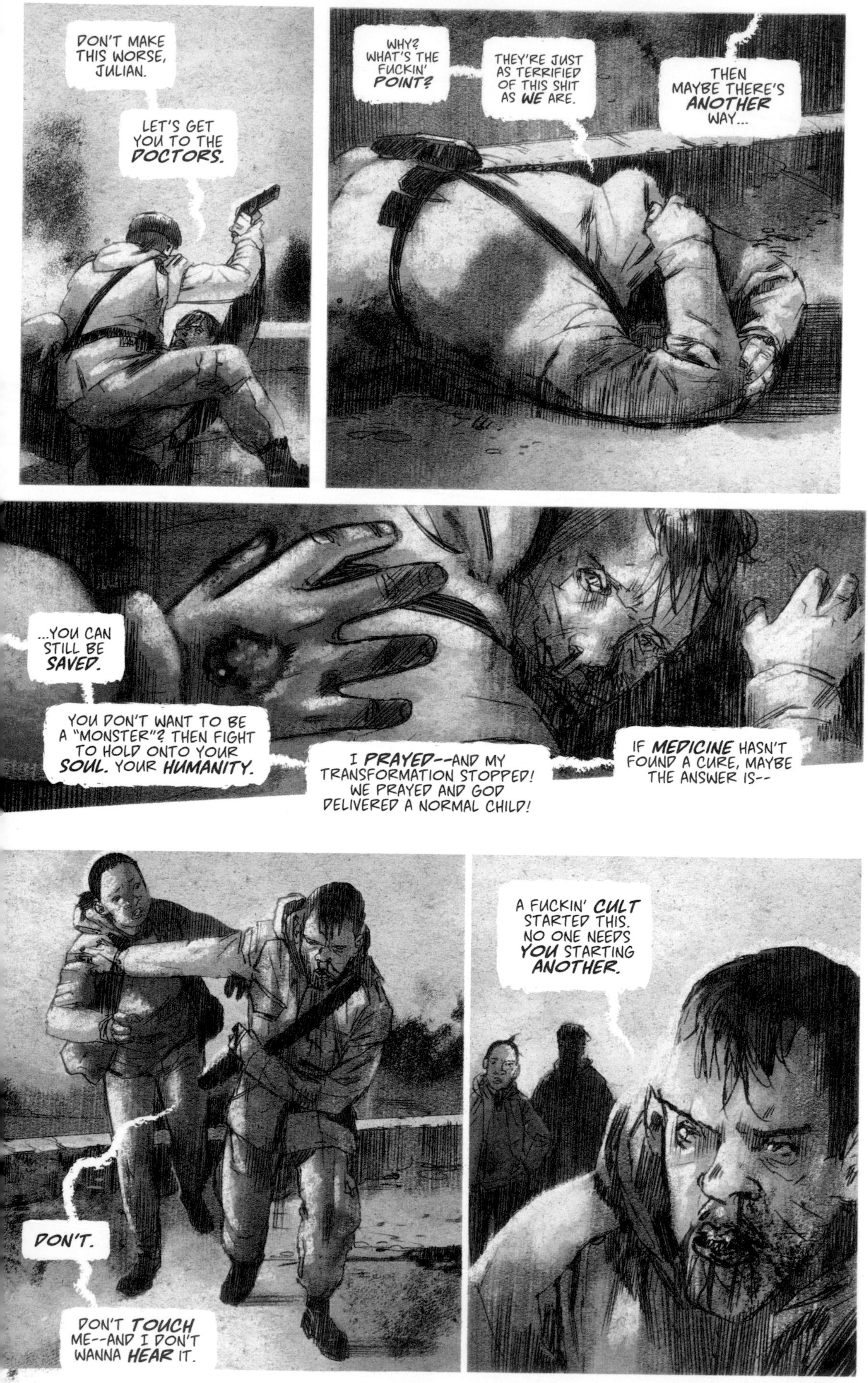
DON'T MAKE THIS WORSE, JULIAN.
LET'S GET YOU TO THE DOCTORS.
WHY? WHAT'S THE FUCKIN' POINT?
THEY'RE JUST AS TERRIFIED OF THIS SHIT AS WE ARE.
THEN MAYBE THERE'S ANOTHER WAY...
...YOU CAN STILL BE SAVED.
YOU DON'T WANT TO BE A "MONSTER"? THEN FIGHT TO HOLD ONTO YOUR SOUL. YOUR HUMANITY.
I PRAYED--AND MY TRANSFORMATION STOPPED! WE PRAYED AND GOD DELIVERED A NORMAL CHILD!
IF MEDICINE HASN'T FOUND A CURE, MAYBE THE ANSWER IS--
DON'T.
DON'T TOUCH ME--AND I DON'T WANNA HEAR IT.
A FUCKIN' CULT STARTED THIS. NO ONE NEEDS YOU STARTING ANOTHER.

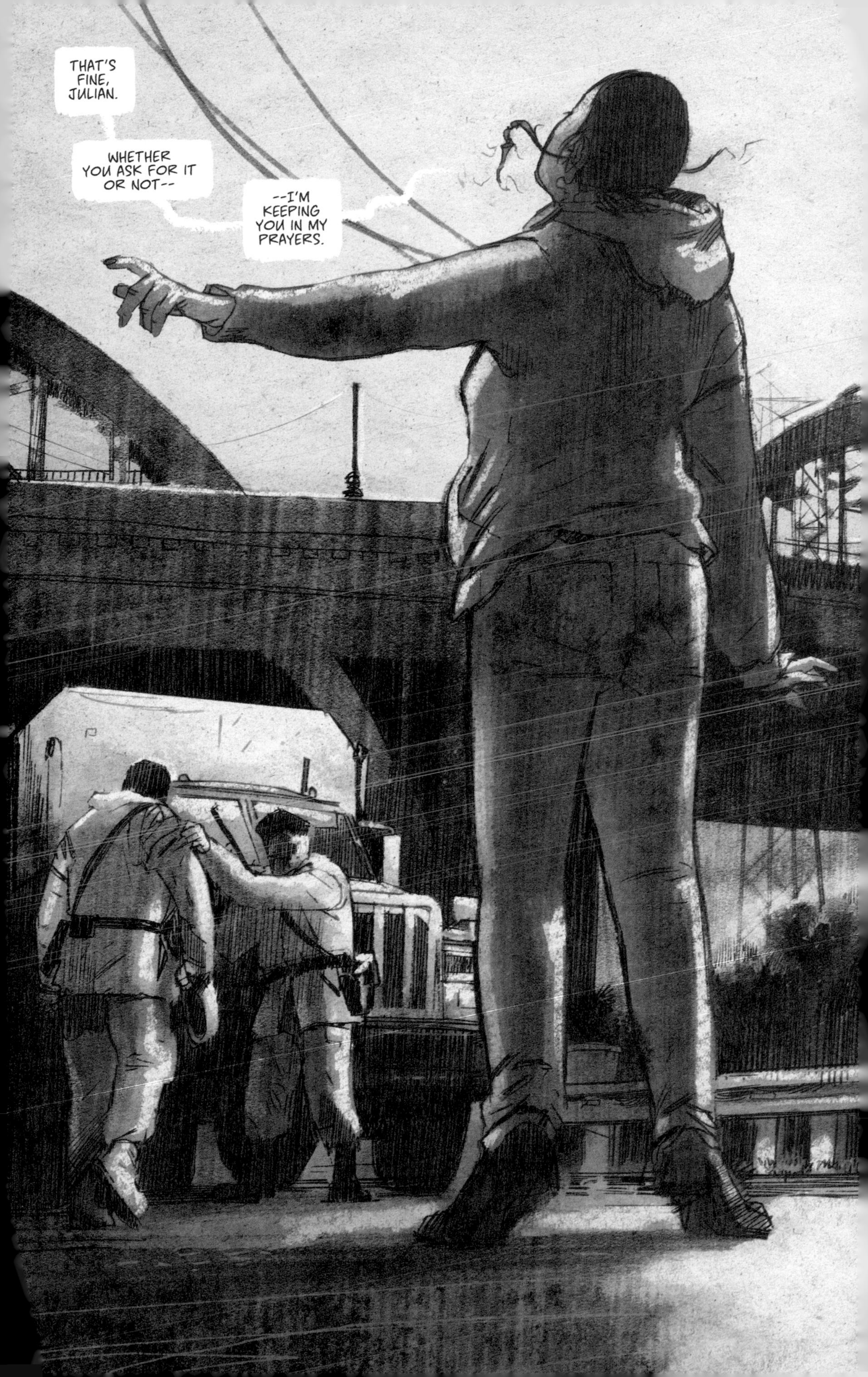
THAT'S FINE, JULIAN.
WHETHER YOU ASK FOR IT OR NOT--
--I'M KEEPING YOU IN MY PRAYERS.

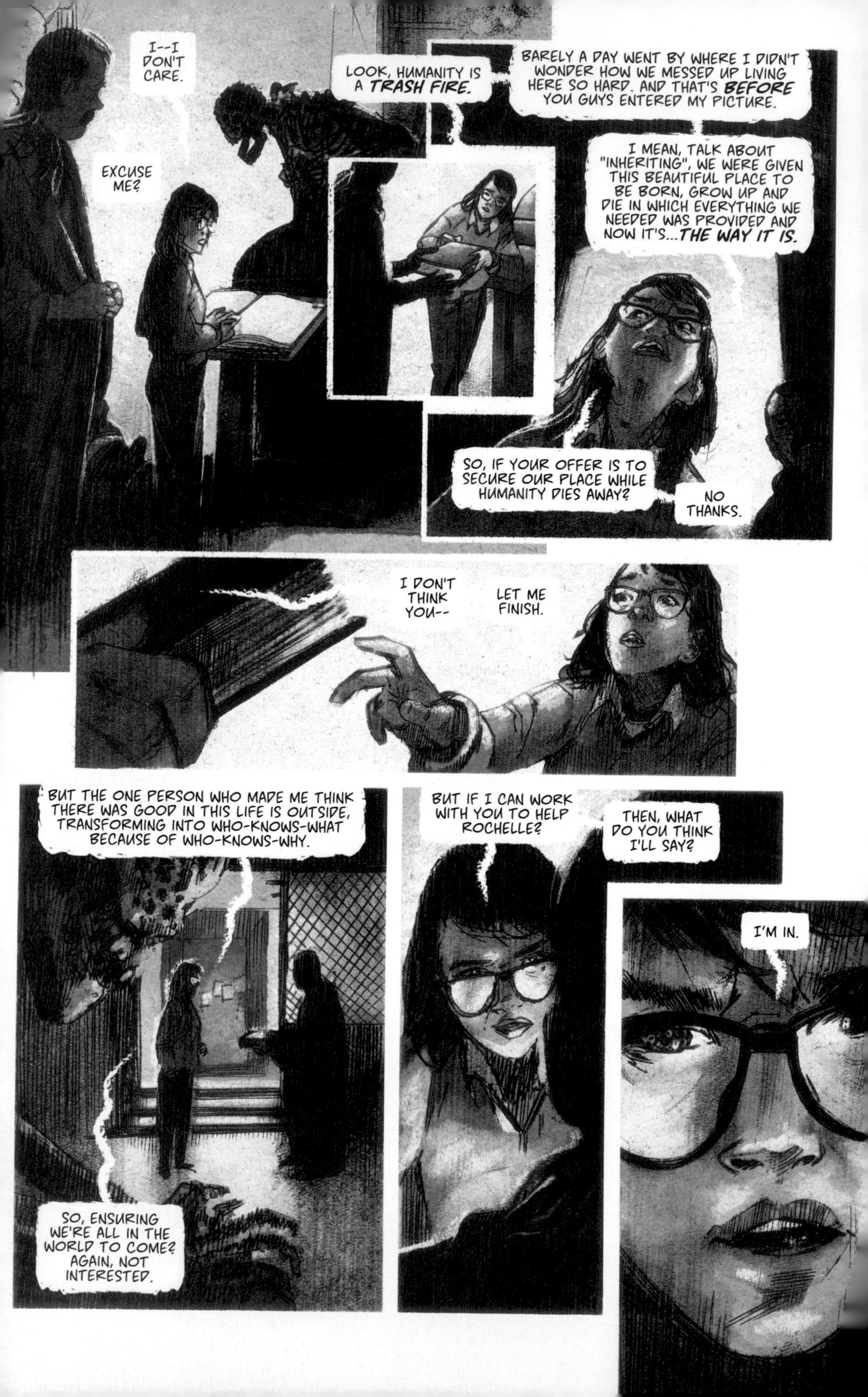
I--I DON'T CARE.
EXCUSE ME?
LOOK, HUMANITY IS A TRASH FIRE.
BARELY A DAY WENT BY WHERE I DIDN'T WONDER HOW WE MESSED UP LIVING HERE SO HARD. AND THAT'S BEFORE YOU GUYS ENTERED MY PICTURE.
I MEAN, TALK ABOUT "INHERITING", WE WERE GIVEN THIS BEAUTIFUL PLACE TO BE BORN, GROW UP AND DIE IN WHICH EVERYTHING WE NEEDED WAS PROVIDED AND NOW IT'S...THE WAY IT IS.
SO, IF YOUR OFFER IS TO SECURE OUR PLACE WHILE HUMANITY DIES AWAY?
NO THANKS.
I DON'T THINK YOU--
LET ME FINISH.
BUT THE ONE PERSON WHO MADE ME THINK THERE WAS GOOD IN THIS LIFE IS OUTSIDE, TRANSFORMING INTO WHO-KNOWS-WHAT BECAUSE OF WHO-KNOWS-WHY.
SO, ENSURING WE'RE ALL IN THE WORLD TO COME? AGAIN, NOT INTERESTED.
BUT IF I CAN WORK WITH YOU TO HELP ROCHELLE?
THEN, WHAT DO YOU THINK I'LL SAY?
I'M IN.

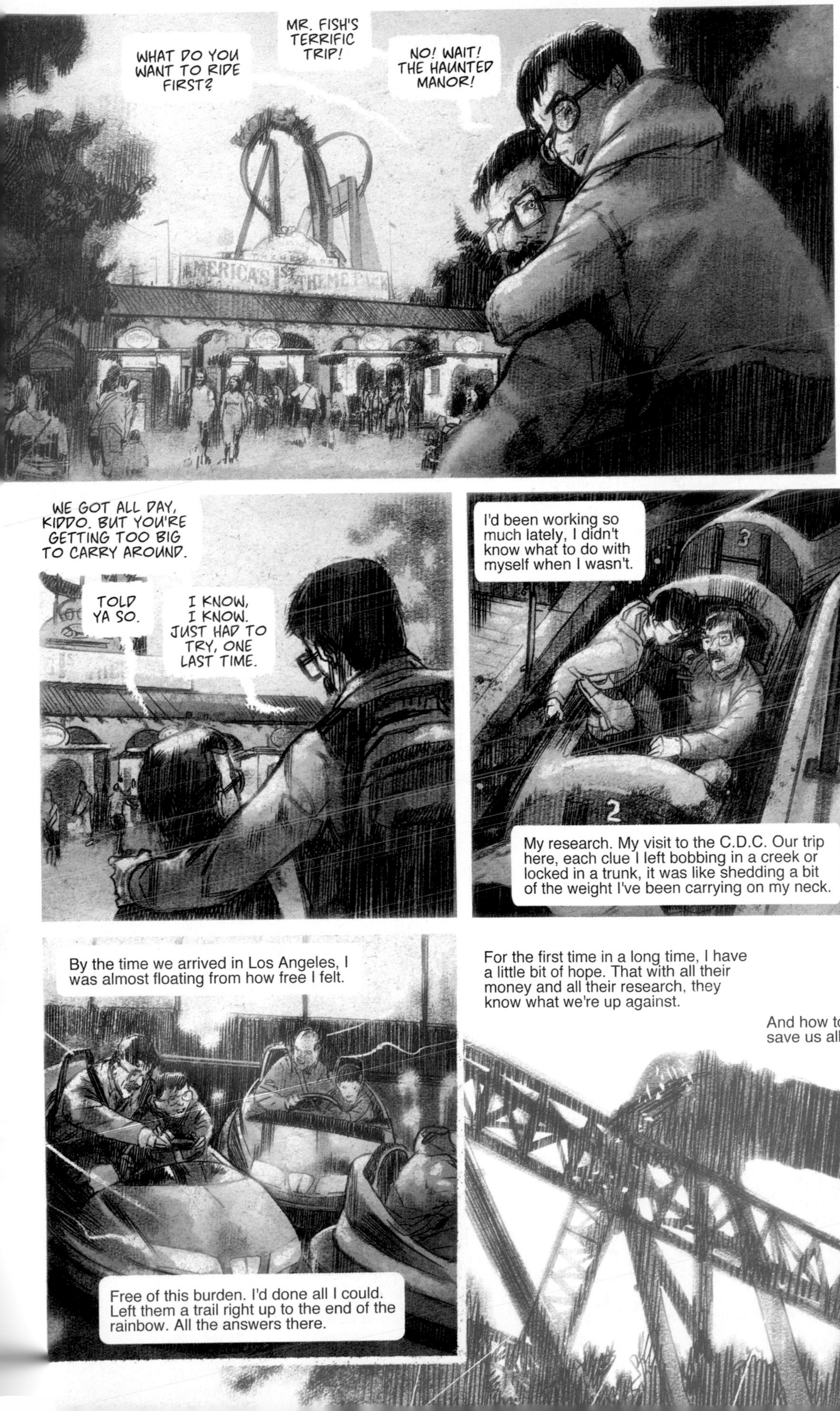
WHAT DO YOU WANT TO RIDE FIRST?
MR. FISH'S TERRIFIC TRIP!
NO! WAIT! THE HAUNTED MANOR!
AMERICA'S 1ST THEME PARK
WE GOT ALL DAY, KIDDO. BUT YOU'RE GETTING TOO BIG TO CARRY AROUND.
TOLD YA SO.
I KNOW, I KNOW. JUST HAD TO TRY, ONE LAST TIME.
I'd been working so much lately, I didn't know what to do with myself when I wasn't.
My research. My visit to the C.D.C. Our trip here, each clue I left bobbing in a creek or locked in a trunk, it was like shedding a bit of the weight I've been carrying on my neck.
By the time we arrived in Los Angeles, I was almost floating from how free I felt.
Free of this burden. I'd done all I could. Left them a trail right up to the end of the rainbow. All the answers there.
For the first time in a long time, I have a little bit of hope. That with all their money and all their research, they know what we're up against.
And how to save us all.

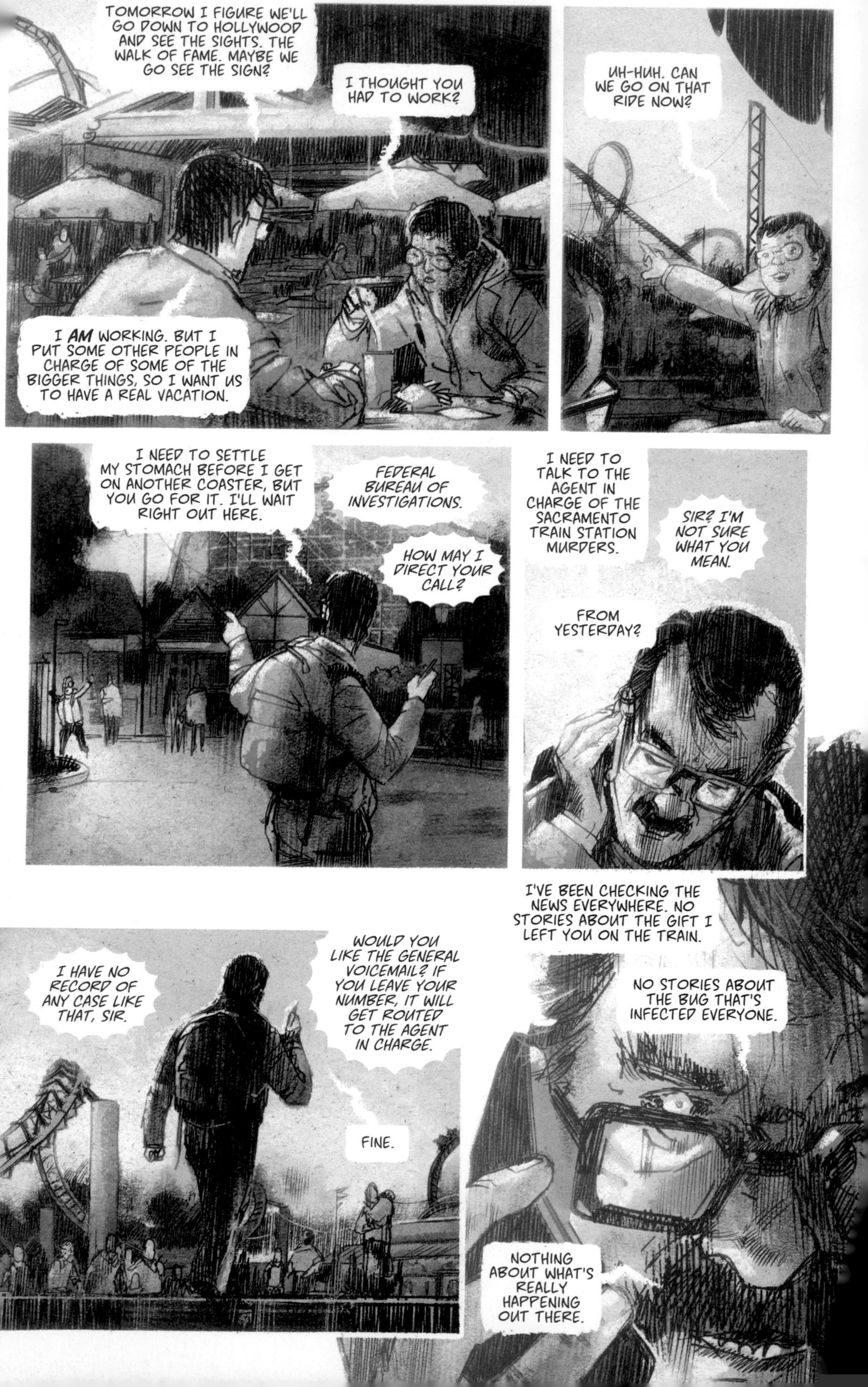
TOMORROW I FIGURE WE'LL GO DOWN TO HOLLYWOOD AND SEE THE SIGHTS. THE WALK OF FAME. MAYBE WE GO SEE THE SIGN?
I THOUGHT YOU HAD TO WORK?
I AM WORKING. BUT I PUT SOME OTHER PEOPLE IN CHARGE OF SOME OF THE BIGGER THINGS, SO I WANT US TO HAVE A REAL VACATION.
UH-HUH. CAN WE GO ON THAT RIDE NOW?
I NEED TO SETTLE MY STOMACH BEFORE I GET ON ANOTHER COASTER, BUT YOU GO FOR IT. I'LL WAIT RIGHT OUT HERE.
FEDERAL BUREAU OF INVESTIGATIONS.
HOW MAY I DIRECT YOUR CALL?
I NEED TO TALK TO THE AGENT IN CHARGE OF THE SACRAMENTO TRAIN STATION MURDERS.
SIR? I'M NOT SURE WHAT YOU MEAN.
FROM YESTERDAY?
I HAVE NO RECORD OF ANY CASE LIKE THAT, SIR.
WOULD YOU LIKE THE GENERAL VOICEMAIL? IF YOU LEAVE YOUR NUMBER, IT WILL GET ROUTED TO THE AGENT IN CHARGE.
FINE.
I'VE BEEN CHECKING THE NEWS EVERYWHERE. NO STORIES ABOUT THE GIFT I LEFT YOU ON THE TRAIN.
NO STORIES ABOUT THE BUG THAT'S INFECTED EVERYONE.
NOTHING ABOUT WHAT'S REALLY HAPPENING OUT THERE.

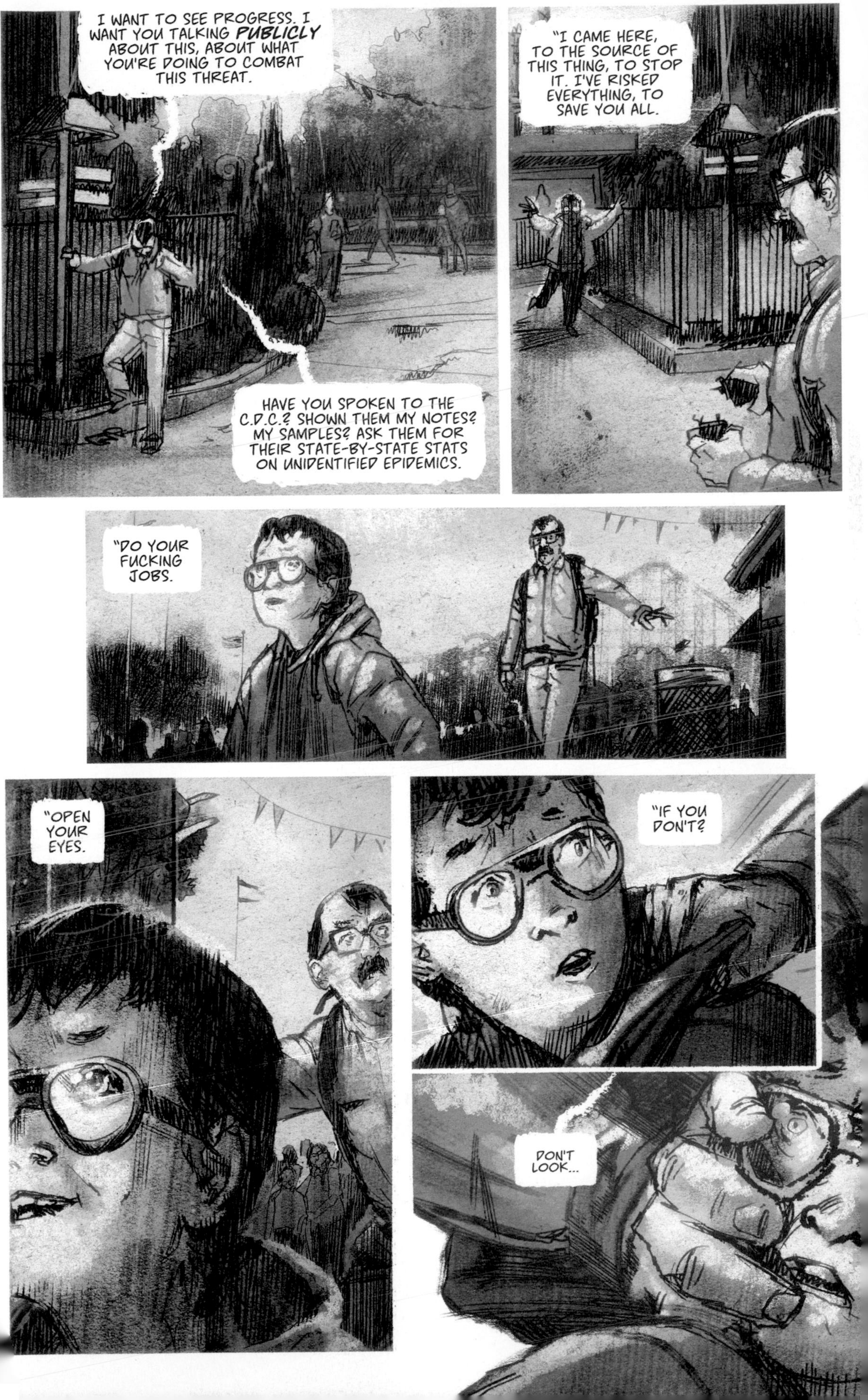
I WANT TO SEE PROGRESS. I WANT YOU TALKING PUBLICLY ABOUT THIS, ABOUT WHAT YOU'RE DOING TO COMBAT THIS THREAT.
HAVE YOU SPOKEN TO THE C.D.C.? SHOWN THEM MY NOTES? MY SAMPLES? ASK THEM FOR THEIR STATE-BY-STATE STATS ON UNIDENTIFIED EPIDEMICS.
"I CAME HERE, TO THE SOURCE OF THIS THING, TO STOP IT. I'VE RISKED EVERYTHING, TO SAVE YOU ALL.
"DO YOUR FUCKING JOBS.
"OPEN YOUR EYES.
"IF YOU DON'T?
DON'T LOOK...

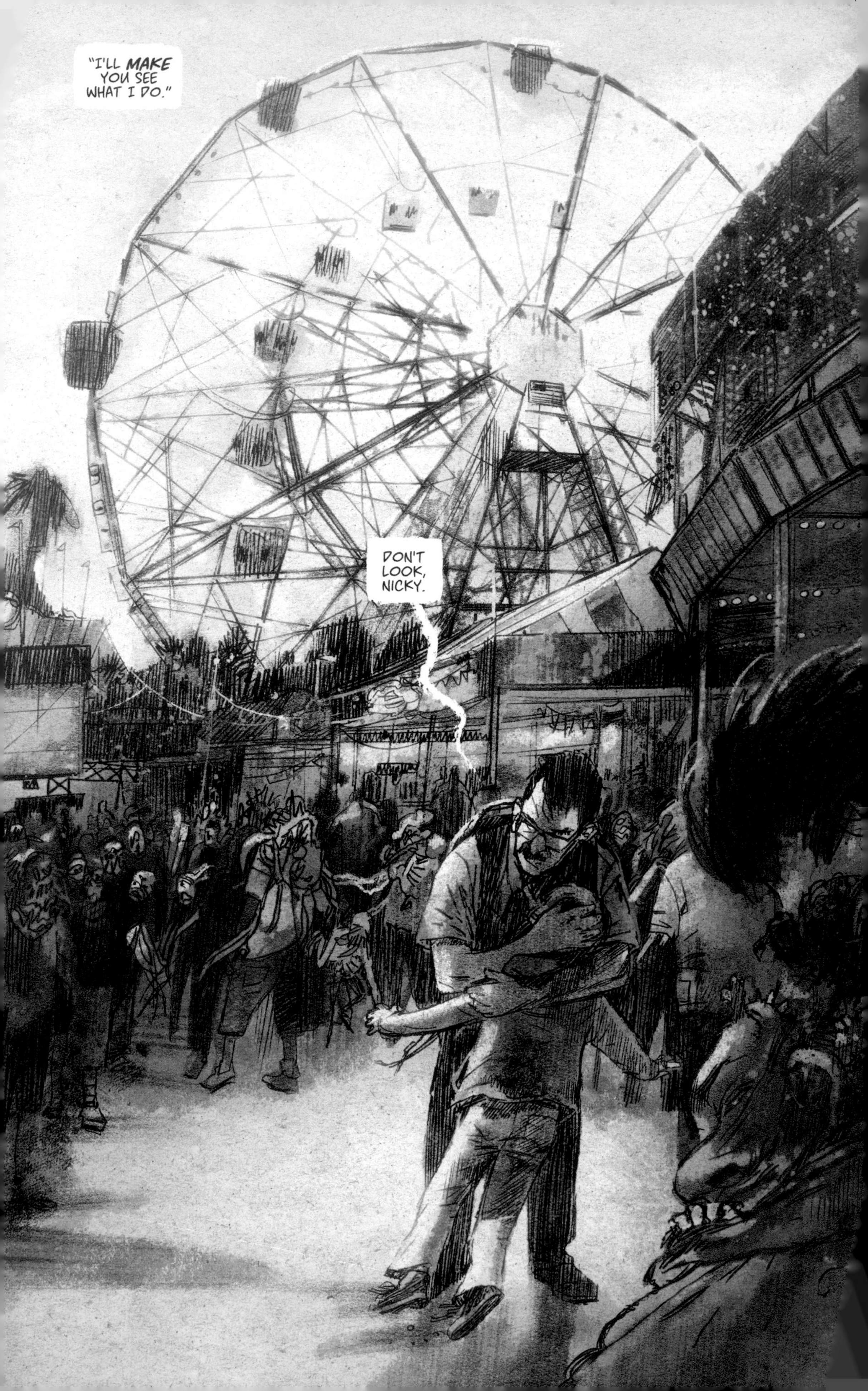
"I'LL MAKE YOU SEE WHAT I DO."
DON'T LOOK, NICKY.

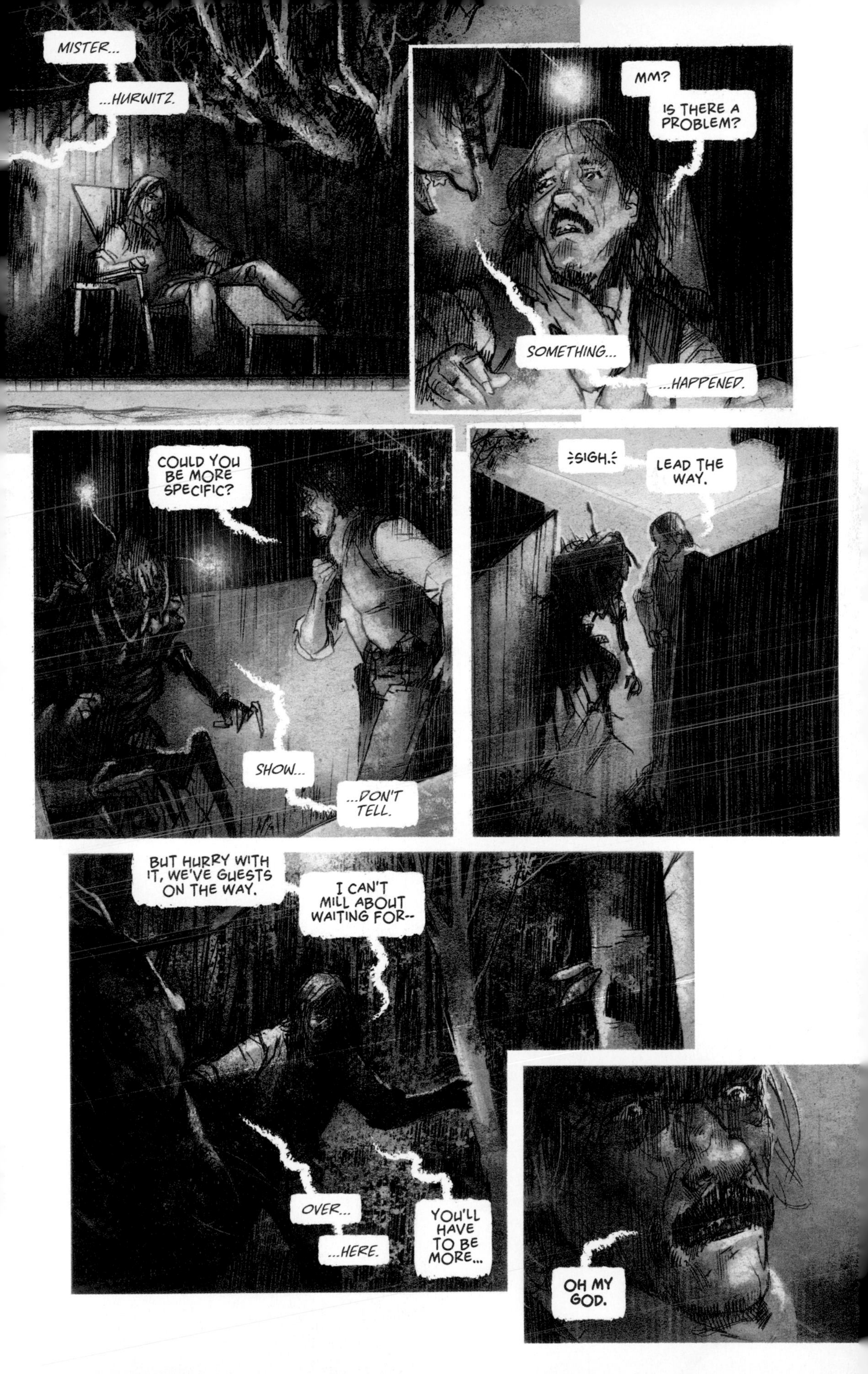
MISTER...
...HURWITZ.
MM?
IS THERE A PROBLEM?
SOMETHING...
...HAPPENED.
COULD YOU BE MORE SPECIFIC?
SHOW...
...DON'T TELL.
⁝SIGH.⁝
LEAD THE WAY.
BUT HURRY WITH IT, WE'VE GUESTS ON THE WAY.
I CAN'T MILL ABOUT WAITING FOR--
OVER...
...HERE.
YOU'LL HAVE TO BE MORE...
OH MY GOD.

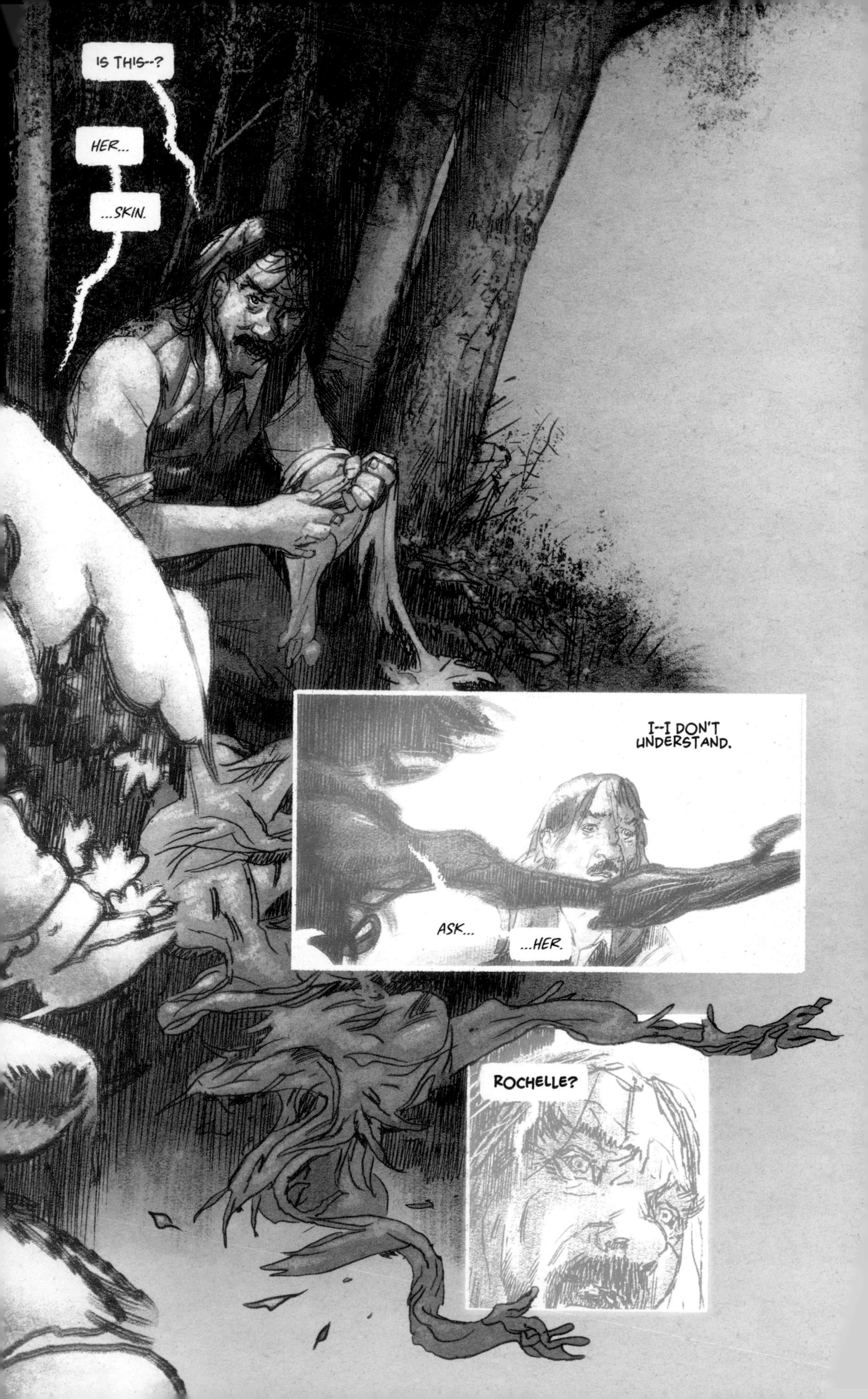
IS THIS--?
HER...
...SKIN.
I--I DON'T UNDERSTAND.
ASK...
...HER.
ROCHELLE?

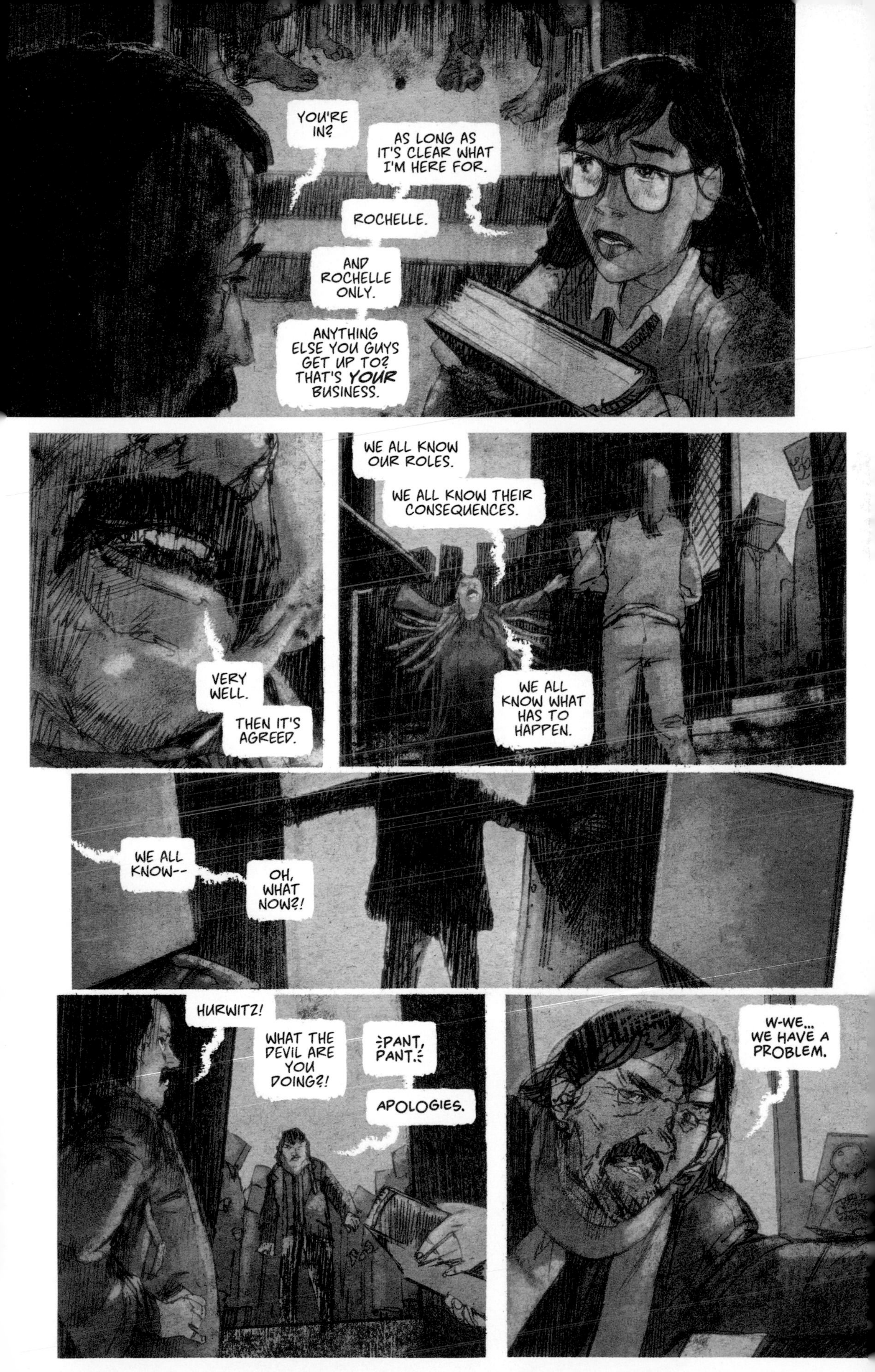
YOU'RE IN?
AS LONG AS IT'S CLEAR WHAT I'M HERE FOR.
ROCHELLE.
AND ROCHELLE ONLY.
ANYTHING ELSE YOU GUYS GET UP TO? THAT'S YOUR BUSINESS.
VERY WELL.
THEN IT'S AGREED.
WE ALL KNOW OUR ROLES.
WE ALL KNOW THEIR CONSEQUENCES.
WE ALL KNOW WHAT HAS TO HAPPEN.
WE ALL KNOW--
OH, WHAT NOW?!
HURWITZ!
WHAT THE DEVIL ARE YOU DOING?!
PANT, PANT.
APOLOGIES.
W-WE... WE HAVE A PROBLEM.

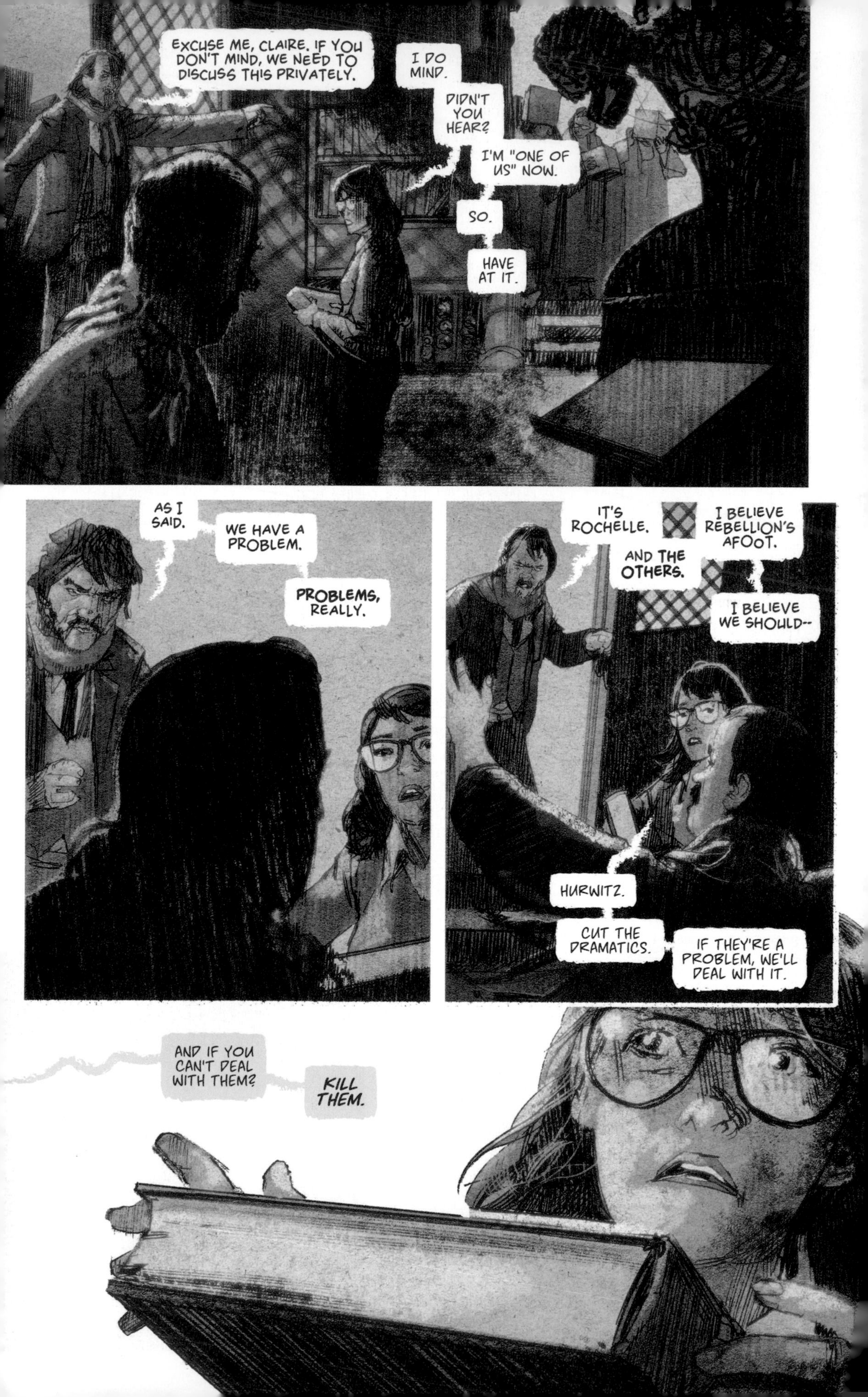
EXCUSE ME, CLAIRE. IF YOU DON'T MIND, WE NEED TO DISCUSS THIS PRIVATELY.
I DO MIND.
DIDN'T YOU HEAR?
I'M "ONE OF US" NOW.
SO.
HAVE AT IT.
AS I SAID.
WE HAVE A PROBLEM.
PROBLEMS, REALLY.
IT'S ROCHELLE.
AND THE OTHERS.
I BELIEVE REBELLION'S AFOOT.
I BELIEVE WE SHOULD--
HURWITZ.
CUT THE DRAMATICS.
IF THEY'RE A PROBLEM, WE'LL DEAL WITH IT.
AND IF YOU CAN'T DEAL WITH THEM?
KILL THEM.

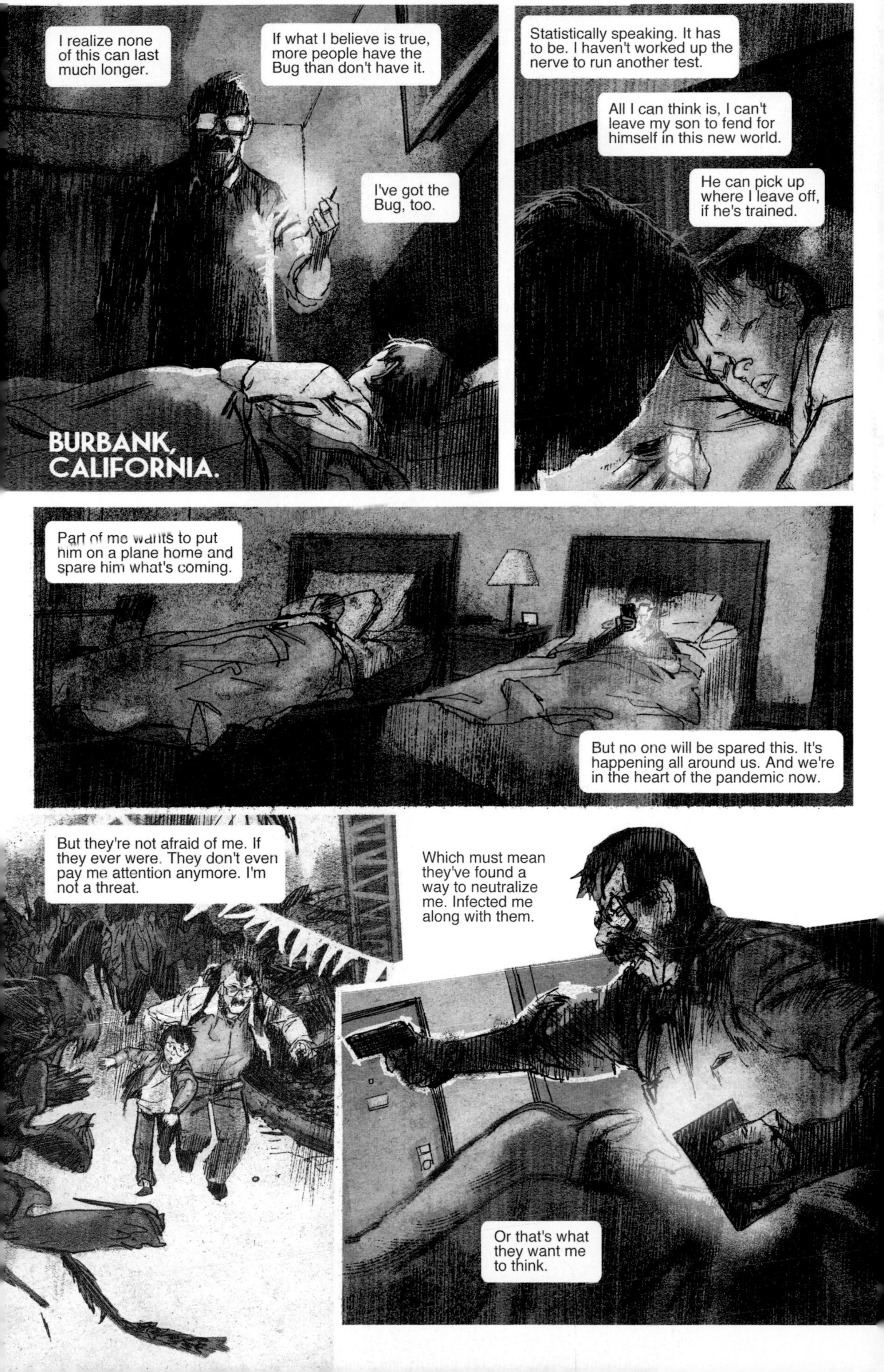
I realize none of this can last much longer.
If what I believe is true, more people have the Bug than don't have it.
I've got the Bug, too.
BURBANK, CALIFORNIA.
Statistically speaking. It has to be. I haven't worked up the nerve to run another test.
All I can think is, I can't leave my son to fend for himself in this new world.
He can pick up where I leave off, if he's trained.
Part of me wants to put him on a plane home and spare him what's coming.
But no one will be spared this. It's happening all around us. And we're in the heart of the pandemic now.
But they're not afraid of me. If they ever were. They don't even pay me attention anymore. I'm not a threat.
Which must mean they've found a way to neutralize me. Infected me along with them.
Or that's what they want me to think.

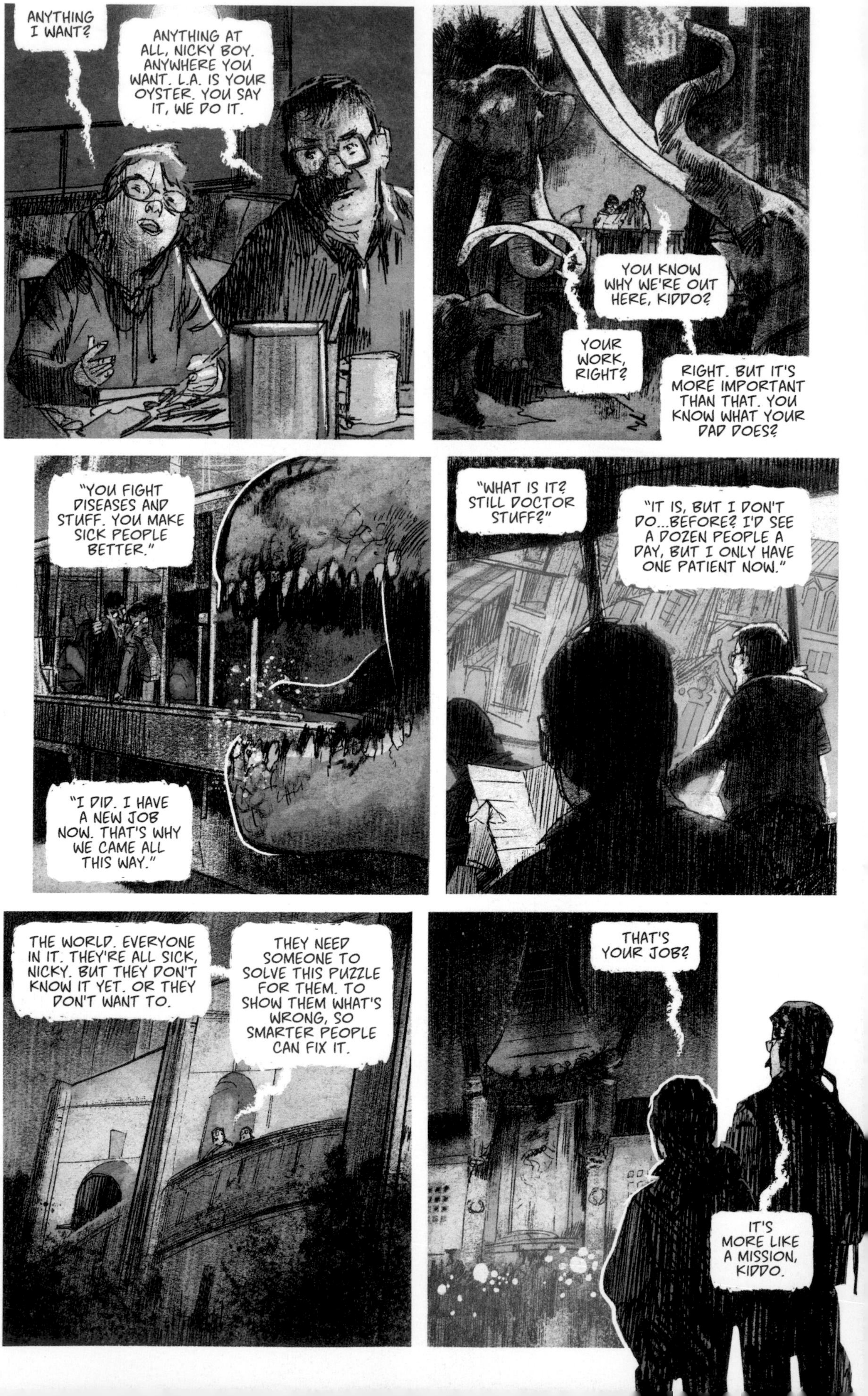
ANYTHING I WANT?
ANYTHING AT ALL, NICKY BOY. ANYWHERE YOU WANT. L.A. IS YOUR OYSTER. YOU SAY IT, WE DO IT.
YOU KNOW WHY WE'RE OUT HERE, KIDDO?
YOUR WORK, RIGHT?
RIGHT. BUT IT'S MORE IMPORTANT THAN THAT. YOU KNOW WHAT YOUR DAD DOES?
"YOU FIGHT DISEASES AND STUFF. YOU MAKE SICK PEOPLE BETTER."
"I DID. I HAVE A NEW JOB NOW. THAT'S WHY WE CAME ALL THIS WAY."
"WHAT IS IT? STILL DOCTOR STUFF?"
"IT IS, BUT I DON'T DO...BEFORE? I'D SEE A DOZEN PEOPLE A DAY, BUT I ONLY HAVE ONE PATIENT NOW."
THE WORLD. EVERYONE IN IT. THEY'RE ALL SICK, NICKY. BUT THEY DON'T KNOW IT YET. OR THEY DON'T WANT TO.
THEY NEED SOMEONE TO SOLVE THIS PUZZLE FOR THEM. TO SHOW THEM WHAT'S WRONG, SO SMARTER PEOPLE CAN FIX IT.
THAT'S YOUR JOB?
IT'S MORE LIKE A MISSION, KIDDO.

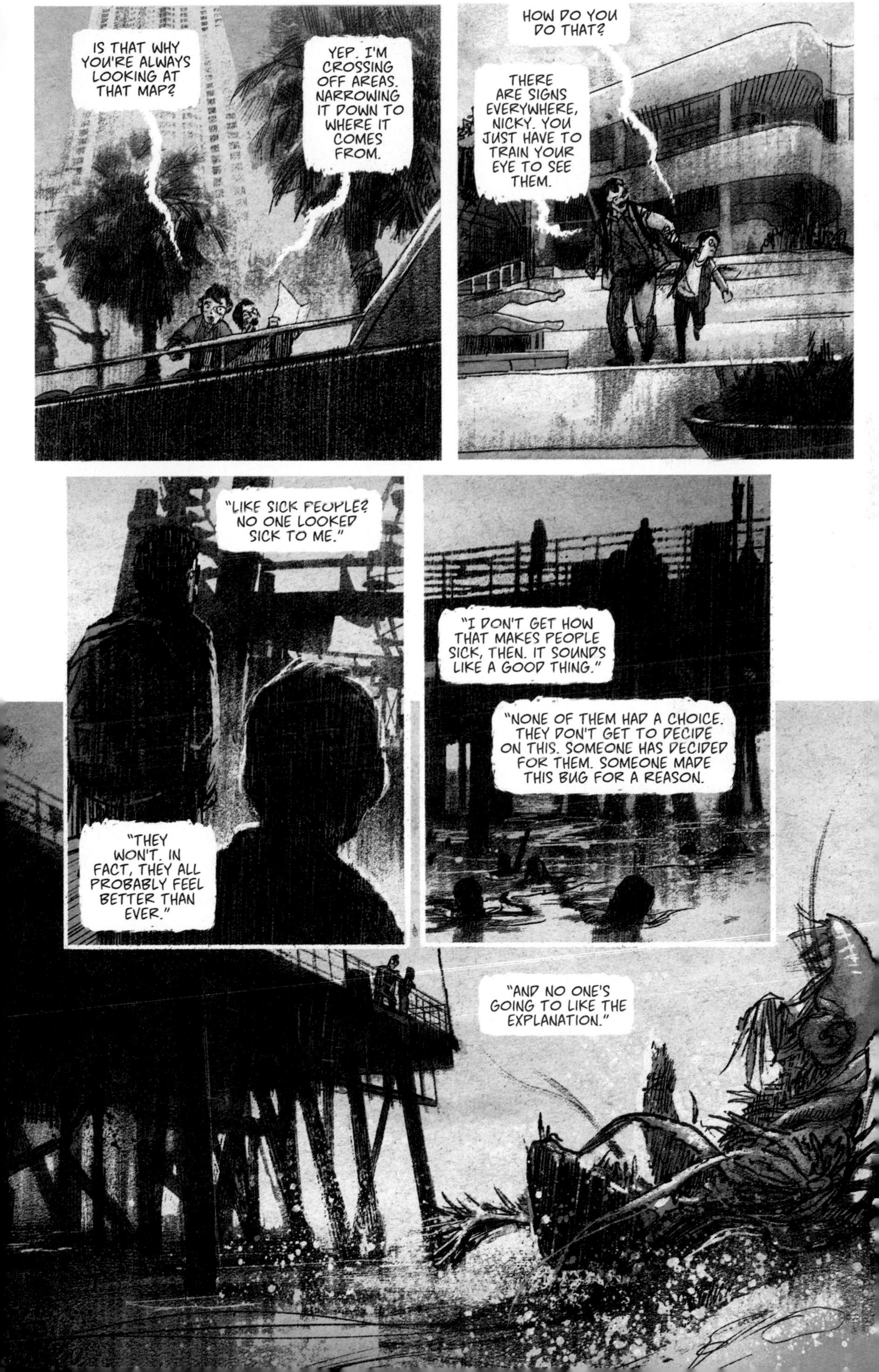
IS THAT WHY YOU'RE ALWAYS LOOKING AT THAT MAP?
YEP. I'M CROSSING OFF AREAS. NARROWING IT DOWN TO WHERE IT COMES FROM.
HOW DO YOU DO THAT?
THERE ARE SIGNS EVERYWHERE, NICKY. YOU JUST HAVE TO TRAIN YOUR EYE TO SEE THEM.
"LIKE SICK PEOPLE? NO ONE LOOKED SICK TO ME."
"THEY WON'T. IN FACT, THEY ALL PROBABLY FEEL BETTER THAN EVER."
"I DON'T GET HOW THAT MAKES PEOPLE SICK, THEN. IT SOUNDS LIKE A GOOD THING."
"NONE OF THEM HAD A CHOICE. THEY DON'T GET TO DECIDE ON THIS. SOMEONE HAS DECIDED FOR THEM. SOMEONE MADE THIS BUG FOR A REASON.
"AND NO ONE'S GOING TO LIKE THE EXPLANATION."

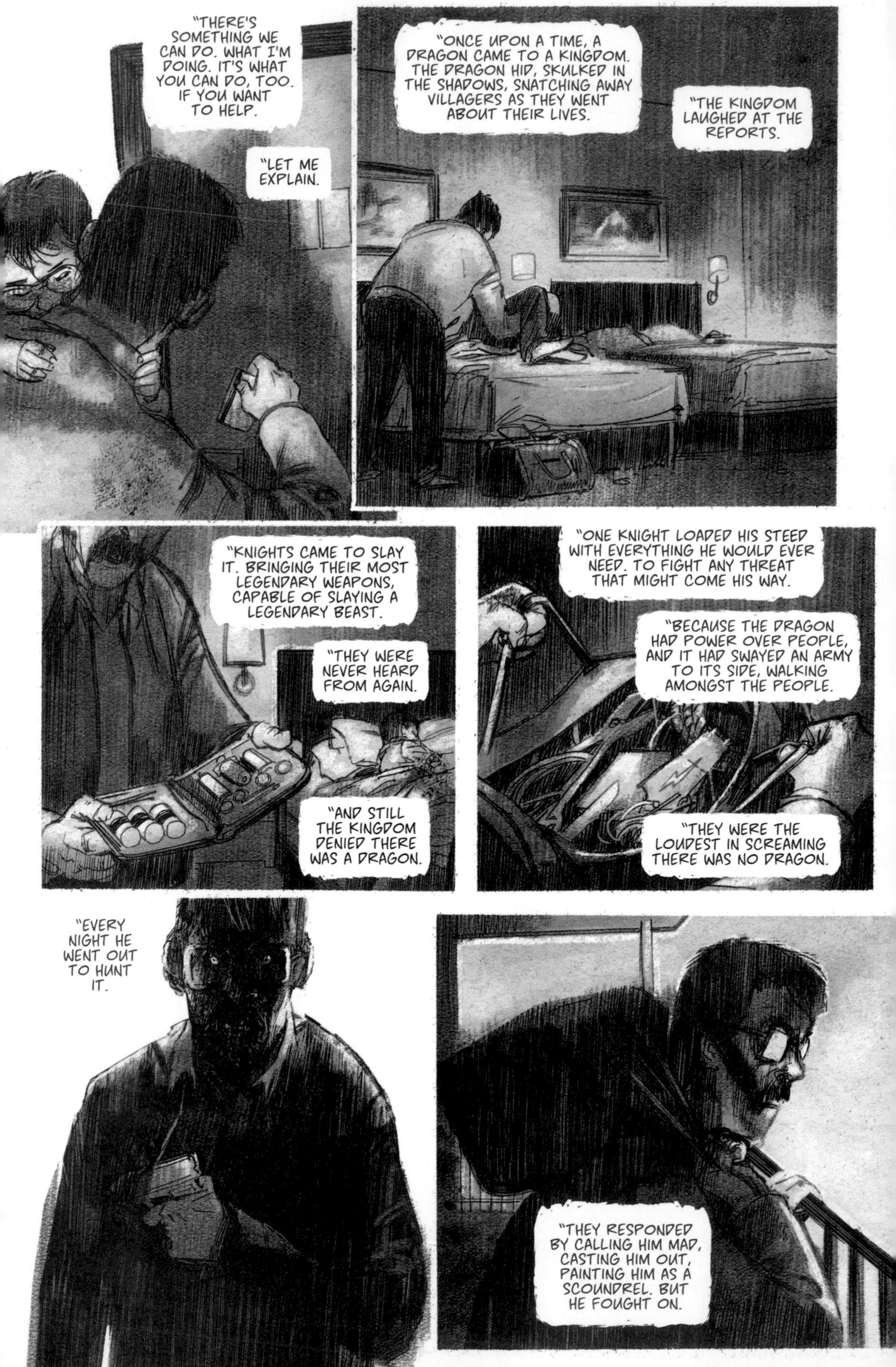
"THERE'S SOMETHING WE CAN DO. WHAT I'M DOING. IT'S WHAT YOU CAN DO, TOO. IF YOU WANT TO HELP.
"LET ME EXPLAIN.
"ONCE UPON A TIME, A DRAGON CAME TO A KINGDOM. THE DRAGON HID, SKULKED IN THE SHADOWS, SNATCHING AWAY VILLAGERS AS THEY WENT ABOUT THEIR LIVES.
"THE KINGDOM LAUGHED AT THE REPORTS.
"KNIGHTS CAME TO SLAY IT. BRINGING THEIR MOST LEGENDARY WEAPONS, CAPABLE OF SLAYING A LEGENDARY BEAST.
"THEY WERE NEVER HEARD FROM AGAIN.
"AND STILL THE KINGDOM DENIED THERE WAS A DRAGON.
"ONE KNIGHT LOADED HIS STEED WITH EVERYTHING HE WOULD EVER NEED. TO FIGHT ANY THREAT THAT MIGHT COME HIS WAY.
"BECAUSE THE DRAGON HAD POWER OVER PEOPLE, AND IT HAD SWAYED AN ARMY TO ITS SIDE, WALKING AMONGST THE PEOPLE.
"THEY WERE THE LOUDEST IN SCREAMING THERE WAS NO DRAGON.
"EVERY NIGHT HE WENT OUT TO HUNT IT.
"THEY RESPONDED BY CALLING HIM MAD, CASTING HIM OUT, PAINTING HIM AS A SCOUNDREL. BUT HE FOUGHT ON.

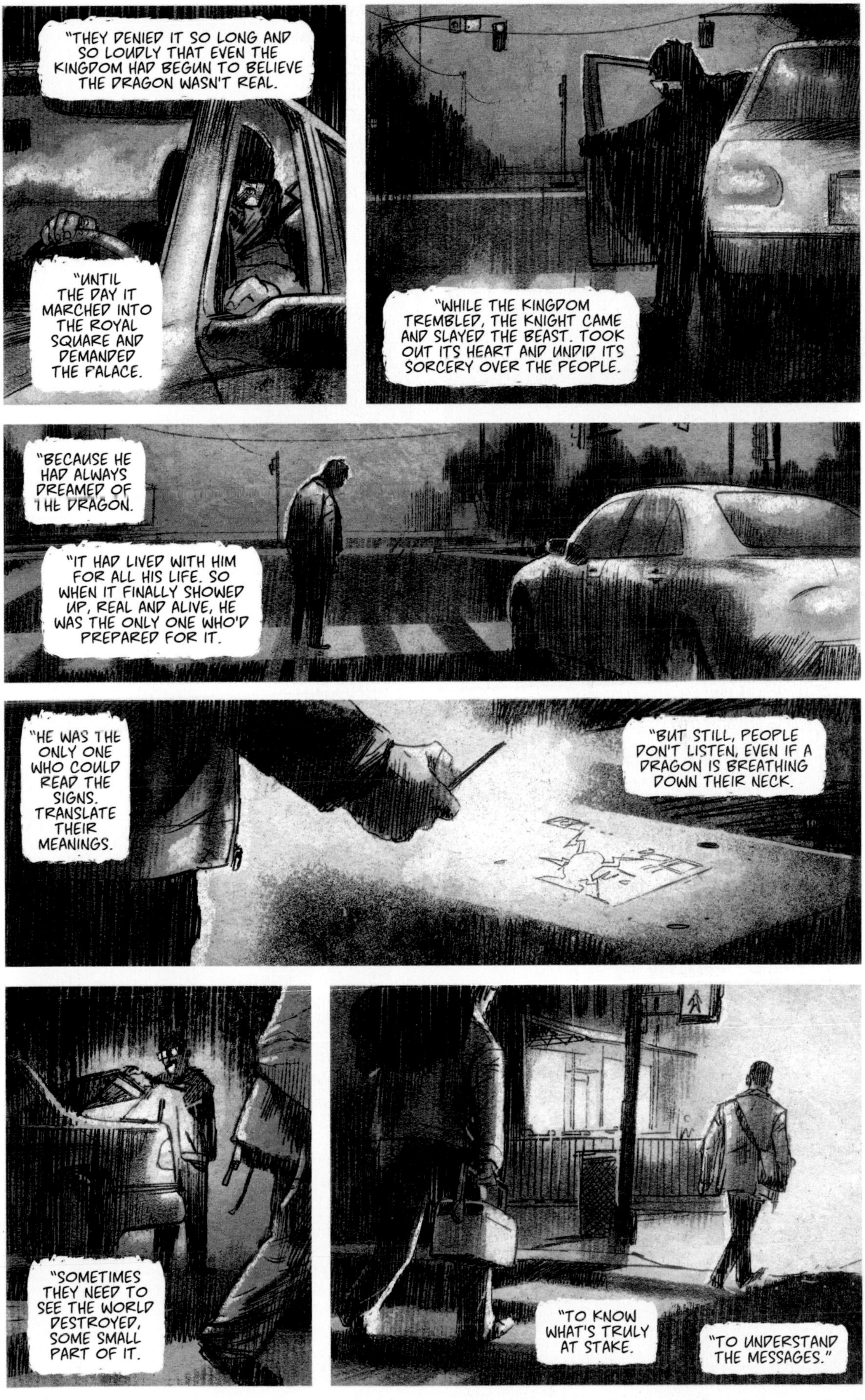
"THEY DENIED IT SO LONG AND SO LOUDLY THAT EVEN THE KINGDOM HAD BEGUN TO BELIEVE THE DRAGON WASN'T REAL.
"UNTIL THE DAY IT MARCHED INTO THE ROYAL SQUARE AND DEMANDED THE PALACE.
"WHILE THE KINGDOM TREMBLED, THE KNIGHT CAME AND SLAYED THE BEAST. TOOK OUT ITS HEART AND UNDID ITS SORCERY OVER THE PEOPLE.
"BECAUSE HE HAD ALWAYS DREAMED OF THE DRAGON.
"IT HAD LIVED WITH HIM FOR ALL HIS LIFE. SO WHEN IT FINALLY SHOWED UP, REAL AND ALIVE, HE WAS THE ONLY ONE WHO'D PREPARED FOR IT.
"HE WAS THE ONLY ONE WHO COULD READ THE SIGNS. TRANSLATE THEIR MEANINGS.
"BUT STILL, PEOPLE DON'T LISTEN, EVEN IF A DRAGON IS BREATHING DOWN THEIR NECK.
"SOMETIMES THEY NEED TO SEE THE WORLD DESTROYED, SOME SMALL PART OF IT.
"TO KNOW WHAT'S TRULY AT STAKE.
"TO UNDERSTAND THE MESSAGES."

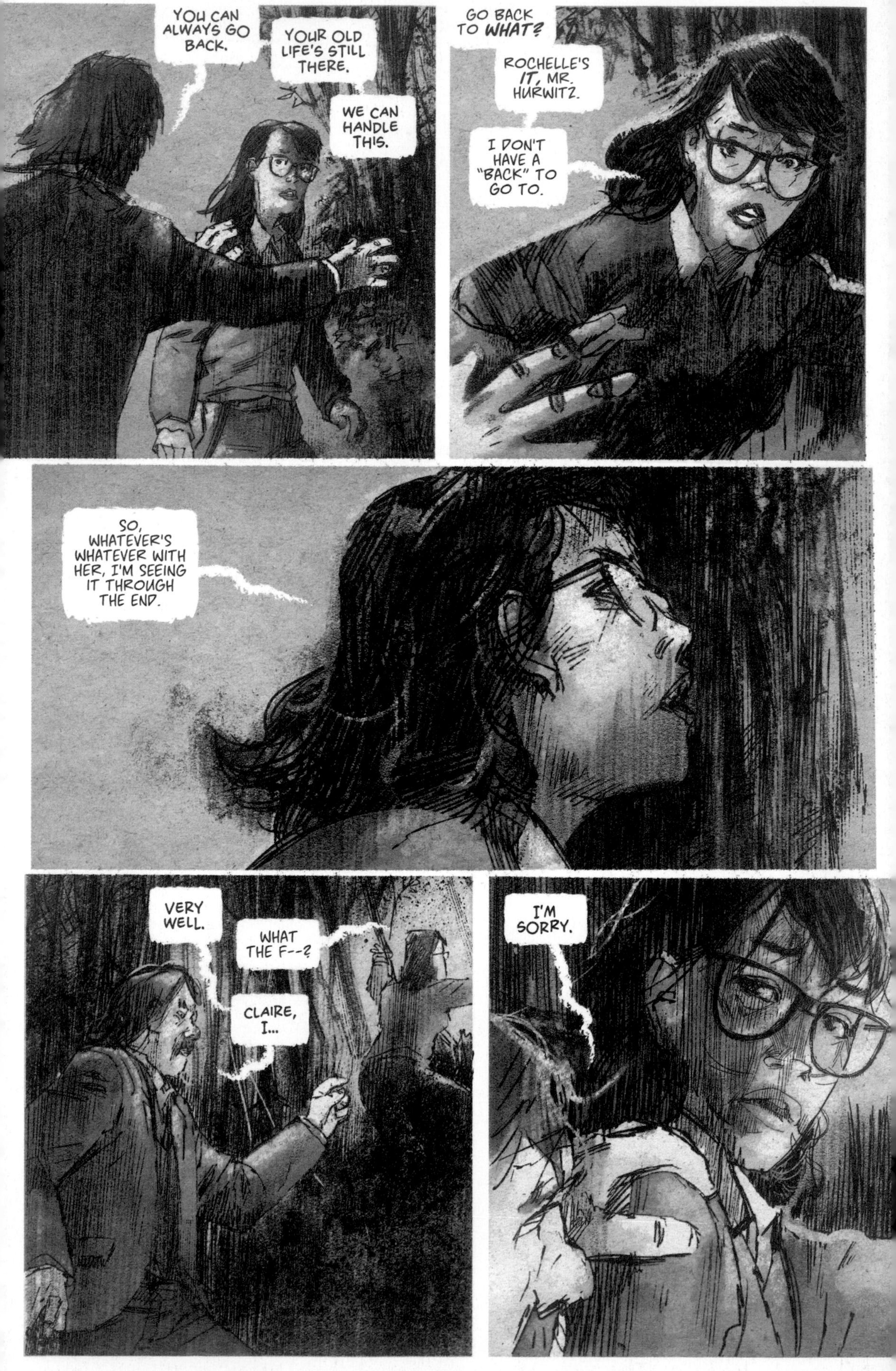
YOU CAN ALWAYS GO BACK.
YOUR OLD LIFE'S STILL THERE.
WE CAN HANDLE THIS.
GO BACK TO WHAT?
ROCHELLE'S IT, MR. HURWITZ.
I DON'T HAVE A "BACK" TO GO TO.
SO, WHATEVER'S WHATEVER WITH HER, I'M SEEING IT THROUGH THE END.
VERY WELL.
WHAT THE F--?
CLAIRE, I...
I'M SORRY.

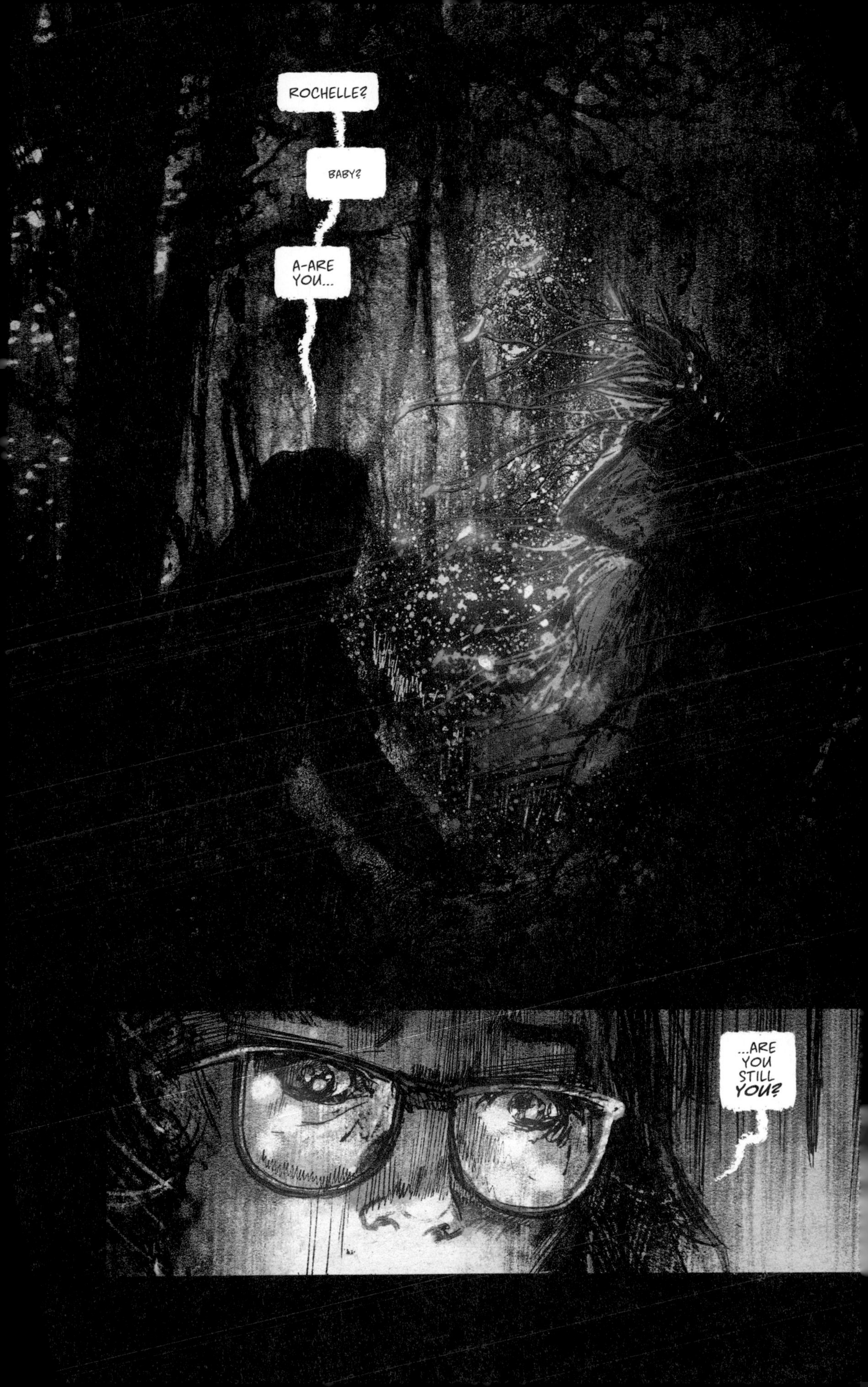
ROCHELLE?
BABY?
A-ARE YOU...
...ARE YOU STILL YOU?

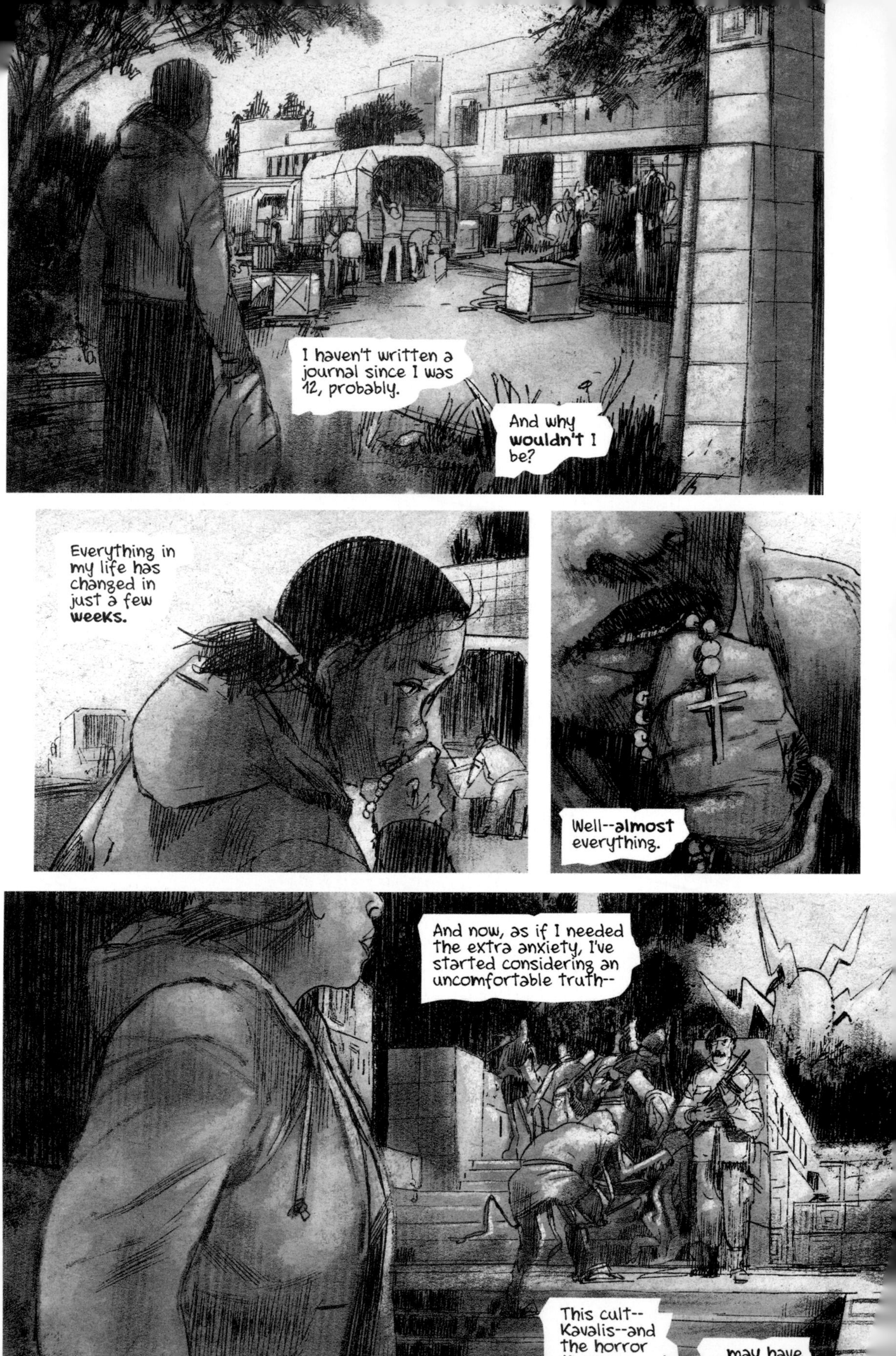
I haven't written a journal since I was 12, probably.
And why **wouldn't** I be?
Everything in my life has changed in just a few **weeks.**
Well--**almost** everything.
And now, as if I needed the extra anxiety, I've started considering an uncomfortable truth--
This cult--Kavalis--and the horror they exposed me to...
...may have **saved** my soul.

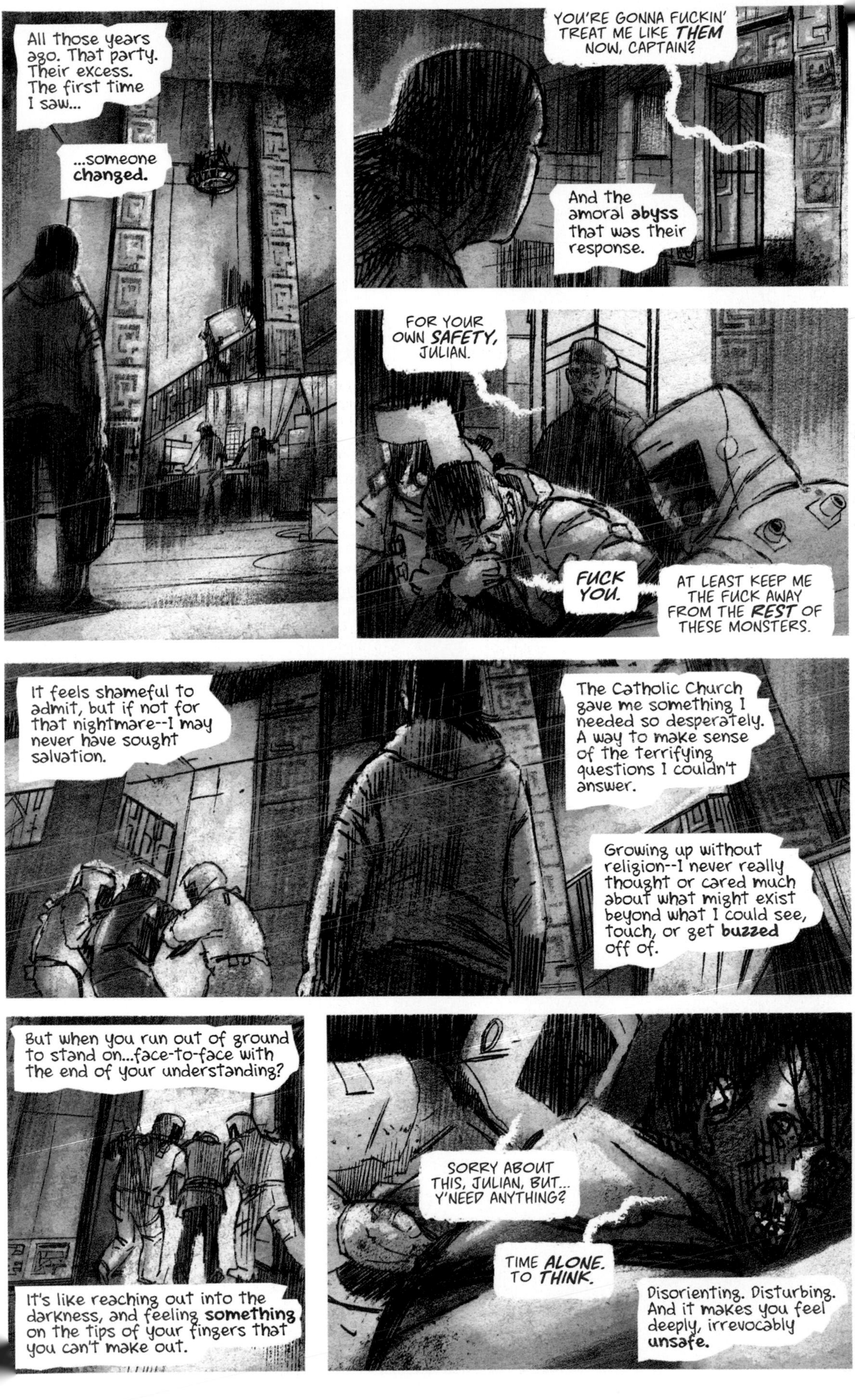
All those years ago. That party. Their excess. The first time I saw...
...someone changed.
YOU'RE GONNA FUCKIN' TREAT ME LIKE THEM NOW, CAPTAIN?
And the amoral abyss that was their response.
FOR YOUR OWN SAFETY, JULIAN.
FUCK YOU.
AT LEAST KEEP ME THE FUCK AWAY FROM THE REST OF THESE MONSTERS.
It feels shameful to admit, but if not for that nightmare--I may never have sought salvation.
The Catholic Church gave me something I needed so desperately. A way to make sense of the terrifying questions I couldn't answer.
Growing up without religion--I never really thought or cared much about what might exist beyond what I could see, touch, or get buzzed off of.
But when you run out of ground to stand on...face-to-face with the end of your understanding?
It's like reaching out into the darkness, and feeling something on the tips of your fingers that you can't make out.
SORRY ABOUT THIS, JULIAN, BUT... Y'NEED ANYTHING?
TIME ALONE. TO THINK.
Disorienting. Disturbing. And it makes you feel deeply, irrevocably unsafe.

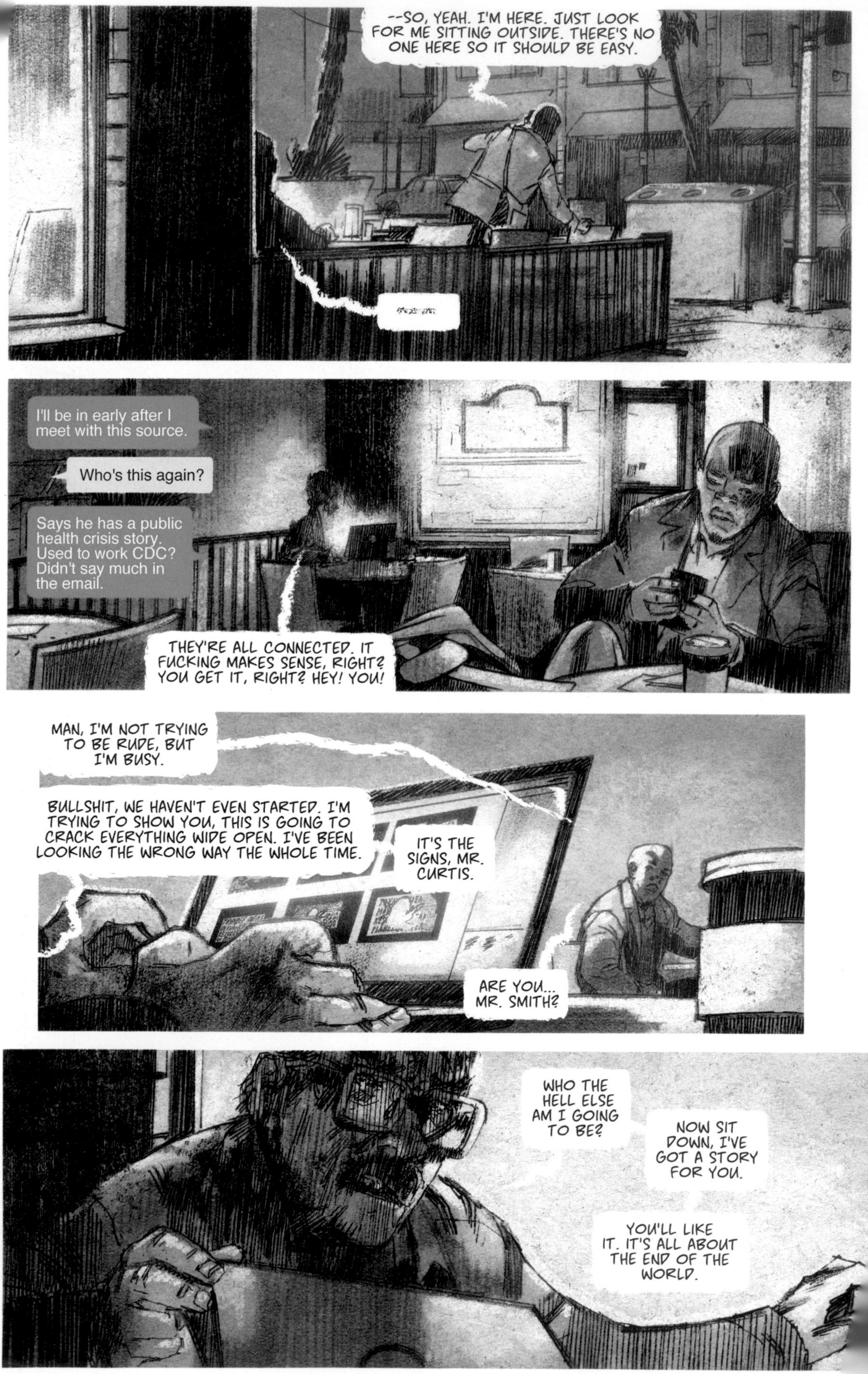
--SO, YEAH. I'M HERE. JUST LOOK FOR ME SITTING OUTSIDE. THERE'S NO ONE HERE SO IT SHOULD BE EASY.
I'll be in early after I meet with this source.
Who's this again?
Says he has a public health crisis story. Used to work CDC? Didn't say much in the email.
THEY'RE ALL CONNECTED. IT FUCKING MAKES SENSE, RIGHT? YOU GET IT, RIGHT? HEY! YOU!
MAN, I'M NOT TRYING TO BE RUDE, BUT I'M BUSY.
BULLSHIT, WE HAVEN'T EVEN STARTED. I'M TRYING TO SHOW YOU, THIS IS GOING TO CRACK EVERYTHING WIDE OPEN. I'VE BEEN LOOKING THE WRONG WAY THE WHOLE TIME.
IT'S THE SIGNS, MR. CURTIS.
ARE YOU... MR. SMITH?
WHO THE HELL ELSE AM I GOING TO BE?
NOW SIT DOWN, I'VE GOT A STORY FOR YOU.
YOU'LL LIKE IT. IT'S ALL ABOUT THE END OF THE WORLD.

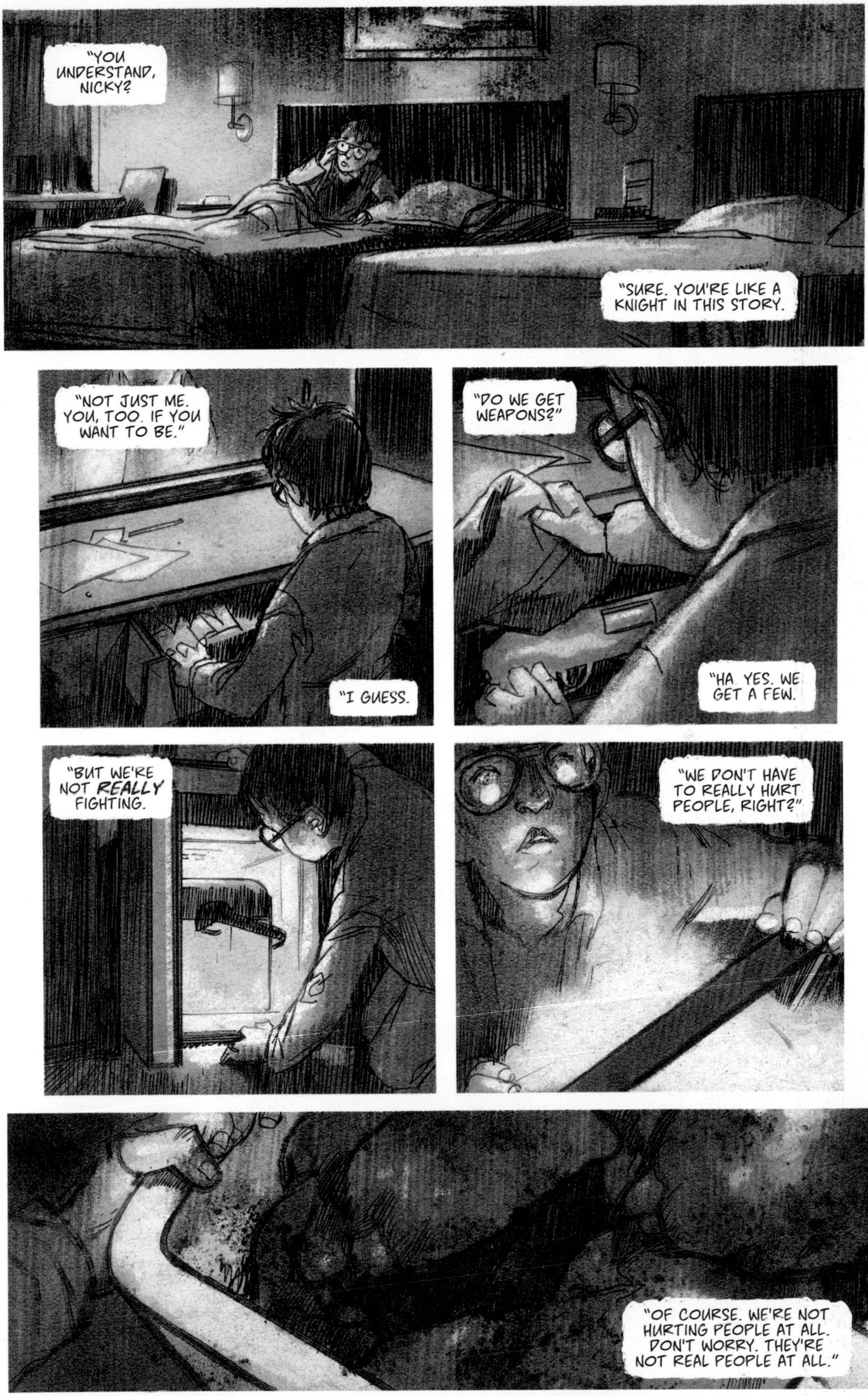
"YOU UNDERSTAND, NICKY?
"SURE. YOU'RE LIKE A KNIGHT IN THIS STORY.
"NOT JUST ME. YOU, TOO. IF YOU WANT TO BE."
"I GUESS.
"DO WE GET WEAPONS?"
"HA. YES. WE GET A FEW.
"BUT WE'RE NOT REALLY FIGHTING.
"WE DON'T HAVE TO REALLY HURT PEOPLE, RIGHT?"
"OF COURSE. WE'RE NOT HURTING PEOPLE AT ALL. DON'T WORRY. THEY'RE NOT REAL PEOPLE AT ALL."

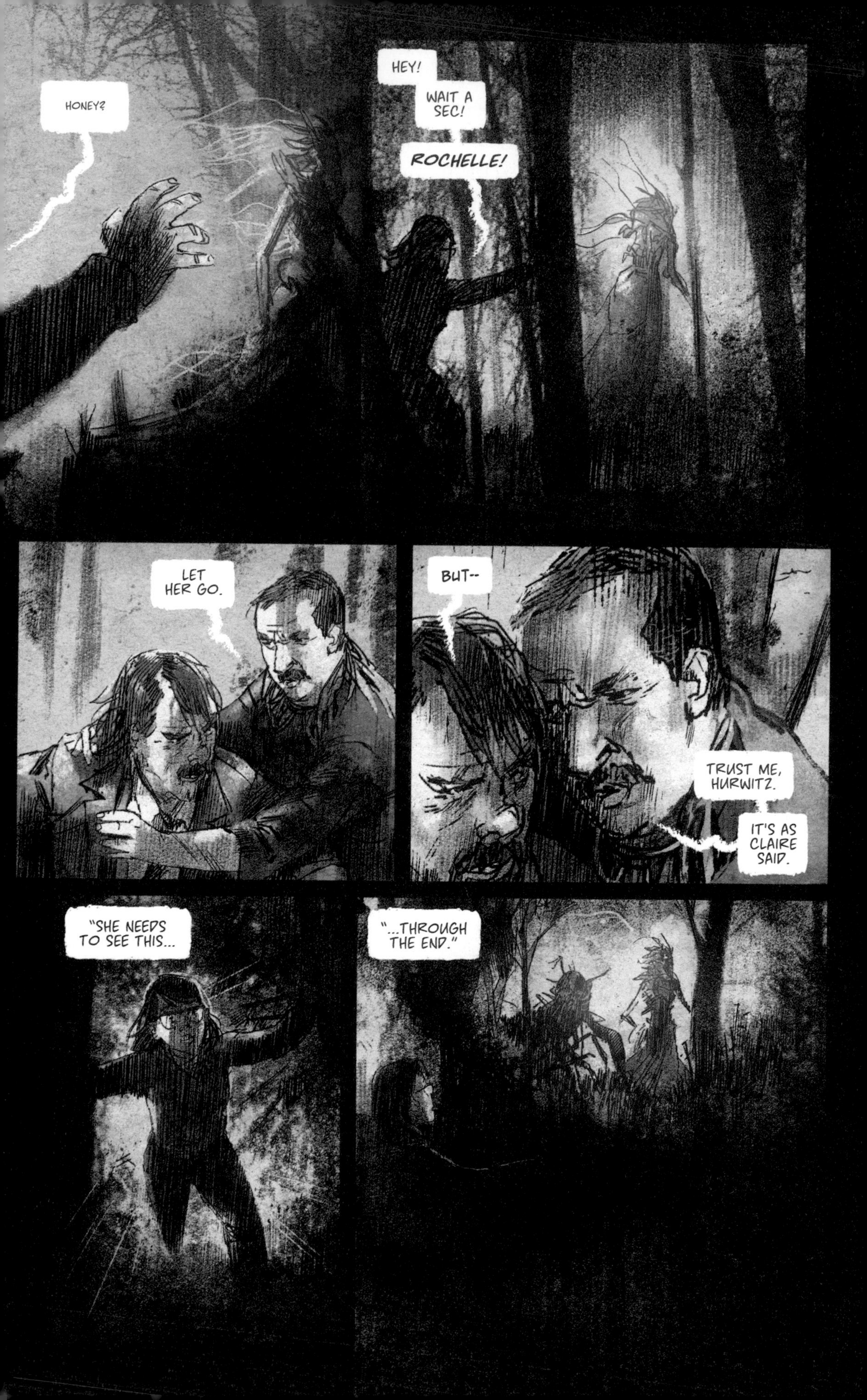
HONEY?
HEY!
WAIT A SEC!
ROCHELLE!
LET HER GO.
BUT--
TRUST ME, HURWITZ.
IT'S AS CLAIRE SAID.
"SHE NEEDS TO SEE THIS...
"...THROUGH THE END."

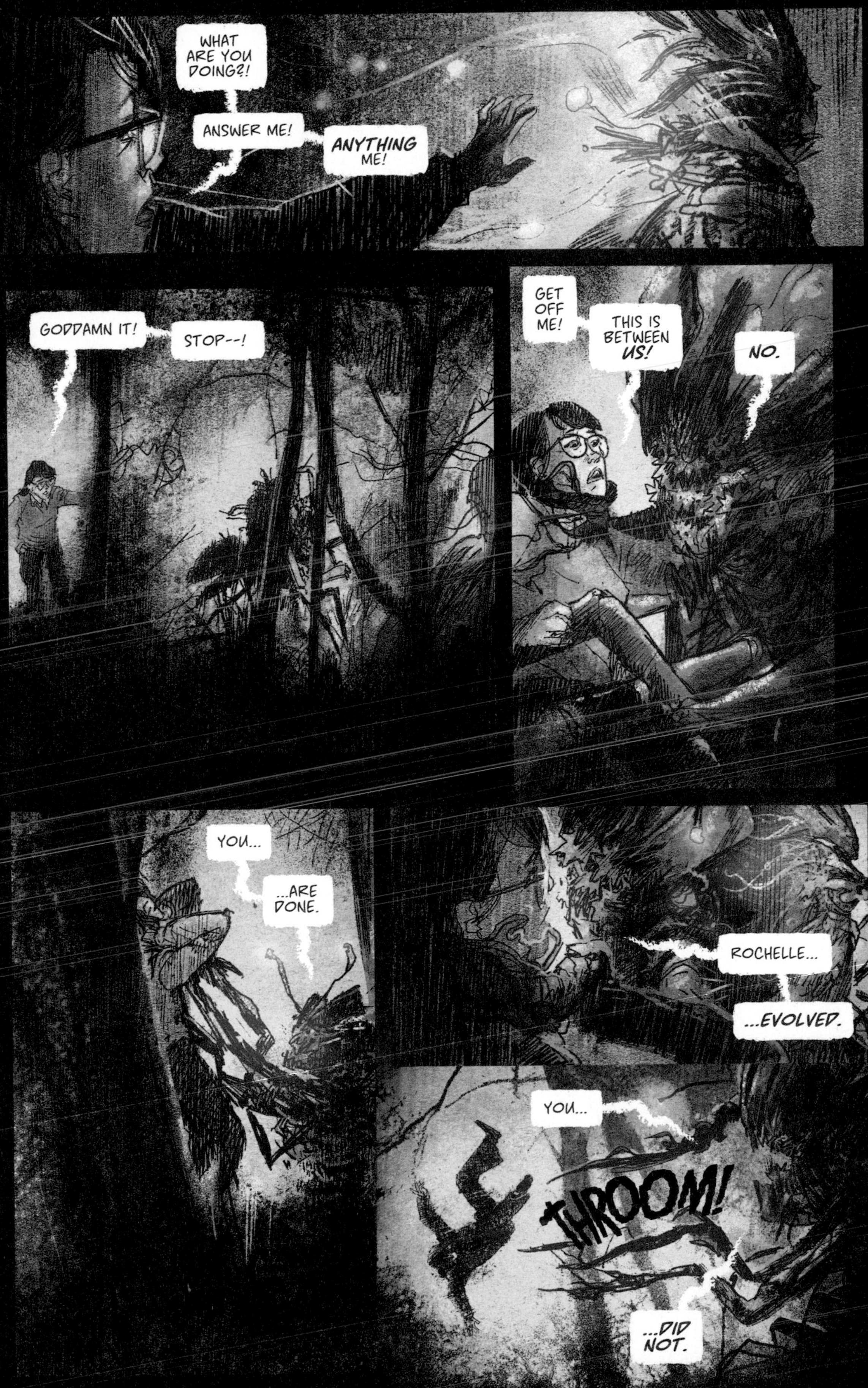
WHAT ARE YOU DOING?!
ANSWER ME!
ANYTHING ME!
GODDAMN IT!
STOP--!
GET OFF ME!
THIS IS BETWEEN US!
NO.
YOU...
...ARE DONE.
ROCHELLE...
...EVOLVED.
YOU...
THROOM!
...DID NOT.

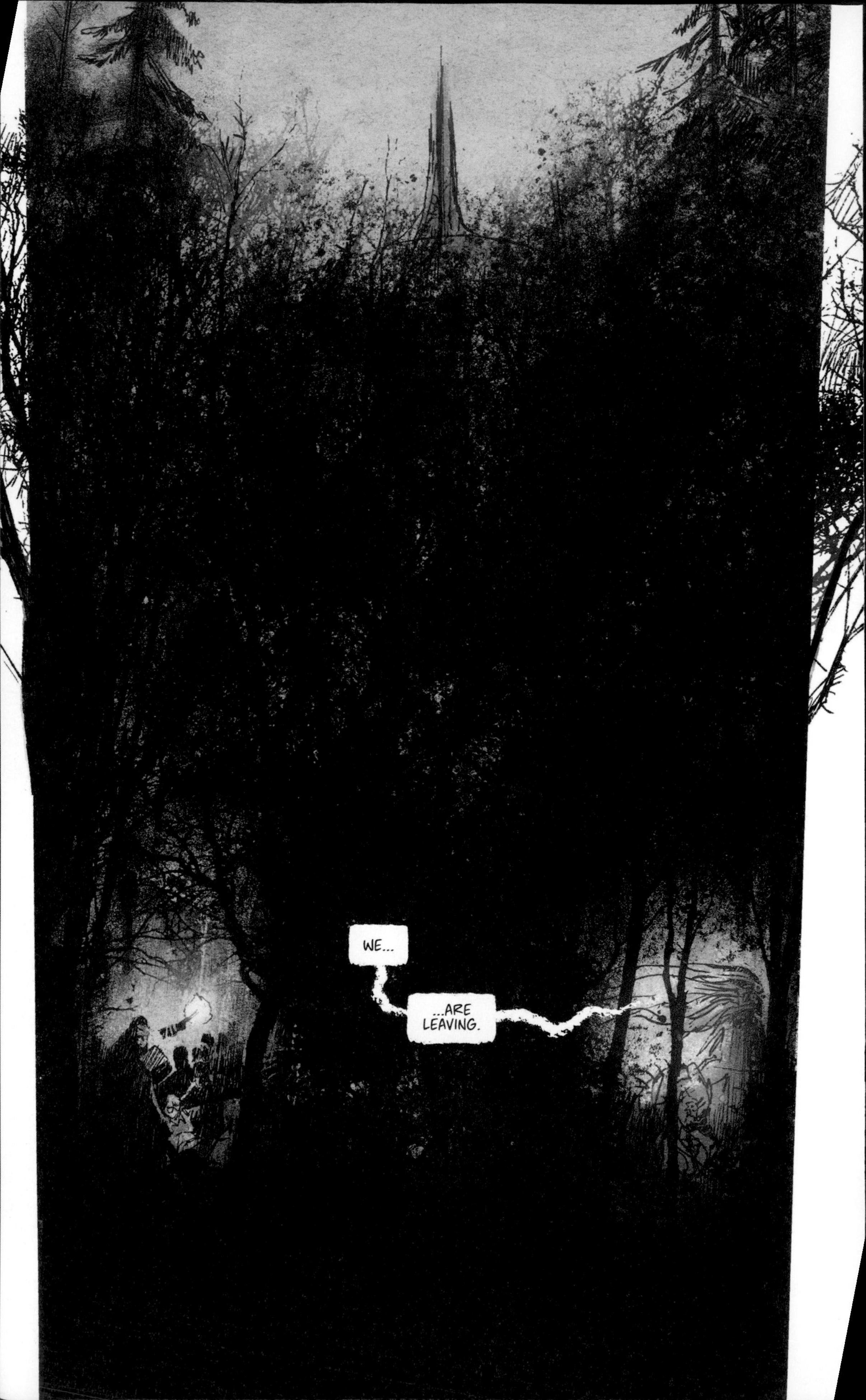
WE...
...ARE LEAVING.

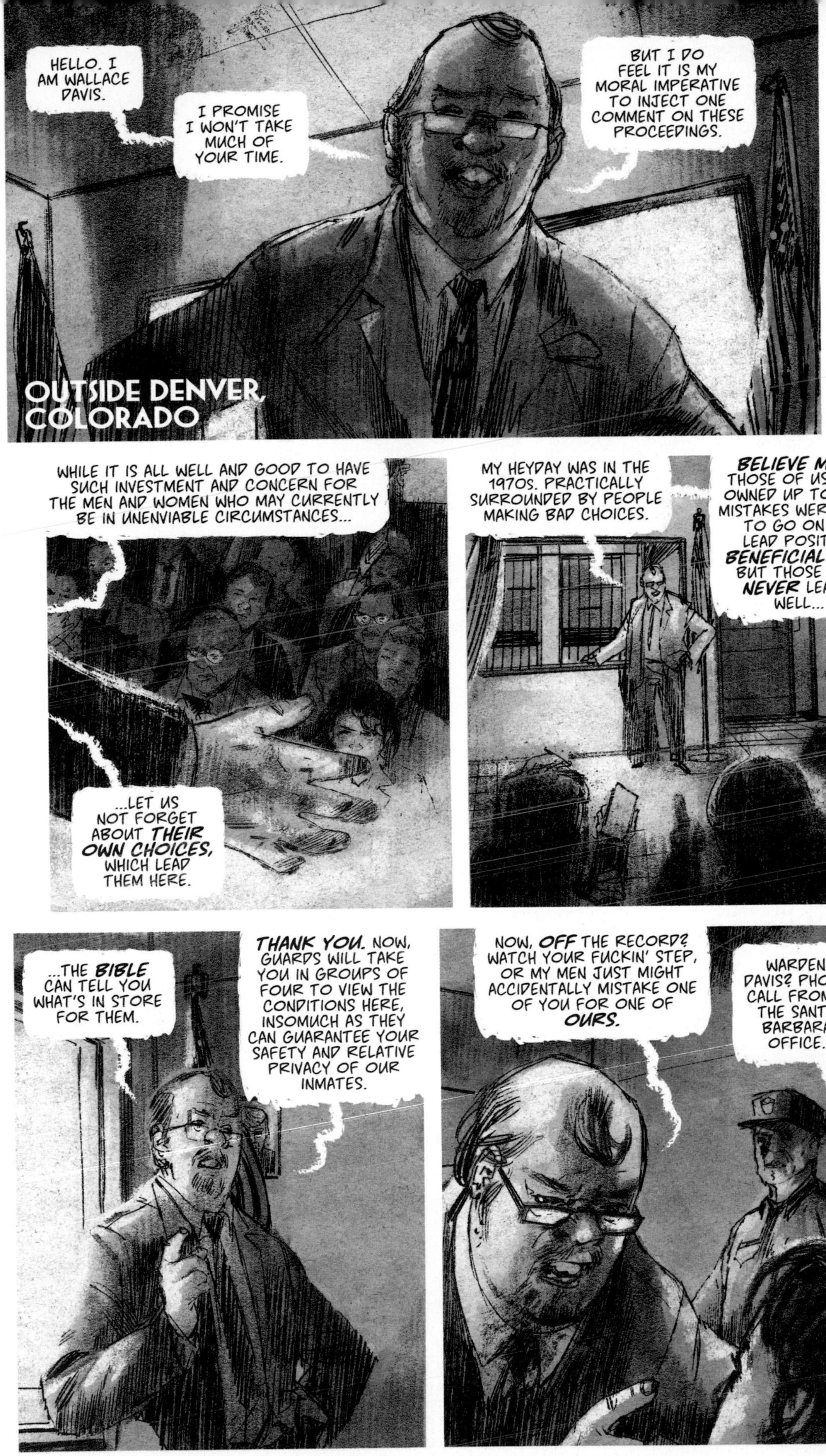
HELLO. I AM WALLACE DAVIS.
I PROMISE I WON'T TAKE MUCH OF YOUR TIME.
BUT I DO FEEL IT IS MY MORAL IMPERATIVE TO INJECT ONE COMMENT ON THESE PROCEEDINGS.
OUTSIDE DENVER, COLORADO
WHILE IT IS ALL WELL AND GOOD TO HAVE SUCH INVESTMENT AND CONCERN FOR THE MEN AND WOMEN WHO MAY CURRENTLY BE IN UNENVIABLE CIRCUMSTANCES...
...LET US NOT FORGET ABOUT THEIR OWN CHOICES, WHICH LEAD THEM HERE.
MY HEYDAY WAS IN THE 1970s. PRACTICALLY SURROUNDED BY PEOPLE MAKING BAD CHOICES.
BELIEVE ME-- THOSE OF US WHO OWNED UP TO OUR MISTAKES WERE ABLE TO GO ON TO LEAD POSITIVE, BENEFICIAL LIVES. BUT THOSE WHO NEVER LEARN, WELL...
...THE BIBLE CAN TELL YOU WHAT'S IN STORE FOR THEM.
THANK YOU. NOW, GUARDS WILL TAKE YOU IN GROUPS OF FOUR TO VIEW THE CONDITIONS HERE, INSOMUCH AS THEY CAN GUARANTEE YOUR SAFETY AND RELATIVE PRIVACY OF OUR INMATES.
NOW, OFF THE RECORD? WATCH YOUR FUCKIN' STEP, OR MY MEN JUST MIGHT ACCIDENTALLY MISTAKE ONE OF YOU FOR ONE OF OURS.
WARDEN DAVIS? PHONE CALL FROM... THE SANTA BARBARA OFFICE.

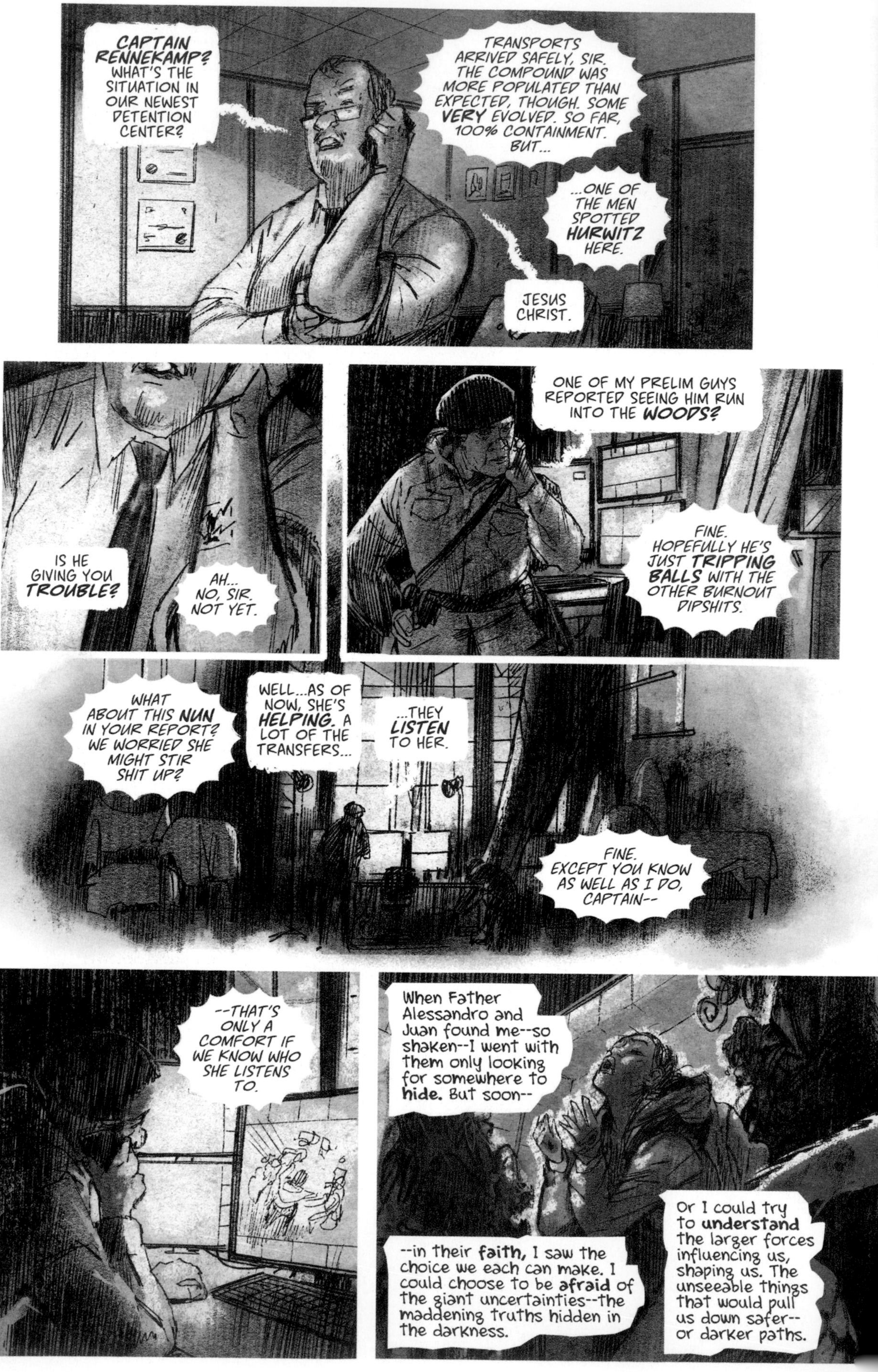
CAPTAIN RENNEKAMP? WHAT'S THE SITUATION IN OUR NEWEST DETENTION CENTER?
TRANSPORTS ARRIVED SAFELY, SIR. THE COMPOUND WAS MORE POPULATED THAN EXPECTED, THOUGH. SOME VERY EVOLVED. SO FAR, 100% CONTAINMENT. BUT...
...ONE OF THE MEN SPOTTED HURWITZ HERE.
JESUS CHRIST.
ONE OF MY PRELIM GUYS REPORTED SEEING HIM RUN INTO THE WOODS?
IS HE GIVING YOU TROUBLE?
AH... NO, SIR. NOT YET.
FINE. HOPEFULLY HE'S JUST TRIPPING BALLS WITH THE OTHER BURNOUT DIPSHITS.
WHAT ABOUT THIS NUN IN YOUR REPORT? WE WORRIED SHE MIGHT STIR SHIT UP?
WELL...AS OF NOW, SHE'S HELPING. A LOT OF THE TRANSFERS...
...THEY LISTEN TO HER.
FINE. EXCEPT YOU KNOW AS WELL AS I DO, CAPTAIN--
--THAT'S ONLY A COMFORT IF WE KNOW WHO SHE LISTENS TO.
When Father Alessandro and Juan found me--so shaken--I went with them only looking for somewhere to hide. But soon--
--in their faith, I saw the choice we each can make. I could choose to be afraid of the giant uncertainties--the maddening truths hidden in the darkness.
Or I could try to understand the larger forces influencing us, shaping us. The unseeable things that would pull us down safer-- or darker paths.

And at first, **their** faith was a comfort. There were easy answers that fit so neatly with what life had already taught me to be true.

The peace and happiness that came from simple virtues.

Kindness. Dedication. Honesty.

It was those virtues--and the good work I saw **sisters** doing in the name of the Church--that inspired me to take up my vows so quickly.

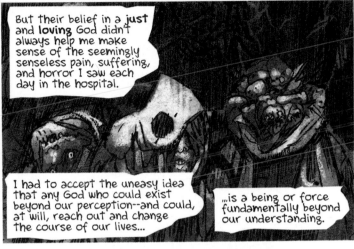

But their belief in a **just** and **loving** God didn't always help me make sense of the seemingly senseless pain, suffering, and horror I saw each day in the hospital.

I had to accept the uneasy idea that any God who could exist beyond our perception--and could, at will, reach out and change the course of our lives...

...is a being or force fundamentally beyond our understanding.

To me, that meant a **greater** dependence on faith. On looking for **cues** from the things I **could** see.

And that belief allowed me to find guidance and direction in even the most unsettling circumstances.

But it also lead me into conflict with Father Alessandro. He wielded Church dogma like a measuring stick--as both **test** and **punishment.**

And even before all this, I saw in him a warning.

That faith can **calcify.** Harden itself, so defensive against anything from the outside--

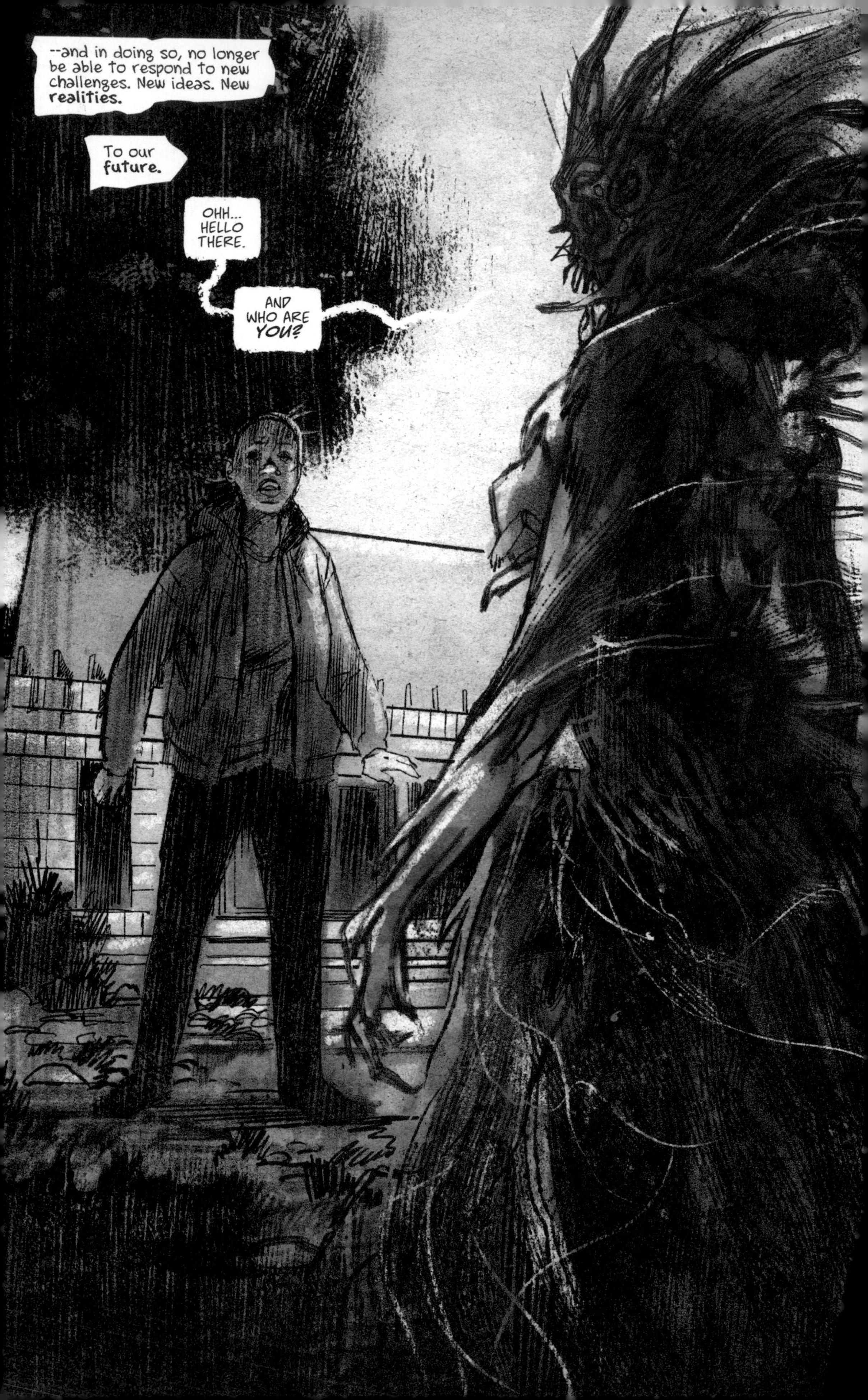
--and in doing so, no longer be able to respond to new challenges. New ideas. New **realities.**
To our **future.**
OHH... HELLO THERE.
AND WHO ARE *YOU?*

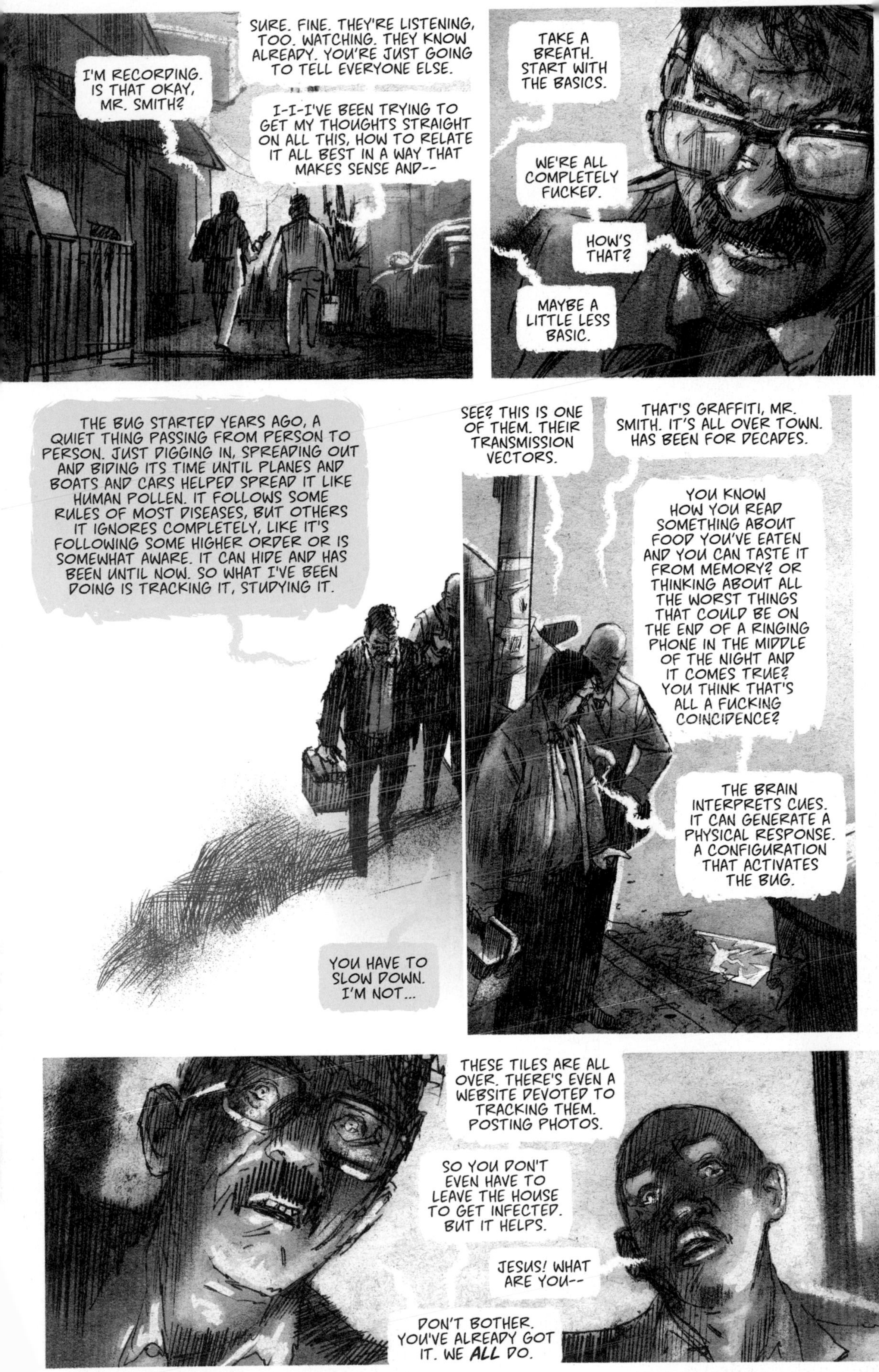
I'M RECORDING. IS THAT OKAY, MR. SMITH?
SURE. FINE. THEY'RE LISTENING, TOO. WATCHING. THEY KNOW ALREADY. YOU'RE JUST GOING TO TELL EVERYONE ELSE.
I-I-I'VE BEEN TRYING TO GET MY THOUGHTS STRAIGHT ON ALL THIS, HOW TO RELATE IT ALL BEST IN A WAY THAT MAKES SENSE AND--
TAKE A BREATH. START WITH THE BASICS.
WE'RE ALL COMPLETELY FUCKED.
HOW'S THAT?
MAYBE A LITTLE LESS BASIC.
THE BUG STARTED YEARS AGO, A QUIET THING PASSING FROM PERSON TO PERSON. JUST DIGGING IN, SPREADING OUT AND BIDING ITS TIME UNTIL PLANES AND BOATS AND CARS HELPED SPREAD IT LIKE HUMAN POLLEN. IT FOLLOWS SOME RULES OF MOST DISEASES, BUT OTHERS IT IGNORES COMPLETELY, LIKE IT'S FOLLOWING SOME HIGHER ORDER OR IS SOMEWHAT AWARE. IT CAN HIDE AND HAS BEEN UNTIL NOW. SO WHAT I'VE BEEN DOING IS TRACKING IT, STUDYING IT.
YOU HAVE TO SLOW DOWN. I'M NOT...
SEE? THIS IS ONE OF THEM. THEIR TRANSMISSION VECTORS.
THAT'S GRAFFITI, MR. SMITH. IT'S ALL OVER TOWN. HAS BEEN FOR DECADES.
YOU KNOW HOW YOU READ SOMETHING ABOUT FOOD YOU'VE EATEN AND YOU CAN TASTE IT FROM MEMORY? OR THINKING ABOUT ALL THE WORST THINGS THAT COULD BE ON THE END OF A RINGING PHONE IN THE MIDDLE OF THE NIGHT AND IT COMES TRUE? YOU THINK THAT'S ALL A FUCKING COINCIDENCE?
THE BRAIN INTERPRETS CUES. IT CAN GENERATE A PHYSICAL RESPONSE. A CONFIGURATION THAT ACTIVATES THE BUG.
THESE TILES ARE ALL OVER. THERE'S EVEN A WEBSITE DEVOTED TO TRACKING THEM. POSTING PHOTOS.
SO YOU DON'T EVEN HAVE TO LEAVE THE HOUSE TO GET INFECTED. BUT IT HELPS.
JESUS! WHAT ARE YOU--
DON'T BOTHER. YOU'VE ALREADY GOT IT. WE ALL DO.

THE TILES HAVE BEEN AROUND FOR DECADES.

THEY'VE FOUND THEM AS FAR AWAY AS SOUTH AMERICA AND EUROPE.

ADVERTISEMENTS FOR NONSENSE. OR SEEDS TO DESTROY HUMANITY. CHECK YOUR EMAIL.

WHY KILL EVERYONE? LIKE, WHAT DOES THAT GET ANYONE?

HA. YOU SIMPLE...THEY'RE NOT KILLING ANYONE. THEY'RE UNLOCKING US. WE'RE PEOPLE, SO WE MAKE THE LEAP TO THAT NEXT STEP PRETTY QUICKLY.

THAT'S WHAT BRAIN FLUID LOOKS LIKE. THAT'S WHAT EVERYONE LOOKS LIKE WHEN YOU LOOK AT THEM. UP CLOSE. EVERYONE'S THE GODDAMN SAME IF YOU ZOOM IN ENOUGH.

THWK THWK THWK

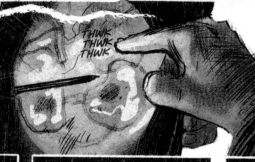

BUT IT'S SNEAKY.

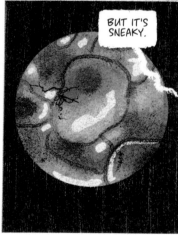

IT KNOWS. WHEN IT THINKS YOU'RE NOT LOOKING, WHEN NO ONE IS AWARE, IT UNFOLDS.

INVASIVE, SPREAD ALL THROUGHOUT THE SYSTEM, ALL THROUGHOUT HUMANITY.

SO WHAT IS--

THE TRANSMISSION. *THAT*, I GET.

HOW IT WORKS. MOSTLY UNDERSTAND THAT.

BUT WHO THE FUCK KNOWS WHY ANYONE DOES ANYTHING? I CAN'T TELL ANYMORE. MAYBE THEY'RE SAVING THE WORLD BY KILLING US ALL. WHO CARES.

I DON'T NEED TO KNOW THAT SHIT TO STOP THEM. TO STOP THE BUG.

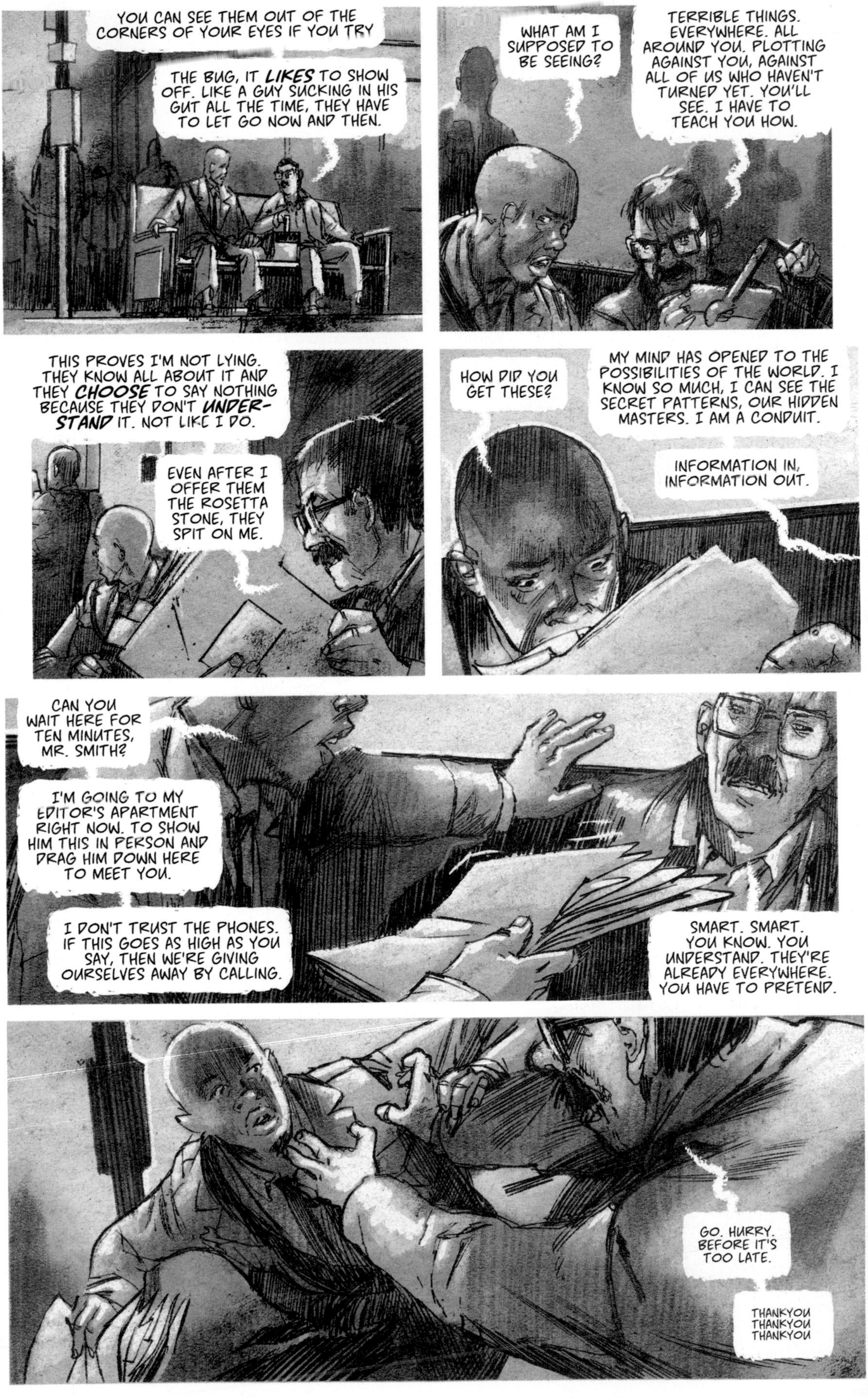
YOU CAN SEE THEM OUT OF THE CORNERS OF YOUR EYES IF YOU TRY
THE BUG, IT LIKES TO SHOW OFF. LIKE A GUY SUCKING IN HIS GUT ALL THE TIME, THEY HAVE TO LET GO NOW AND THEN.
WHAT AM I SUPPOSED TO BE SEEING?
TERRIBLE THINGS. EVERYWHERE. ALL AROUND YOU. PLOTTING AGAINST YOU, AGAINST ALL OF US WHO HAVEN'T TURNED YET. YOU'LL SEE. I HAVE TO TEACH YOU HOW.
THIS PROVES I'M NOT LYING. THEY KNOW ALL ABOUT IT AND THEY CHOOSE TO SAY NOTHING BECAUSE THEY DON'T UNDER-STAND IT. NOT LIKE I DO.
EVEN AFTER I OFFER THEM THE ROSETTA STONE, THEY SPIT ON ME.
HOW DID YOU GET THESE?
MY MIND HAS OPENED TO THE POSSIBILITIES OF THE WORLD. I KNOW SO MUCH, I CAN SEE THE SECRET PATTERNS, OUR HIDDEN MASTERS. I AM A CONDUIT.
INFORMATION IN, INFORMATION OUT.
CAN YOU WAIT HERE FOR TEN MINUTES, MR. SMITH?
I'M GOING TO MY EDITOR'S APARTMENT RIGHT NOW. TO SHOW HIM THIS IN PERSON AND DRAG HIM DOWN HERE TO MEET YOU.
I DON'T TRUST THE PHONES. IF THIS GOES AS HIGH AS YOU SAY, THEN WE'RE GIVING OURSELVES AWAY BY CALLING.
SMART. SMART. YOU KNOW. YOU UNDERSTAND. THEY'RE ALREADY EVERYWHERE. YOU HAVE TO PRETEND.
GO. HURRY. BEFORE IT'S TOO LATE.
THANKYOU THANKYOU THANKYOU

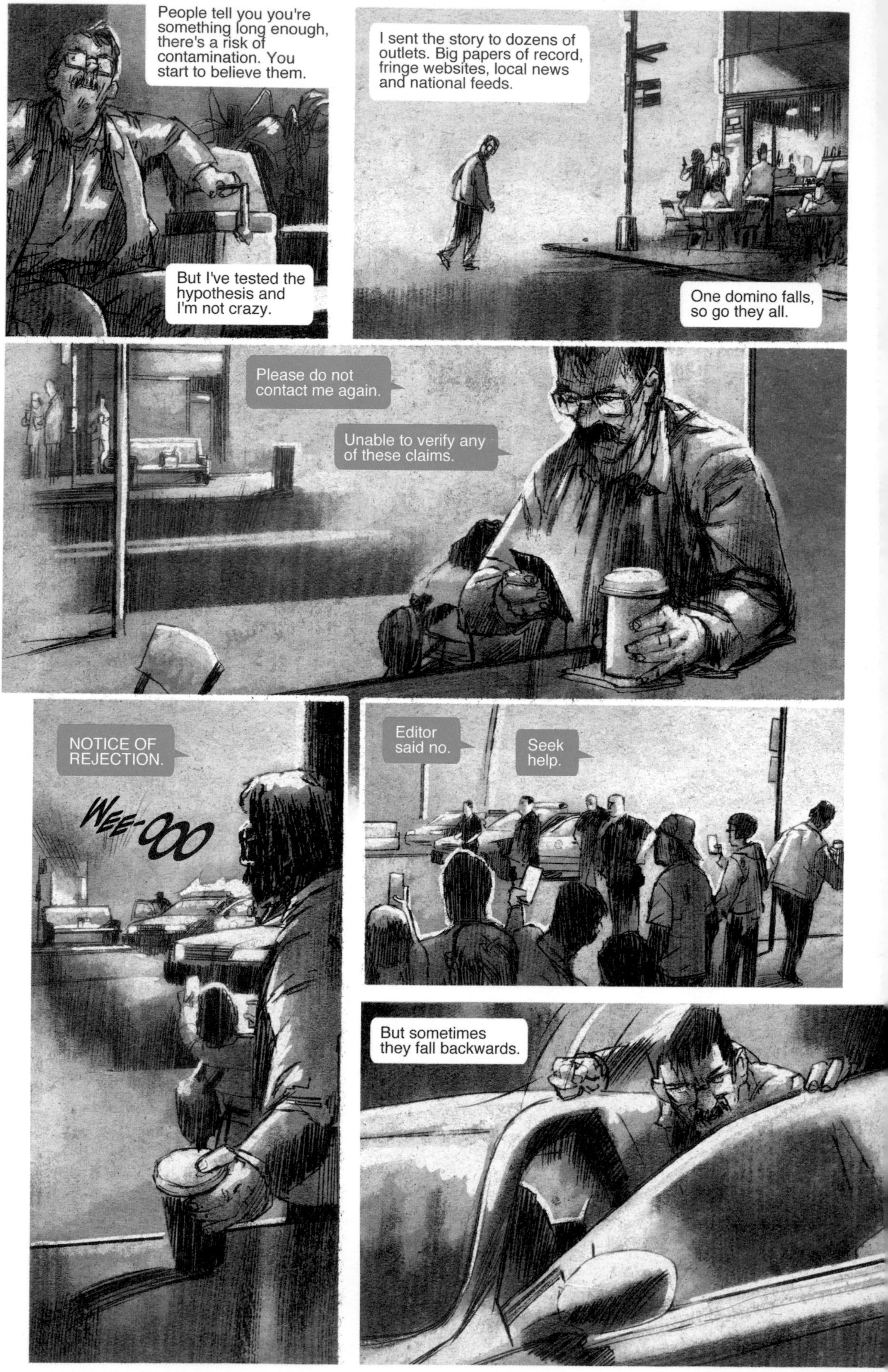
People tell you you're something long enough, there's a risk of contamination. You start to believe them.
But I've tested the hypothesis and I'm not crazy.
I sent the story to dozens of outlets. Big papers of record, fringe websites, local news and national feeds.
One domino falls, so go they all.
Please do not contact me again.
Unable to verify any of these claims.
NOTICE OF REJECTION.
WEE-OOO
Editor said no.
Seek help.
But sometimes they fall backwards.

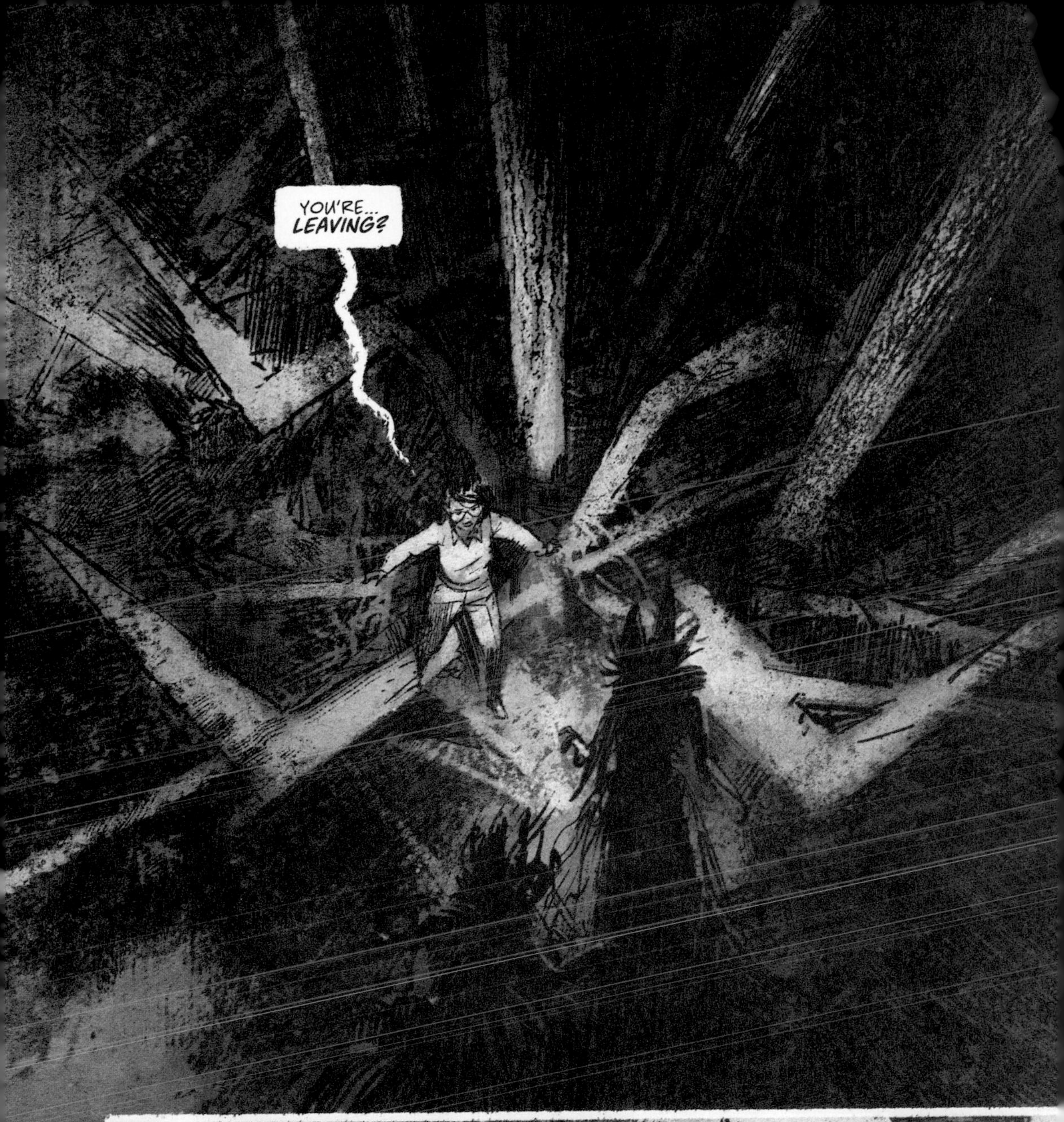
YOU'RE... LEAVING?

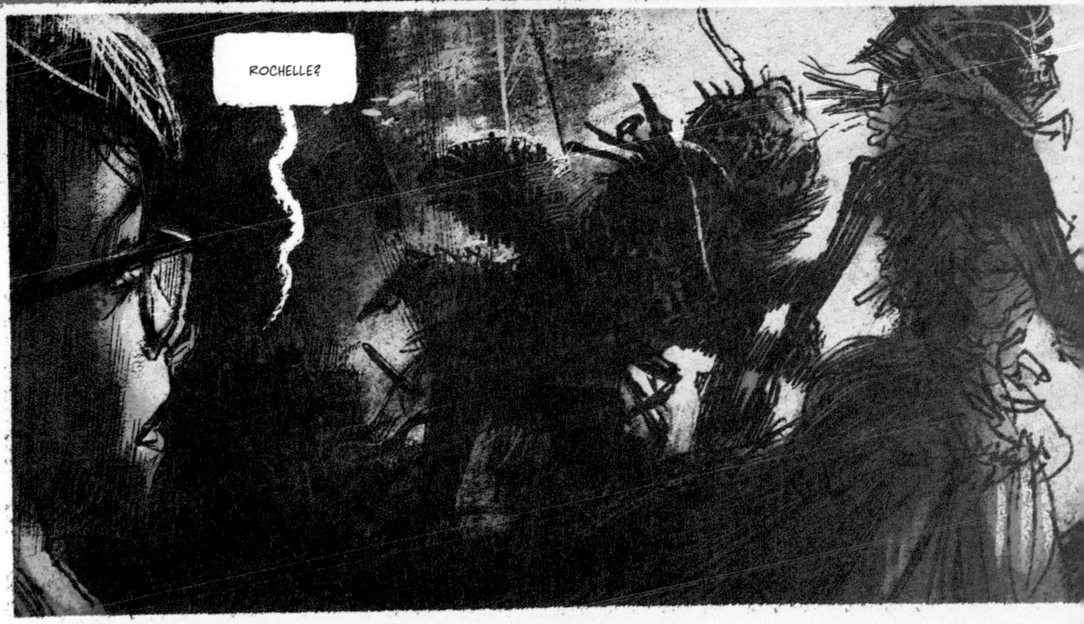
ROCHELLE?

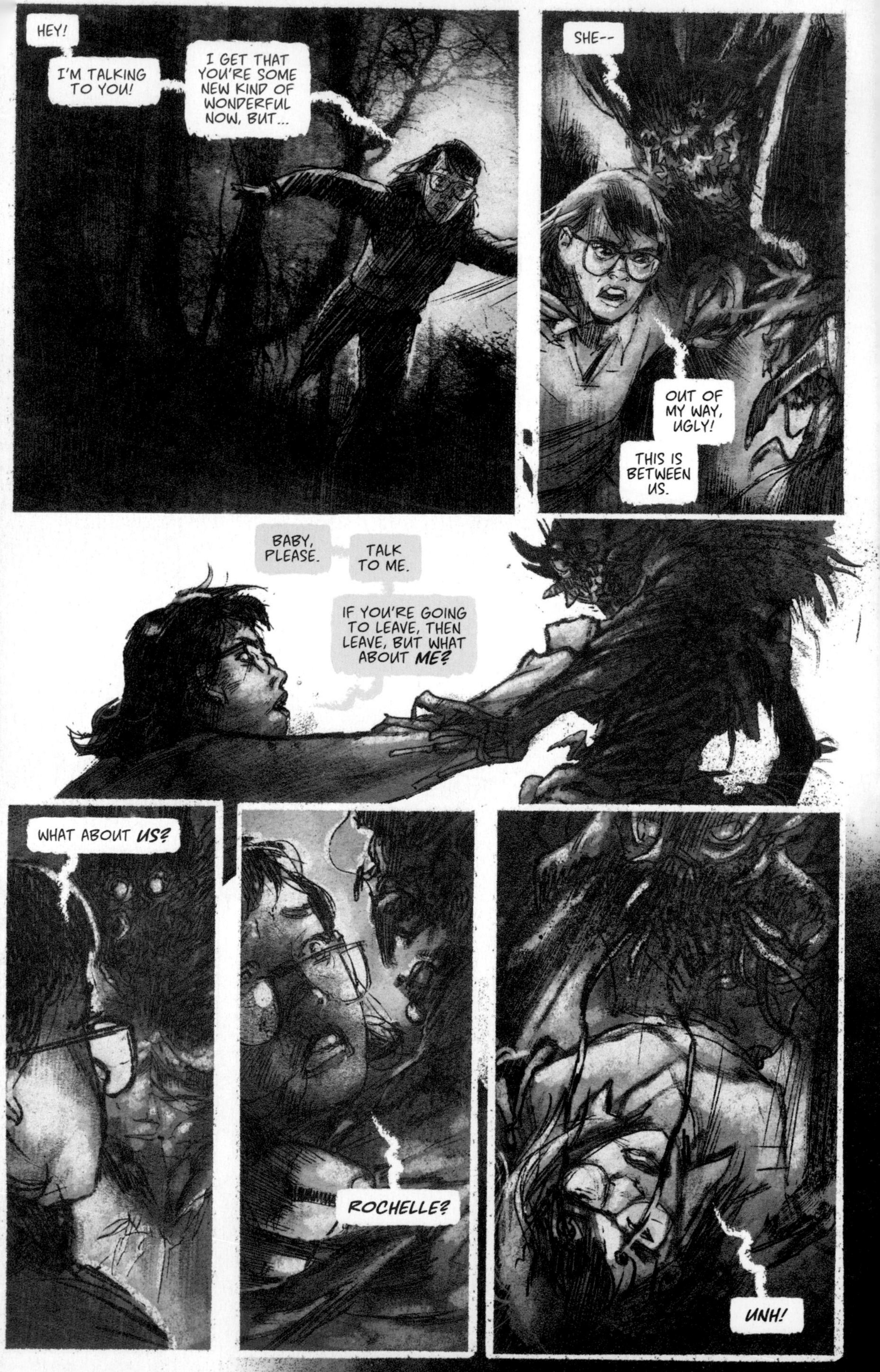
HEY!
I'M TALKING TO YOU!
I GET THAT YOU'RE SOME NEW KIND OF WONDERFUL NOW, BUT...
SHE--
OUT OF MY WAY, UGLY!
THIS IS BETWEEN US.
BABY, PLEASE.
TALK TO ME.
IF YOU'RE GOING TO LEAVE, THEN LEAVE, BUT WHAT ABOUT ME?
WHAT ABOUT US?
ROCHELLE?
UNH!

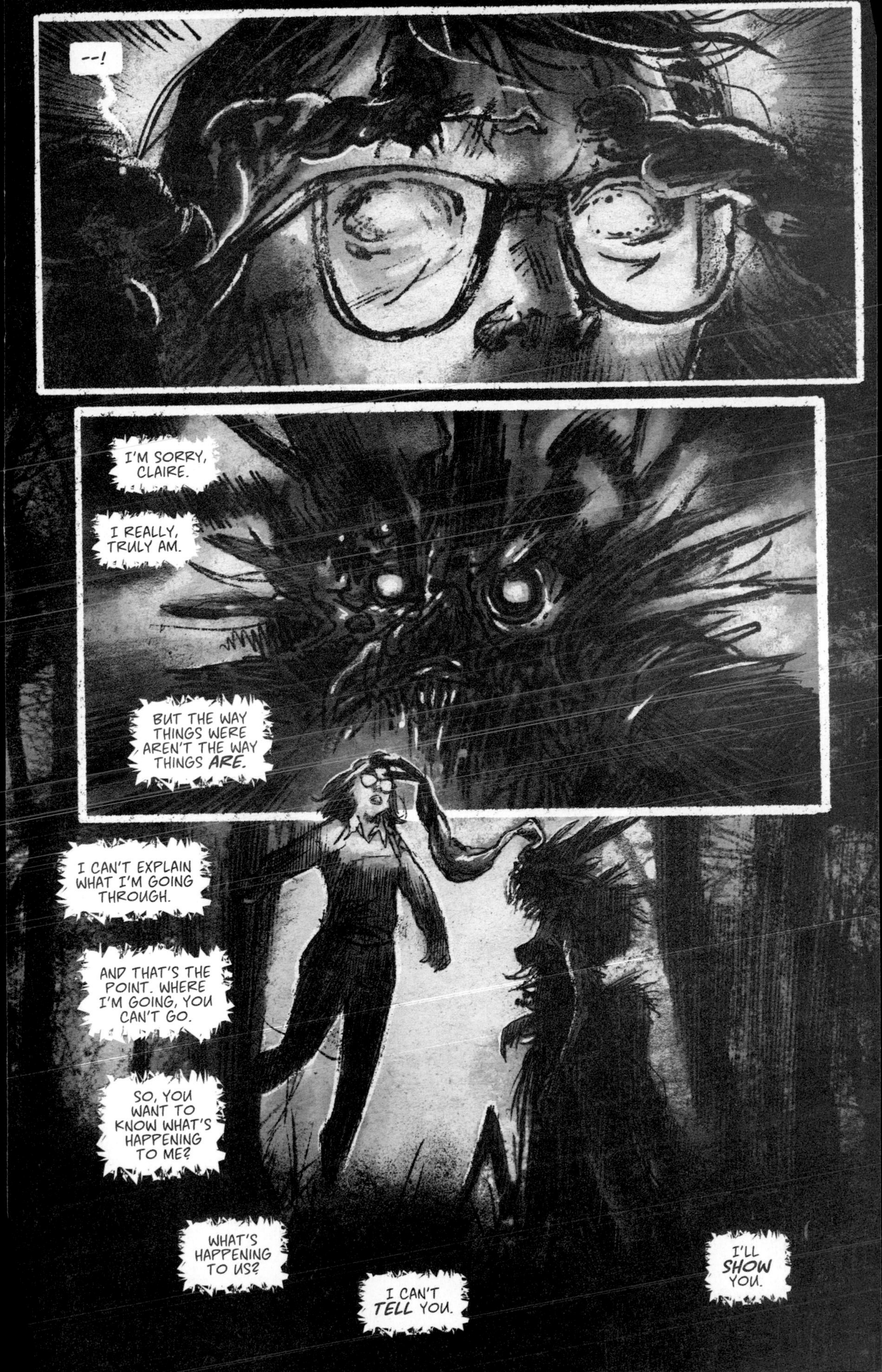
--!
I'M SORRY, CLAIRE.
I REALLY, TRULY AM.
BUT THE WAY THINGS WERE AREN'T THE WAY THINGS *ARE.*
I CAN'T EXPLAIN WHAT I'M GOING THROUGH.
AND THAT'S THE POINT. WHERE I'M GOING, YOU CAN'T GO.
SO, YOU WANT TO KNOW WHAT'S HAPPENING TO ME?
WHAT'S HAPPENING TO US?
I CAN'T **TELL** YOU.
I'LL **SHOW** YOU.

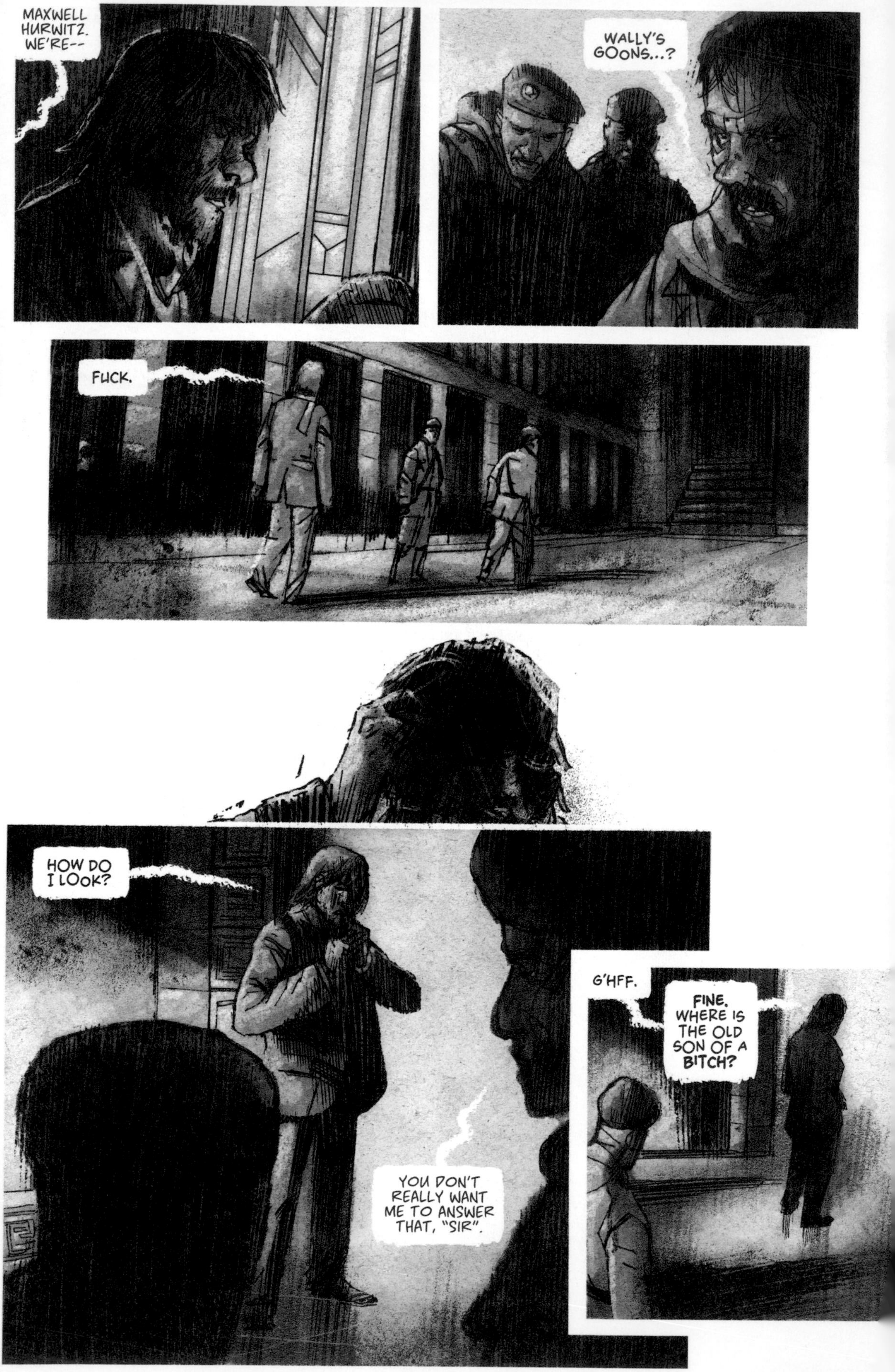
MAXWELL HURWITZ. WE'RE--
WALLY'S GOONS...?
FUCK.
HOW DO I LOOK?
YOU DON'T REALLY WANT ME TO ANSWER THAT, "SIR".
G'HFF.
FINE. WHERE IS THE OLD SON OF A BITCH?

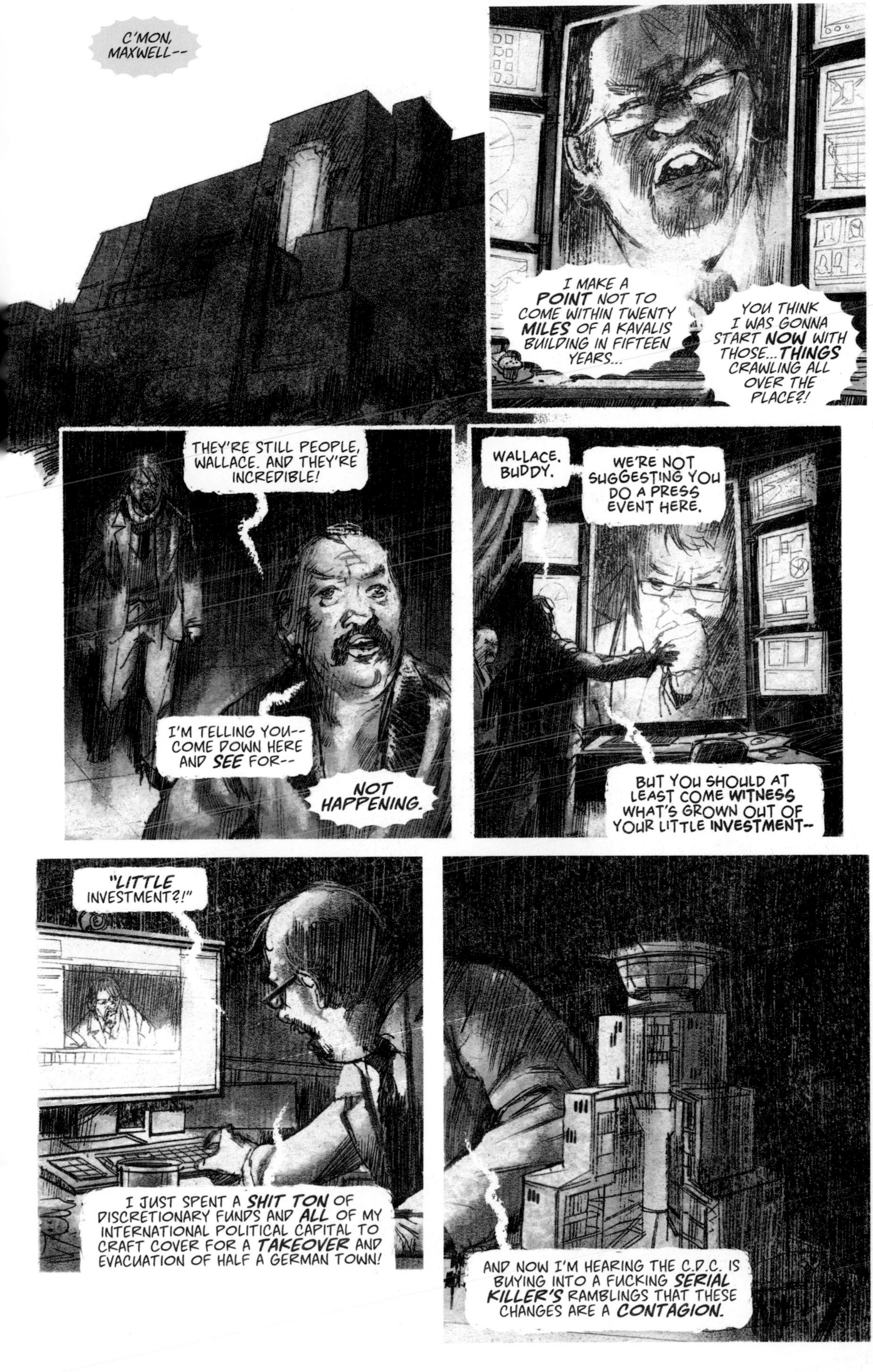
C'MON, MAXWELL--
I MAKE A POINT NOT TO COME WITHIN TWENTY MILES OF A KAVALIS BUILDING IN FIFTEEN YEARS...
YOU THINK I WAS GONNA START NOW WITH THOSE...THINGS CRAWLING ALL OVER THE PLACE?!
THEY'RE STILL PEOPLE, WALLACE. AND THEY'RE INCREDIBLE!
I'M TELLING YOU-- COME DOWN HERE AND SEE FOR--
NOT HAPPENING.
WALLACE. BUDDY.
WE'RE NOT SUGGESTING YOU DO A PRESS EVENT HERE.
BUT YOU SHOULD AT LEAST COME WITNESS WHAT'S GROWN OUT OF YOUR LITTLE INVESTMENT--
"LITTLE INVESTMENT?!"
I JUST SPENT A SHIT TON OF DISCRETIONARY FUNDS AND ALL OF MY INTERNATIONAL POLITICAL CAPITAL TO CRAFT COVER FOR A TAKEOVER AND EVACUATION OF HALF A GERMAN TOWN!
AND NOW I'M HEARING THE C.D.C. IS BUYING INTO A FUCKING SERIAL KILLER'S RAMBLINGS THAT THESE CHANGES ARE A CONTAGION.

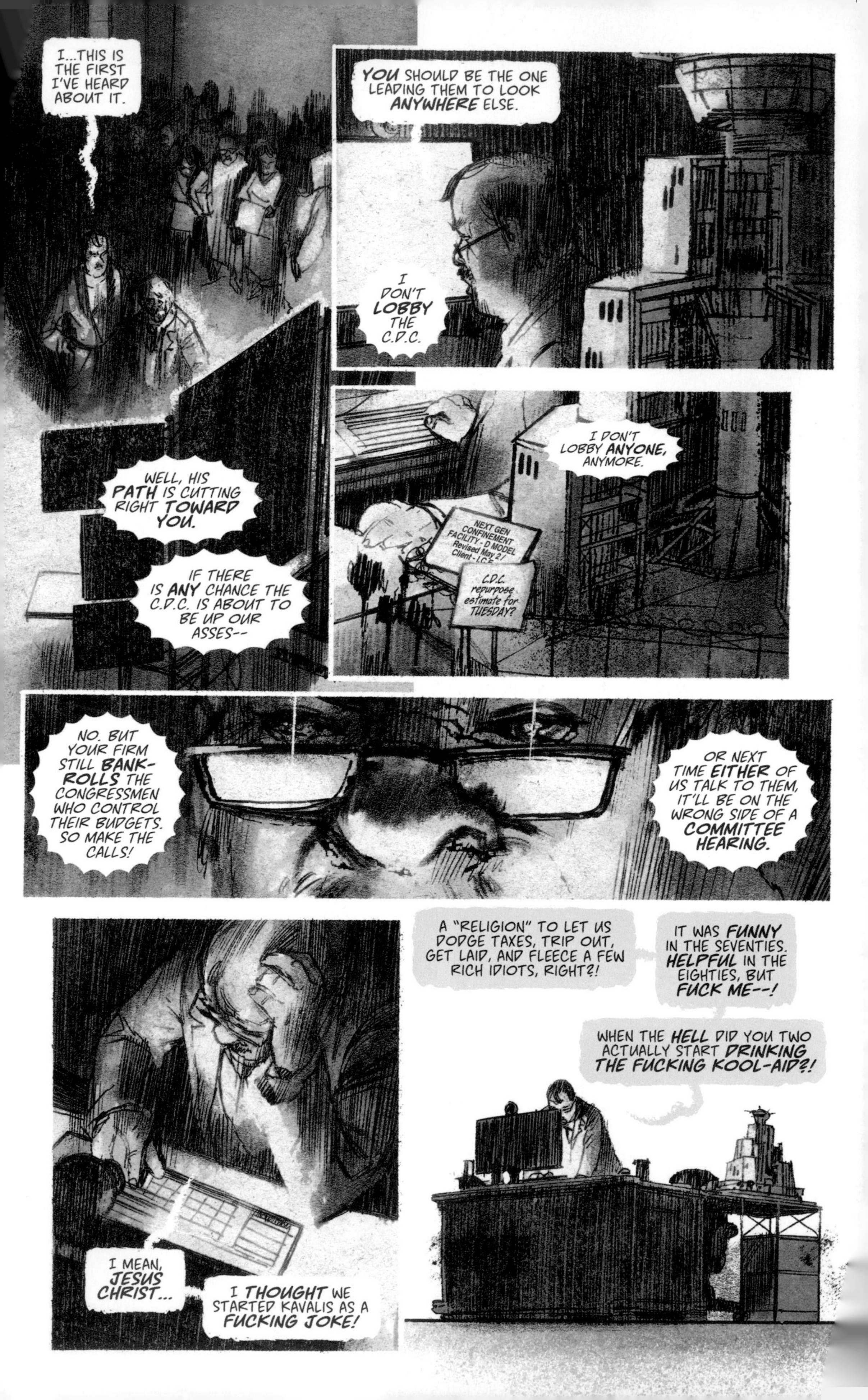
I...THIS IS THE FIRST I'VE HEARD ABOUT IT.
YOU SHOULD BE THE ONE LEADING THEM TO LOOK ANYWHERE ELSE.
I DON'T LOBBY THE C.D.C.
WELL, HIS PATH IS CUTTING RIGHT TOWARD YOU.
IF THERE IS ANY CHANCE THE C.D.C. IS ABOUT TO BE UP OUR ASSES--
I DON'T LOBBY ANYONE, ANYMORE.
NEXT GEN CONFINEMENT FACILITY - D MODEL Revised May 2 / Client - I.C.E.
C.D.C. repurpose estimate for TUESDAY?
NO. BUT YOUR FIRM STILL BANKROLLS THE CONGRESSMEN WHO CONTROL THEIR BUDGETS. SO MAKE THE CALLS!
OR NEXT TIME EITHER OF US TALK TO THEM, IT'LL BE ON THE WRONG SIDE OF A COMMITTEE HEARING.
I MEAN, JESUS CHRIST...
I THOUGHT WE STARTED KAVALIS AS A FUCKING JOKE!
A "RELIGION" TO LET US DODGE TAXES, TRIP OUT, GET LAID, AND FLEECE A FEW RICH IDIOTS, RIGHT?!
IT WAS FUNNY IN THE SEVENTIES. HELPFUL IN THE EIGHTIES, BUT FUCK ME--!
WHEN THE HELL DID YOU TWO ACTUALLY START DRINKING THE FUCKING KOOL-AID?!

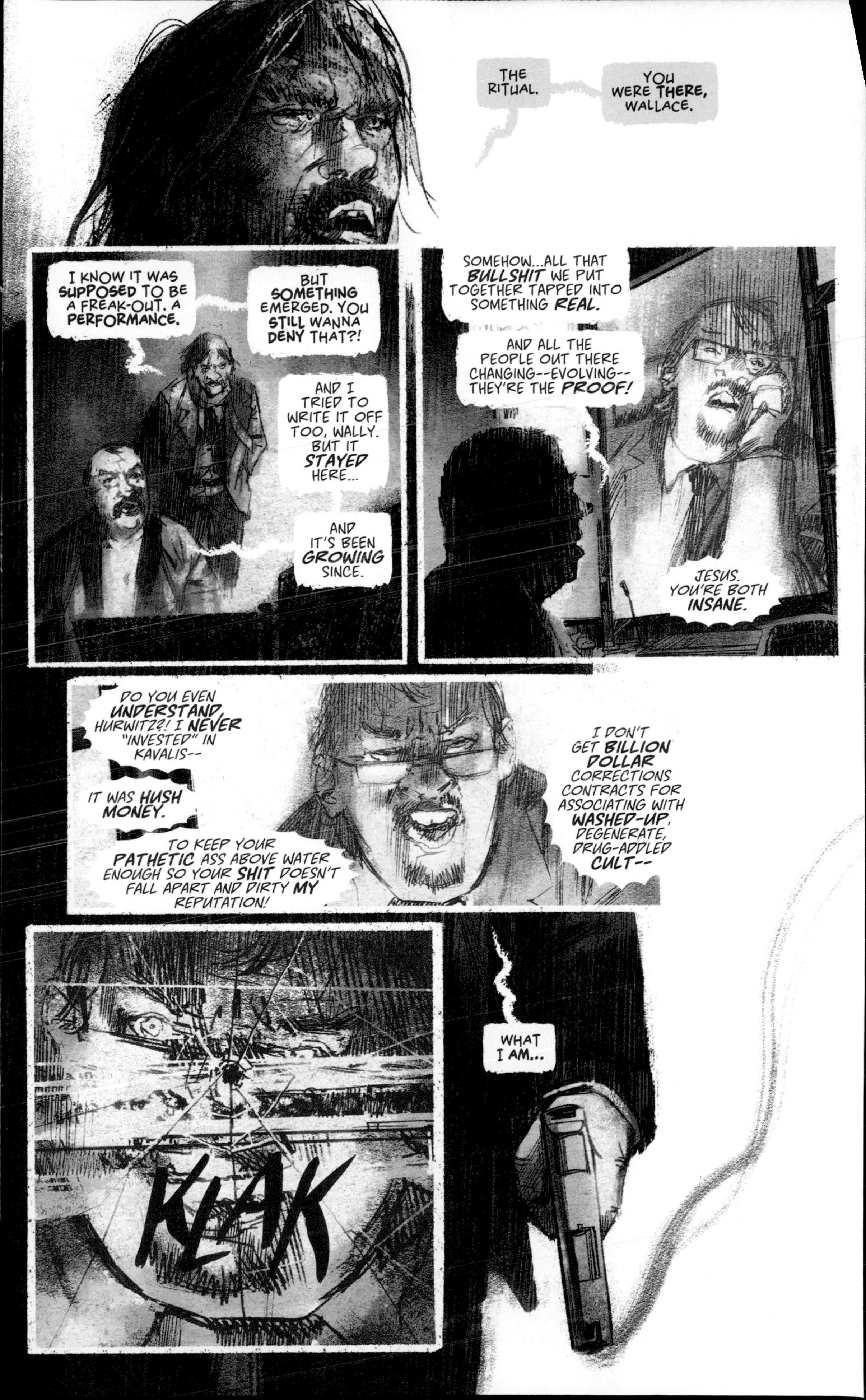
THE RITUAL.
YOU WERE THERE, WALLACE.
I KNOW IT WAS SUPPOSED TO BE A FREAK-OUT. A PERFORMANCE.
BUT SOMETHING EMERGED. YOU STILL WANNA DENY THAT?!
AND I TRIED TO WRITE IT OFF TOO, WALLY. BUT IT STAYED HERE...
AND IT'S BEEN GROWING SINCE.
SOMEHOW...ALL THAT BULLSHIT WE PUT TOGETHER TAPPED INTO SOMETHING REAL.
AND ALL THE PEOPLE OUT THERE CHANGING--EVOLVING--THEY'RE THE PROOF!
JESUS. YOU'RE BOTH INSANE.
DO YOU EVEN UNDERSTAND, HURWITZ?! I NEVER "INVESTED" IN KAVALIS--
IT WAS HUSH MONEY.
TO KEEP YOUR PATHETIC ASS ABOVE WATER ENOUGH SO YOUR SHIT DOESN'T FALL APART AND DIRTY MY REPUTATION!
I DON'T GET BILLION DOLLAR CORRECTIONS CONTRACTS FOR ASSOCIATING WITH WASHED-UP, DEGENERATE, DRUG-ADDLED CULT--
WHAT I AM...
KLAK

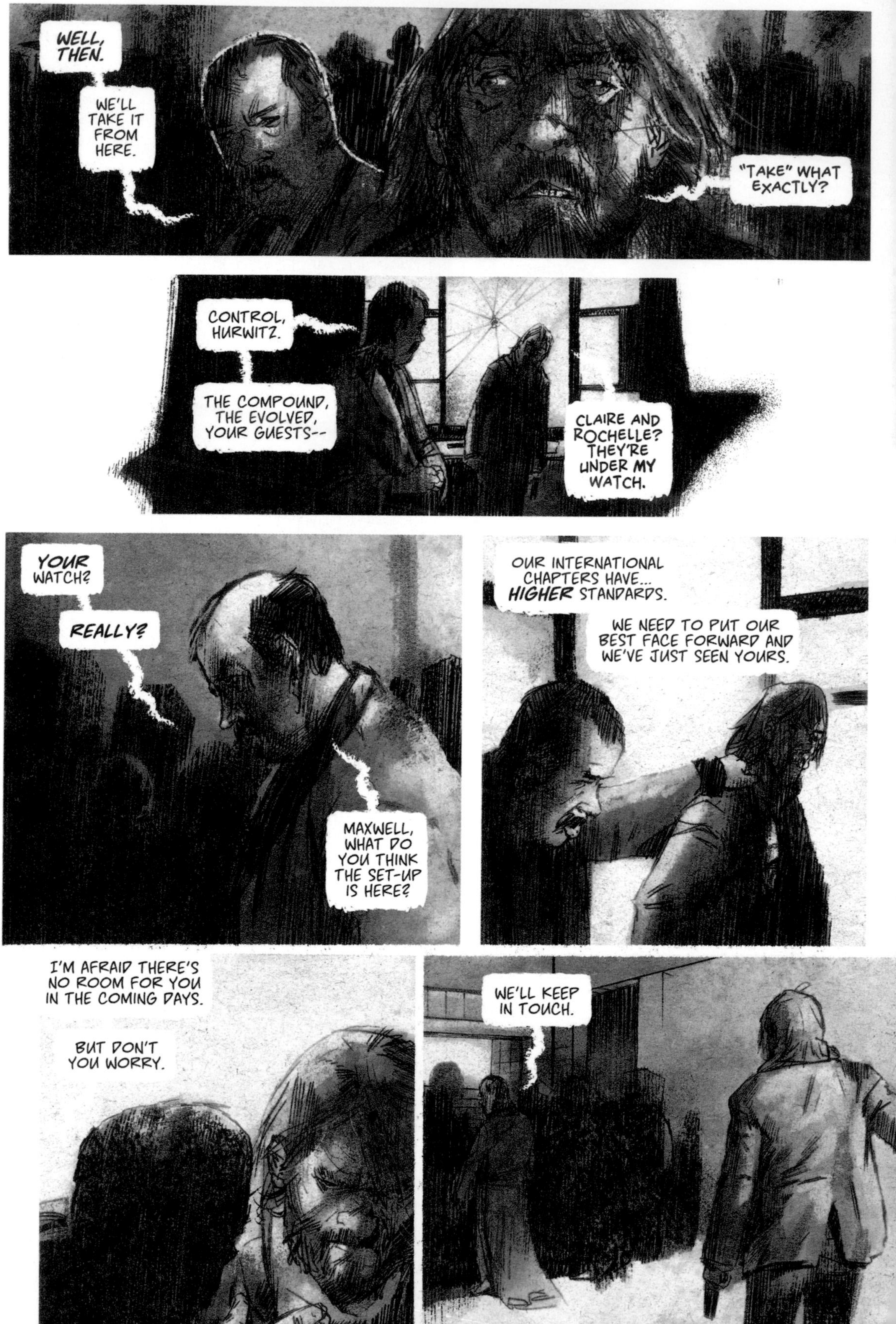
WELL, THEN.
WE'LL TAKE IT FROM HERE.
"TAKE" WHAT EXACTLY?
CONTROL, HURWITZ.
THE COMPOUND, THE EVOLVED, YOUR GUESTS--
CLAIRE AND ROCHELLE? THEY'RE UNDER MY WATCH.
YOUR WATCH?
REALLY?
MAXWELL, WHAT DO YOU THINK THE SET-UP IS HERE?
OUR INTERNATIONAL CHAPTERS HAVE... HIGHER STANDARDS.
WE NEED TO PUT OUR BEST FACE FORWARD AND WE'VE JUST SEEN YOURS.
I'M AFRAID THERE'S NO ROOM FOR YOU IN THE COMING DAYS.
BUT DON'T YOU WORRY.
WE'LL KEEP IN TOUCH.

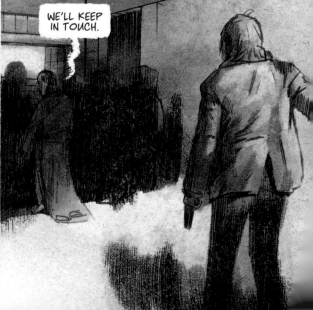

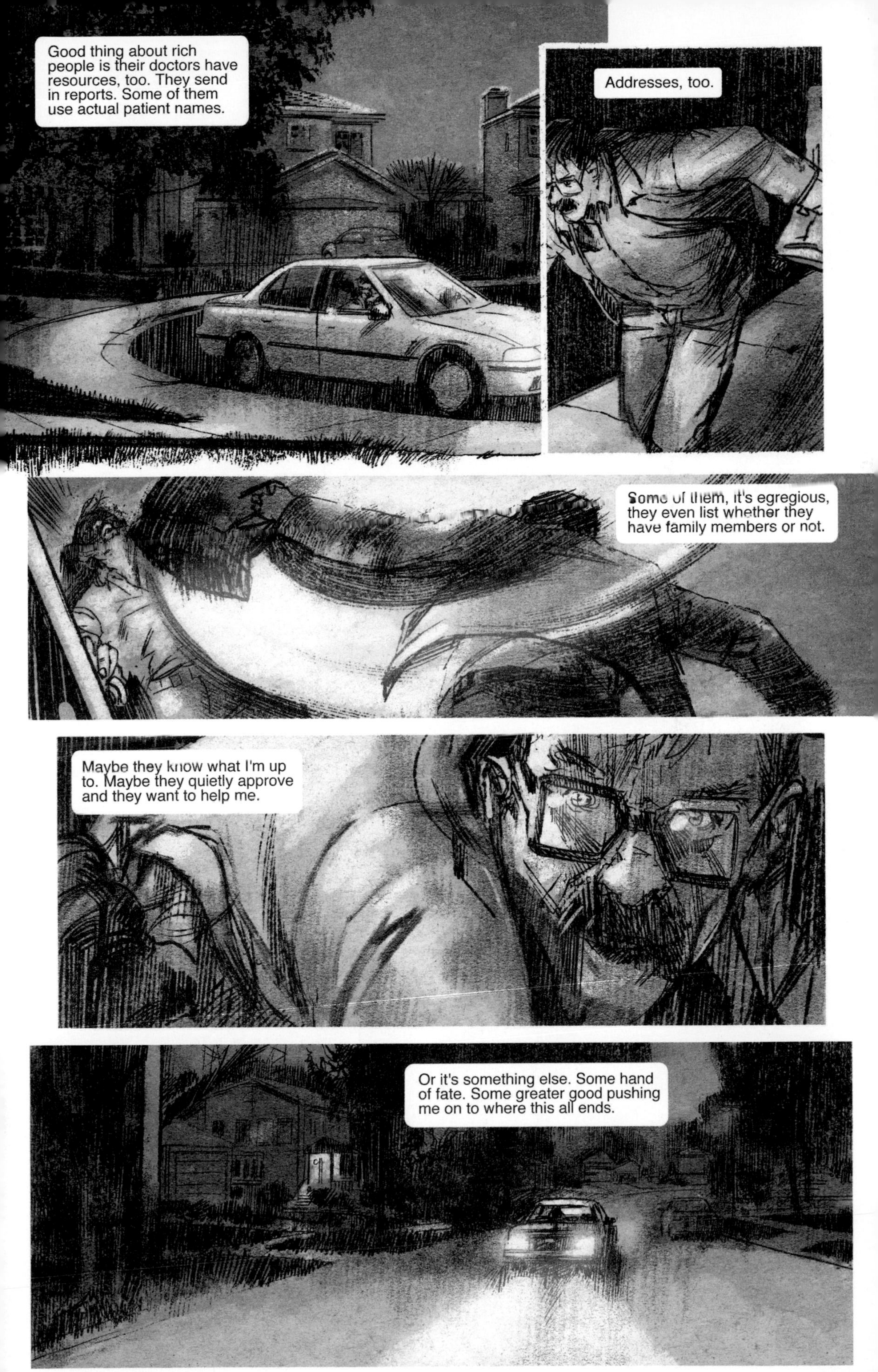
Good thing about rich people is their doctors have resources, too. They send in reports. Some of them use actual patient names.
Addresses, too.
Some of them, it's egregious, they even list whether they have family members or not.
Maybe they know what I'm up to. Maybe they quietly approve and they want to help me.
Or it's something else. Some hand of fate. Some greater good pushing me on to where this all ends.

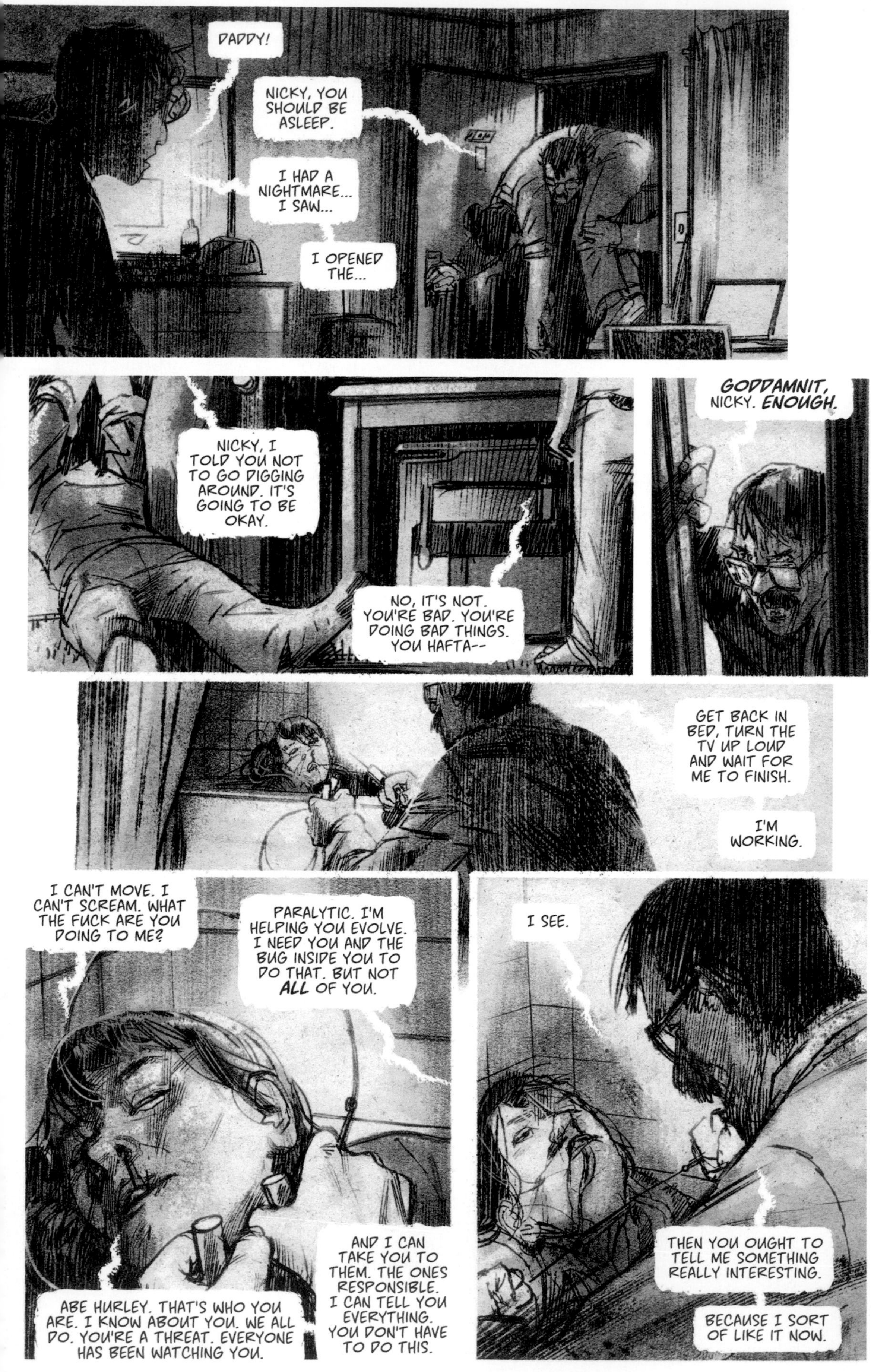
DADDY!
NICKY, YOU SHOULD BE ASLEEP.
I HAD A NIGHTMARE... I SAW...
I OPENED THE...
NICKY, I TOLD YOU NOT TO GO DIGGING AROUND. IT'S GOING TO BE OKAY.
NO, IT'S NOT. YOU'RE BAD. YOU'RE DOING BAD THINGS. YOU HAFTA--
GODDAMNIT, NICKY. ENOUGH.
GET BACK IN BED, TURN THE TV UP LOUD AND WAIT FOR ME TO FINISH.
I'M WORKING.
I CAN'T MOVE. I CAN'T SCREAM. WHAT THE FUCK ARE YOU DOING TO ME?
PARALYTIC. I'M HELPING YOU EVOLVE. I NEED YOU AND THE BUG INSIDE YOU TO DO THAT. BUT NOT ALL OF YOU.
ABE HURLEY. THAT'S WHO YOU ARE. I KNOW ABOUT YOU. WE ALL DO. YOU'RE A THREAT. EVERYONE HAS BEEN WATCHING YOU.
AND I CAN TAKE YOU TO THEM. THE ONES RESPONSIBLE. I CAN TELL YOU EVERYTHING. YOU DON'T HAVE TO DO THIS.
I SEE.
THEN YOU OUGHT TO TELL ME SOMETHING REALLY INTERESTING.
BECAUSE I SORT OF LIKE IT NOW.

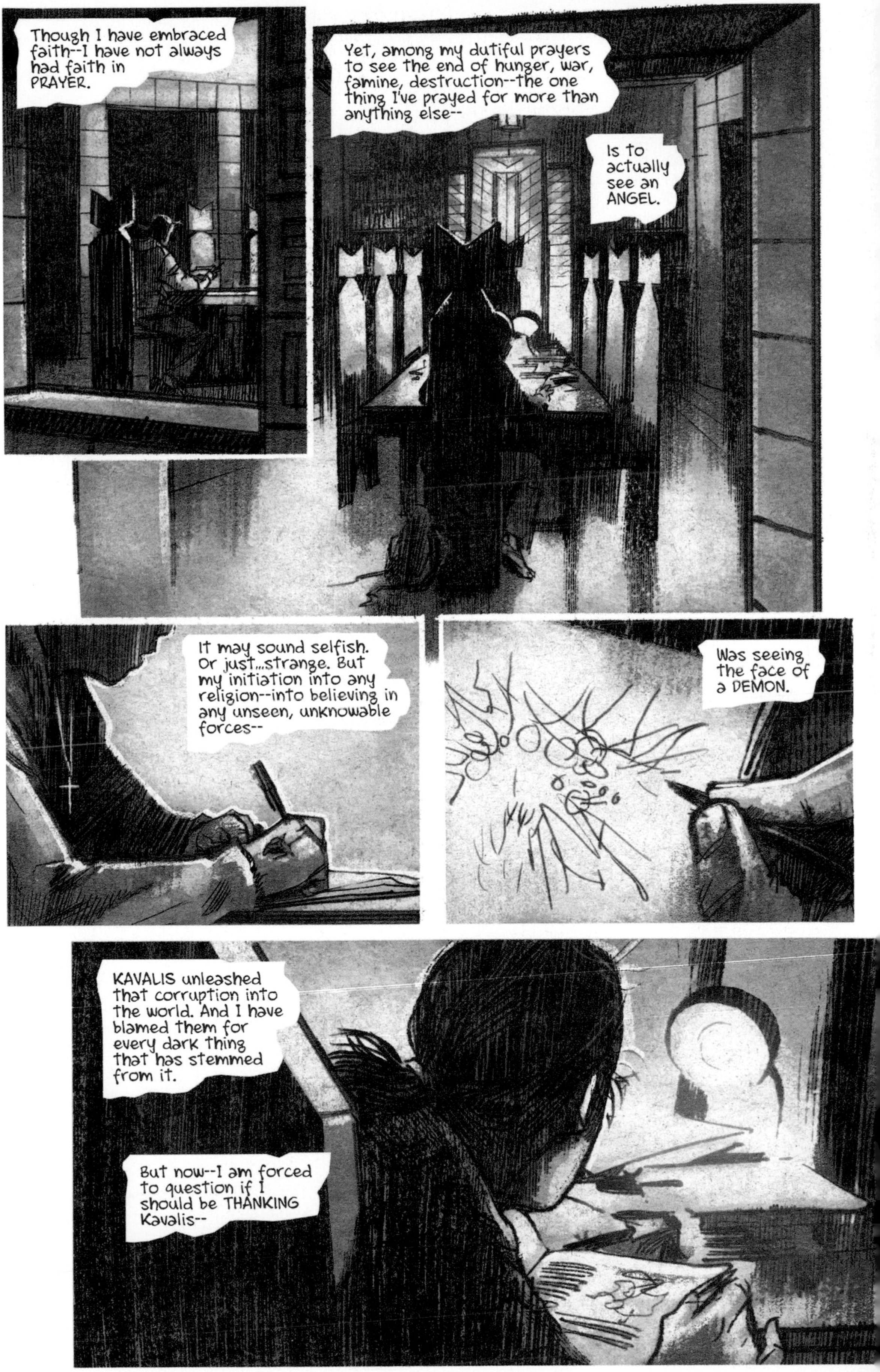

Though I have embraced faith--I have not always had faith in PRAYER.
Yet, among my dutiful prayers to see the end of hunger, war, famine, destruction--the one thing I've prayed for more than anything else--
Is to actually see an ANGEL.
It may sound selfish. Or just...strange. But my initiation into any religion--into believing in any unseen, unknowable forces--
Was seeing the face of a DEMON.
KAVALIS unleashed that corruption into the world. And I have blamed them for every dark thing that has stemmed from it.
But now--I am forced to question if I should be THANKING Kavalis--

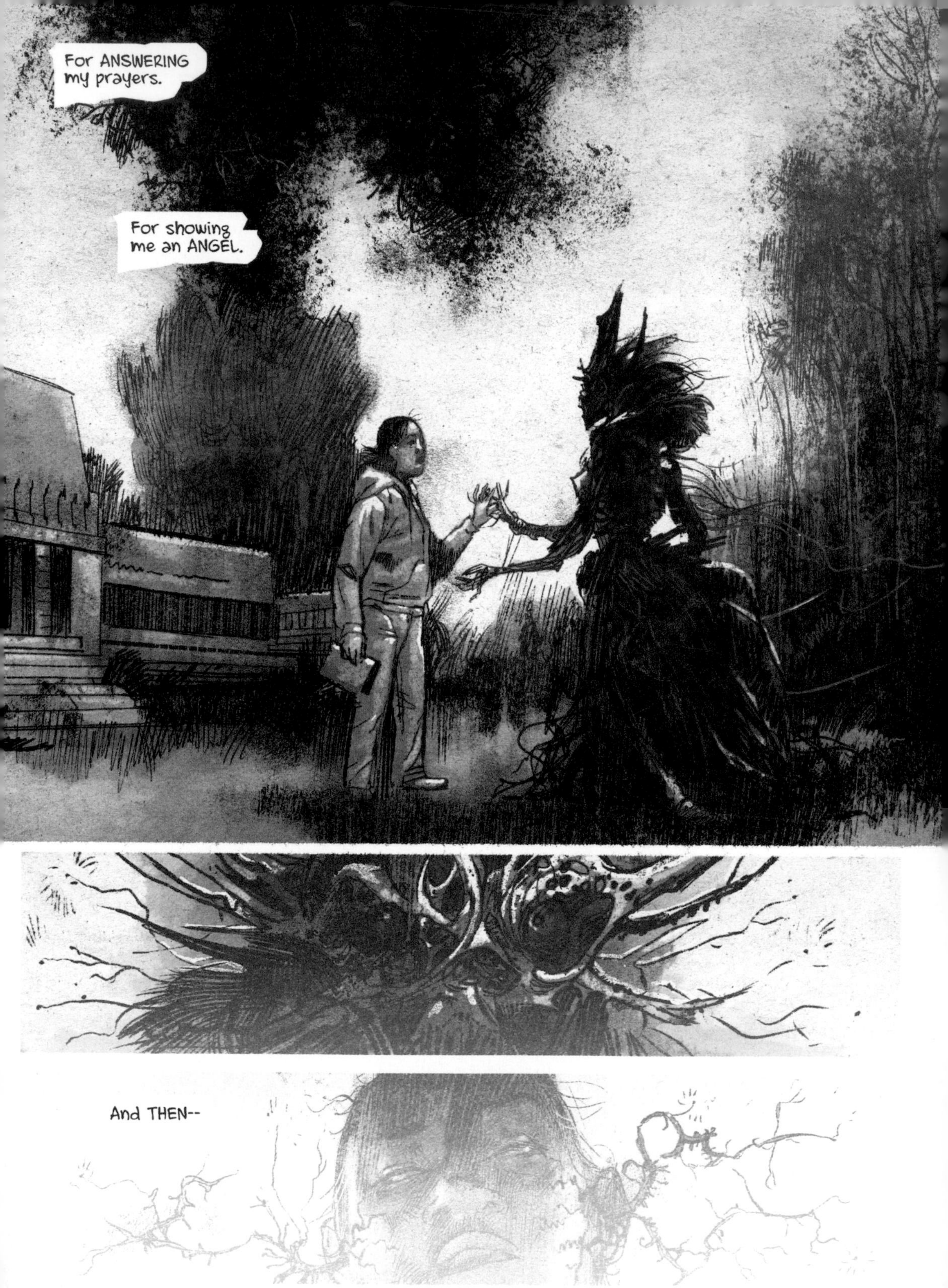
For ANSWERING my prayers.
For showing me an ANGEL.
And THEN--

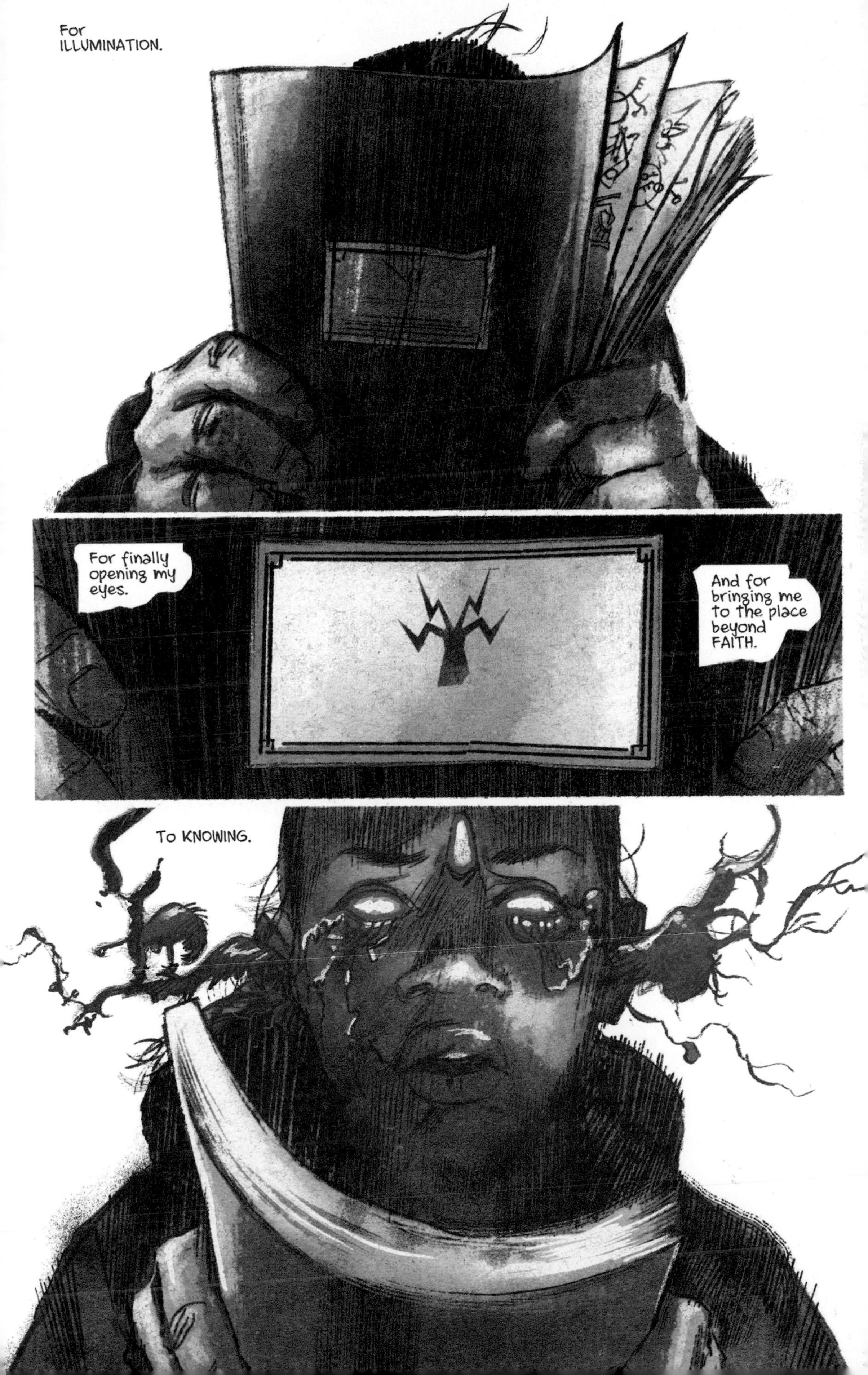
For ILLUMINATION.
For finally opening my eyes.
And for bringing me to the place beyond FAITH.
To KNOWING.

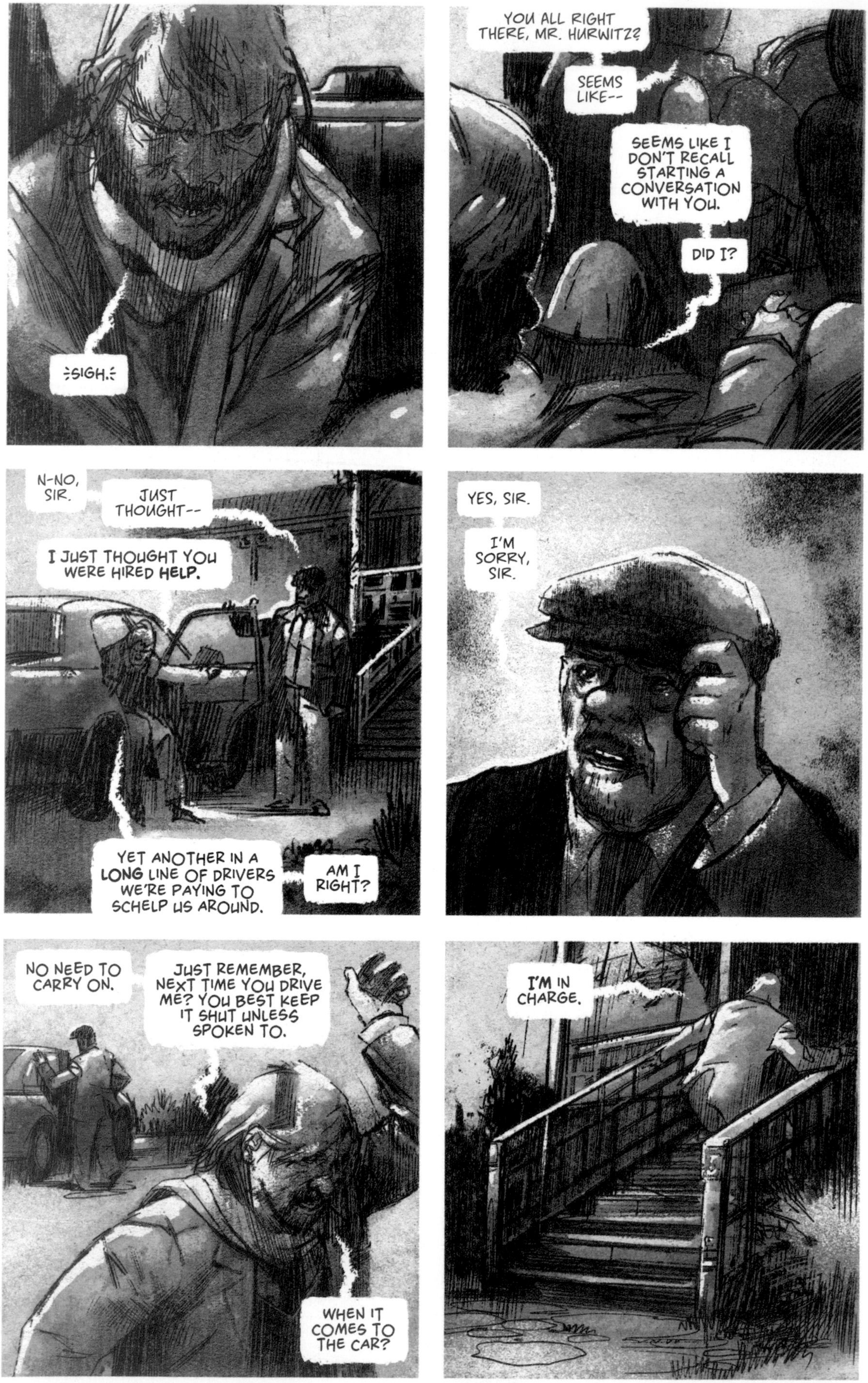

SIGH.
YOU ALL RIGHT THERE, MR. HURWITZ?
SEEMS LIKE--
SEEMS LIKE I DON'T RECALL STARTING A CONVERSATION WITH YOU.
DID I?
N-NO, SIR.
JUST THOUGHT--
I JUST THOUGHT YOU WERE HIRED **HELP.**
YET ANOTHER IN A **LONG** LINE OF DRIVERS WE'RE PAYING TO SCHELP US AROUND.
AM I RIGHT?
YES, SIR.
I'M SORRY, SIR.
NO NEED TO CARRY ON.
JUST REMEMBER, NEXT TIME YOU DRIVE ME? YOU BEST KEEP IT SHUT UNLESS SPOKEN TO.
WHEN IT COMES TO THE CAR?
I'M IN CHARGE.

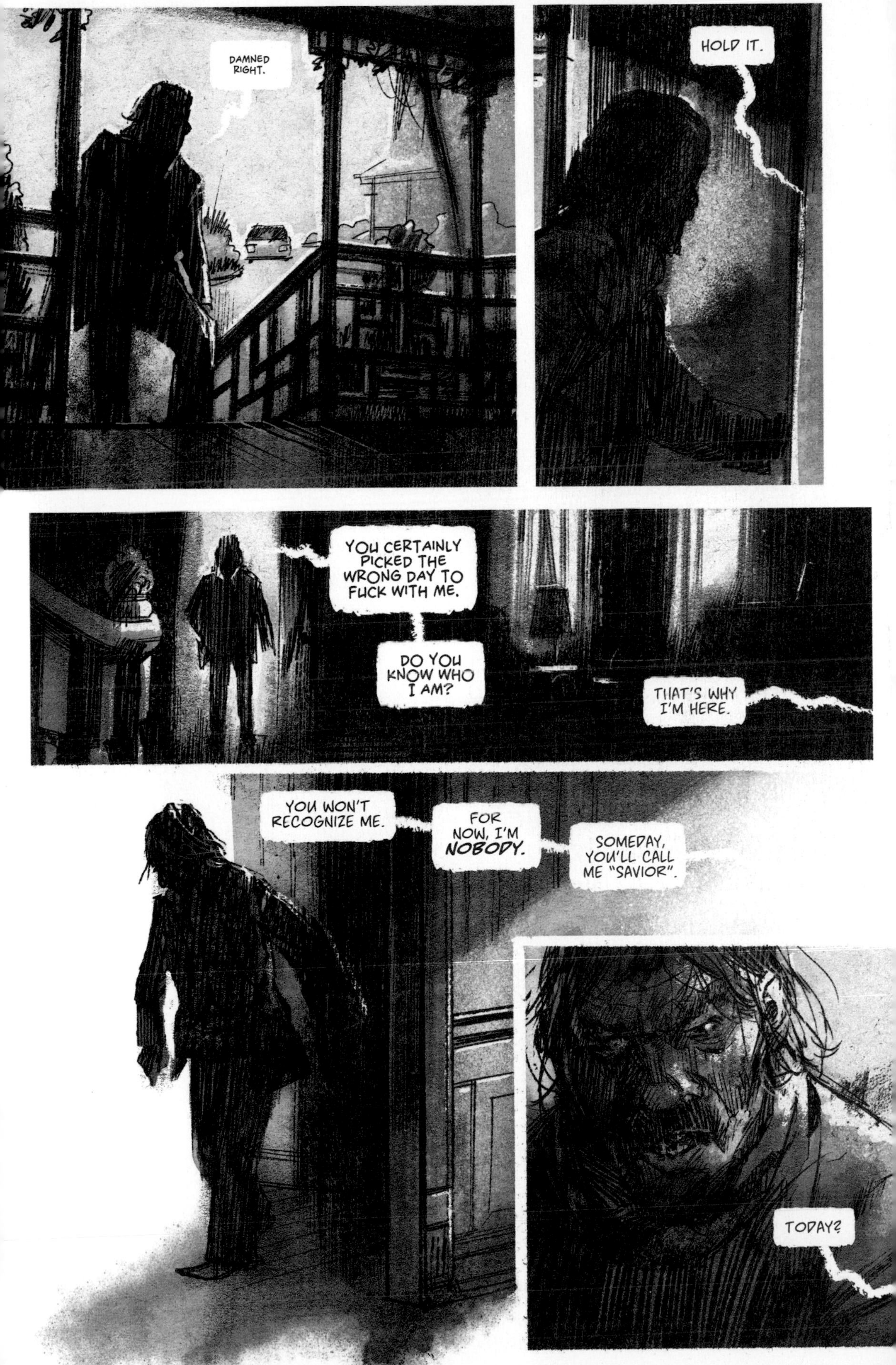
DAMNED RIGHT.
HOLD IT.
YOU CERTAINLY PICKED THE WRONG DAY TO FUCK WITH ME.
DO YOU KNOW WHO I AM?
THAT'S WHY I'M HERE.
YOU WON'T RECOGNIZE ME.
FOR NOW, I'M ***NOBODY.***
SOMEDAY, YOU'LL CALL ME "SAVIOR".
TODAY?

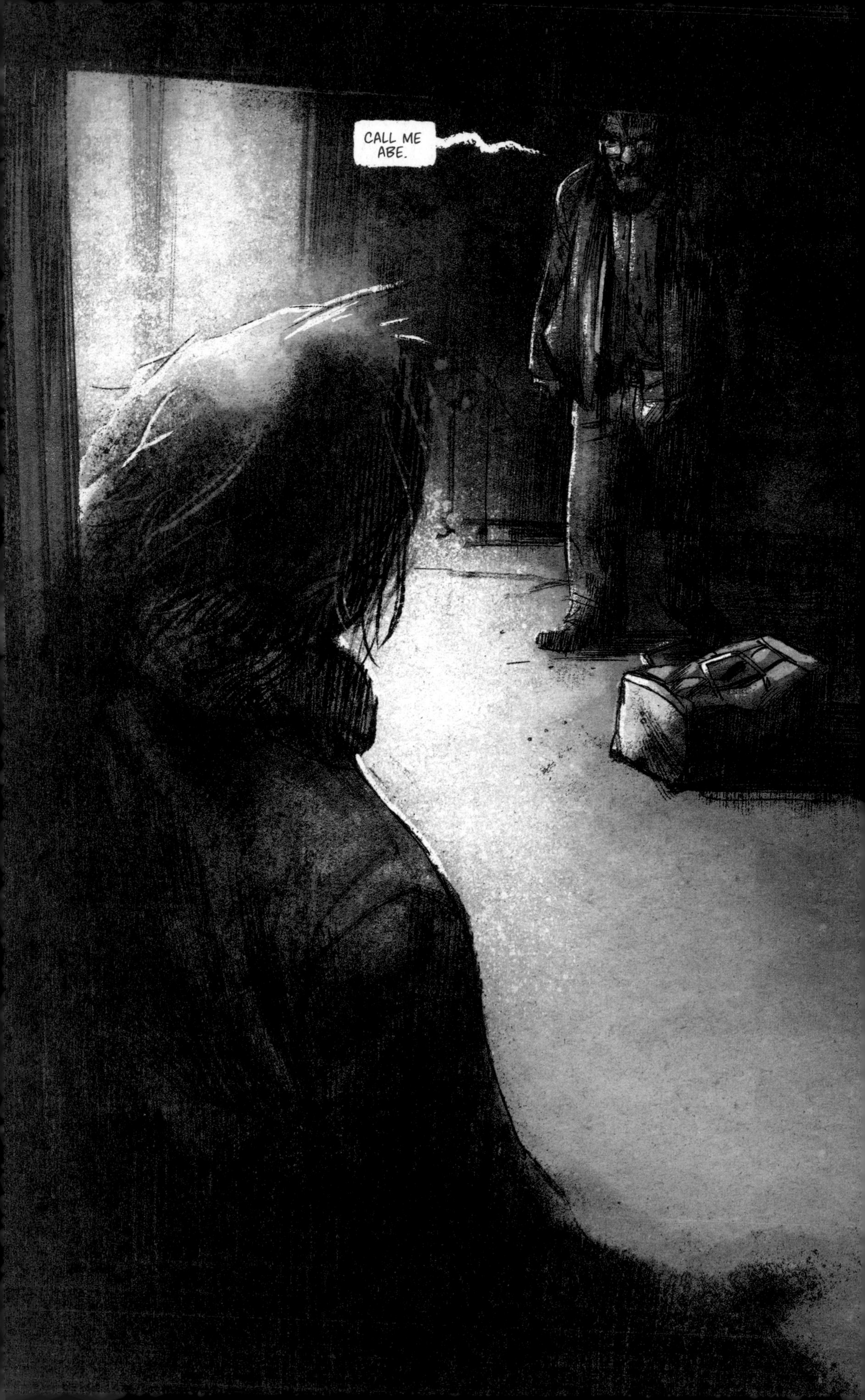
CALL ME ABE.

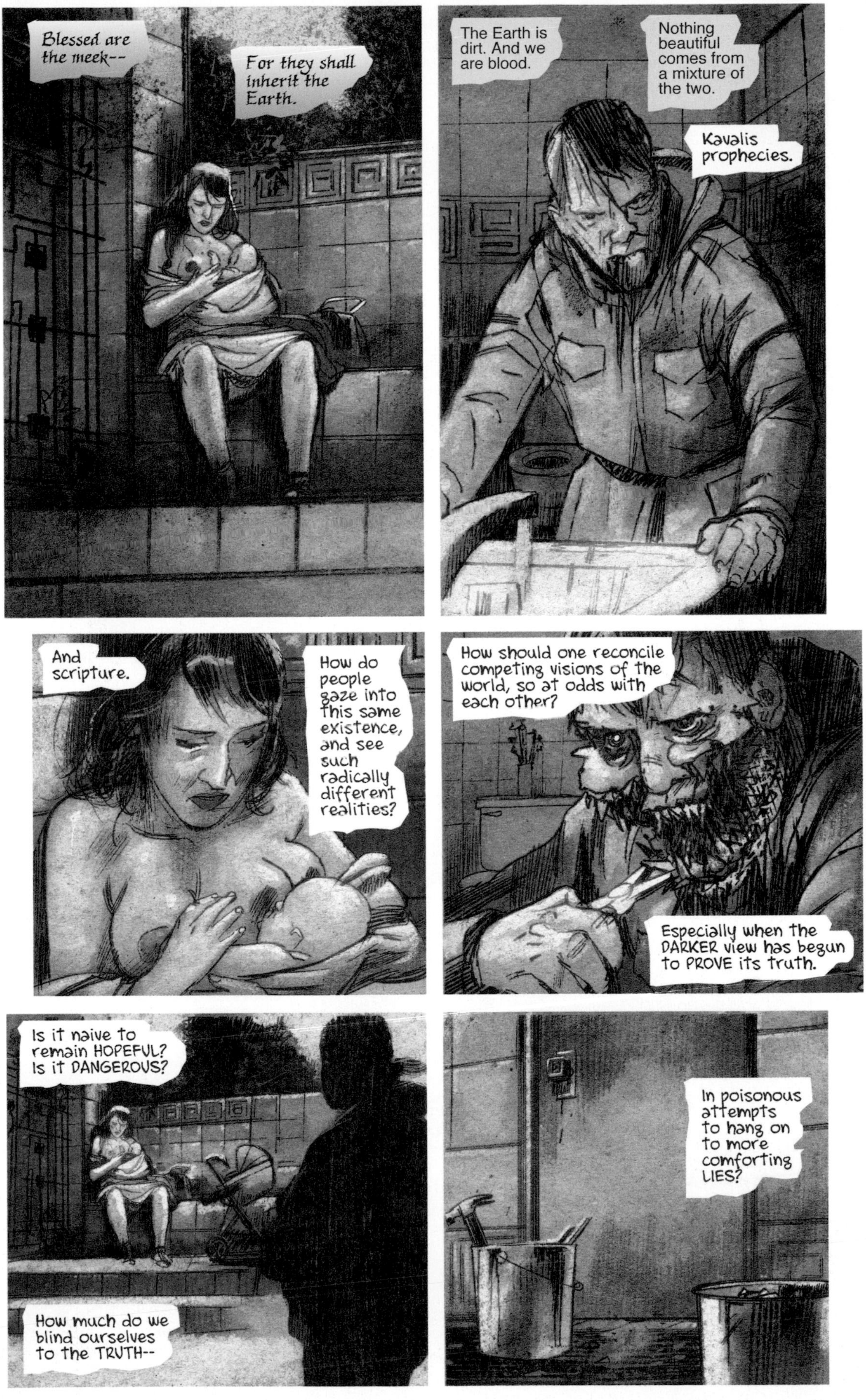
Blessed are the meek--
For they shall inherit the Earth.
The Earth is dirt. And we are blood.
Nothing beautiful comes from a mixture of the two.
Kavalis prophecies.
And scripture.
How do people gaze into this same existence, and see such radically different realities?
How should one reconcile competing visions of the world, so at odds with each other?
Especially when the DARKER view has begun to PROVE its truth.
Is it naive to remain HOPEFUL? Is it DANGEROUS?
How much do we blind ourselves to the TRUTH--
In poisonous attempts to hang on to more comforting LIES?

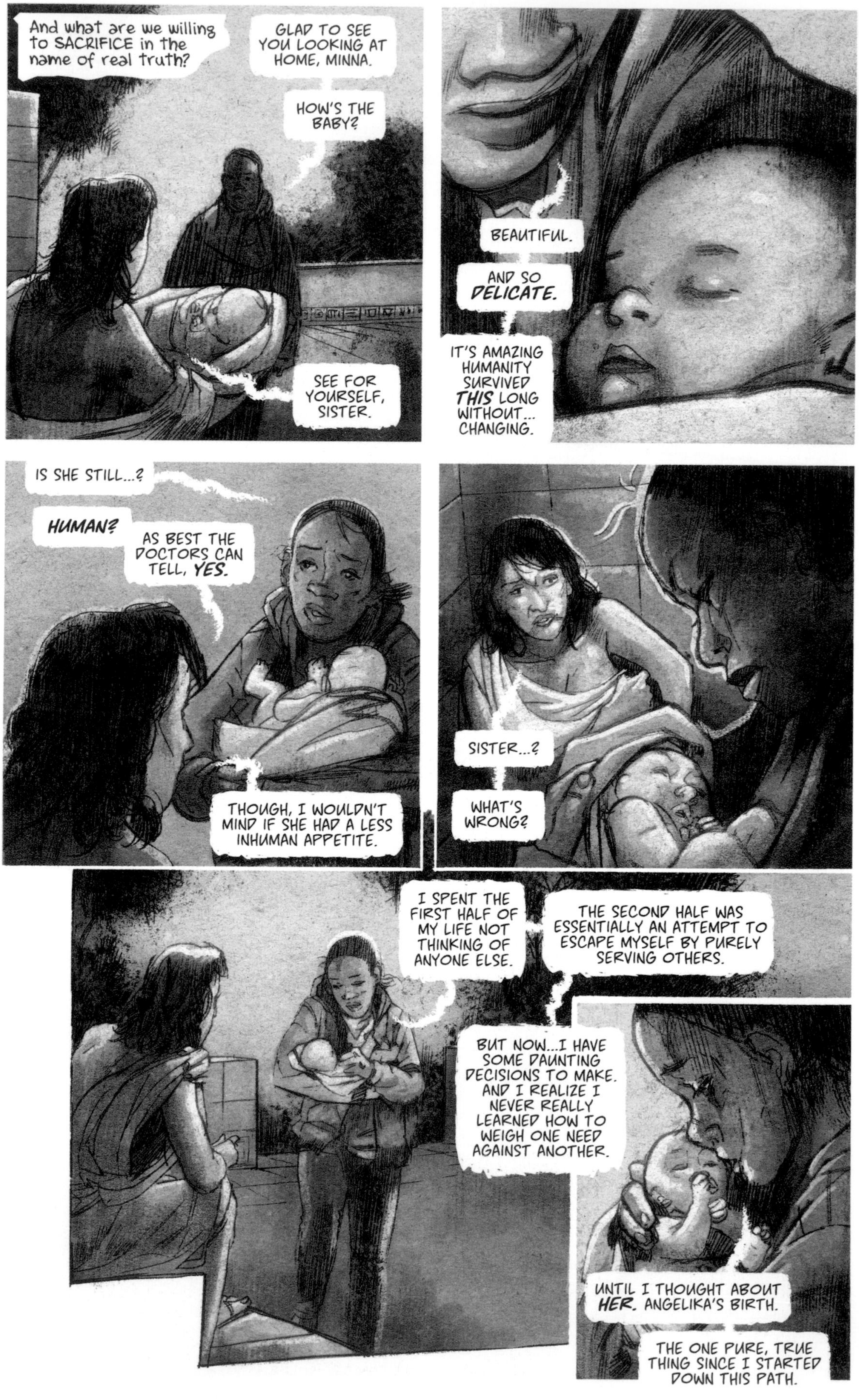
And what are we willing to SACRIFICE in the name of real truth?
GLAD TO SEE YOU LOOKING AT HOME, MINNA.
HOW'S THE BABY?
SEE FOR YOURSELF, SISTER.
BEAUTIFUL.
AND SO DELICATE.
IT'S AMAZING HUMANITY SURVIVED THIS LONG WITHOUT... CHANGING.
IS SHE STILL...?
HUMAN?
AS BEST THE DOCTORS CAN TELL, YES.
THOUGH, I WOULDN'T MIND IF SHE HAD A LESS INHUMAN APPETITE.
SISTER...?
WHAT'S WRONG?
I SPENT THE FIRST HALF OF MY LIFE NOT THINKING OF ANYONE ELSE.
THE SECOND HALF WAS ESSENTIALLY AN ATTEMPT TO ESCAPE MYSELF BY PURELY SERVING OTHERS.
BUT NOW...I HAVE SOME DAUNTING DECISIONS TO MAKE. AND I REALIZE I NEVER REALLY LEARNED HOW TO WEIGH ONE NEED AGAINST ANOTHER.
UNTIL I THOUGHT ABOUT HER. ANGELIKA'S BIRTH.
THE ONE PURE, TRUE THING SINCE I STARTED DOWN THIS PATH.

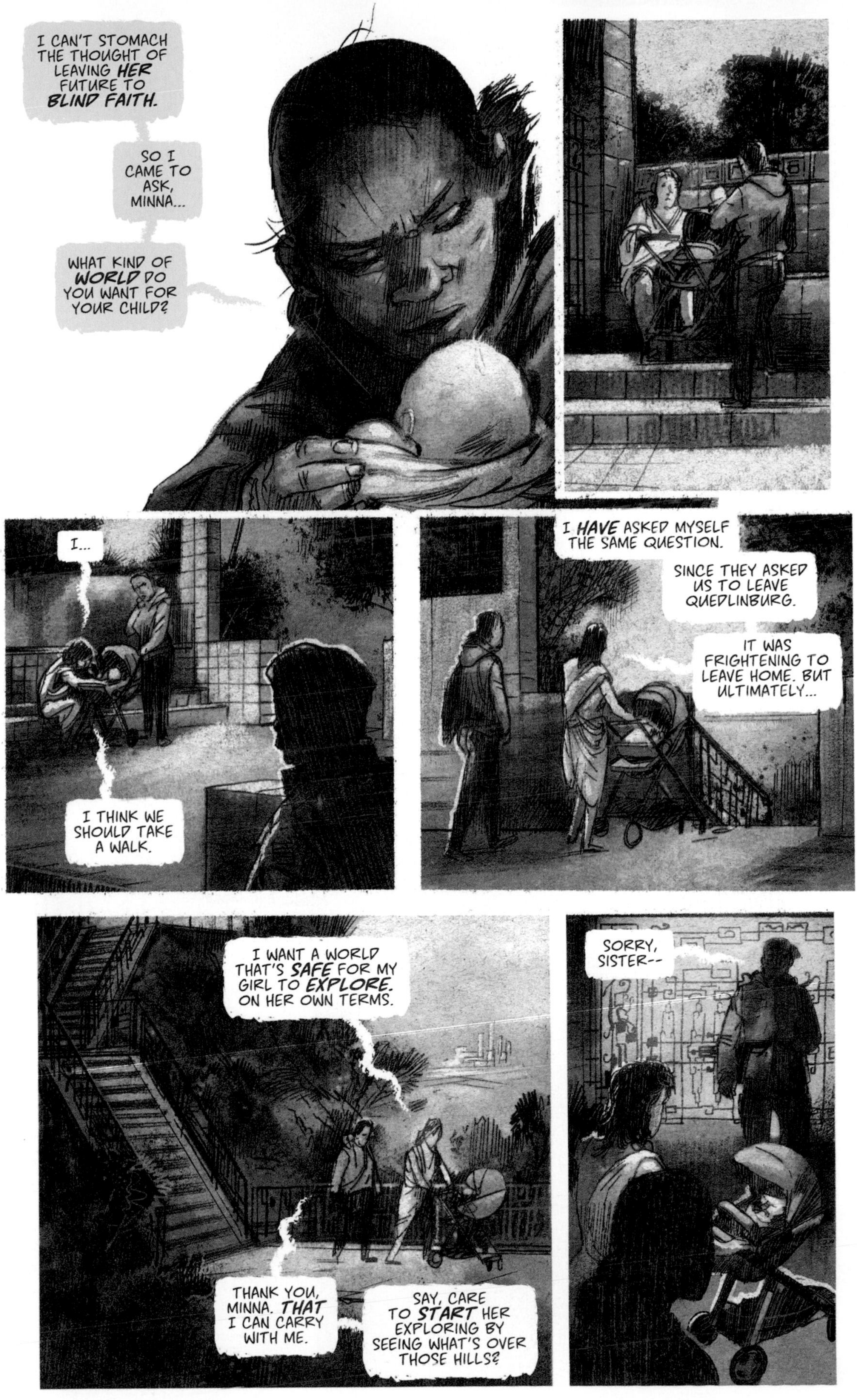
I CAN'T STOMACH THE THOUGHT OF LEAVING HER FUTURE TO BLIND FAITH.
SO I CAME TO ASK, MINNA...
WHAT KIND OF WORLD DO YOU WANT FOR YOUR CHILD?
I...
I THINK WE SHOULD TAKE A WALK.
I HAVE ASKED MYSELF THE SAME QUESTION.
SINCE THEY ASKED US TO LEAVE QUEDLINBURG.
IT WAS FRIGHTENING TO LEAVE HOME. BUT ULTIMATELY...
I WANT A WORLD THAT'S SAFE FOR MY GIRL TO EXPLORE. ON HER OWN TERMS.
THANK YOU, MINNA. THAT I CAN CARRY WITH ME.
SAY, CARE TO START HER EXPLORING BY SEEING WHAT'S OVER THOSE HILLS?
SORRY, SISTER--

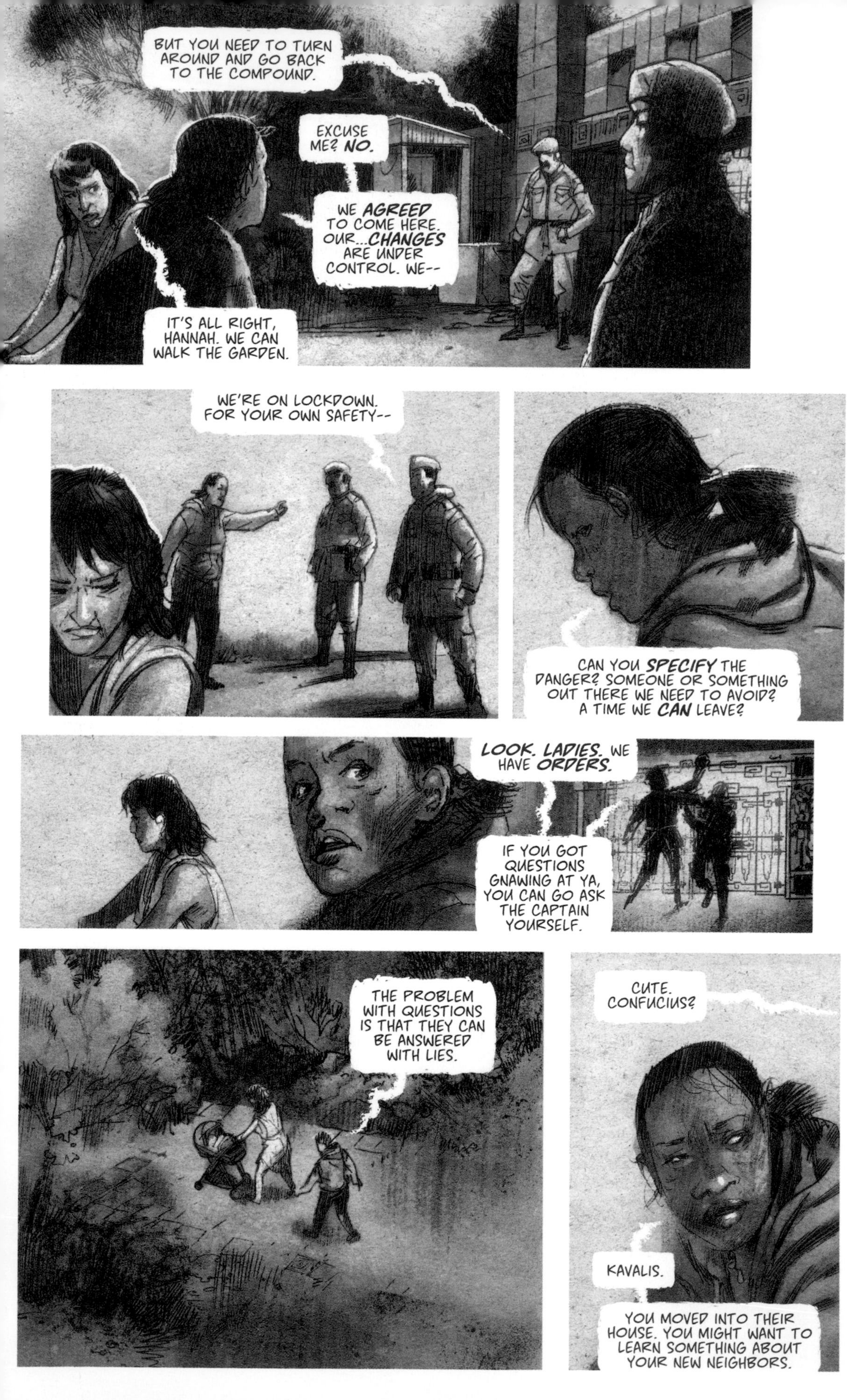
BUT YOU NEED TO TURN AROUND AND GO BACK TO THE COMPOUND.
EXCUSE ME? **NO.**
WE **AGREED** TO COME HERE. OUR... **CHANGES** ARE UNDER CONTROL. WE--
IT'S ALL RIGHT, HANNAH. WE CAN WALK THE GARDEN.
WE'RE ON LOCKDOWN. FOR YOUR OWN SAFETY--
CAN YOU **SPECIFY** THE DANGER? SOMEONE OR SOMETHING OUT THERE WE NEED TO AVOID? A TIME WE **CAN** LEAVE?
LOOK. LADIES. WE HAVE **ORDERS.**
IF YOU GOT QUESTIONS GNAWING AT YA, YOU CAN GO ASK THE CAPTAIN YOURSELF.
THE PROBLEM WITH QUESTIONS IS THAT THEY CAN BE ANSWERED WITH LIES.
CUTE. CONFUCIUS?
KAVALIS.
YOU MOVED INTO THEIR HOUSE. YOU MIGHT WANT TO LEARN SOMETHING ABOUT YOUR NEW NEIGHBORS.

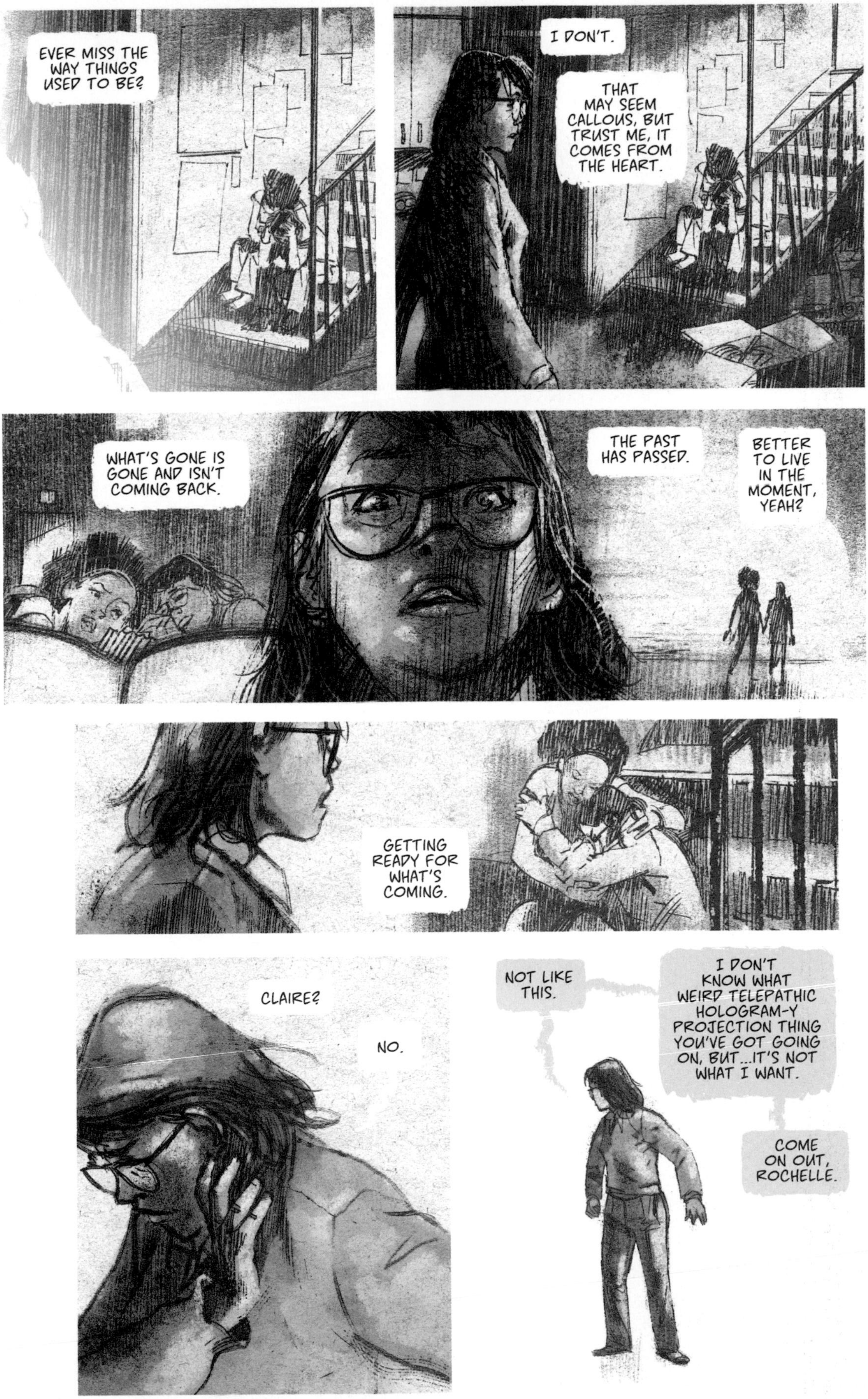
EVER MISS THE WAY THINGS USED TO BE?
I DON'T.
THAT MAY SEEM CALLOUS, BUT TRUST ME, IT COMES FROM THE HEART.
WHAT'S GONE IS GONE AND ISN'T COMING BACK.
THE PAST HAS PASSED.
BETTER TO LIVE IN THE MOMENT, YEAH?
GETTING READY FOR WHAT'S COMING.
CLAIRE?
NO.
NOT LIKE THIS.
I DON'T KNOW WHAT WEIRD TELEPATHIC HOLOGRAM-Y PROJECTION THING YOU'VE GOT GOING ON, BUT...IT'S NOT WHAT I WANT.
COME ON OUT, ROCHELLE.

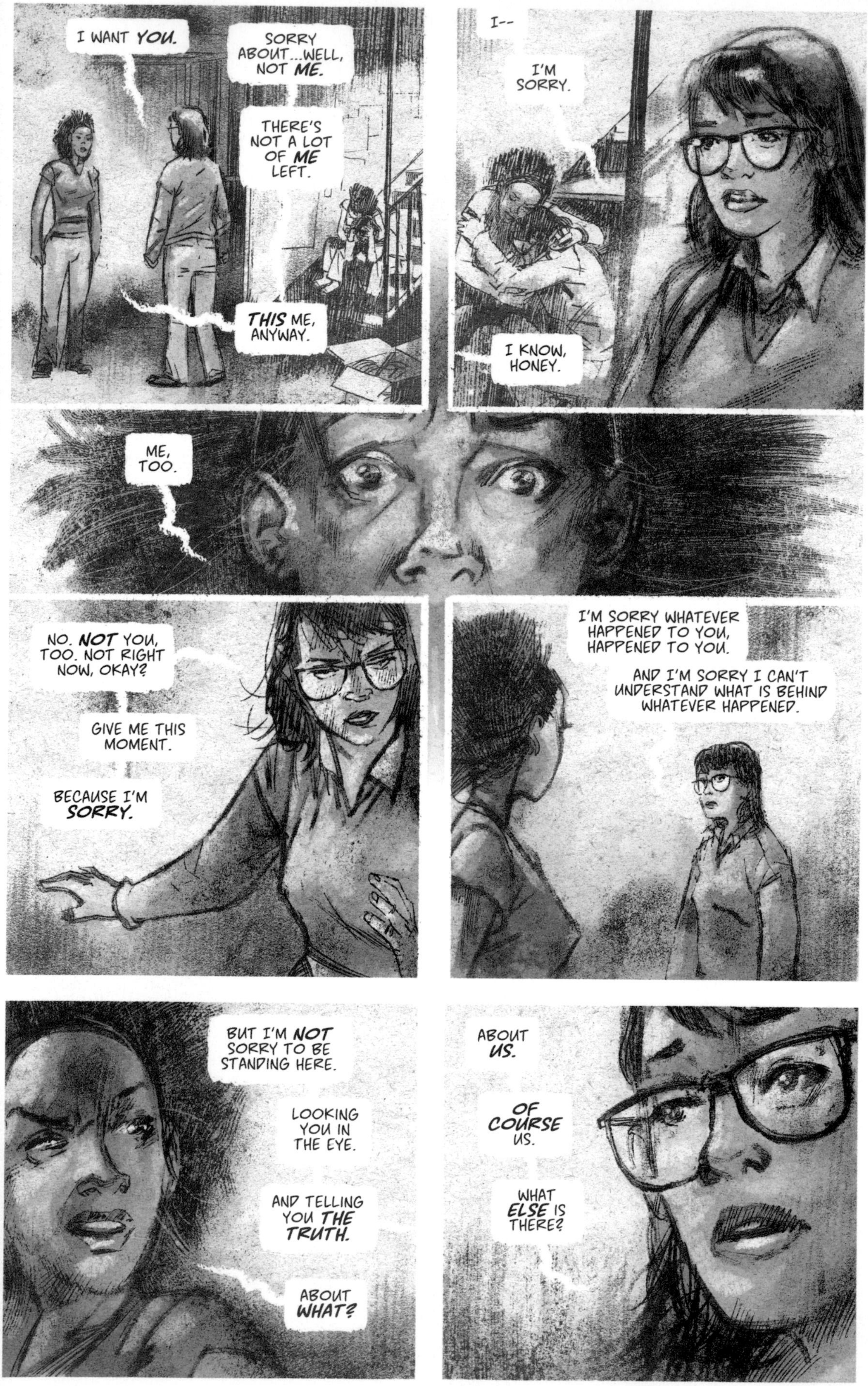
I WANT YOU.
SORRY ABOUT...WELL, NOT ME.
THERE'S NOT A LOT OF ME LEFT.
THIS ME, ANYWAY.
I--
I'M SORRY.
I KNOW, HONEY.
ME, TOO.
NO. NOT YOU, TOO. NOT RIGHT NOW, OKAY?
GIVE ME THIS MOMENT.
BECAUSE I'M SORRY.
I'M SORRY WHATEVER HAPPENED TO YOU, HAPPENED TO YOU.
AND I'M SORRY I CAN'T UNDERSTAND WHAT IS BEHIND WHATEVER HAPPENED.
BUT I'M NOT SORRY TO BE STANDING HERE.
LOOKING YOU IN THE EYE.
AND TELLING YOU THE TRUTH.
ABOUT WHAT?
ABOUT US.
OF COURSE US.
WHAT ELSE IS THERE?

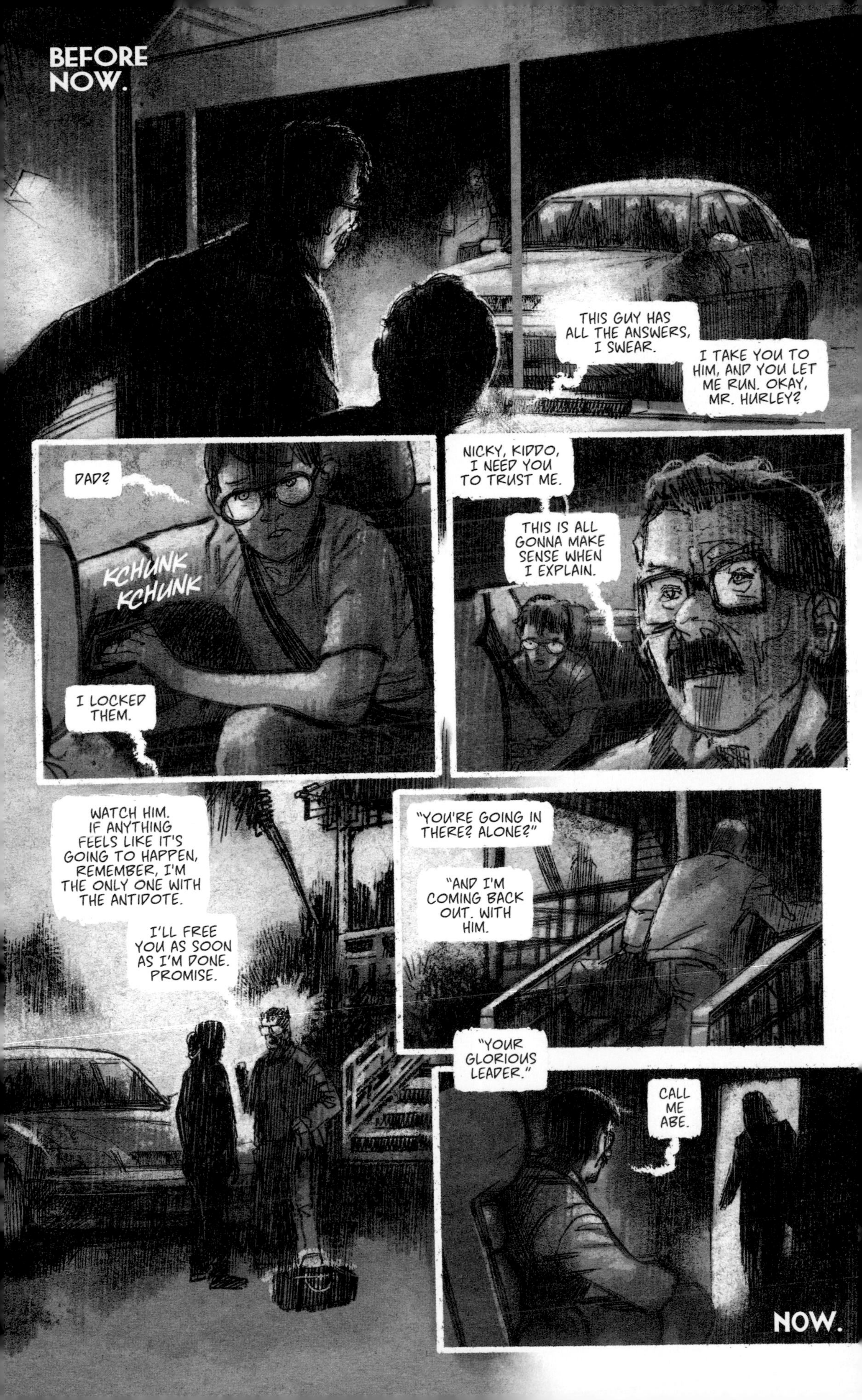
BEFORE NOW.
THIS GUY HAS ALL THE ANSWERS, I SWEAR.
I TAKE YOU TO HIM, AND YOU LET ME RUN. OKAY, MR. HURLEY?
DAD?
KCHUNK KCHUNK
I LOCKED THEM.
NICKY, KIDDO, I NEED YOU TO TRUST ME.
THIS IS ALL GONNA MAKE SENSE WHEN I EXPLAIN.
WATCH HIM. IF ANYTHING FEELS LIKE IT'S GOING TO HAPPEN, REMEMBER, I'M THE ONLY ONE WITH THE ANTIDOTE.
I'LL FREE YOU AS SOON AS I'M DONE. PROMISE.
"YOU'RE GOING IN THERE? ALONE?"
"AND I'M COMING BACK OUT. WITH HIM.
"YOUR GLORIOUS LEADER."
CALL ME ABE.
NOW.

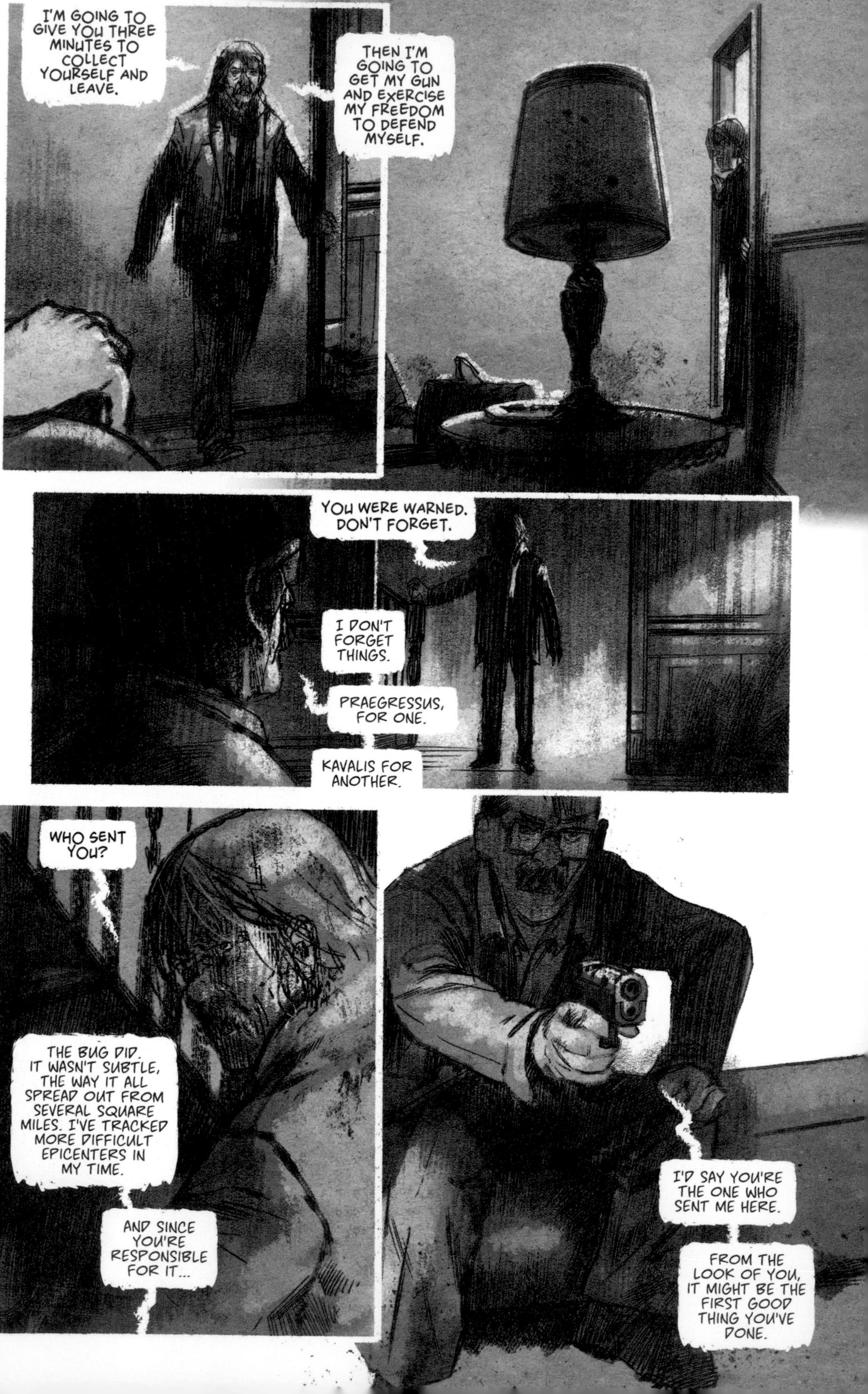
I'M GOING TO GIVE YOU THREE MINUTES TO COLLECT YOURSELF AND LEAVE.
THEN I'M GOING TO GET MY GUN AND EXERCISE MY FREEDOM TO DEFEND MYSELF.
YOU WERE WARNED. DON'T FORGET.
I DON'T FORGET THINGS.
PRAEGRESSUS, FOR ONE.
KAVALIS FOR ANOTHER.
WHO SENT YOU?
THE BUG DID. IT WASN'T SUBTLE, THE WAY IT ALL SPREAD OUT FROM SEVERAL SQUARE MILES. I'VE TRACKED MORE DIFFICULT EPICENTERS IN MY TIME.
AND SINCE YOU'RE RESPONSIBLE FOR IT...
I'D SAY YOU'RE THE ONE WHO SENT ME HERE.
FROM THE LOOK OF YOU, IT MIGHT BE THE FIRST GOOD THING YOU'VE DONE.

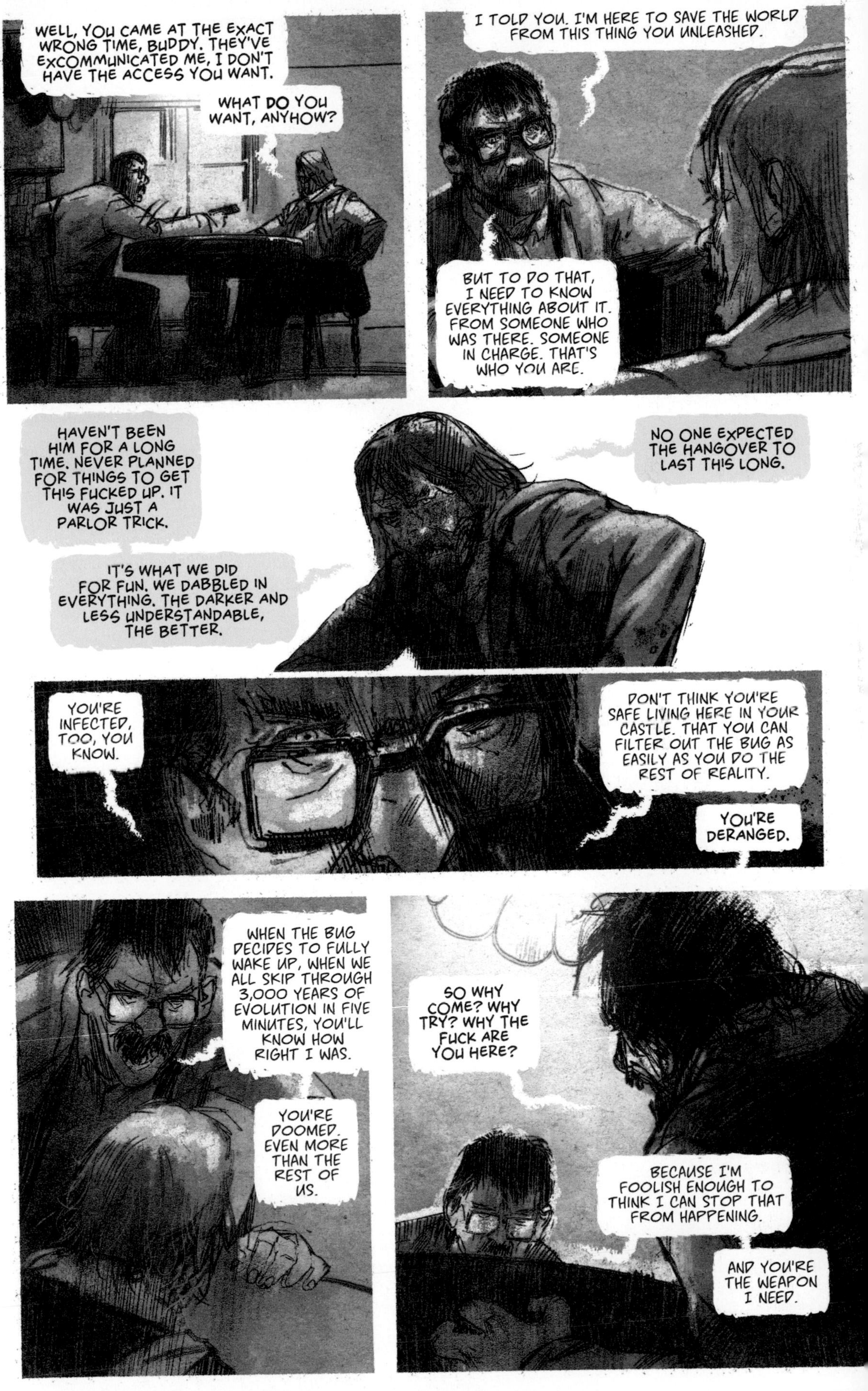
WELL, YOU CAME AT THE EXACT WRONG TIME, BUDDY. THEY'VE EXCOMMUNICATED ME, I DON'T HAVE THE ACCESS YOU WANT.
WHAT DO YOU WANT, ANYHOW?
I TOLD YOU. I'M HERE TO SAVE THE WORLD FROM THIS THING YOU UNLEASHED.
BUT TO DO THAT, I NEED TO KNOW EVERYTHING ABOUT IT. FROM SOMEONE WHO WAS THERE. SOMEONE IN CHARGE. THAT'S WHO YOU ARE.
HAVEN'T BEEN HIM FOR A LONG TIME. NEVER PLANNED FOR THINGS TO GET THIS FUCKED UP. IT WAS JUST A PARLOR TRICK.
IT'S WHAT WE DID FOR FUN. WE DABBLED IN EVERYTHING. THE DARKER AND LESS UNDERSTANDABLE, THE BETTER.
NO ONE EXPECTED THE HANGOVER TO LAST THIS LONG.
YOU'RE INFECTED, TOO, YOU KNOW.
DON'T THINK YOU'RE SAFE LIVING HERE IN YOUR CASTLE. THAT YOU CAN FILTER OUT THE BUG AS EASILY AS YOU DO THE REST OF REALITY.
YOU'RE DERANGED.
WHEN THE BUG DECIDES TO FULLY WAKE UP, WHEN WE ALL SKIP THROUGH 3,000 YEARS OF EVOLUTION IN FIVE MINUTES, YOU'LL KNOW HOW RIGHT I WAS.
YOU'RE DOOMED. EVEN MORE THAN THE REST OF US.
SO WHY COME? WHY TRY? WHY THE FUCK ARE YOU HERE?
BECAUSE I'M FOOLISH ENOUGH TO THINK I CAN STOP THAT FROM HAPPENING.
AND YOU'RE THE WEAPON I NEED.

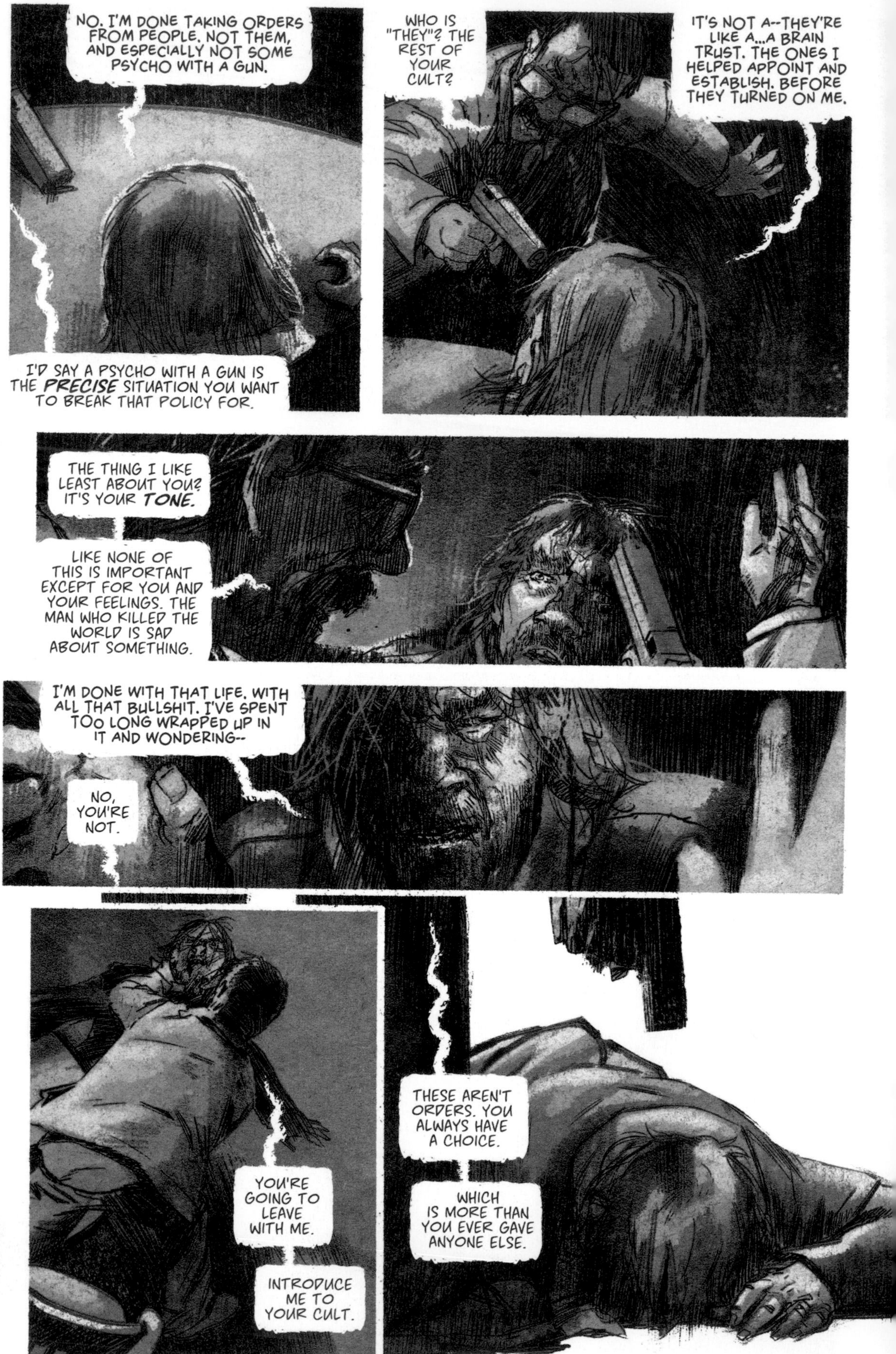
NO. I'M DONE TAKING ORDERS FROM PEOPLE. NOT THEM, AND ESPECIALLY NOT SOME PSYCHO WITH A GUN.
I'D SAY A PSYCHO WITH A GUN IS THE PRECISE SITUATION YOU WANT TO BREAK THAT POLICY FOR.
WHO IS "THEY"? THE REST OF YOUR CULT?
IT'S NOT A--THEY'RE LIKE A...A BRAIN TRUST. THE ONES I HELPED APPOINT AND ESTABLISH. BEFORE THEY TURNED ON ME.
THE THING I LIKE LEAST ABOUT YOU? IT'S YOUR TONE.
LIKE NONE OF THIS IS IMPORTANT EXCEPT FOR YOU AND YOUR FEELINGS. THE MAN WHO KILLED THE WORLD IS SAD ABOUT SOMETHING.
I'M DONE WITH THAT LIFE. WITH ALL THAT BULLSHIT. I'VE SPENT TOO LONG WRAPPED UP IN IT AND WONDERING--
NO, YOU'RE NOT.
YOU'RE GOING TO LEAVE WITH ME.
INTRODUCE ME TO YOUR CULT.
THESE AREN'T ORDERS. YOU ALWAYS HAVE A CHOICE.
WHICH IS MORE THAN YOU EVER GAVE ANYONE ELSE.

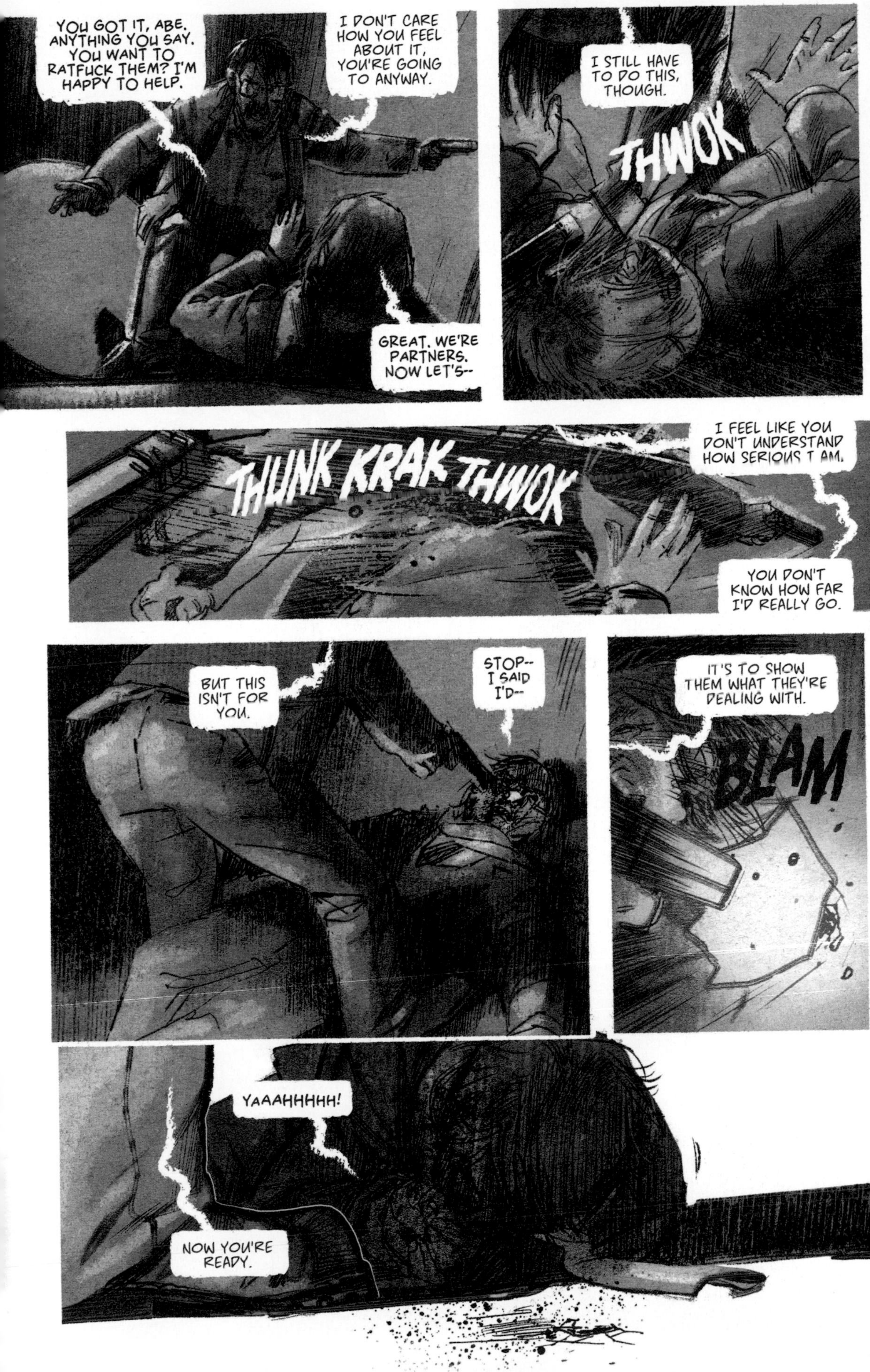
YOU GOT IT, ABE. ANYTHING YOU SAY. YOU WANT TO RATFUCK THEM? I'M HAPPY TO HELP.
I DON'T CARE HOW YOU FEEL ABOUT IT, YOU'RE GOING TO ANYWAY.
GREAT. WE'RE PARTNERS. NOW LET'S--
I STILL HAVE TO DO THIS, THOUGH.
THWOK
THUNK KRAK THWOK
I FEEL LIKE YOU DON'T UNDERSTAND HOW SERIOUS I AM.
YOU DON'T KNOW HOW FAR I'D REALLY GO.
BUT THIS ISN'T FOR YOU.
STOP-- I SAID I'D--
IT'S TO SHOW THEM WHAT THEY'RE DEALING WITH.
BLAM
YAAAHHHHH!
NOW YOU'RE READY.

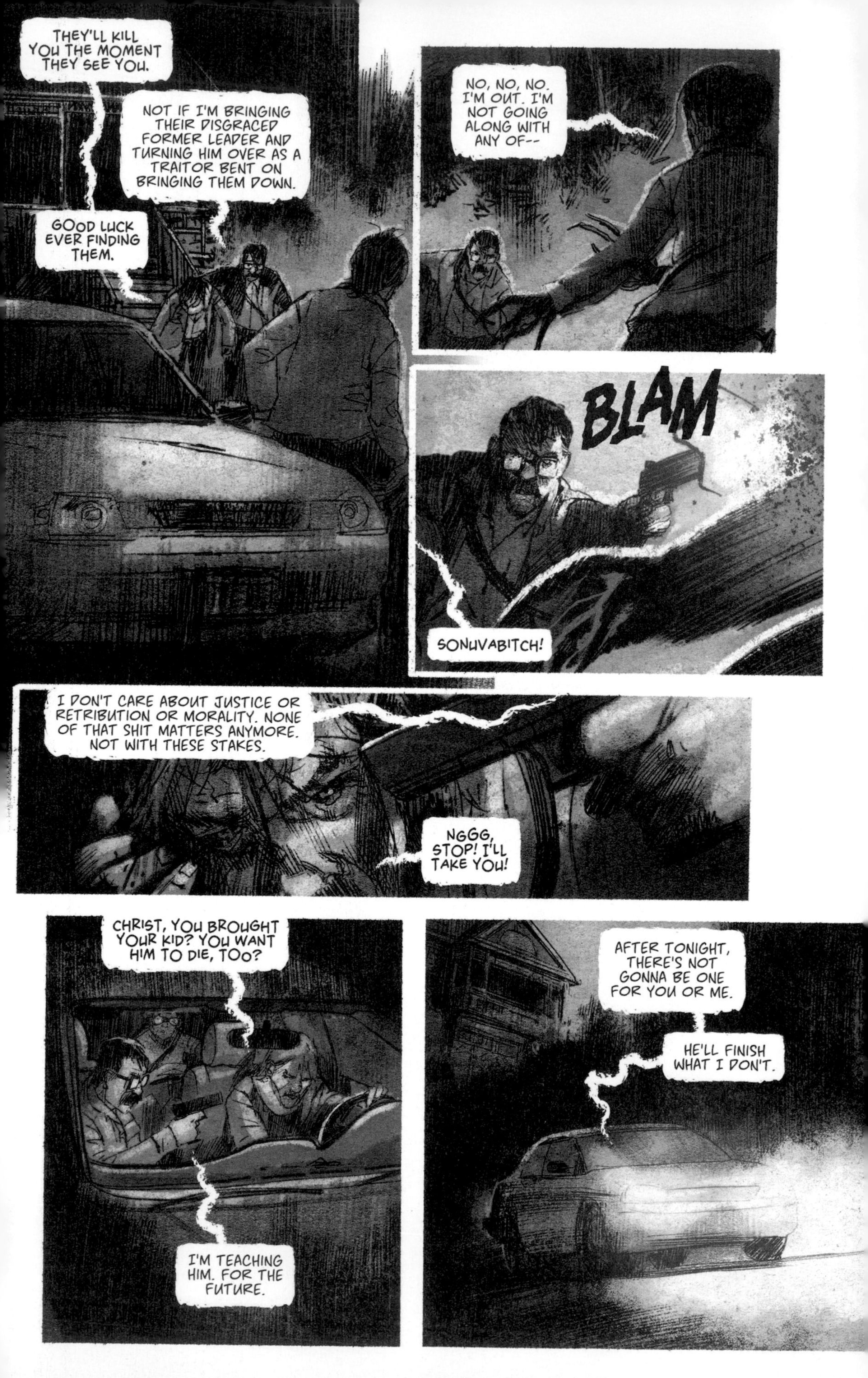
THEY'LL KILL YOU THE MOMENT THEY SEE YOU.
NOT IF I'M BRINGING THEIR DISGRACED FORMER LEADER AND TURNING HIM OVER AS A TRAITOR BENT ON BRINGING THEM DOWN.
GOOD LUCK EVER FINDING THEM.
NO, NO, NO. I'M OUT. I'M NOT GOING ALONG WITH ANY OF--
BLAM
SONUVABITCH!
I DON'T CARE ABOUT JUSTICE OR RETRIBUTION OR MORALITY. NONE OF THAT SHIT MATTERS ANYMORE. NOT WITH THESE STAKES.
NGGG, STOP! I'LL TAKE YOU!
CHRIST, YOU BROUGHT YOUR KID? YOU WANT HIM TO DIE, TOO?
I'M TEACHING HIM. FOR THE FUTURE.
AFTER TONIGHT, THERE'S NOT GONNA BE ONE FOR YOU OR ME.
HE'LL FINISH WHAT I DON'T.

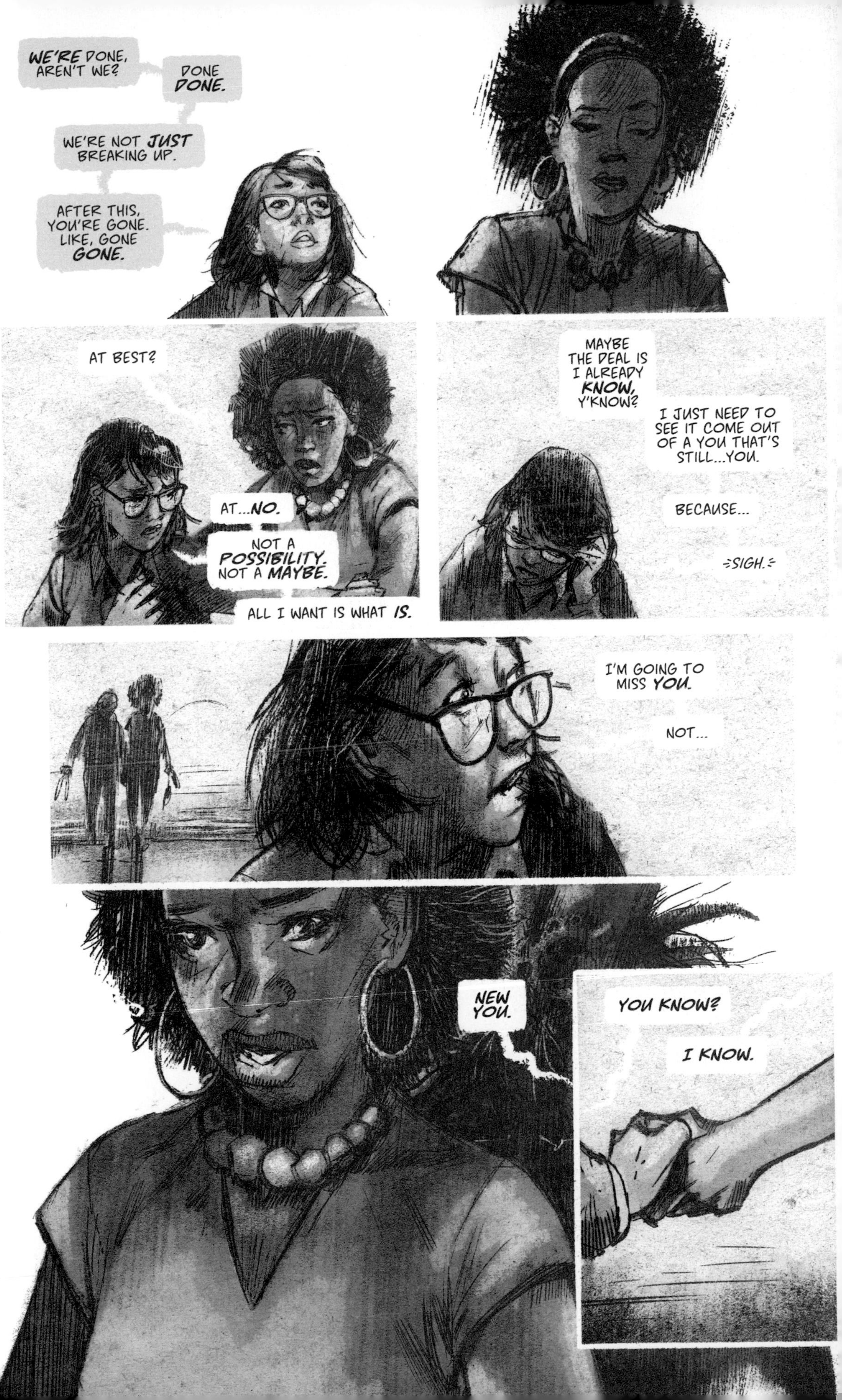

WE'RE DONE, AREN'T WE?
DONE DONE.
WE'RE NOT JUST BREAKING UP.
AFTER THIS, YOU'RE GONE. LIKE, GONE GONE.
AT BEST?
AT...NO.
NOT A POSSIBILITY. NOT A MAYBE.
ALL I WANT IS WHAT IS.
MAYBE THE DEAL IS I ALREADY KNOW, Y'KNOW?
I JUST NEED TO SEE IT COME OUT OF A YOU THAT'S STILL...YOU.
BECAUSE...
=SIGH.=
I'M GOING TO MISS YOU.
NOT...
NEW YOU.
YOU KNOW?
I KNOW.

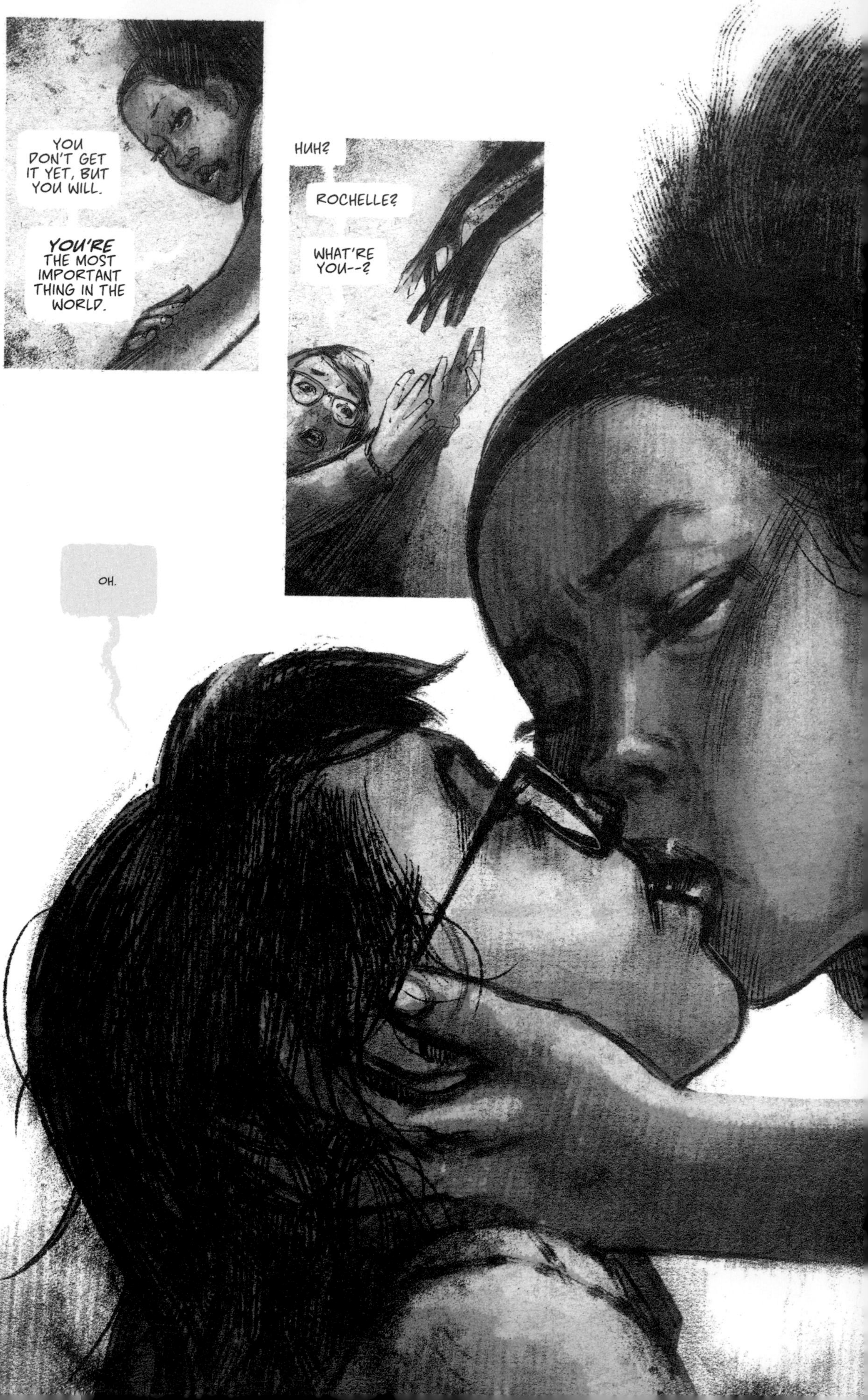
YOU DON'T GET IT YET, BUT YOU WILL.
YOU'RE THE MOST IMPORTANT THING IN THE WORLD.
HUH?
ROCHELLE?
WHAT'RE YOU--?
OH.

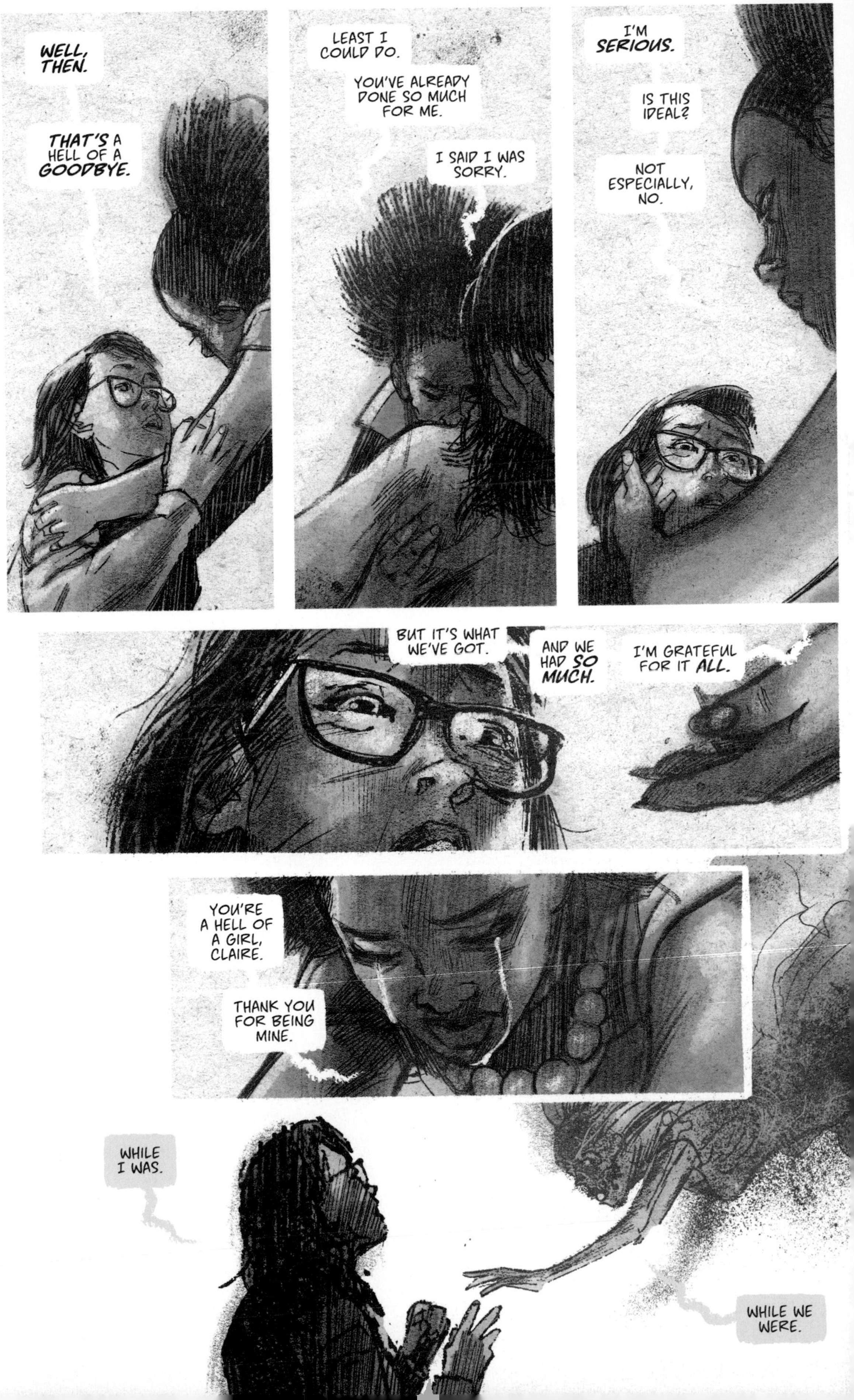
WELL, THEN.
THAT'S A HELL OF A GOODBYE.
LEAST I COULD DO.
YOU'VE ALREADY DONE SO MUCH FOR ME.
I SAID I WAS SORRY.
I'M SERIOUS.
IS THIS IDEAL?
NOT ESPECIALLY, NO.
BUT IT'S WHAT WE'VE GOT.
AND WE HAD SO MUCH.
I'M GRATEFUL FOR IT ALL.
YOU'RE A HELL OF A GIRL, CLAIRE.
THANK YOU FOR BEING MINE.
WHILE I WAS.
WHILE WE WERE.

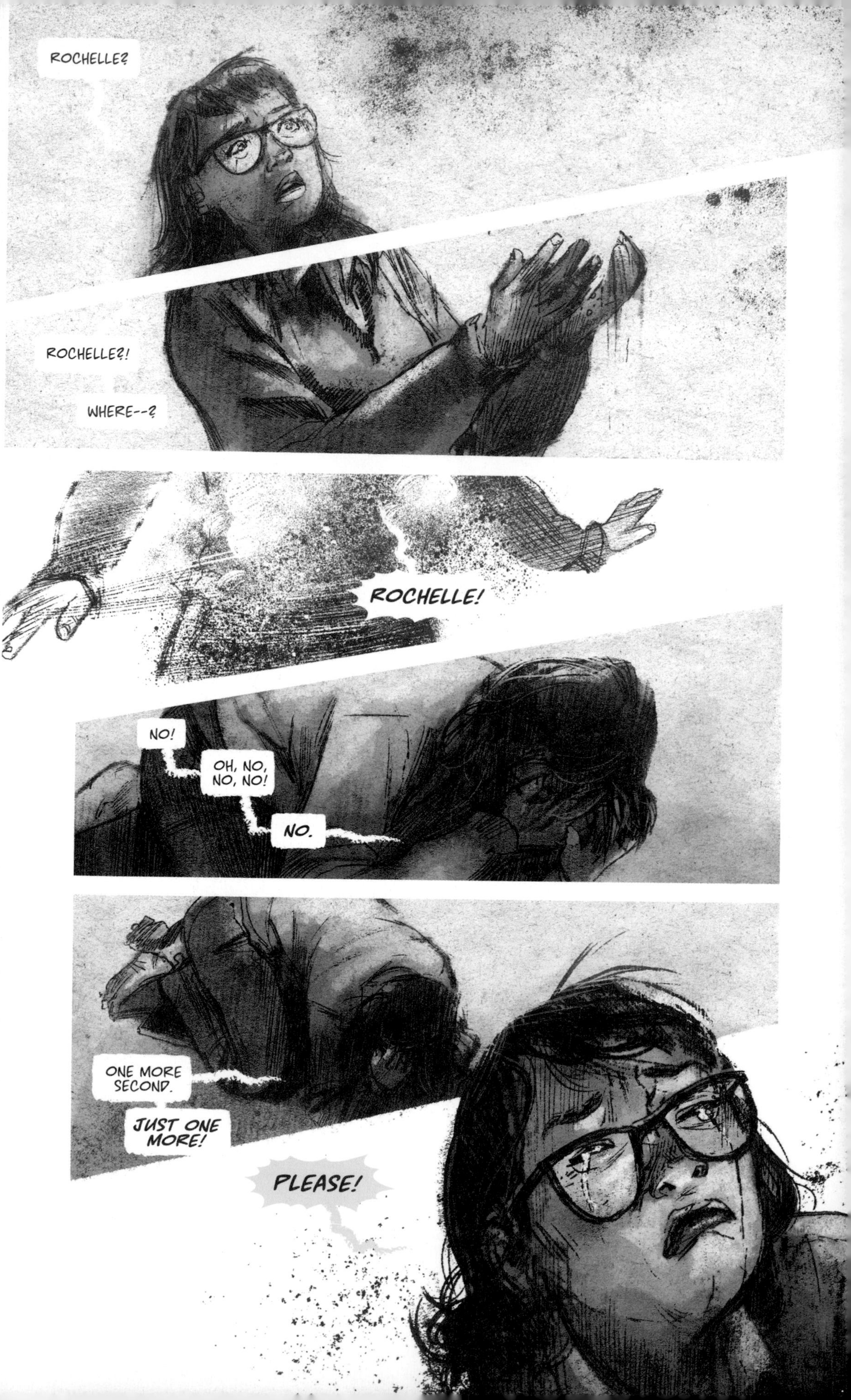
ROCHELLE?
ROCHELLE?!
WHERE--?
ROCHELLE!
NO!
OH, NO, NO, NO!
NO.
ONE MORE SECOND.
JUST ONE MORE!
PLEASE!

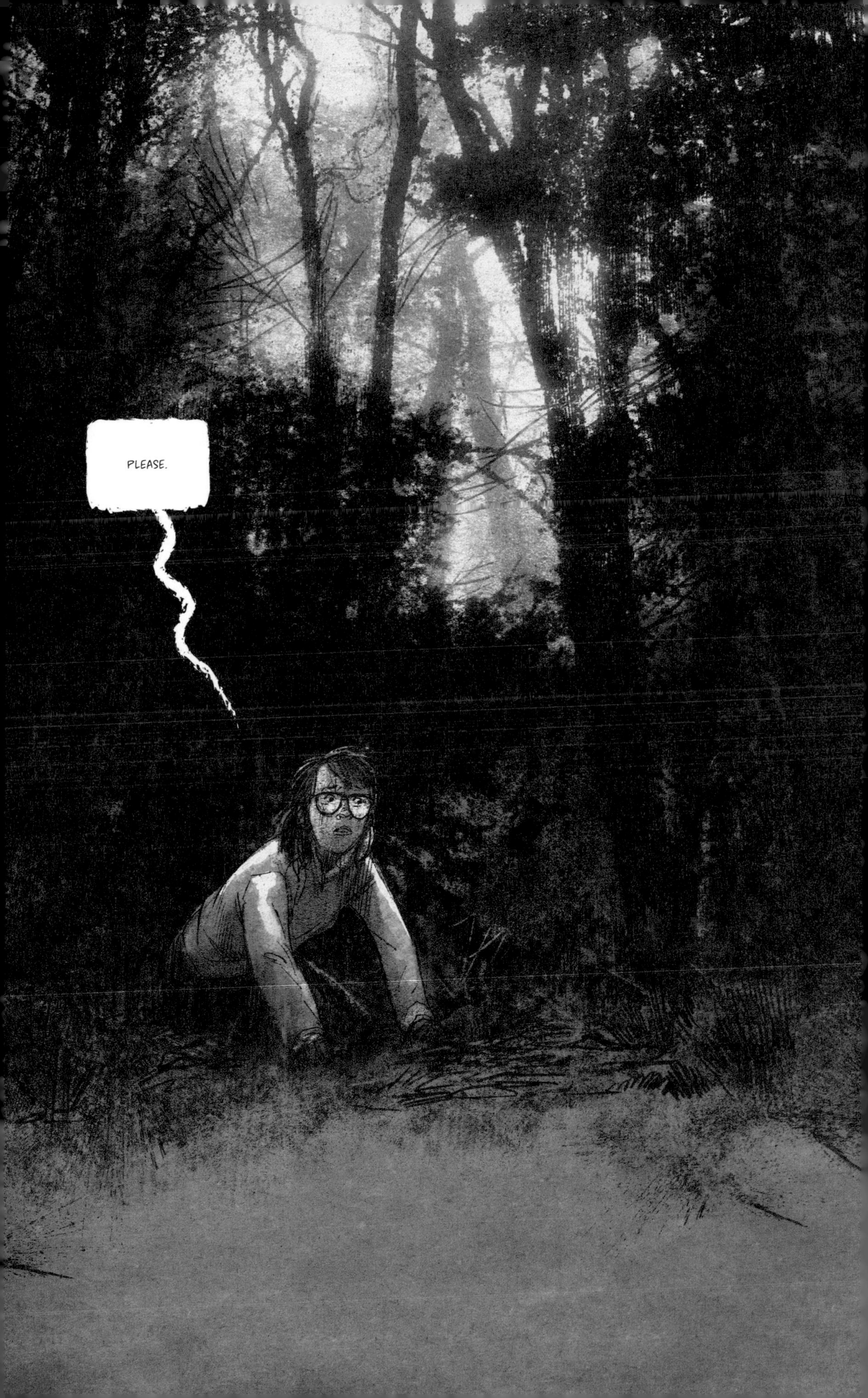
PLEASE.

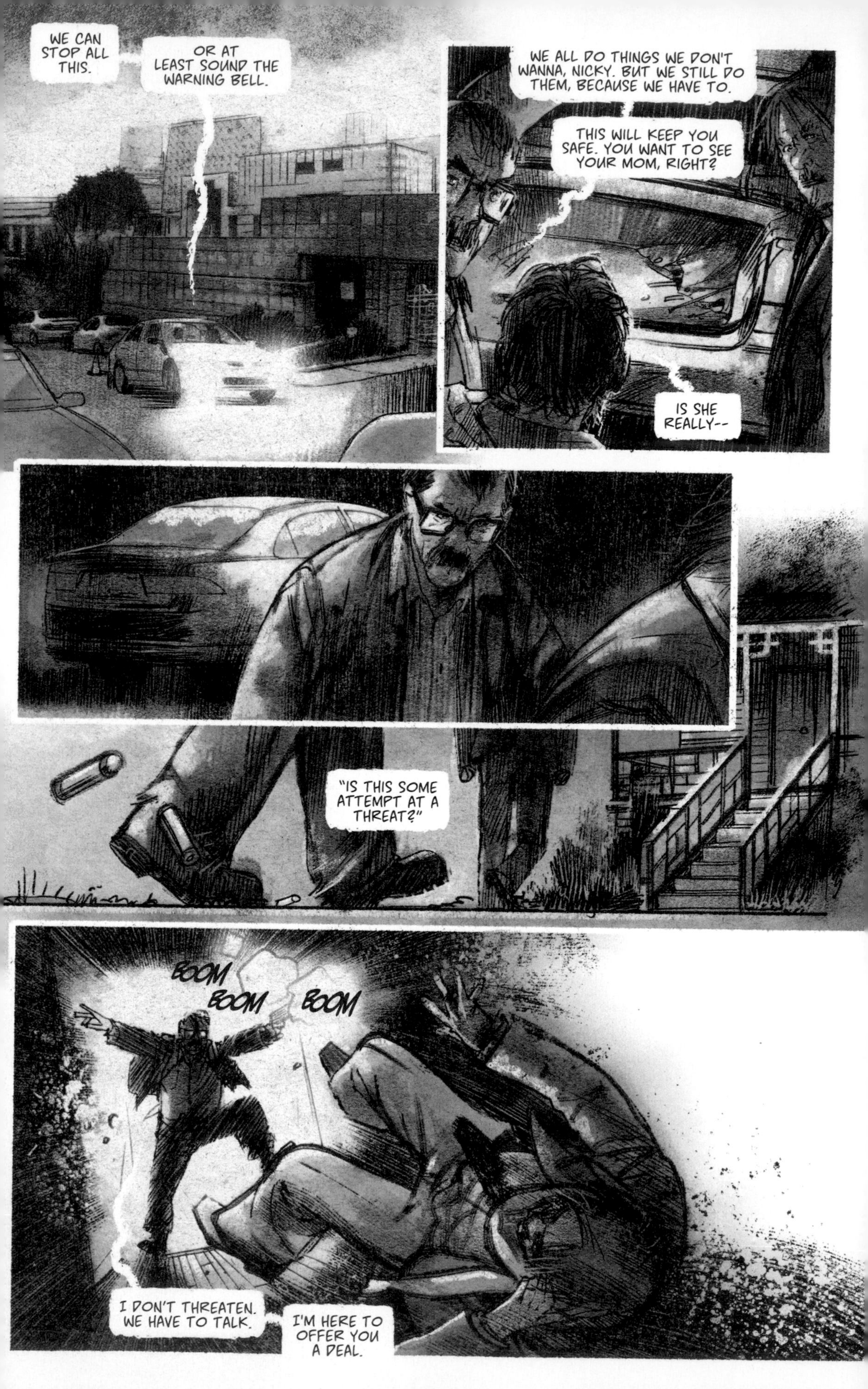
WE CAN STOP ALL THIS.
OR AT LEAST SOUND THE WARNING BELL.
WE ALL DO THINGS WE DON'T WANNA, NICKY. BUT WE STILL DO THEM, BECAUSE WE HAVE TO.
THIS WILL KEEP YOU SAFE. YOU WANT TO SEE YOUR MOM, RIGHT?
IS SHE REALLY--
"IS THIS SOME ATTEMPT AT A THREAT?"
BOOM
BOOM
BOOM
I DON'T THREATEN. WE HAVE TO TALK.
I'M HERE TO OFFER YOU A DEAL.

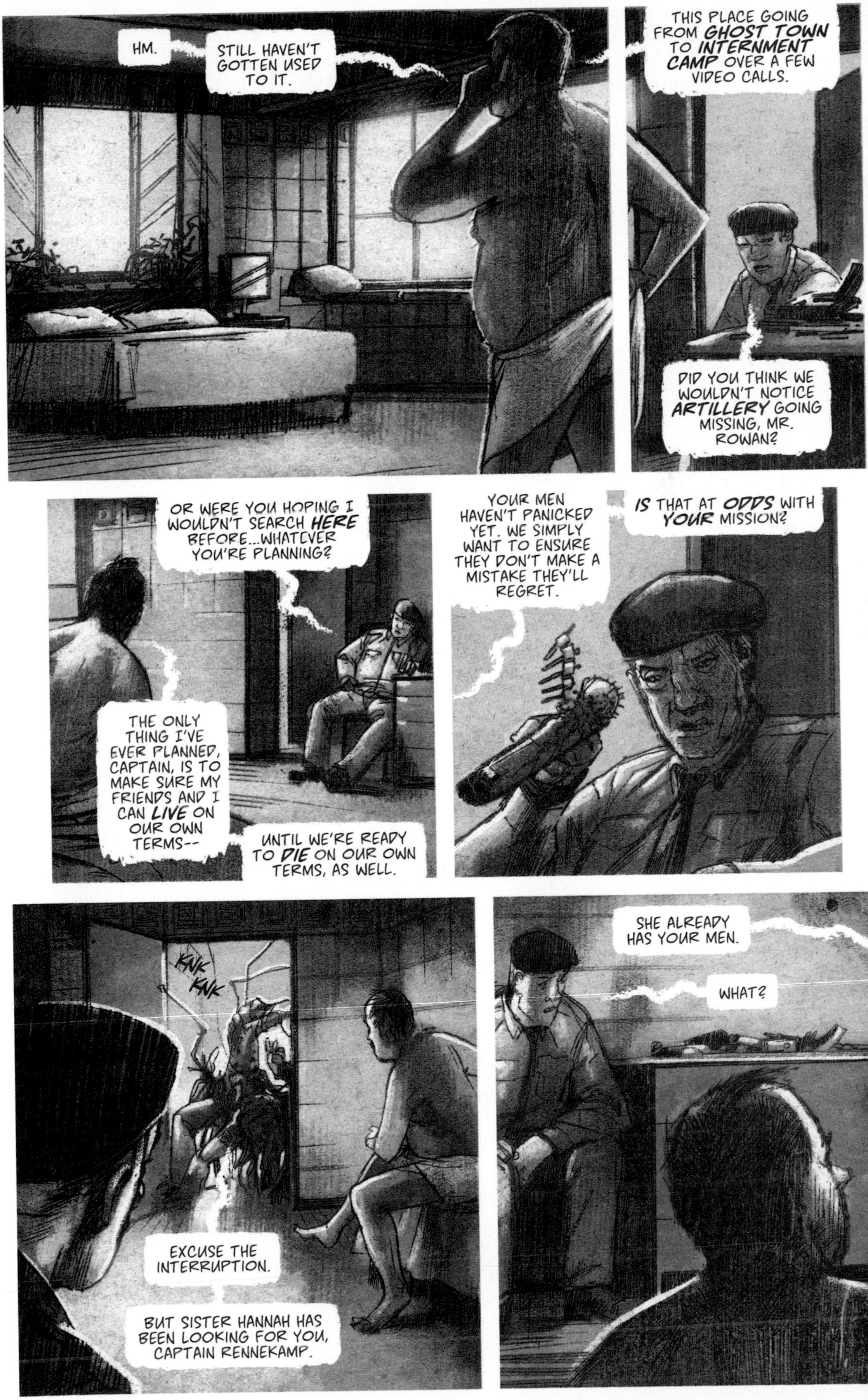
HM.
STILL HAVEN'T GOTTEN USED TO IT.
THIS PLACE GOING FROM GHOST TOWN TO INTERNMENT CAMP OVER A FEW VIDEO CALLS.
DID YOU THINK WE WOULDN'T NOTICE ARTILLERY GOING MISSING, MR. ROWAN?
OR WERE YOU HOPING I WOULDN'T SEARCH HERE BEFORE...WHATEVER YOU'RE PLANNING?
THE ONLY THING I'VE EVER PLANNED, CAPTAIN, IS TO MAKE SURE MY FRIENDS AND I CAN LIVE ON OUR OWN TERMS--
UNTIL WE'RE READY TO DIE ON OUR OWN TERMS, AS WELL.
YOUR MEN HAVEN'T PANICKED YET. WE SIMPLY WANT TO ENSURE THEY DON'T MAKE A MISTAKE THEY'LL REGRET.
IS THAT AT ODDS WITH YOUR MISSION?
KNK KNK
EXCUSE THE INTERRUPTION.
BUT SISTER HANNAH HAS BEEN LOOKING FOR YOU, CAPTAIN RENNEKAMP.
SHE ALREADY HAS YOUR MEN.
WHAT?

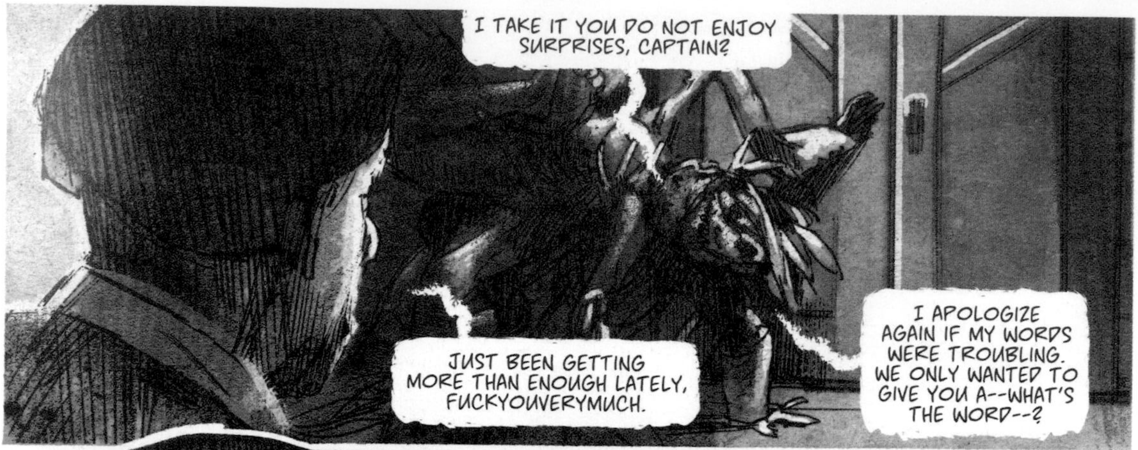
I TAKE IT YOU DO NOT ENJOY SURPRISES, CAPTAIN?
JUST BEEN GETTING MORE THAN ENOUGH LATELY, FUCKYOUVERYMUCH.
I APOLOGIZE AGAIN IF MY WORDS WERE TROUBLING. WE ONLY WANTED TO GIVE YOU A--WHAT'S THE WORD--?

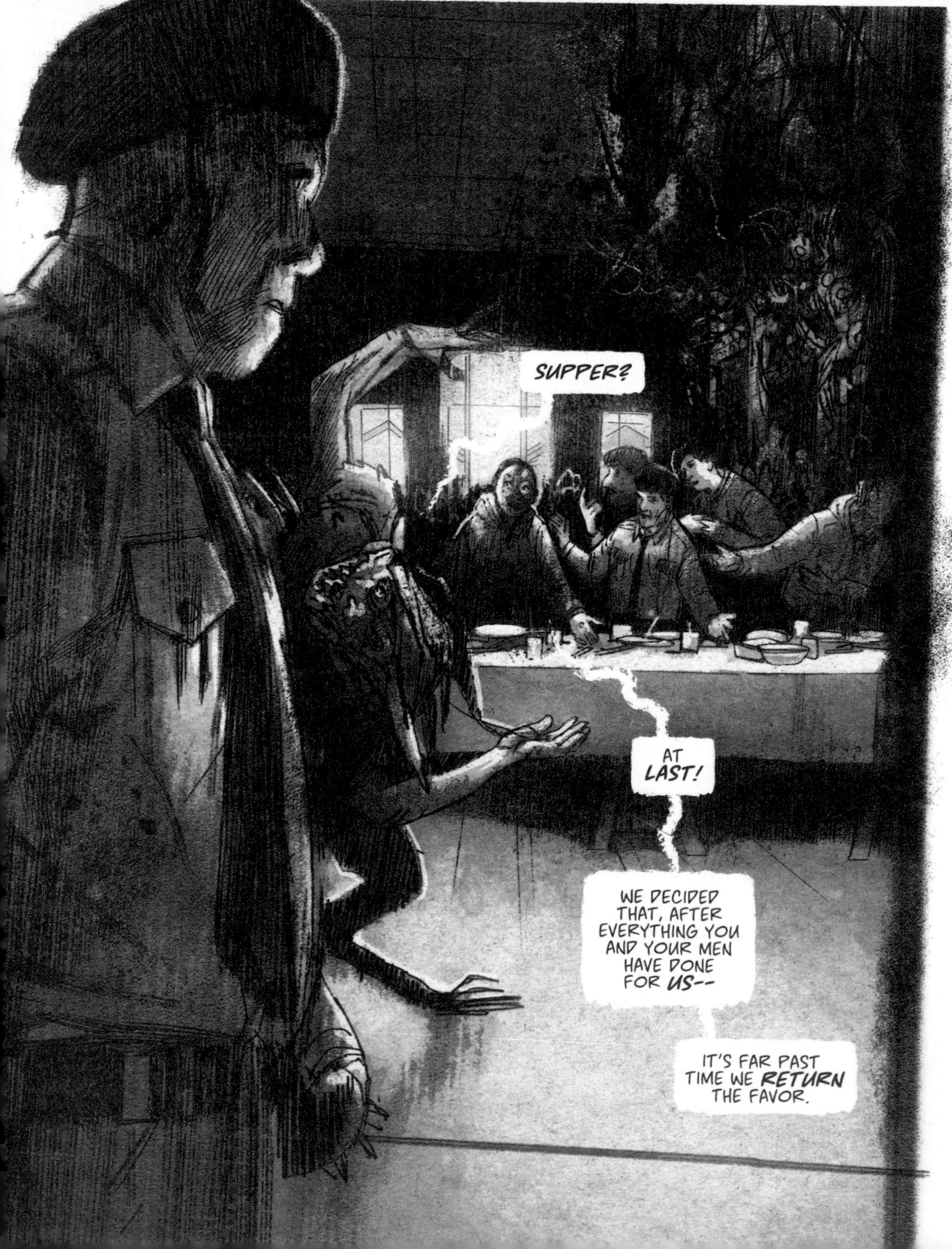
SUPPER?
AT LAST!
WE DECIDED THAT, AFTER EVERYTHING YOU AND YOUR MEN HAVE DONE FOR US--
IT'S FAR PAST TIME WE RETURN THE FAVOR.

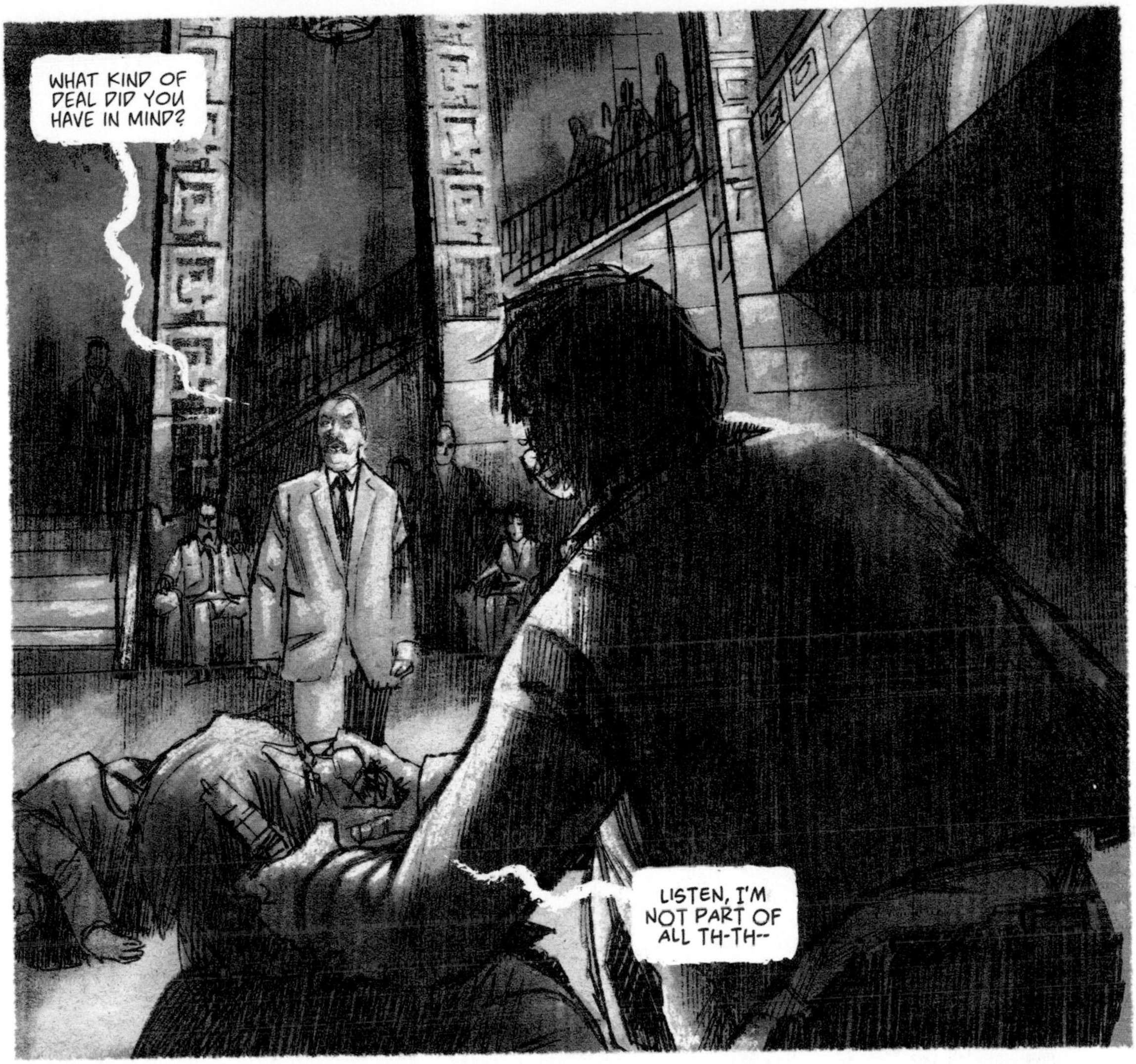
WHAT KIND OF DEAL DID YOU HAVE IN MIND?
LISTEN, I'M NOT PART OF ALL TH-TH--

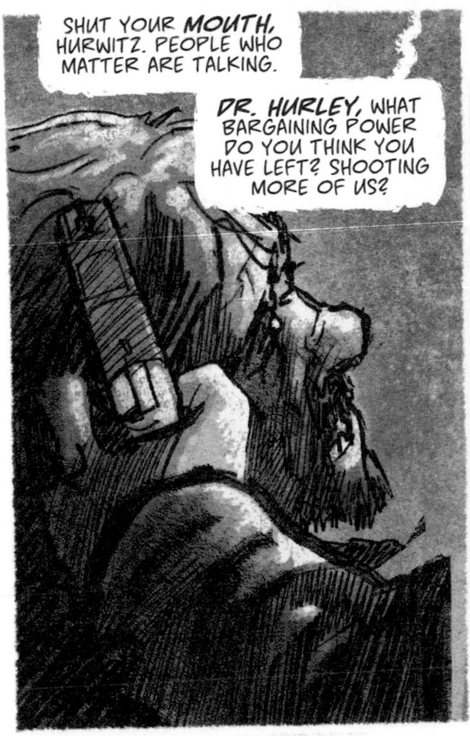
SHUT YOUR MOUTH, HURWITZ. PEOPLE WHO MATTER ARE TALKING.
DR. HURLEY, WHAT BARGAINING POWER DO YOU THINK YOU HAVE LEFT? SHOOTING MORE OF US?

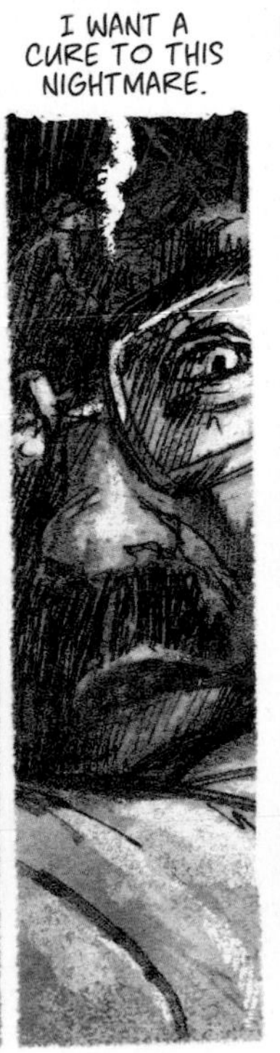
I WANT A CURE TO THIS NIGHTMARE.

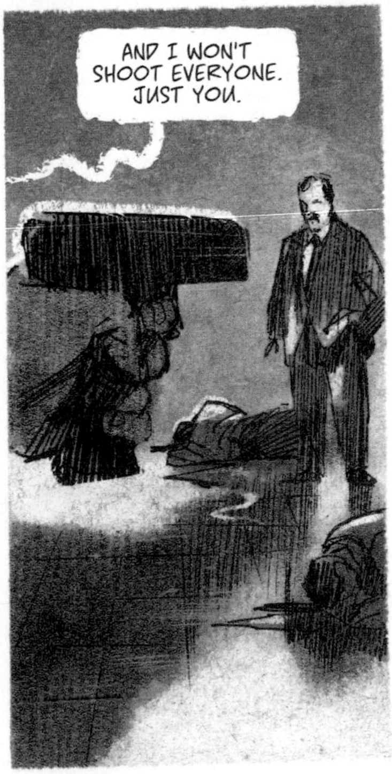
AND I WON'T SHOOT EVERYONE. JUST YOU.

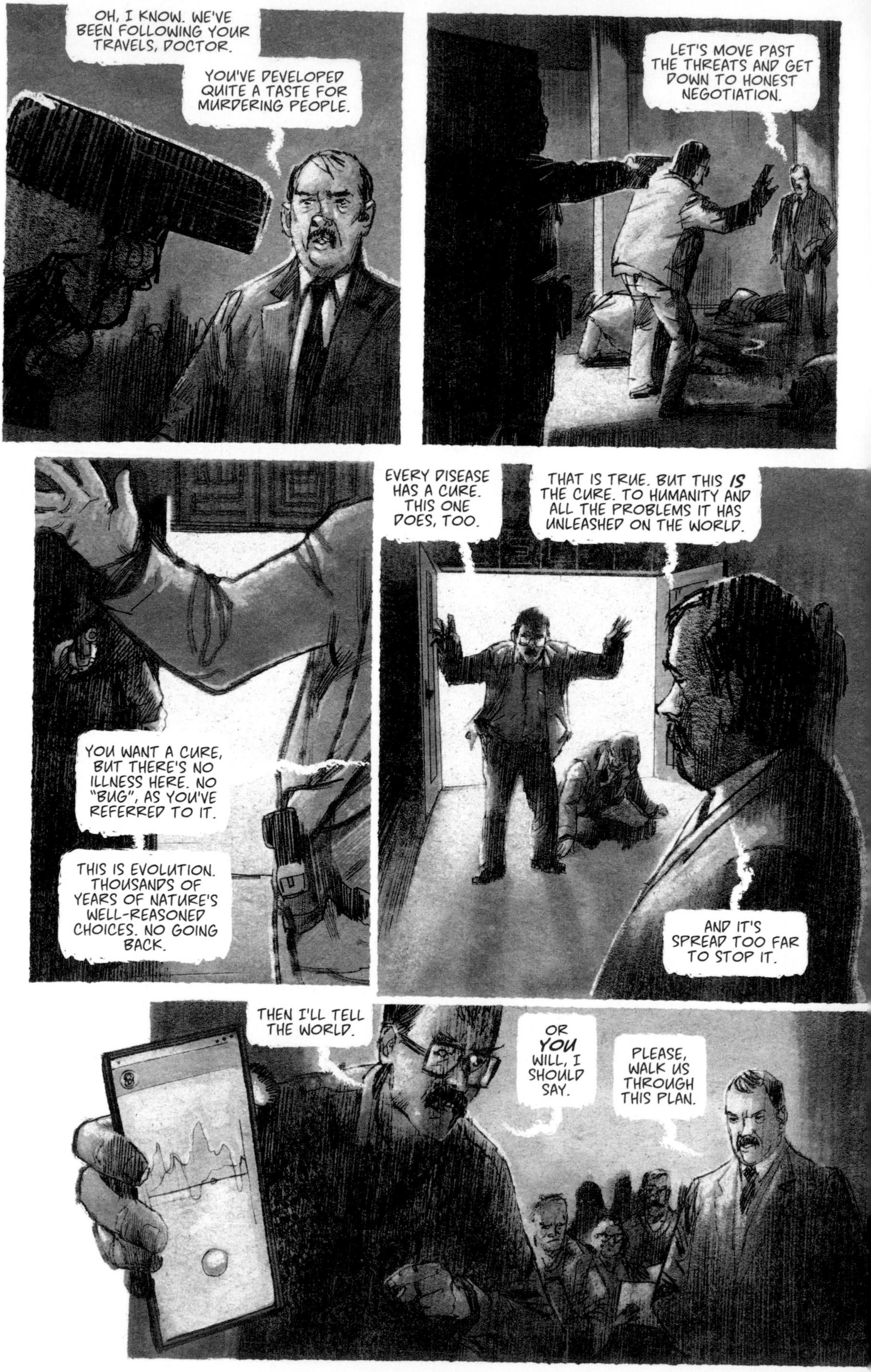
OH, I KNOW. WE'VE BEEN FOLLOWING YOUR TRAVELS, DOCTOR.
YOU'VE DEVELOPED QUITE A TASTE FOR MURDERING PEOPLE.
LET'S MOVE PAST THE THREATS AND GET DOWN TO HONEST NEGOTIATION.
YOU WANT A CURE, BUT THERE'S NO ILLNESS HERE. NO "BUG", AS YOU'VE REFERRED TO IT.
THIS IS EVOLUTION. THOUSANDS OF YEARS OF NATURE'S WELL-REASONED CHOICES. NO GOING BACK.
EVERY DISEASE HAS A CURE. THIS ONE DOES, TOO.
THAT IS TRUE. BUT THIS *IS* THE CURE. TO HUMANITY AND ALL THE PROBLEMS IT HAS UNLEASHED ON THE WORLD.
AND IT'S SPREAD TOO FAR TO STOP IT.
THEN I'LL TELL THE WORLD.
OR ***YOU*** WILL, I SHOULD SAY.
PLEASE, WALK US THROUGH THIS PLAN.

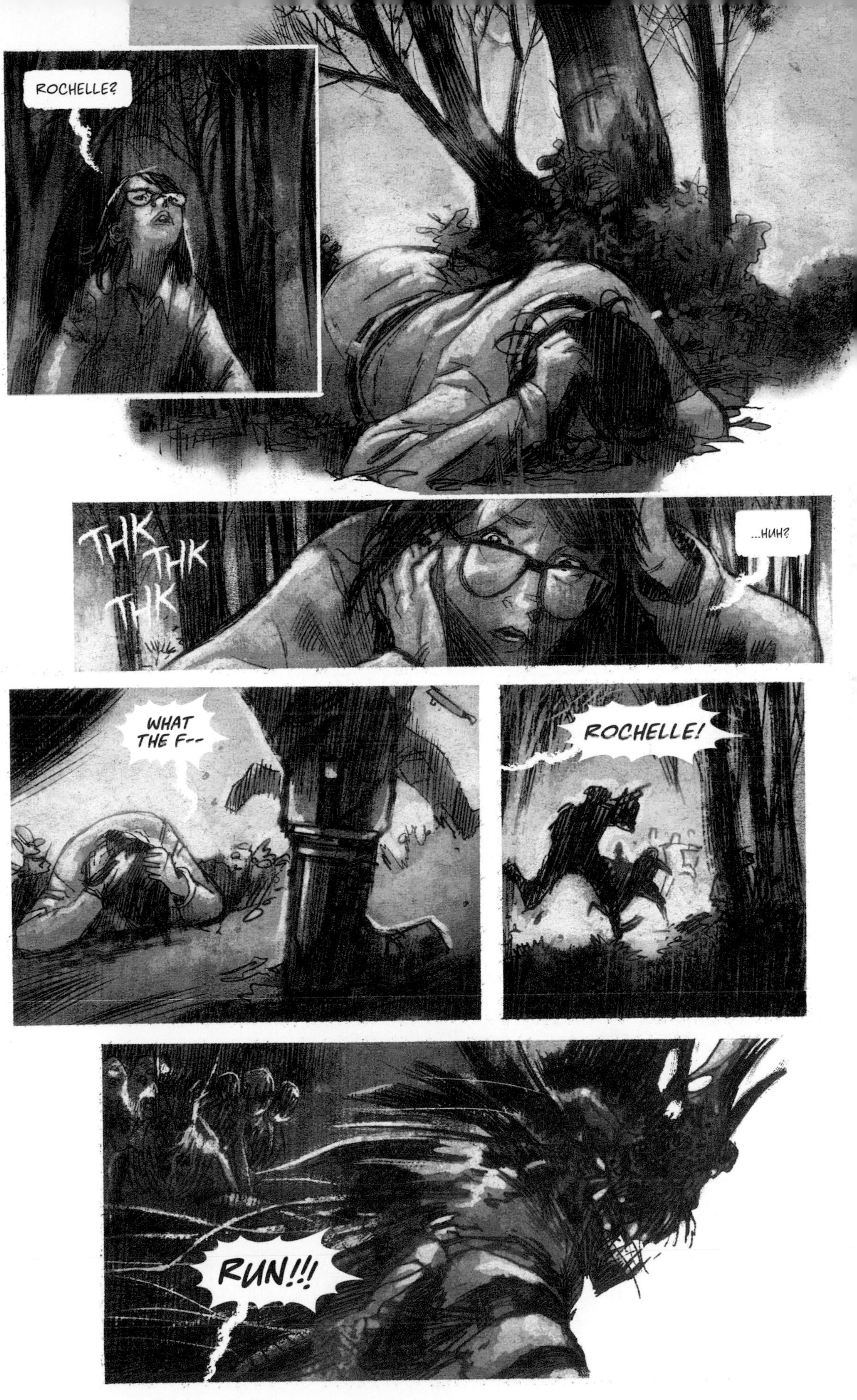
ROCHELLE?
THK THK THK
...HUH?
WHAT THE F--
ROCHELLE!
RUN!!!

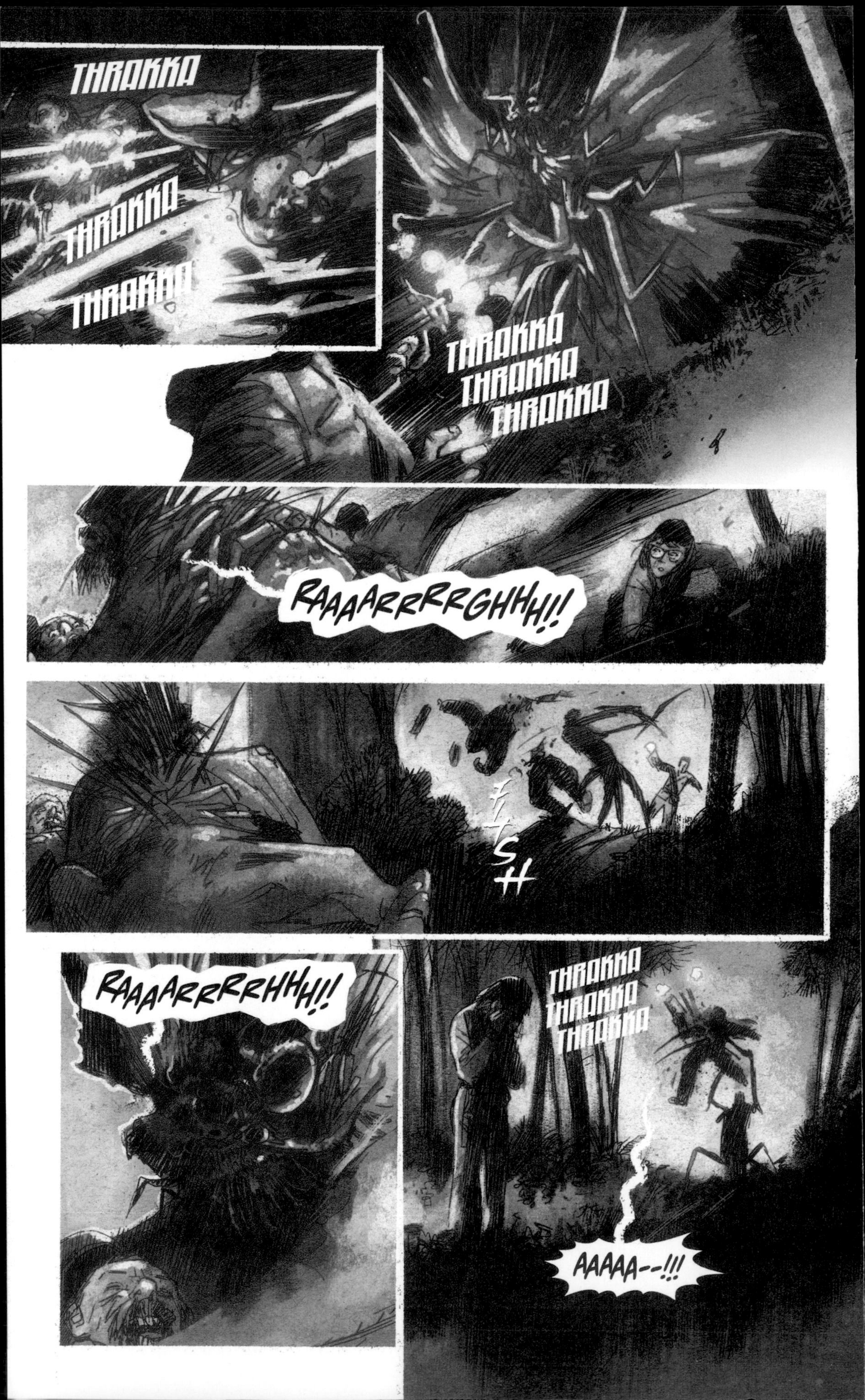
THRAKKA
THRAKKA
THRAKKA
THRAKKA
THRAKKA
THRAKKA
RAAAARRRRGHHH!!
FITSH
RAAAARRRRHHH!!
THRAKKA
THRAKKA
THRAKKA
AAAAA--!!!

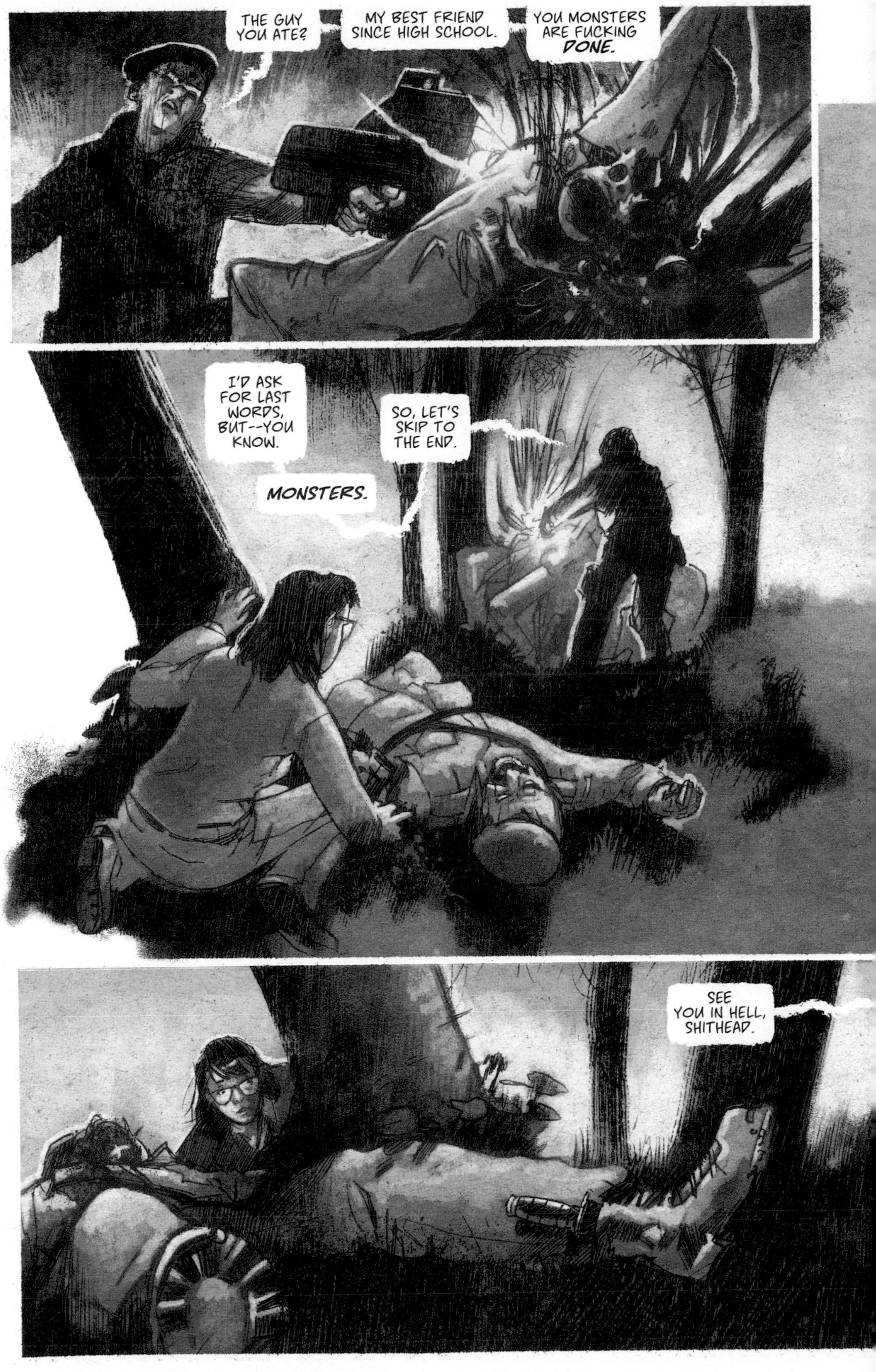
THE GUY YOU ATE?
MY BEST FRIEND SINCE HIGH SCHOOL.
YOU MONSTERS ARE FUCKING DONE.
I'D ASK FOR LAST WORDS, BUT--YOU KNOW.
MONSTERS.
SO, LET'S SKIP TO THE END.
SEE YOU IN HELL, SHITHEAD.

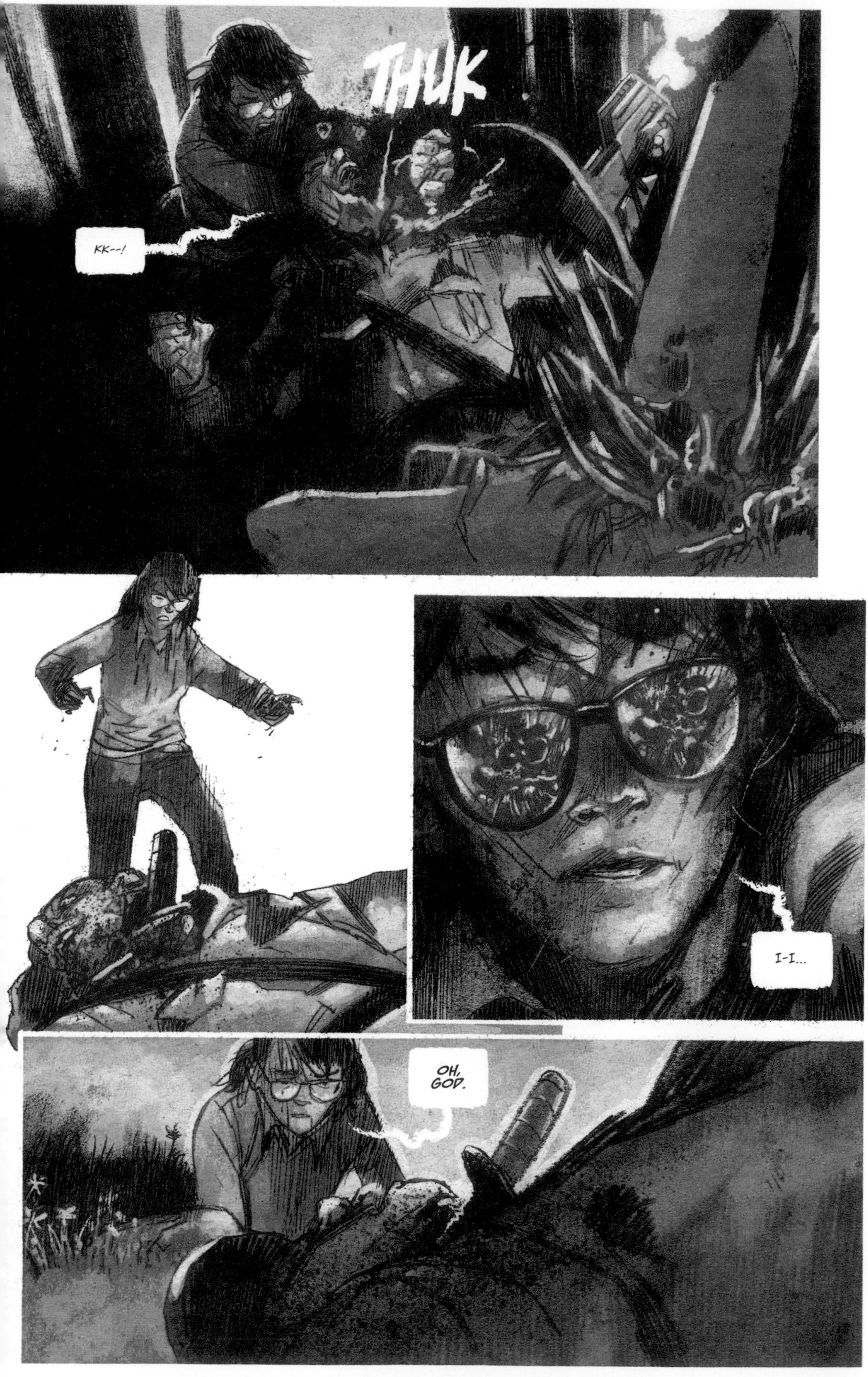
THUK
KK--!
I-I...
OH, GOD.

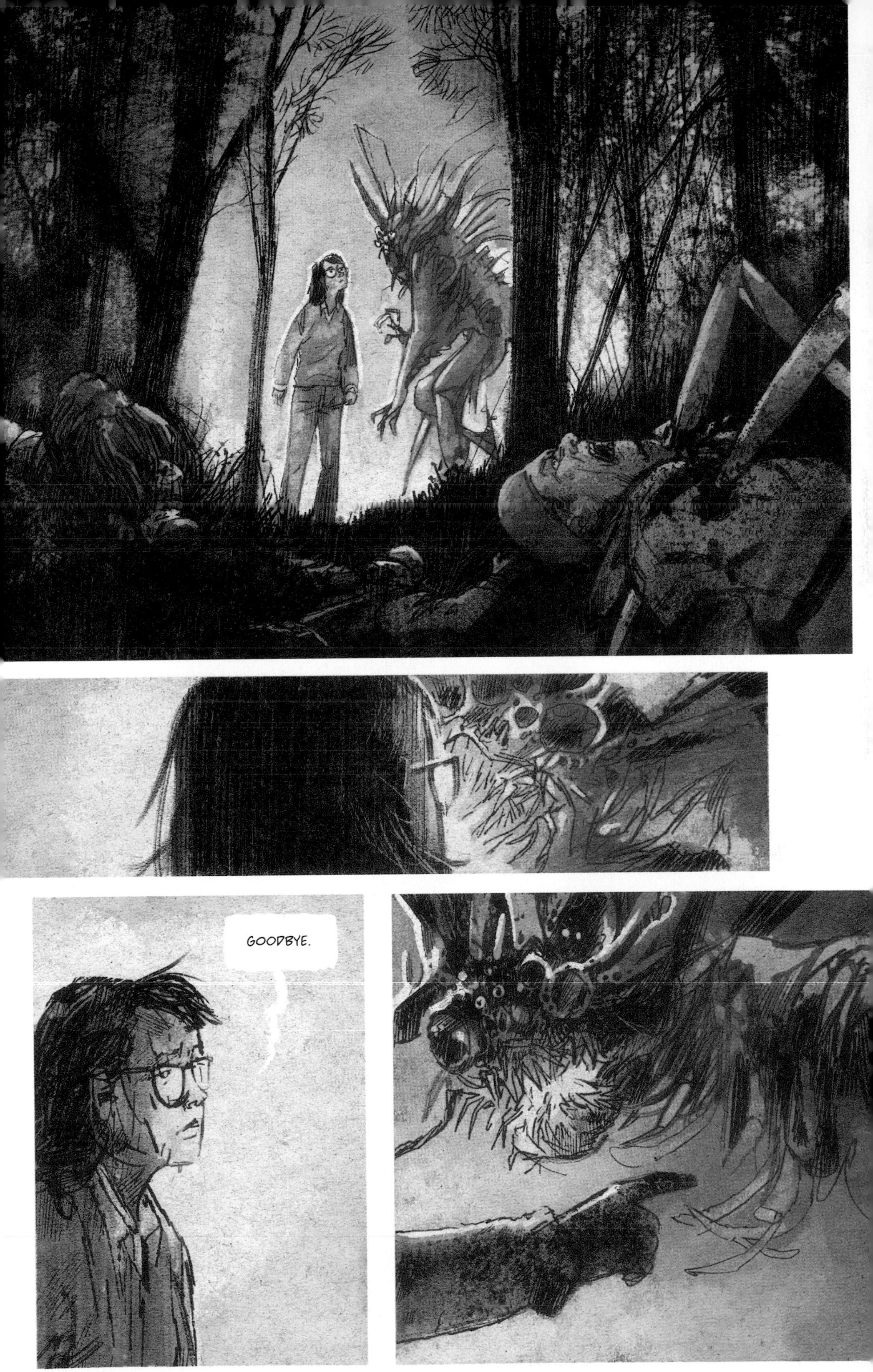
GOODBYE.

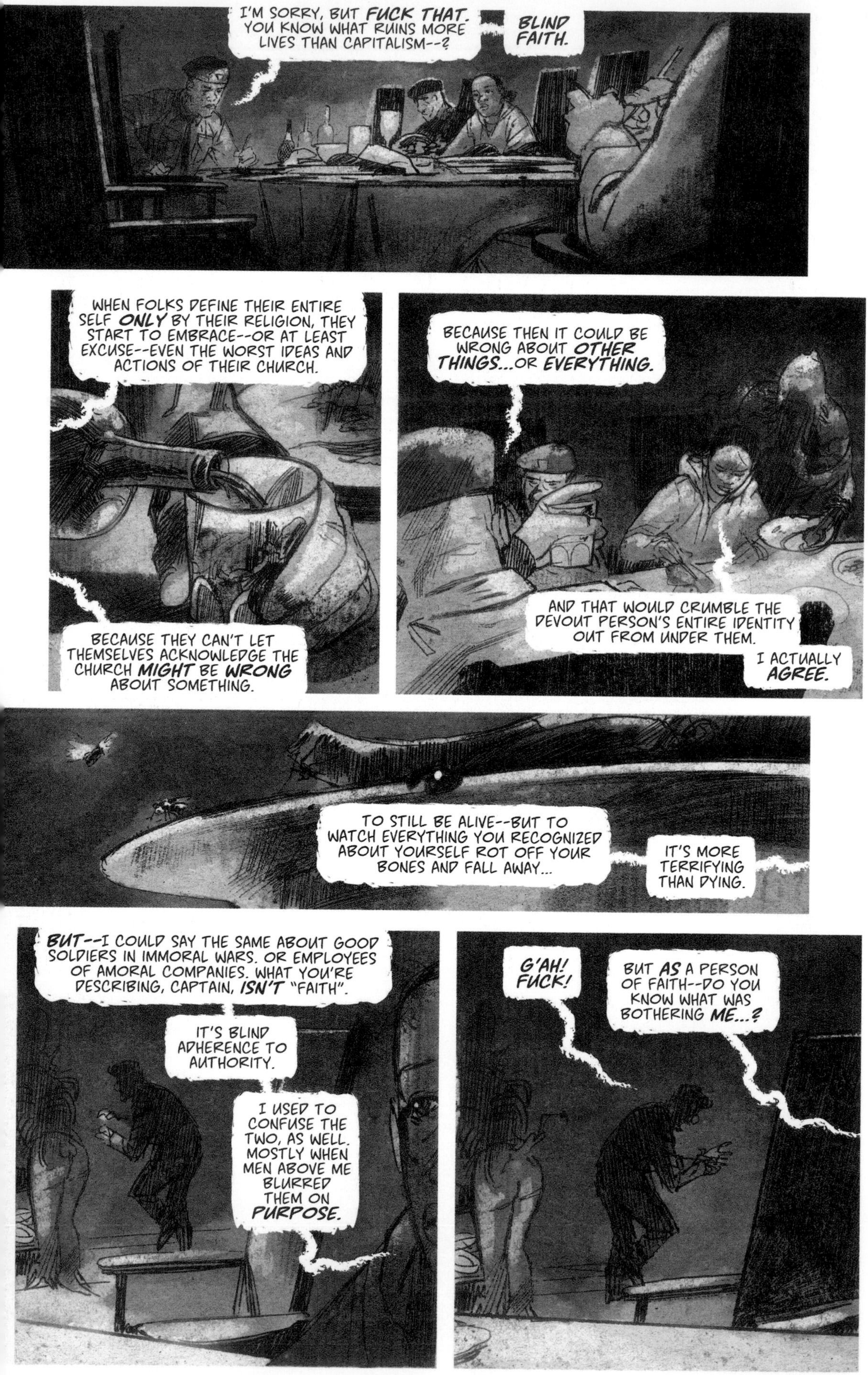
I'M SORRY, BUT FUCK THAT. YOU KNOW WHAT RUINS MORE LIVES THAN CAPITALISM--?
BLIND FAITH.
WHEN FOLKS DEFINE THEIR ENTIRE SELF ONLY BY THEIR RELIGION, THEY START TO EMBRACE--OR AT LEAST EXCUSE--EVEN THE WORST IDEAS AND ACTIONS OF THEIR CHURCH.
BECAUSE THEY CAN'T LET THEMSELVES ACKNOWLEDGE THE CHURCH MIGHT BE WRONG ABOUT SOMETHING.
BECAUSE THEN IT COULD BE WRONG ABOUT OTHER THINGS...OR EVERYTHING.
AND THAT WOULD CRUMBLE THE DEVOUT PERSON'S ENTIRE IDENTITY OUT FROM UNDER THEM.
I ACTUALLY AGREE.
TO STILL BE ALIVE--BUT TO WATCH EVERYTHING YOU RECOGNIZED ABOUT YOURSELF ROT OFF YOUR BONES AND FALL AWAY...
IT'S MORE TERRIFYING THAN DYING.
BUT--I COULD SAY THE SAME ABOUT GOOD SOLDIERS IN IMMORAL WARS. OR EMPLOYEES OF AMORAL COMPANIES. WHAT YOU'RE DESCRIBING, CAPTAIN, ISN'T "FAITH".
IT'S BLIND ADHERENCE TO AUTHORITY.
I USED TO CONFUSE THE TWO, AS WELL. MOSTLY WHEN MEN ABOVE ME BLURRED THEM ON PURPOSE.
G'AH! FUCK!
BUT AS A PERSON OF FAITH--DO YOU KNOW WHAT WAS BOTHERING ME...?

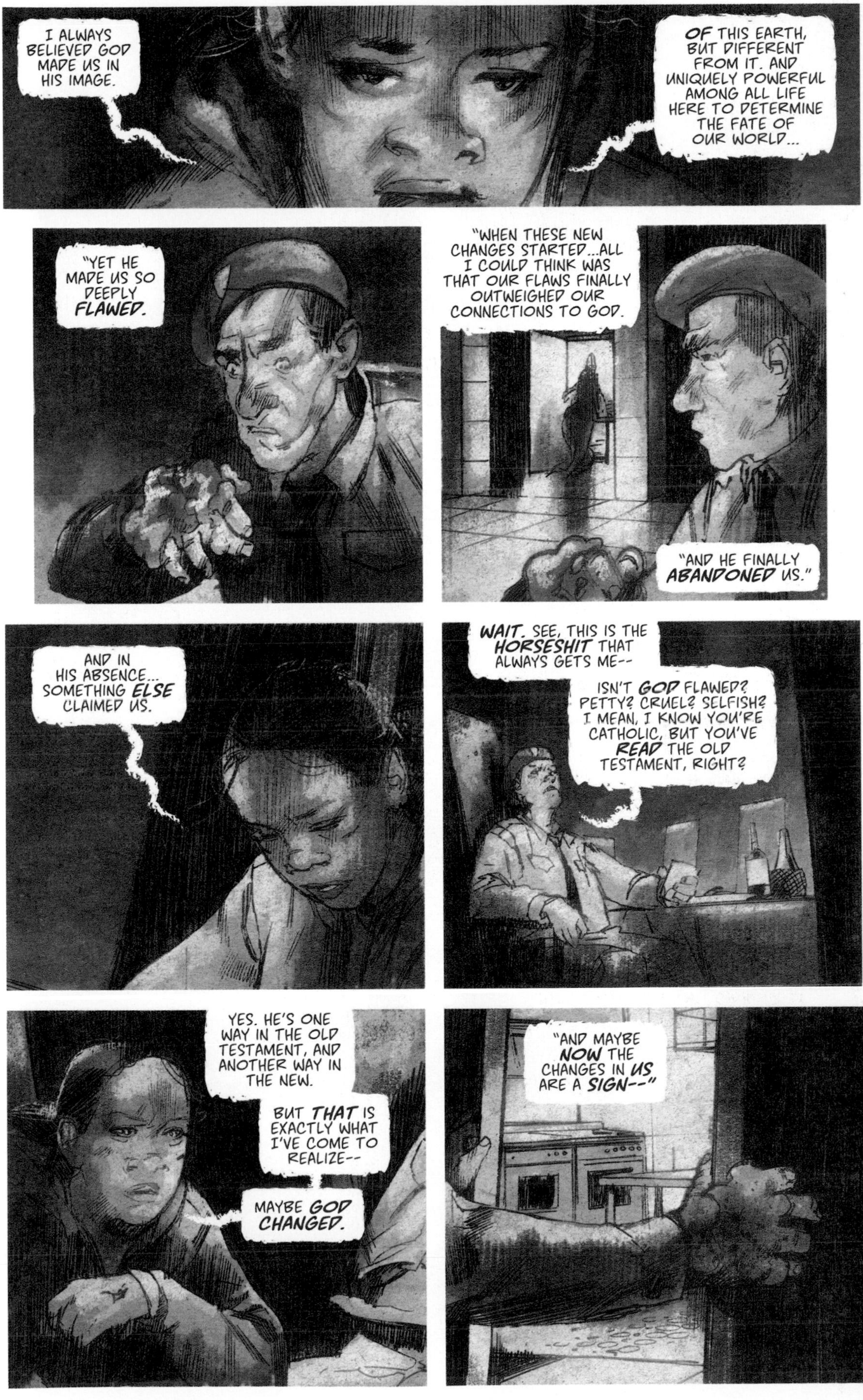
I ALWAYS BELIEVED GOD MADE US IN HIS IMAGE.
OF THIS EARTH, BUT DIFFERENT FROM IT. AND UNIQUELY POWERFUL AMONG ALL LIFE HERE TO DETERMINE THE FATE OF OUR WORLD...
"YET HE MADE US SO DEEPLY FLAWED.
"WHEN THESE NEW CHANGES STARTED...ALL I COULD THINK WAS THAT OUR FLAWS FINALLY OUTWEIGHED OUR CONNECTIONS TO GOD.
"AND HE FINALLY ABANDONED US."
AND IN HIS ABSENCE... SOMETHING ELSE CLAIMED US.
WAIT. SEE, THIS IS THE HORSESHIT THAT ALWAYS GETS ME--
ISN'T GOD FLAWED? PETTY? CRUEL? SELFISH? I MEAN, I KNOW YOU'RE CATHOLIC, BUT YOU'VE READ THE OLD TESTAMENT, RIGHT?
YES. HE'S ONE WAY IN THE OLD TESTAMENT, AND ANOTHER WAY IN THE NEW.
BUT THAT IS EXACTLY WHAT I'VE COME TO REALIZE--
MAYBE GOD CHANGED.
"AND MAYBE NOW THE CHANGES IN US ARE A SIGN--"

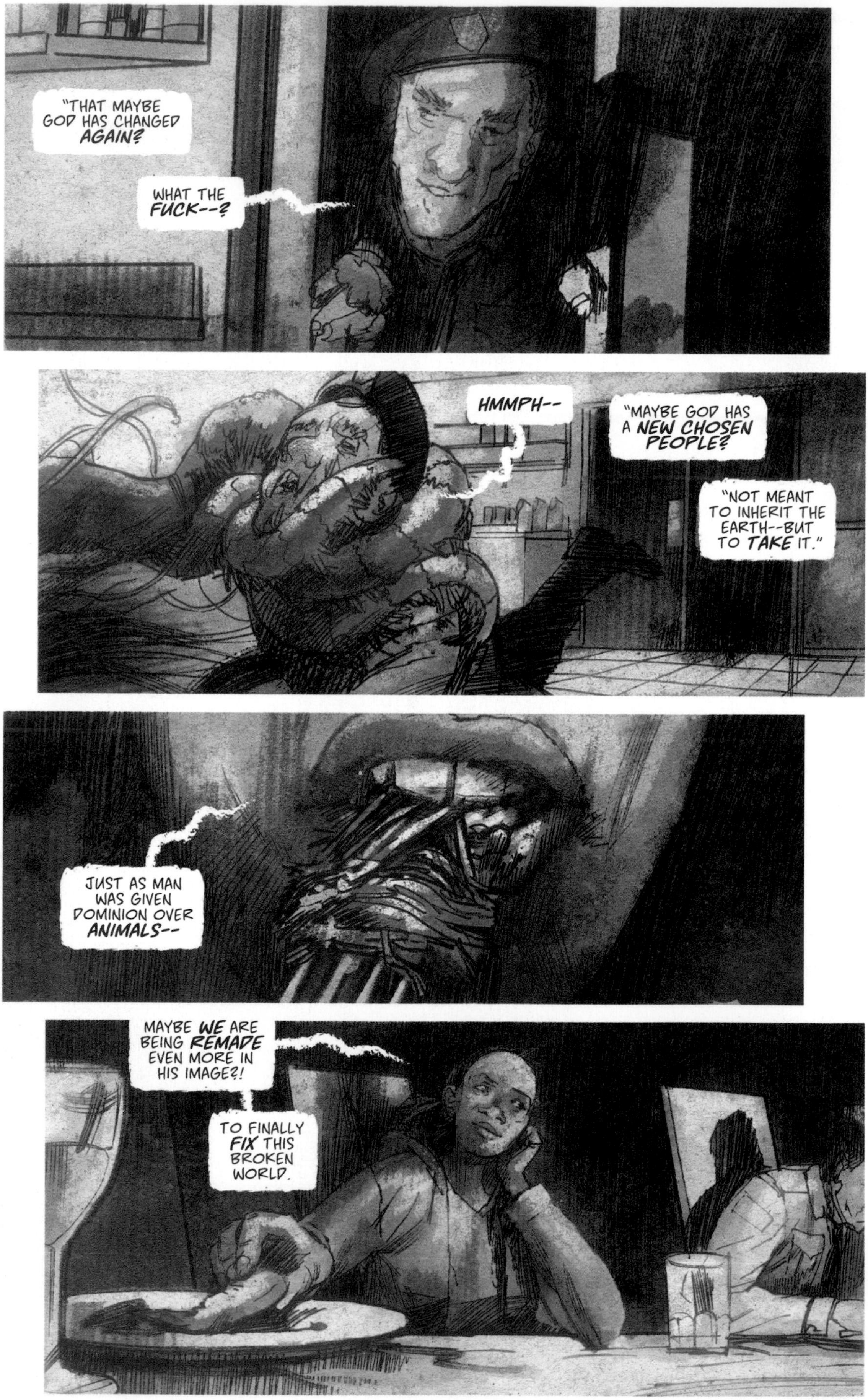
"THAT MAYBE GOD HAS CHANGED AGAIN?
WHAT THE FUCK--?
HMMPH--
"MAYBE GOD HAS A NEW CHOSEN PEOPLE?
"NOT MEANT TO INHERIT THE EARTH--BUT TO TAKE IT."
JUST AS MAN WAS GIVEN DOMINION OVER ANIMALS--
MAYBE WE ARE BEING REMADE EVEN MORE IN HIS IMAGE?!
TO FINALLY FIX THIS BROKEN WORLD.

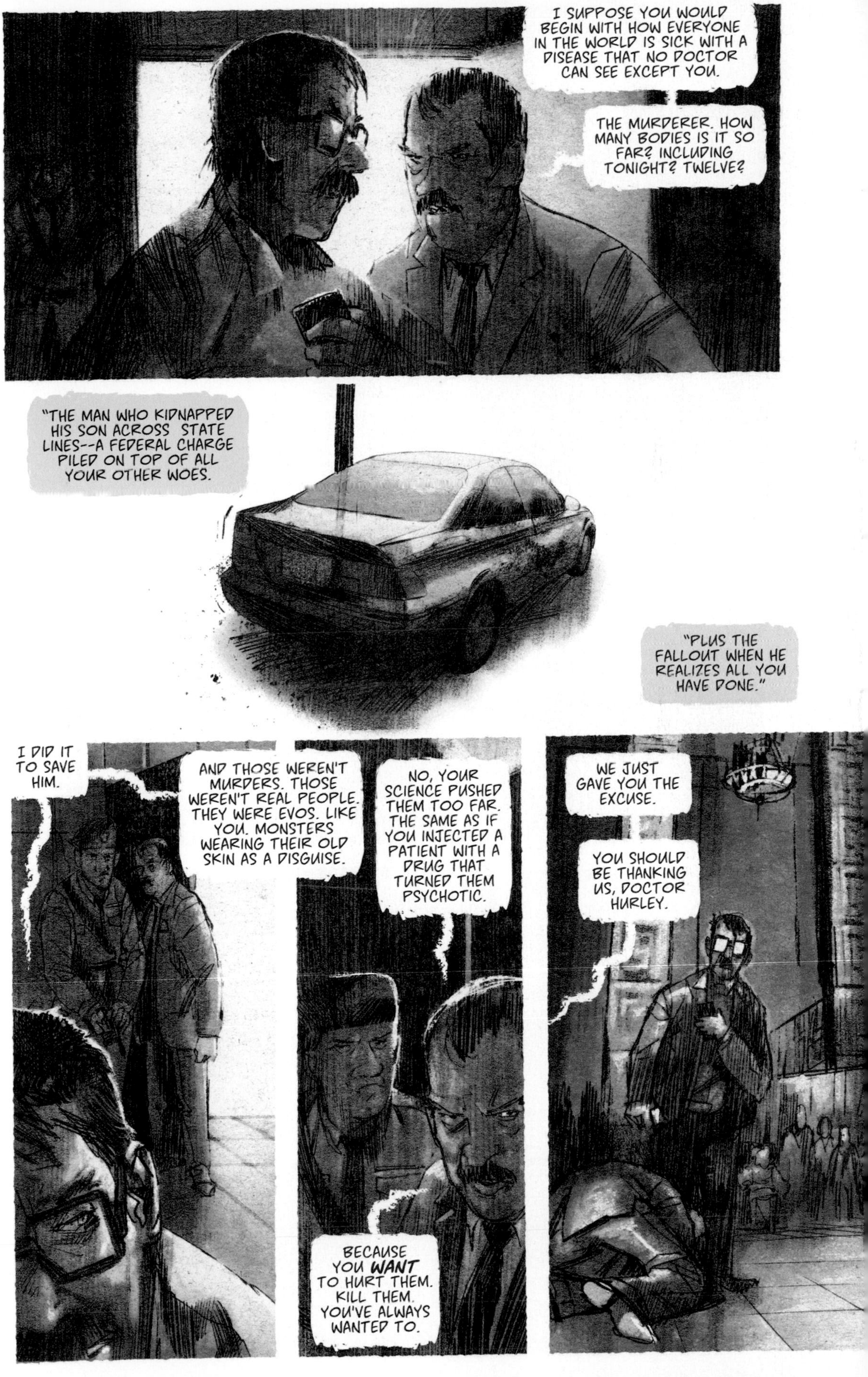

I SUPPOSE YOU WOULD BEGIN WITH HOW EVERYONE IN THE WORLD IS SICK WITH A DISEASE THAT NO DOCTOR CAN SEE EXCEPT YOU.
THE MURDERER. HOW MANY BODIES IS IT SO FAR? INCLUDING TONIGHT? TWELVE?
"THE MAN WHO KIDNAPPED HIS SON ACROSS STATE LINES--A FEDERAL CHARGE PILED ON TOP OF ALL YOUR OTHER WOES.
"PLUS THE FALLOUT WHEN HE REALIZES ALL YOU HAVE DONE."
I DID IT TO SAVE HIM.
AND THOSE WEREN'T MURDERS. THOSE WEREN'T REAL PEOPLE. THEY WERE EVOS. LIKE YOU. MONSTERS WEARING THEIR OLD SKIN AS A DISGUISE.
NO, YOUR SCIENCE PUSHED THEM TOO FAR. THE SAME AS IF YOU INJECTED A PATIENT WITH A DRUG THAT TURNED THEM PSYCHOTIC.
BECAUSE YOU **WANT** TO HURT THEM. KILL THEM. YOU'VE ALWAYS WANTED TO.
WE JUST GAVE YOU THE EXCUSE.
YOU SHOULD BE THANKING US, DOCTOR HURLEY.

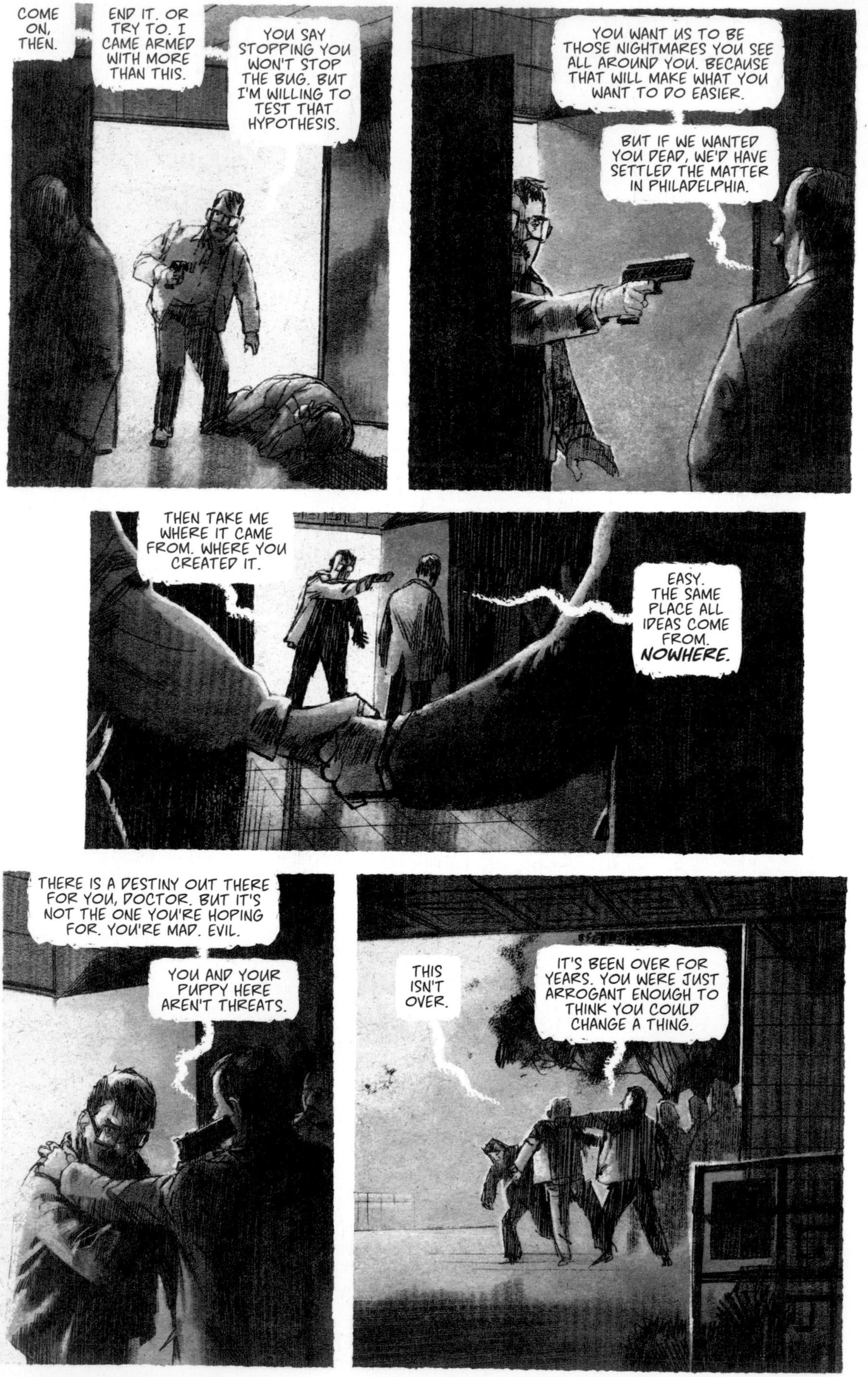
COME ON, THEN.
END IT. OR TRY TO. I CAME ARMED WITH MORE THAN THIS.
YOU SAY STOPPING YOU WON'T STOP THE BUG. BUT I'M WILLING TO TEST THAT HYPOTHESIS.
YOU WANT US TO BE THOSE NIGHTMARES YOU SEE ALL AROUND YOU. BECAUSE THAT WILL MAKE WHAT YOU WANT TO DO EASIER.
BUT IF WE WANTED YOU DEAD, WE'D HAVE SETTLED THE MATTER IN PHILADELPHIA.
THEN TAKE ME WHERE IT CAME FROM. WHERE YOU CREATED IT.
EASY. THE SAME PLACE ALL IDEAS COME FROM. NOWHERE.
THERE IS A DESTINY OUT THERE FOR YOU, DOCTOR. BUT IT'S NOT THE ONE YOU'RE HOPING FOR. YOU'RE MAD. EVIL.
YOU AND YOUR PUPPY HERE AREN'T THREATS.
THIS ISN'T OVER.
IT'S BEEN OVER FOR YEARS. YOU WERE JUST ARROGANT ENOUGH TO THINK YOU COULD CHANGE A THING.

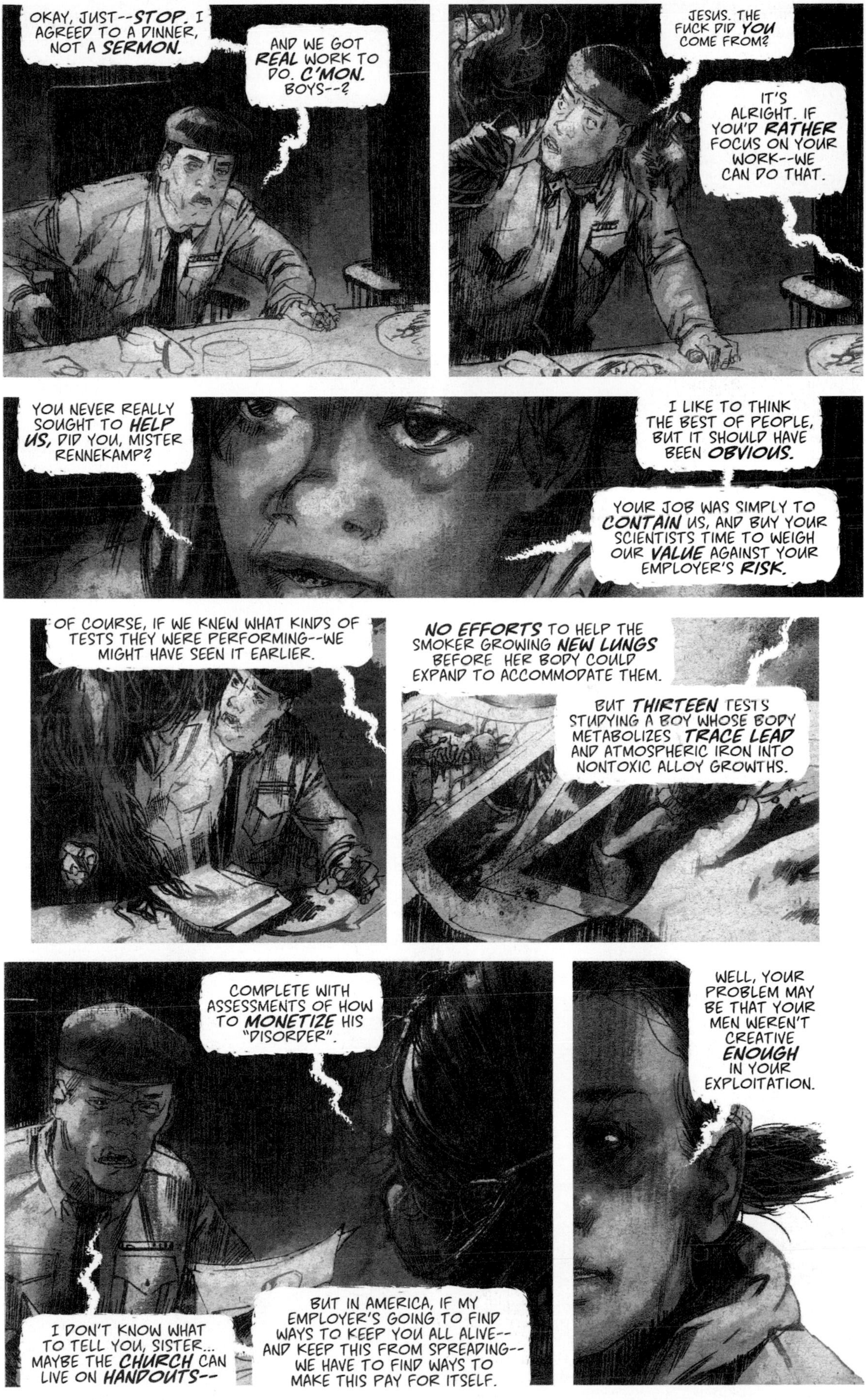

OKAY, JUST--STOP. I AGREED TO A DINNER, NOT A SERMON.
AND WE GOT REAL WORK TO DO. C'MON. BOYS--?
JESUS. THE FUCK DID YOU COME FROM?
IT'S ALRIGHT. IF YOU'D RATHER FOCUS ON YOUR WORK--WE CAN DO THAT.
YOU NEVER REALLY SOUGHT TO HELP US, DID YOU, MISTER RENNEKAMP?
I LIKE TO THINK THE BEST OF PEOPLE, BUT IT SHOULD HAVE BEEN OBVIOUS.
YOUR JOB WAS SIMPLY TO CONTAIN US, AND BUY YOUR SCIENTISTS TIME TO WEIGH OUR VALUE AGAINST YOUR EMPLOYER'S RISK.
OF COURSE, IF WE KNEW WHAT KINDS OF TESTS THEY WERE PERFORMING--WE MIGHT HAVE SEEN IT EARLIER.
NO EFFORTS TO HELP THE SMOKER GROWING NEW LUNGS BEFORE HER BODY COULD EXPAND TO ACCOMMODATE THEM.
BUT THIRTEEN TESTS STUDYING A BOY WHOSE BODY METABOLIZES TRACE LEAD AND ATMOSPHERIC IRON INTO NONTOXIC ALLOY GROWTHS.
COMPLETE WITH ASSESSMENTS OF HOW TO MONETIZE HIS "DISORDER".
I DON'T KNOW WHAT TO TELL YOU, SISTER... MAYBE THE CHURCH CAN LIVE ON HANDOUTS--
BUT IN AMERICA, IF MY EMPLOYER'S GOING TO FIND WAYS TO KEEP YOU ALL ALIVE--AND KEEP THIS FROM SPREADING--WE HAVE TO FIND WAYS TO MAKE THIS PAY FOR ITSELF.
WELL, YOUR PROBLEM MAY BE THAT YOUR MEN WEREN'T CREATIVE ENOUGH IN YOUR EXPLOITATION.

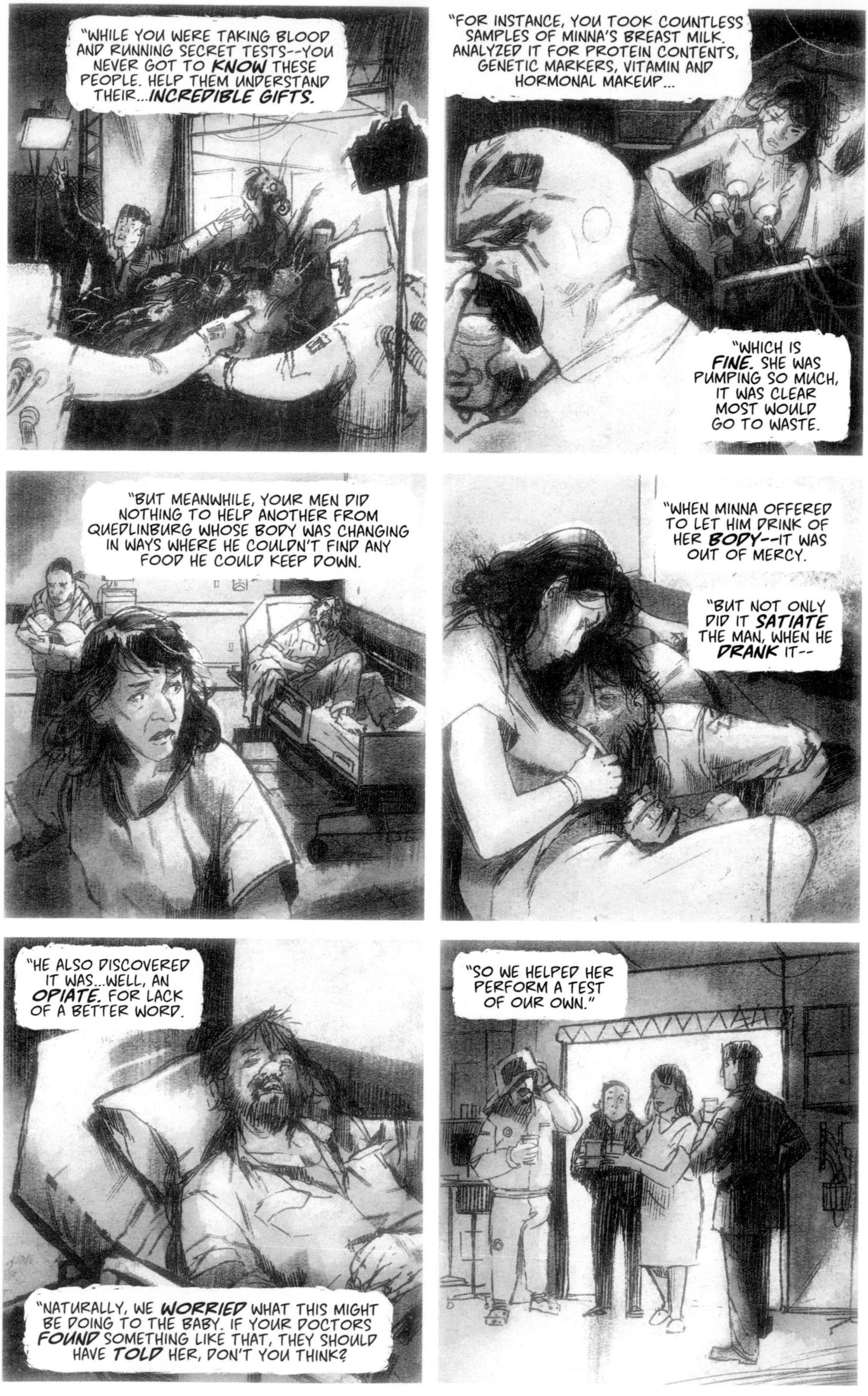
"WHILE YOU WERE TAKING BLOOD AND RUNNING SECRET TESTS--YOU NEVER GOT TO KNOW THESE PEOPLE. HELP THEM UNDERSTAND THEIR...INCREDIBLE GIFTS.
"FOR INSTANCE, YOU TOOK COUNTLESS SAMPLES OF MINNA'S BREAST MILK. ANALYZED IT FOR PROTEIN CONTENTS, GENETIC MARKERS, VITAMIN AND HORMONAL MAKEUP...
"WHICH IS FINE. SHE WAS PUMPING SO MUCH, IT WAS CLEAR MOST WOULD GO TO WASTE.
"BUT MEANWHILE, YOUR MEN DID NOTHING TO HELP ANOTHER FROM QUEDLINBURG WHOSE BODY WAS CHANGING IN WAYS WHERE HE COULDN'T FIND ANY FOOD HE COULD KEEP DOWN.
"WHEN MINNA OFFERED TO LET HIM DRINK OF HER BODY--IT WAS OUT OF MERCY.
"BUT NOT ONLY DID IT SATIATE THE MAN, WHEN HE DRANK IT--
"HE ALSO DISCOVERED IT WAS...WELL, AN OPIATE. FOR LACK OF A BETTER WORD.
"NATURALLY, WE WORRIED WHAT THIS MIGHT BE DOING TO THE BABY. IF YOUR DOCTORS FOUND SOMETHING LIKE THAT, THEY SHOULD HAVE TOLD HER, DON'T YOU THINK?
"SO WE HELPED HER PERFORM A TEST OF OUR OWN."

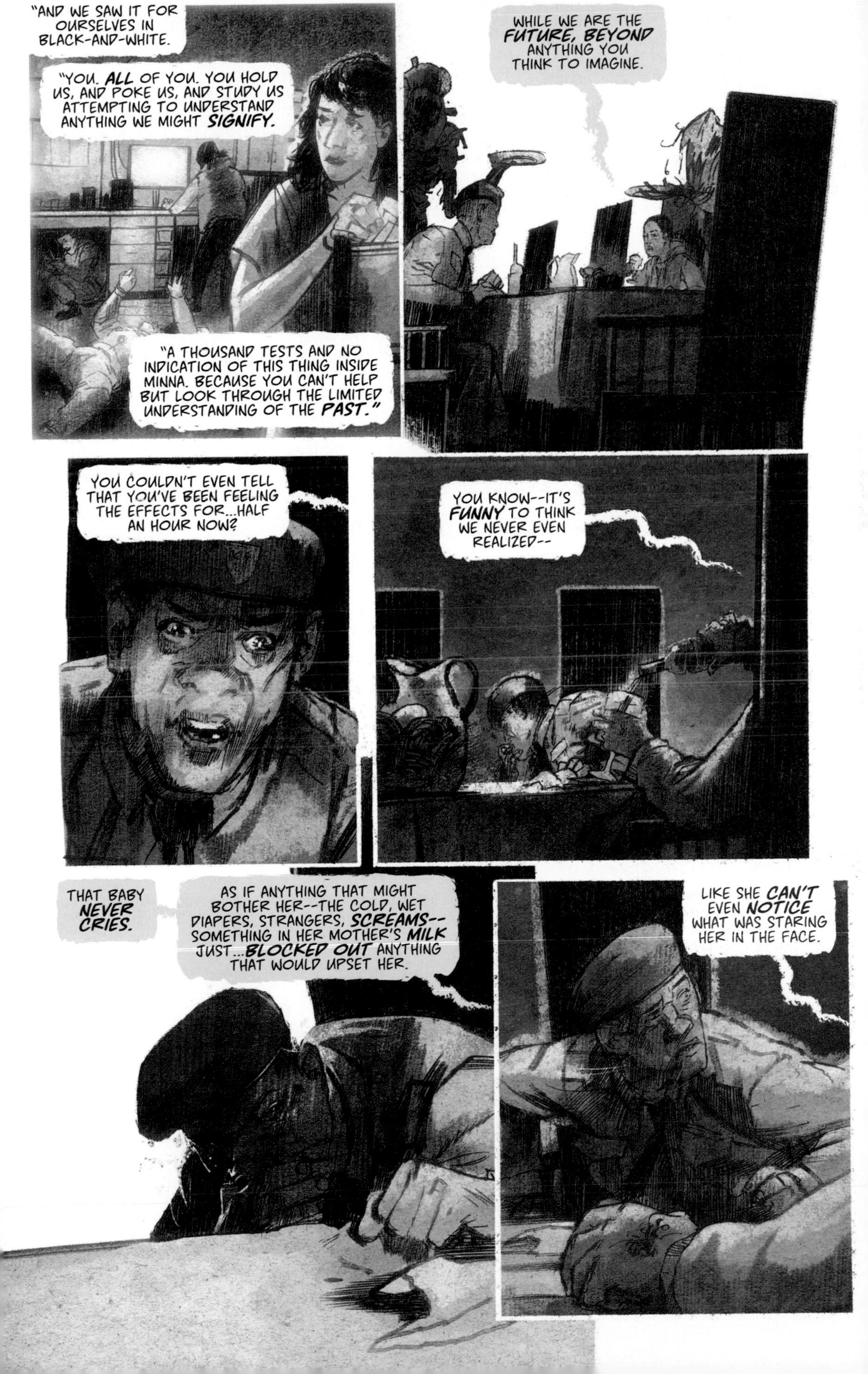
"AND WE SAW IT FOR OURSELVES IN BLACK-AND-WHITE.
"YOU. ALL OF YOU. YOU HOLD US, AND POKE US, AND STUDY US ATTEMPTING TO UNDERSTAND ANYTHING WE MIGHT SIGNIFY.
"A THOUSAND TESTS AND NO INDICATION OF THIS THING INSIDE MINNA. BECAUSE YOU CAN'T HELP BUT LOOK THROUGH THE LIMITED UNDERSTANDING OF THE PAST."
WHILE WE ARE THE FUTURE, BEYOND ANYTHING YOU THINK TO IMAGINE.
YOU COULDN'T EVEN TELL THAT YOU'VE BEEN FEELING THE EFFECTS FOR...HALF AN HOUR NOW?
YOU KNOW--IT'S FUNNY TO THINK WE NEVER EVEN REALIZED--
THAT BABY NEVER CRIES.
AS IF ANYTHING THAT MIGHT BOTHER HER--THE COLD, WET DIAPERS, STRANGERS, SCREAMS--SOMETHING IN HER MOTHER'S MILK JUST...BLOCKED OUT ANYTHING THAT WOULD UPSET HER.
LIKE SHE CAN'T EVEN NOTICE WHAT WAS STARING HER IN THE FACE.

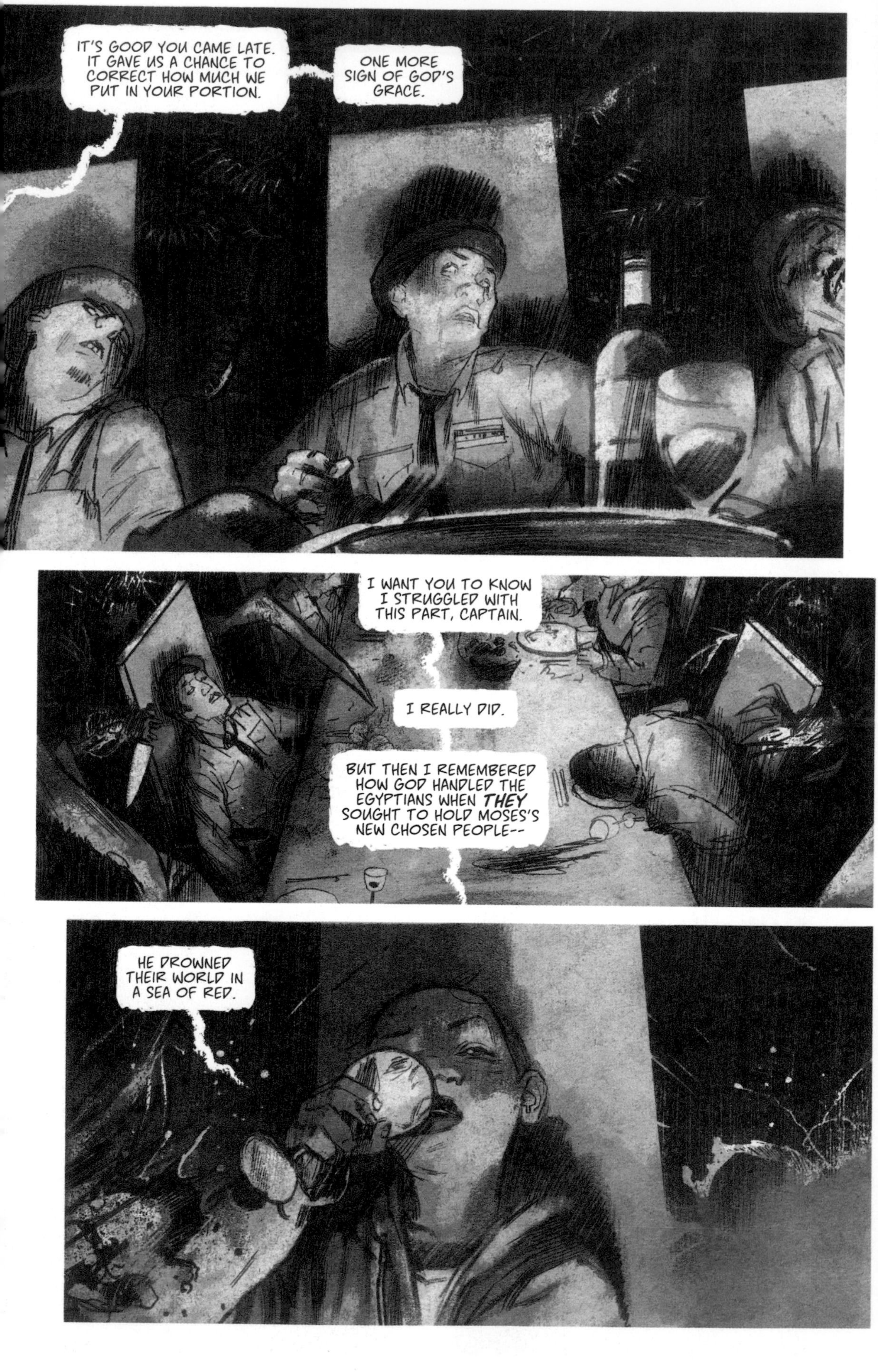
IT'S GOOD YOU CAME LATE. IT GAVE US A CHANCE TO CORRECT HOW MUCH WE PUT IN YOUR PORTION.
ONE MORE SIGN OF GOD'S GRACE.
I WANT YOU TO KNOW I STRUGGLED WITH THIS PART, CAPTAIN.
I REALLY DID.
BUT THEN I REMEMBERED HOW GOD HANDLED THE EGYPTIANS WHEN ***THEY*** SOUGHT TO HOLD MOSES'S NEW CHOSEN PEOPLE--
HE DROWNED THEIR WORLD IN A SEA OF RED.

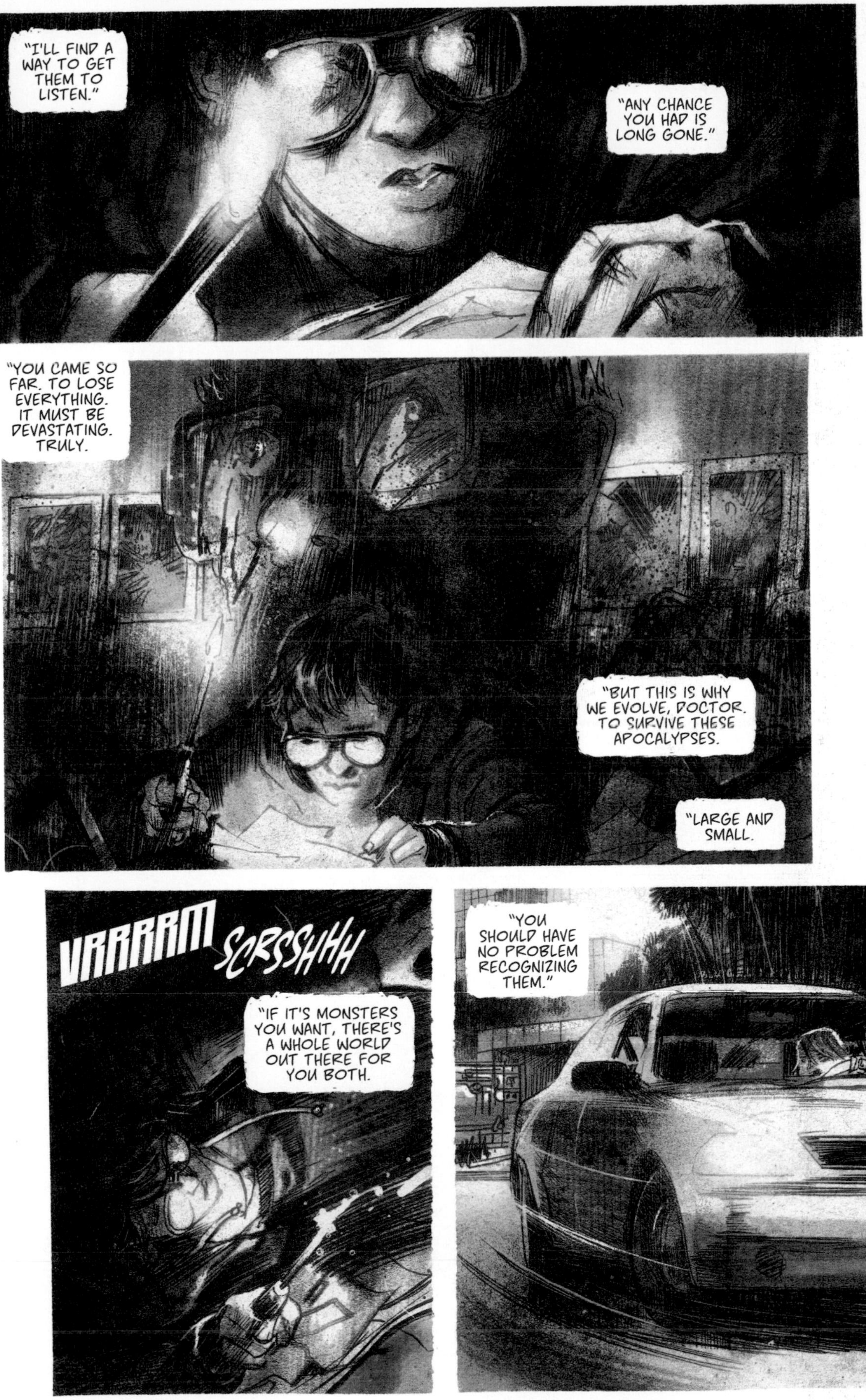
"I'LL FIND A WAY TO GET THEM TO LISTEN."
"ANY CHANCE YOU HAD IS LONG GONE."
"YOU CAME SO FAR. TO LOSE EVERYTHING. IT MUST BE DEVASTATING. TRULY.
"BUT THIS IS WHY WE EVOLVE, DOCTOR. TO SURVIVE THESE APOCALYPSES.
"LARGE AND SMALL.
VRRRRM
SCRSSHHH
"IF IT'S MONSTERS YOU WANT, THERE'S A WHOLE WORLD OUT THERE FOR YOU BOTH.
"YOU SHOULD HAVE NO PROBLEM RECOGNIZING THEM."

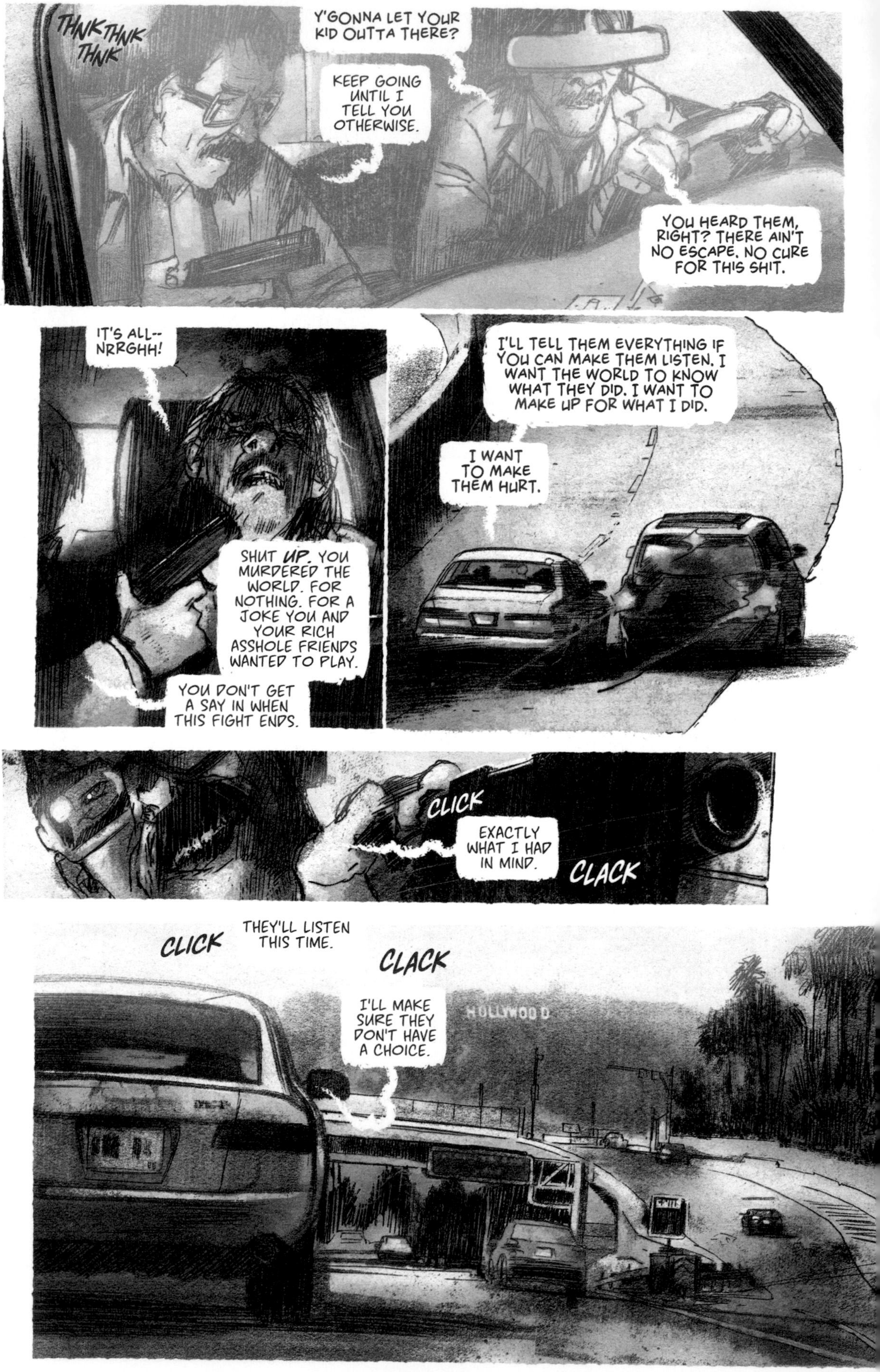
THNK THNK THNK
Y'GONNA LET YOUR KID OUTTA THERE?
KEEP GOING UNTIL I TELL YOU OTHERWISE.
YOU HEARD THEM, RIGHT? THERE AIN'T NO ESCAPE. NO CURE FOR THIS SHIT.
IT'S ALL-- NRRGHH!
SHUT UP. YOU MURDERED THE WORLD. FOR NOTHING. FOR A JOKE YOU AND YOUR RICH ASSHOLE FRIENDS WANTED TO PLAY.
YOU DON'T GET A SAY IN WHEN THIS FIGHT ENDS.
I'LL TELL THEM EVERYTHING IF YOU CAN MAKE THEM LISTEN. I WANT THE WORLD TO KNOW WHAT THEY DID. I WANT TO MAKE UP FOR WHAT I DID.
I WANT TO MAKE THEM HURT.
CLICK
EXACTLY WHAT I HAD IN MIND.
CLACK
CLICK
THEY'LL LISTEN THIS TIME.
CLACK
I'LL MAKE SURE THEY DON'T HAVE A CHOICE.
HOLLYWOOD

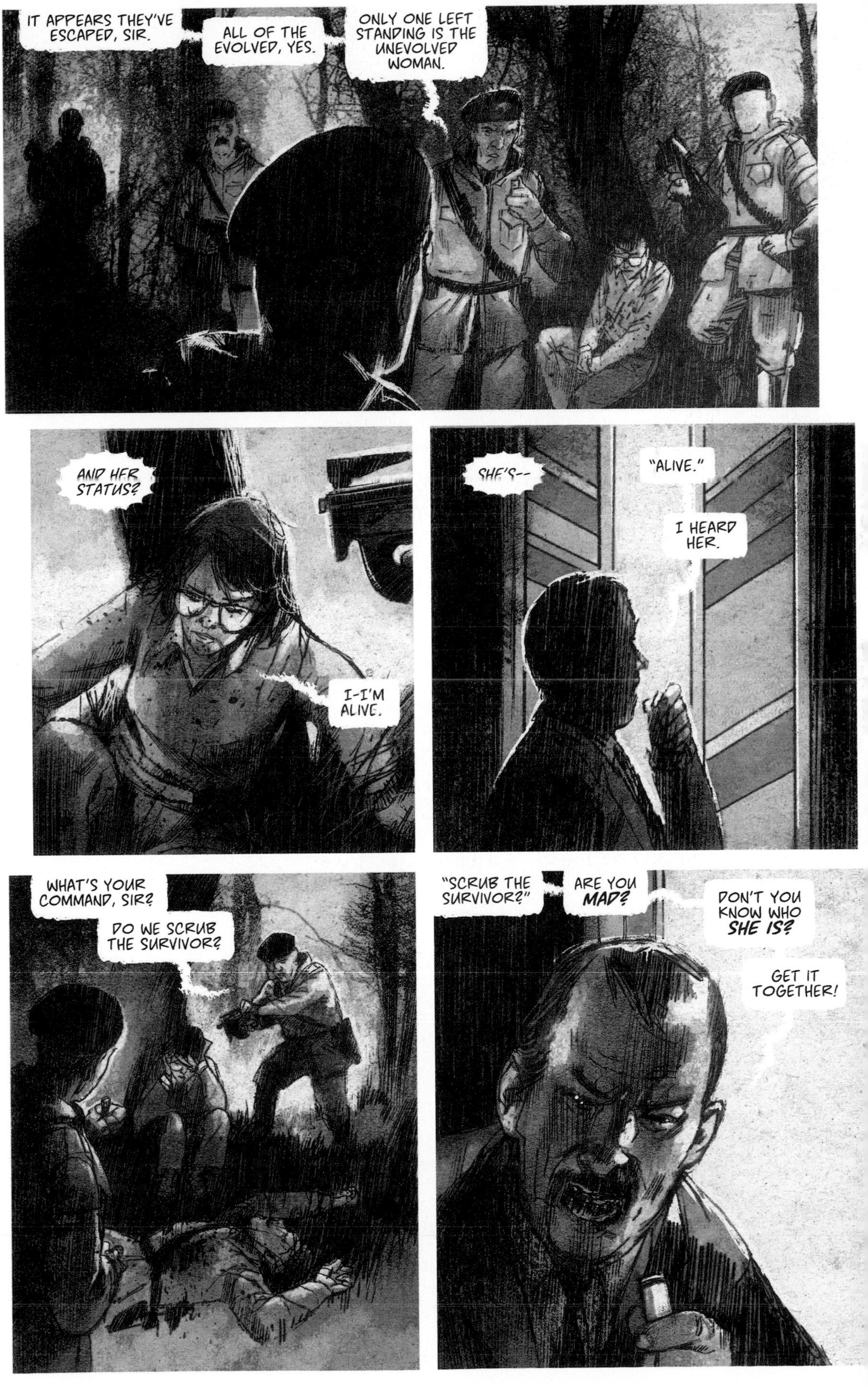
IT APPEARS THEY'VE ESCAPED, SIR.
ALL OF THE EVOLVED, YES.
ONLY ONE LEFT STANDING IS THE UNEVOLVED WOMAN.
AND HER STATUS?
I-I'M ALIVE.
SHE'S--
"ALIVE."
I HEARD HER.
WHAT'S YOUR COMMAND, SIR?
DO WE SCRUB THE SURVIVOR?
"SCRUB THE SURVIVOR?"
ARE YOU MAD?
DON'T YOU KNOW WHO SHE IS?
GET IT TOGETHER!

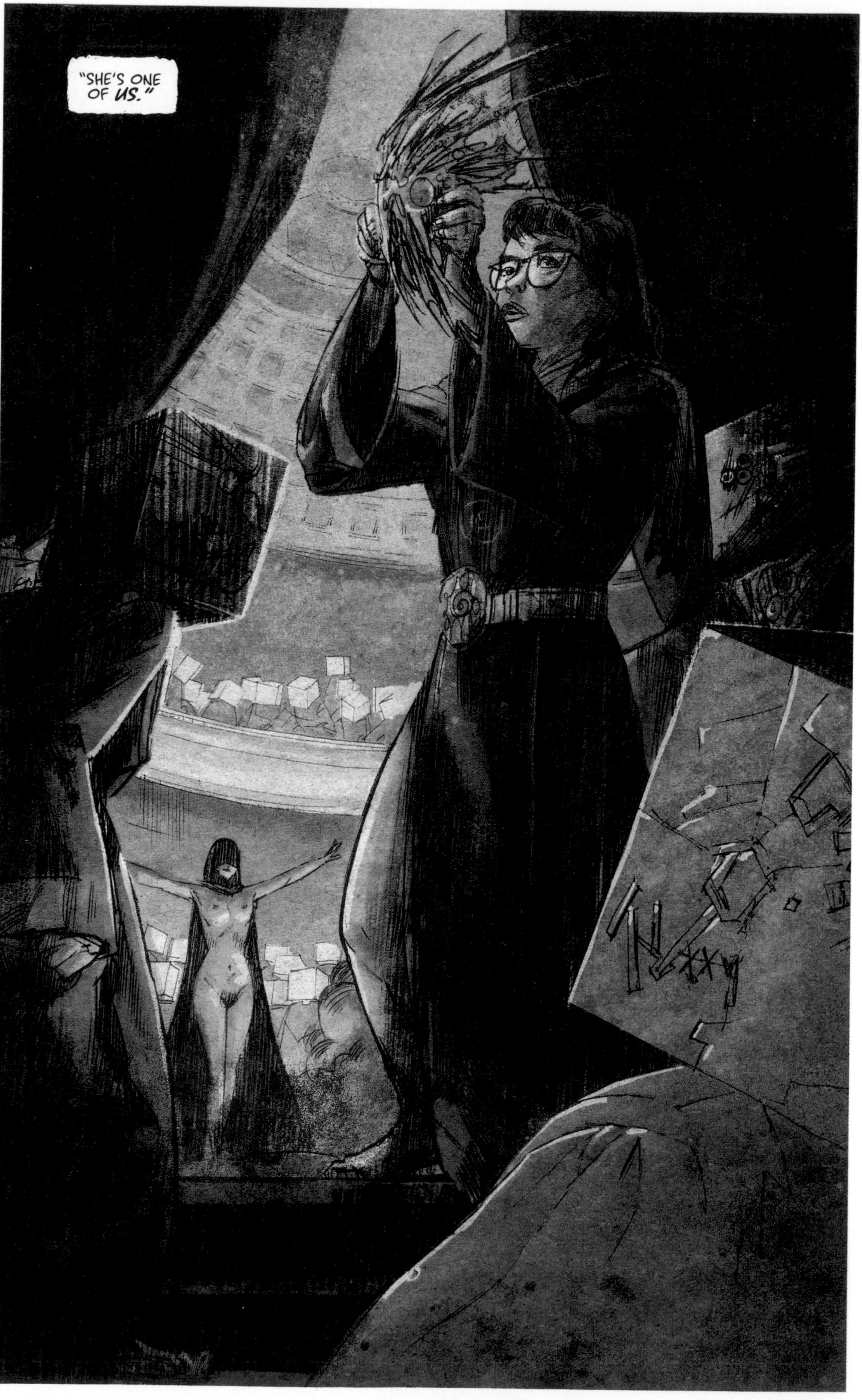
"SHE'S ONE OF *US.*"

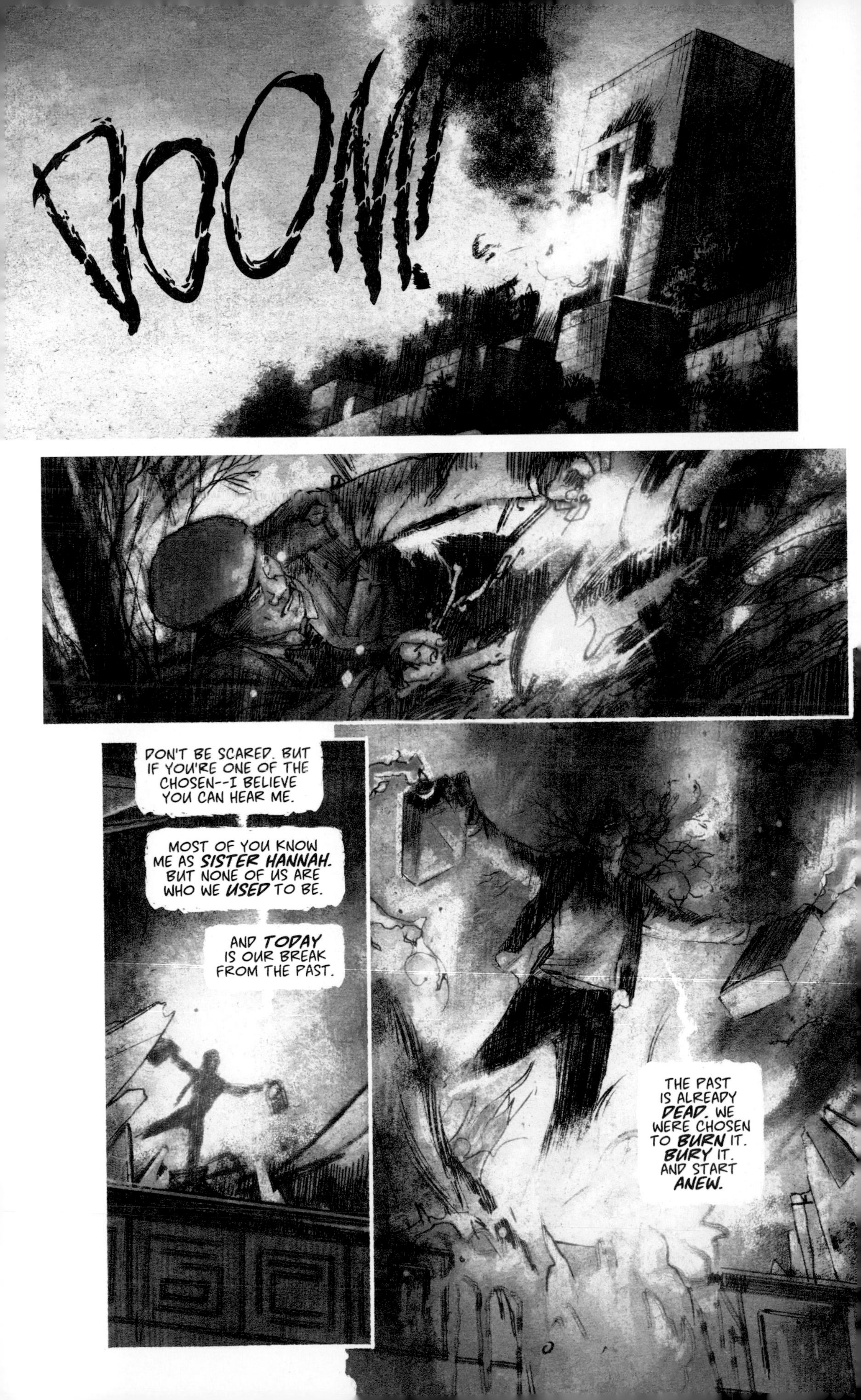
DOOM!
DON'T BE SCARED. BUT IF YOU'RE ONE OF THE CHOSEN--I BELIEVE YOU CAN HEAR ME.
MOST OF YOU KNOW ME AS SISTER HANNAH. BUT NONE OF US ARE WHO WE USED TO BE.
AND TODAY IS OUR BREAK FROM THE PAST.
THE PAST IS ALREADY DEAD. WE WERE CHOSEN TO BURN IT. BURY IT. AND START ANEW.

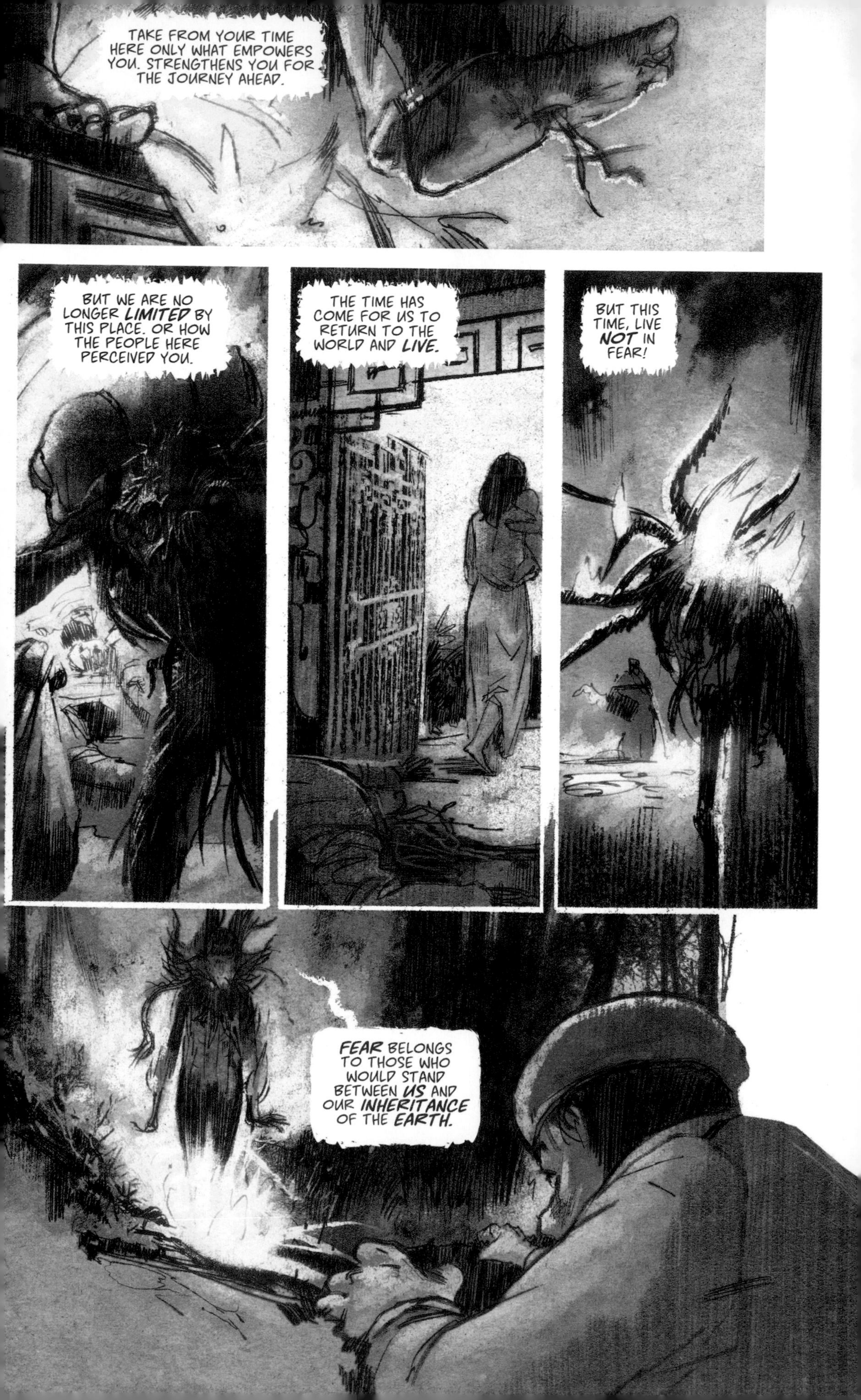
TAKE FROM YOUR TIME HERE ONLY WHAT EMPOWERS YOU. STRENGTHENS YOU FOR THE JOURNEY AHEAD.
BUT WE ARE NO LONGER LIMITED BY THIS PLACE. OR HOW THE PEOPLE HERE PERCEIVED YOU.
THE TIME HAS COME FOR US TO RETURN TO THE WORLD AND LIVE.
BUT THIS TIME, LIVE NOT IN FEAR!
FEAR BELONGS TO THOSE WHO WOULD STAND BETWEEN US AND OUR INHERITANCE OF THE EARTH.

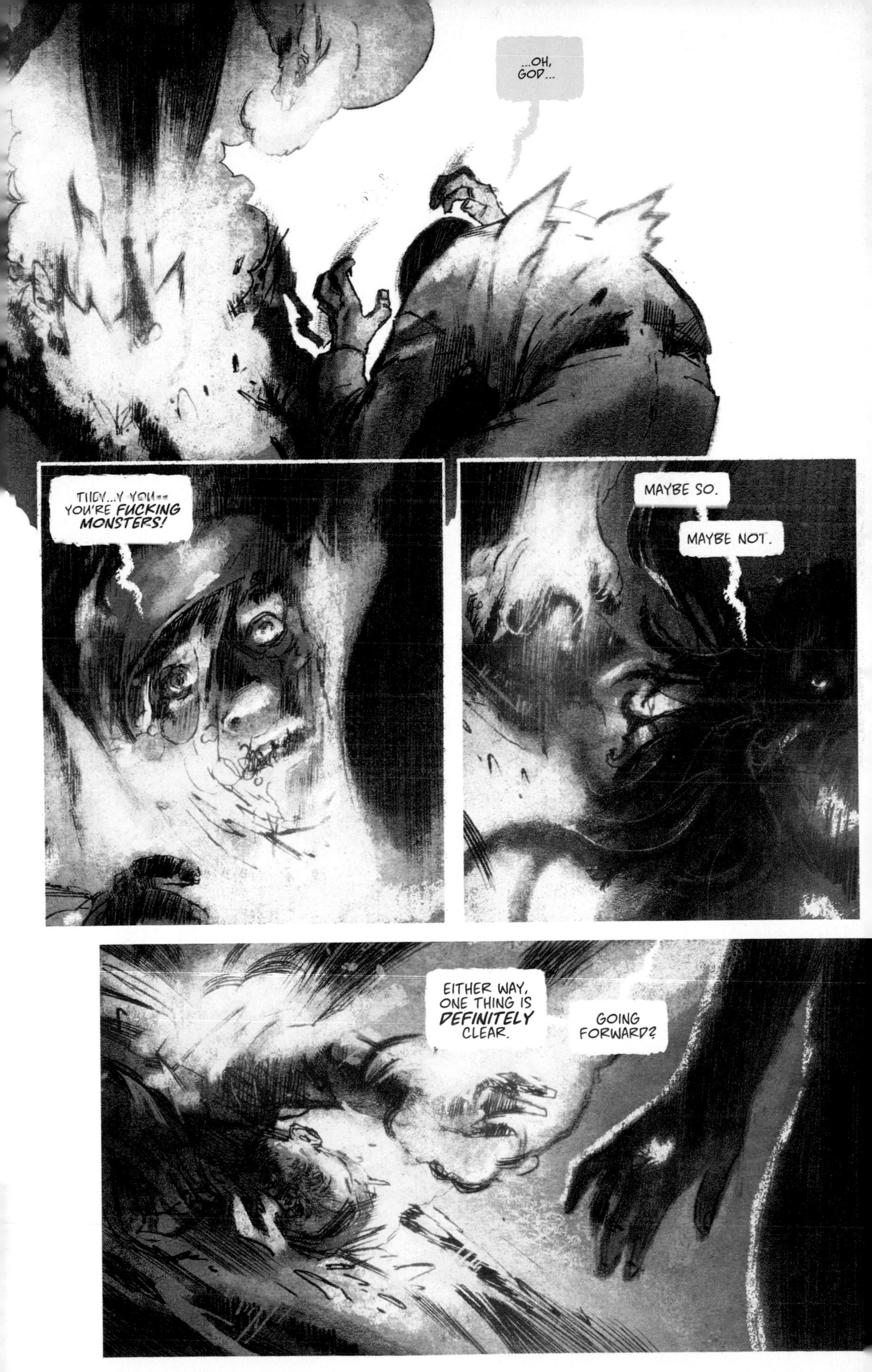
...OH, GOD...
YOU'RE FUCKING MONSTERS!
MAYBE SO.
MAYBE NOT.
EITHER WAY, ONE THING IS DEFINITELY CLEAR.
GOING FORWARD?

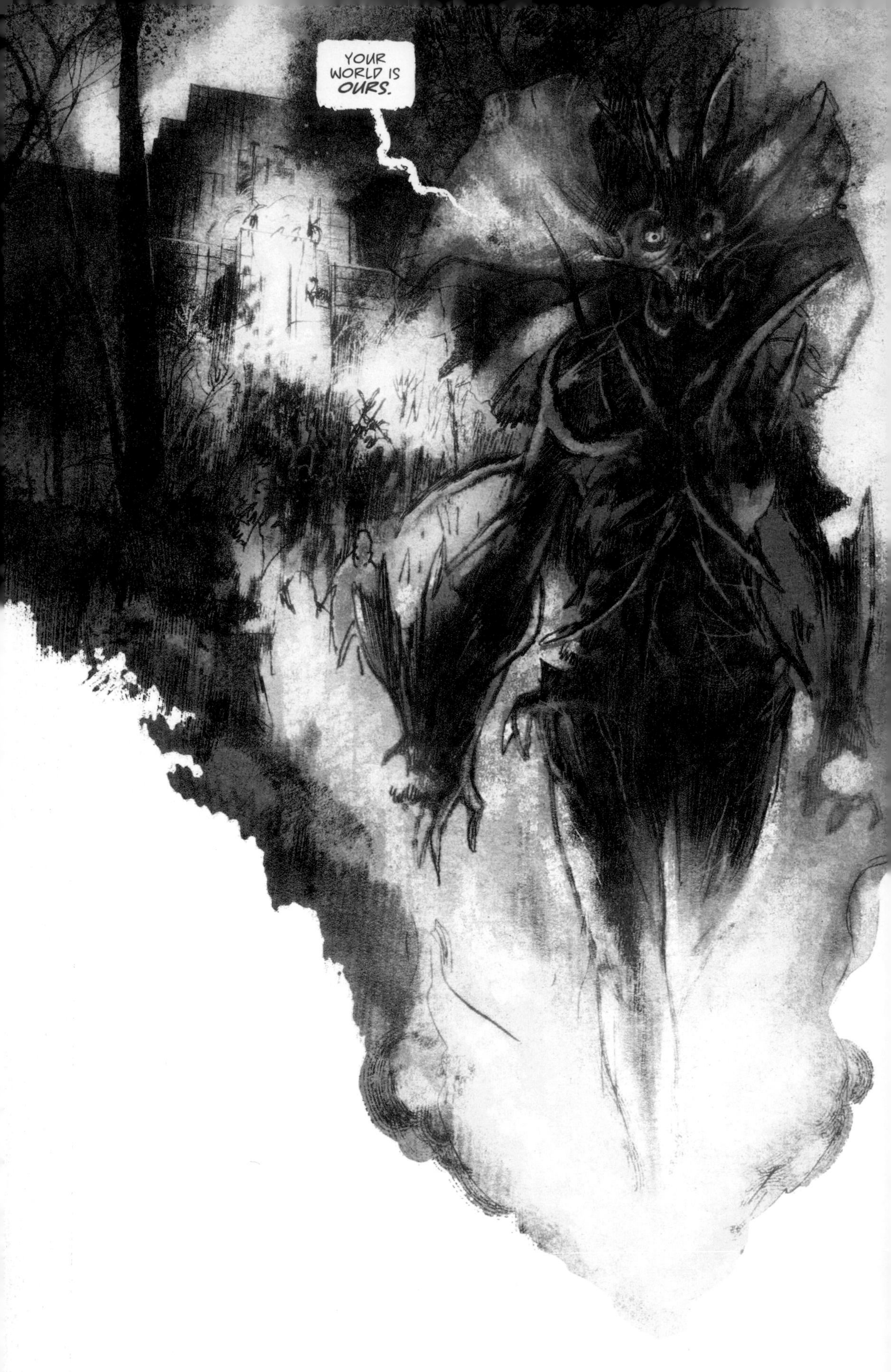
YOUR WORLD IS OURS.

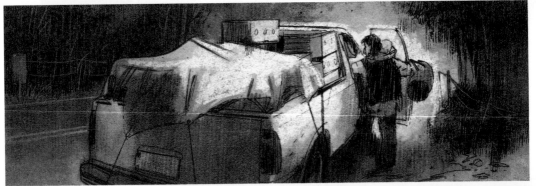

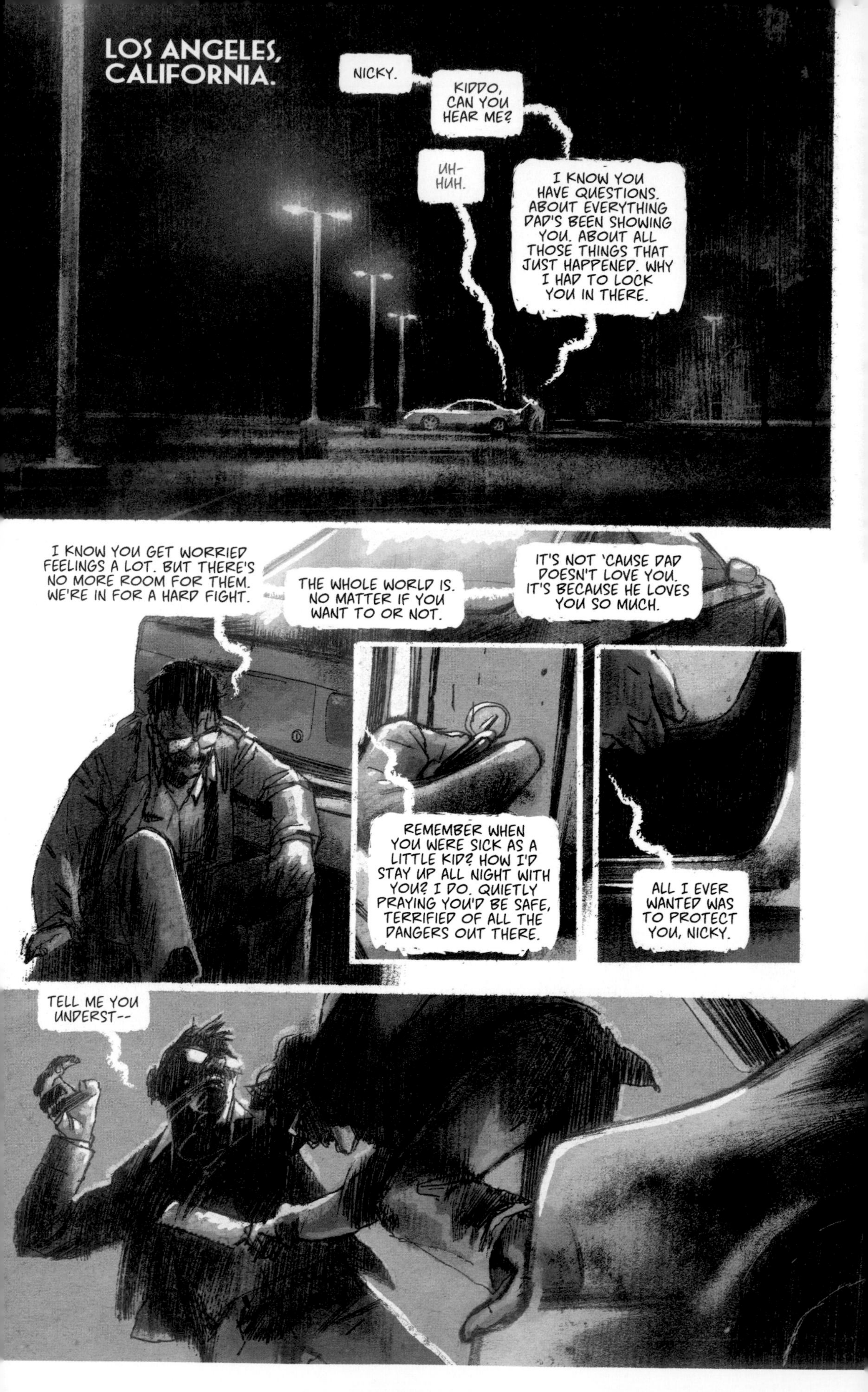
LOS ANGELES, CALIFORNIA.
NICKY.
KIDDO, CAN YOU HEAR ME?
UH-HUH.
I KNOW YOU HAVE QUESTIONS. ABOUT EVERYTHING DAD'S BEEN SHOWING YOU. ABOUT ALL THOSE THINGS THAT JUST HAPPENED. WHY I HAD TO LOCK YOU IN THERE.
I KNOW YOU GET WORRIED FEELINGS A LOT. BUT THERE'S NO MORE ROOM FOR THEM. WE'RE IN FOR A HARD FIGHT.
THE WHOLE WORLD IS. NO MATTER IF YOU WANT TO OR NOT.
IT'S NOT 'CAUSE DAD DOESN'T LOVE YOU. IT'S BECAUSE HE LOVES YOU SO MUCH.
REMEMBER WHEN YOU WERE SICK AS A LITTLE KID? HOW I'D STAY UP ALL NIGHT WITH YOU? I DO. QUIETLY PRAYING YOU'D BE SAFE, TERRIFIED OF ALL THE DANGERS OUT THERE.
ALL I EVER WANTED WAS TO PROTECT YOU, NICKY.
TELL ME YOU UNDERST--

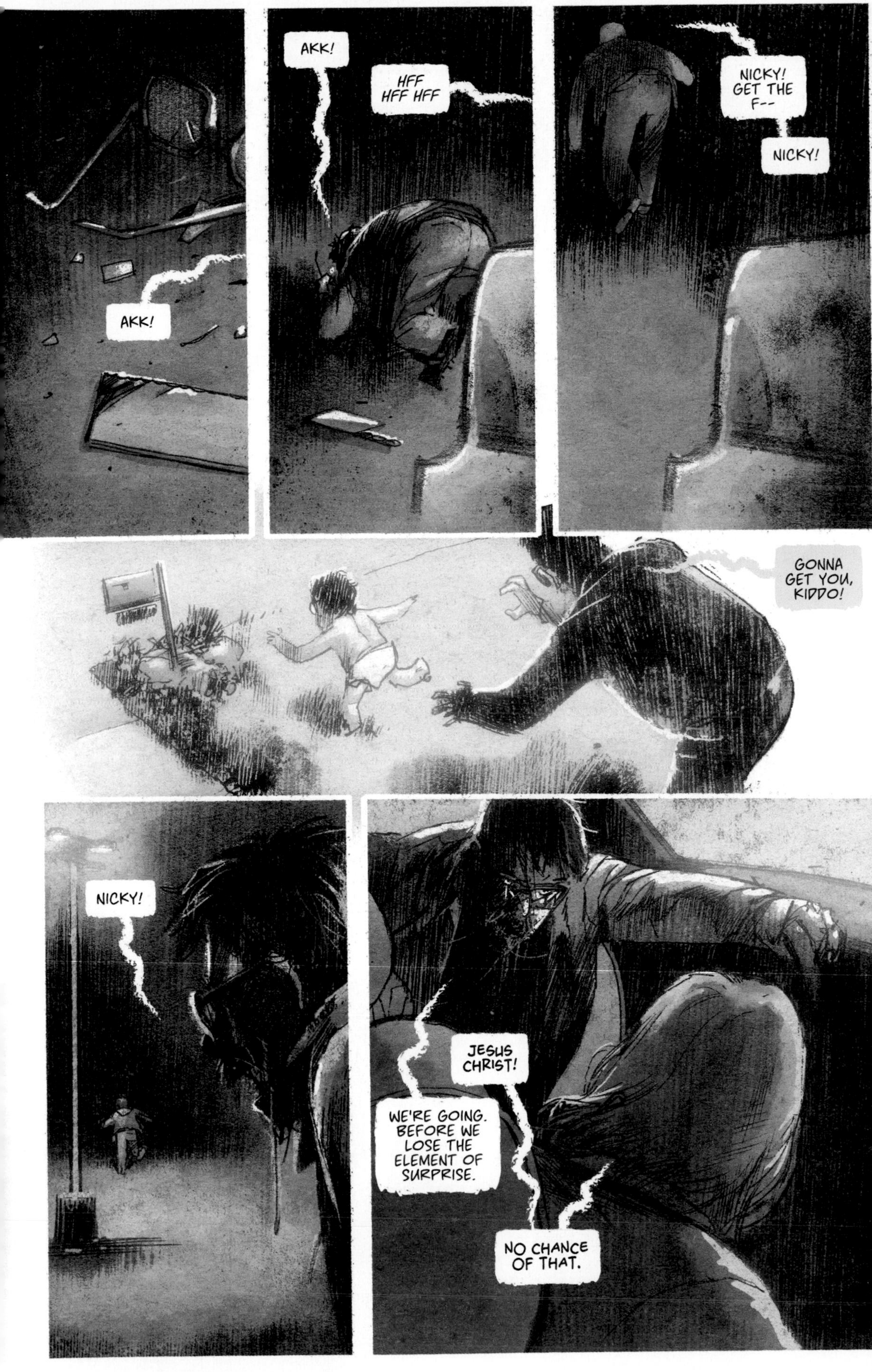
AKK!
AKK!
HFF HFF HFF
NICKY! GET THE F--
NICKY!
GONNA GET YOU, KIDDO!
NICKY!
JESUS CHRIST!
WE'RE GOING. BEFORE WE LOSE THE ELEMENT OF SURPRISE.
NO CHANCE OF THAT.

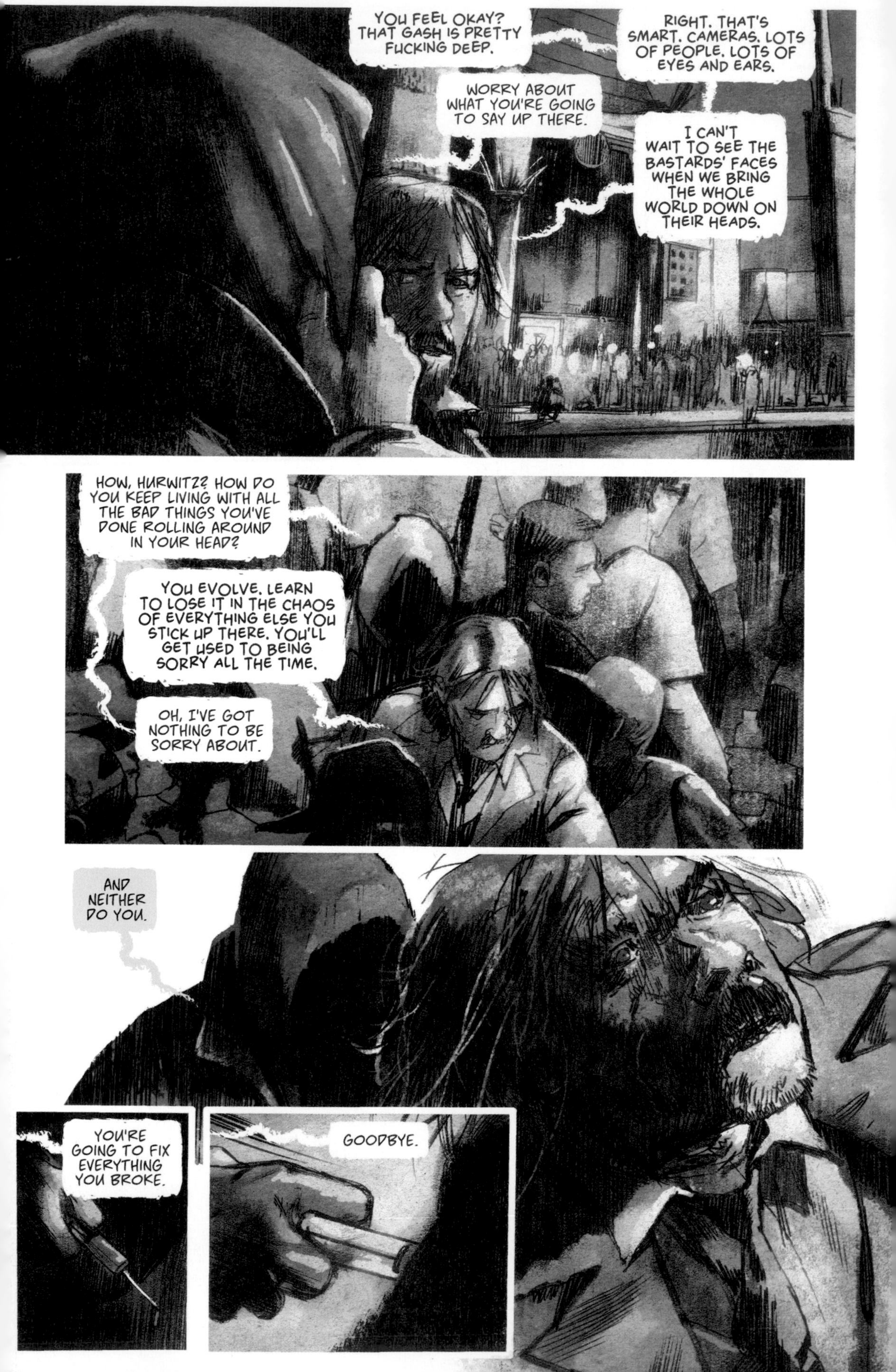
YOU FEEL OKAY? THAT GASH IS PRETTY FUCKING DEEP.
WORRY ABOUT WHAT YOU'RE GOING TO SAY UP THERE.
RIGHT. THAT'S SMART. CAMERAS. LOTS OF PEOPLE. LOTS OF EYES AND EARS.
I CAN'T WAIT TO SEE THE BASTARDS' FACES WHEN WE BRING THE WHOLE WORLD DOWN ON THEIR HEADS.
HOW, HURWITZ? HOW DO YOU KEEP LIVING WITH ALL THE BAD THINGS YOU'VE DONE ROLLING AROUND IN YOUR HEAD?
YOU EVOLVE. LEARN TO LOSE IT IN THE CHAOS OF EVERYTHING ELSE YOU STICK UP THERE. YOU'LL GET USED TO BEING SORRY ALL THE TIME.
OH, I'VE GOT NOTHING TO BE SORRY ABOUT.
AND NEITHER DO YOU.
YOU'RE GOING TO FIX EVERYTHING YOU BROKE.
GOODBYE.

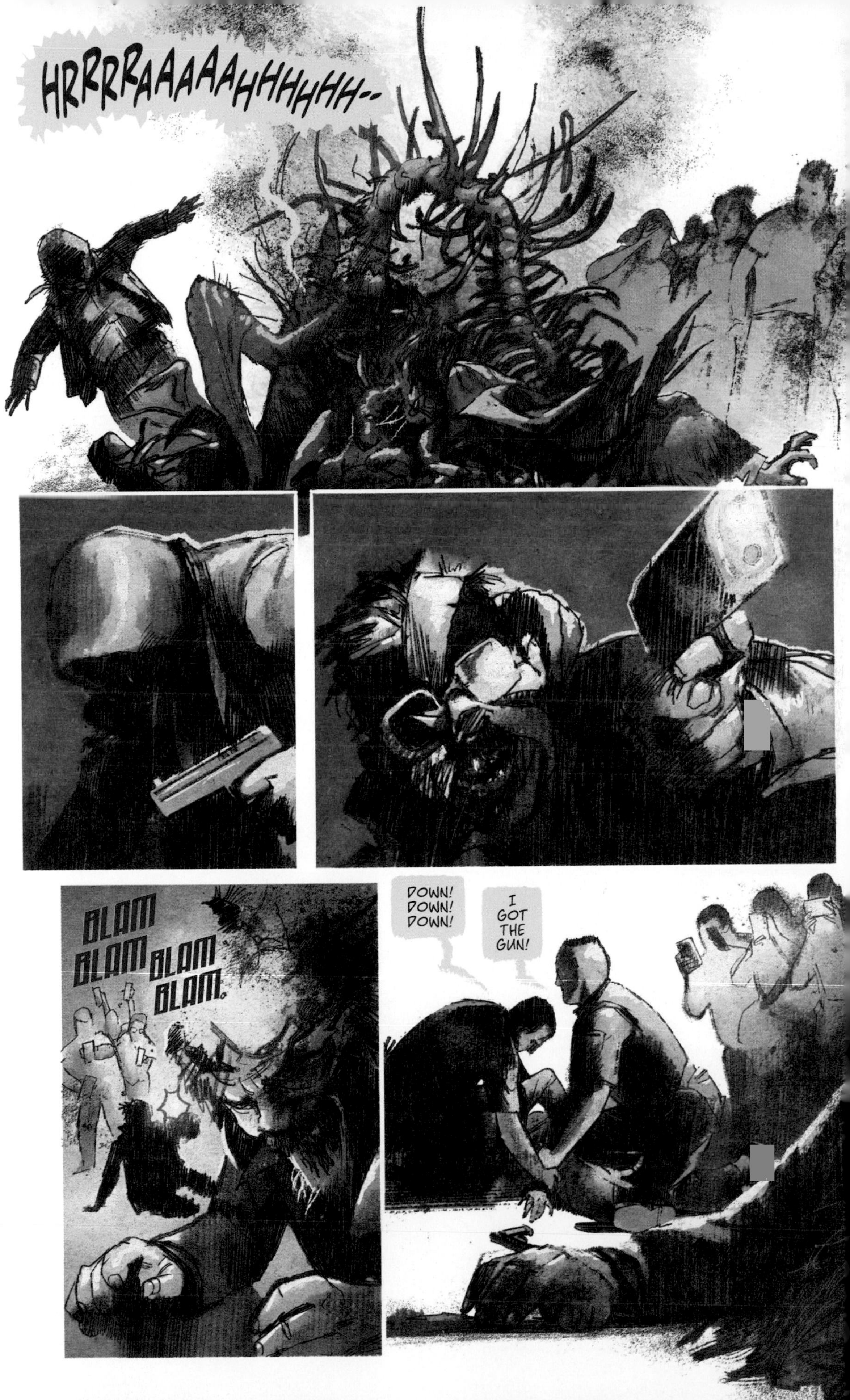
HRRRRAAAAAHHHHH--
BLAM BLAM BLAM BLAM.
DOWN! DOWN! DOWN!
I GOT THE GUN!

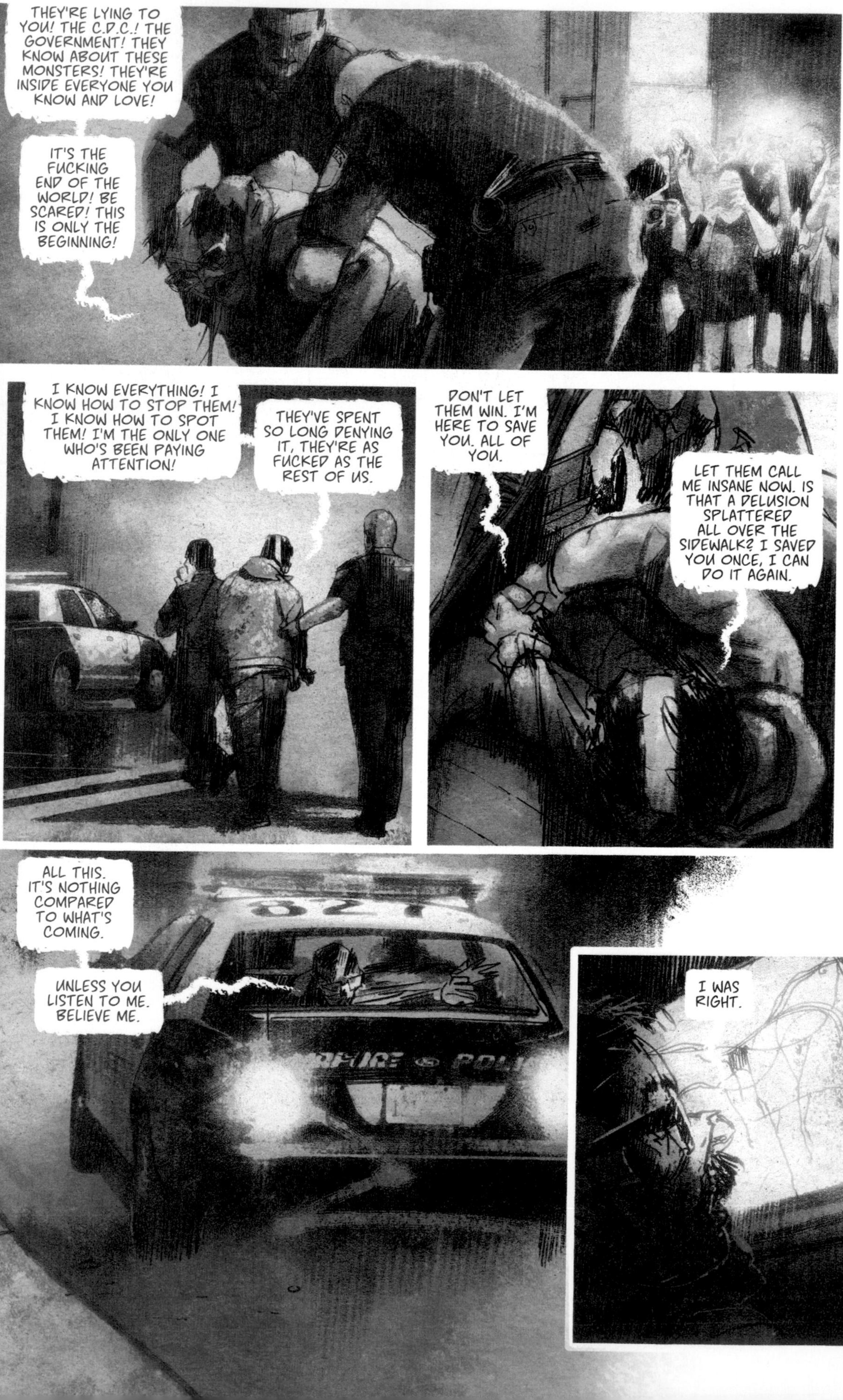
THEY'RE LYING TO YOU! THE C.D.C.! THE GOVERNMENT! THEY KNOW ABOUT THESE MONSTERS! THEY'RE INSIDE EVERYONE YOU KNOW AND LOVE!
IT'S THE FUCKING END OF THE WORLD! BE SCARED! THIS IS ONLY THE BEGINNING!
I KNOW EVERYTHING! I KNOW HOW TO STOP THEM! I KNOW HOW TO SPOT THEM! I'M THE ONLY ONE WHO'S BEEN PAYING ATTENTION!
THEY'VE SPENT SO LONG DENYING IT, THEY'RE AS FUCKED AS THE REST OF US.
DON'T LET THEM WIN. I'M HERE TO SAVE YOU. ALL OF YOU.
LET THEM CALL ME INSANE NOW. IS THAT A DELUSION SPLATTERED ALL OVER THE SIDEWALK? I SAVED YOU ONCE, I CAN DO IT AGAIN.
ALL THIS. IT'S NOTHING COMPARED TO WHAT'S COMING.
UNLESS YOU LISTEN TO ME. BELIEVE ME.
I WAS RIGHT.

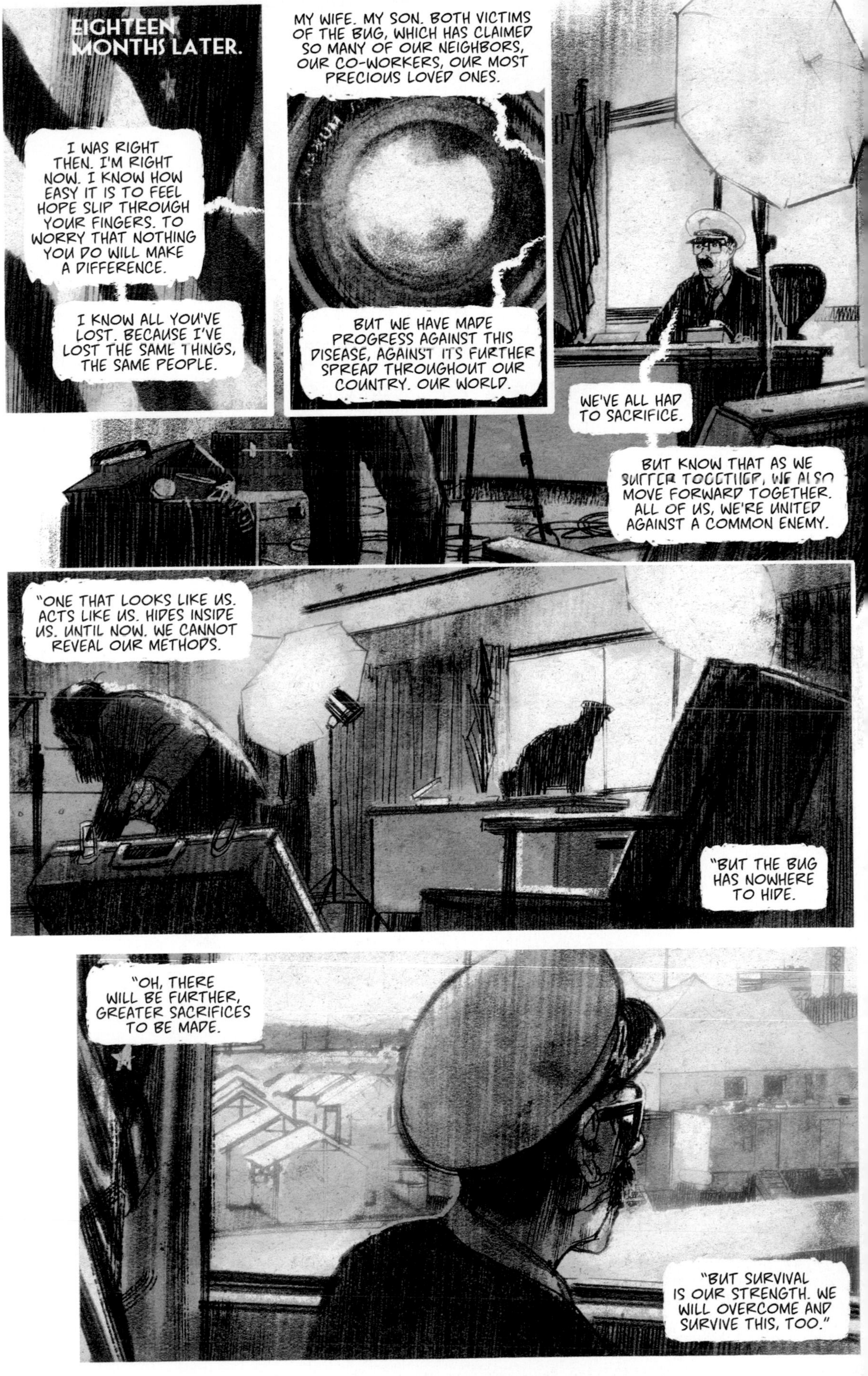
EIGHTEEN MONTHS LATER.
I WAS RIGHT THEN. I'M RIGHT NOW. I KNOW HOW EASY IT IS TO FEEL HOPE SLIP THROUGH YOUR FINGERS. TO WORRY THAT NOTHING YOU DO WILL MAKE A DIFFERENCE.
I KNOW ALL YOU'VE LOST. BECAUSE I'VE LOST THE SAME THINGS, THE SAME PEOPLE.
MY WIFE. MY SON. BOTH VICTIMS OF THE BUG, WHICH HAS CLAIMED SO MANY OF OUR NEIGHBORS, OUR CO-WORKERS, OUR MOST PRECIOUS LOVED ONES.
BUT WE HAVE MADE PROGRESS AGAINST THIS DISEASE, AGAINST ITS FURTHER SPREAD THROUGHOUT OUR COUNTRY. OUR WORLD.
WE'VE ALL HAD TO SACRIFICE.
BUT KNOW THAT AS WE SUFFER TOGETHER, WE ALSO MOVE FORWARD TOGETHER. ALL OF US, WE'RE UNITED AGAINST A COMMON ENEMY.
"ONE THAT LOOKS LIKE US. ACTS LIKE US. HIDES INSIDE US. UNTIL NOW. WE CANNOT REVEAL OUR METHODS.
"BUT THE BUG HAS NOWHERE TO HIDE.
"OH, THERE WILL BE FURTHER, GREATER SACRIFICES TO BE MADE.
"BUT SURVIVAL IS OUR STRENGTH. WE WILL OVERCOME AND SURVIVE THIS, TOO."

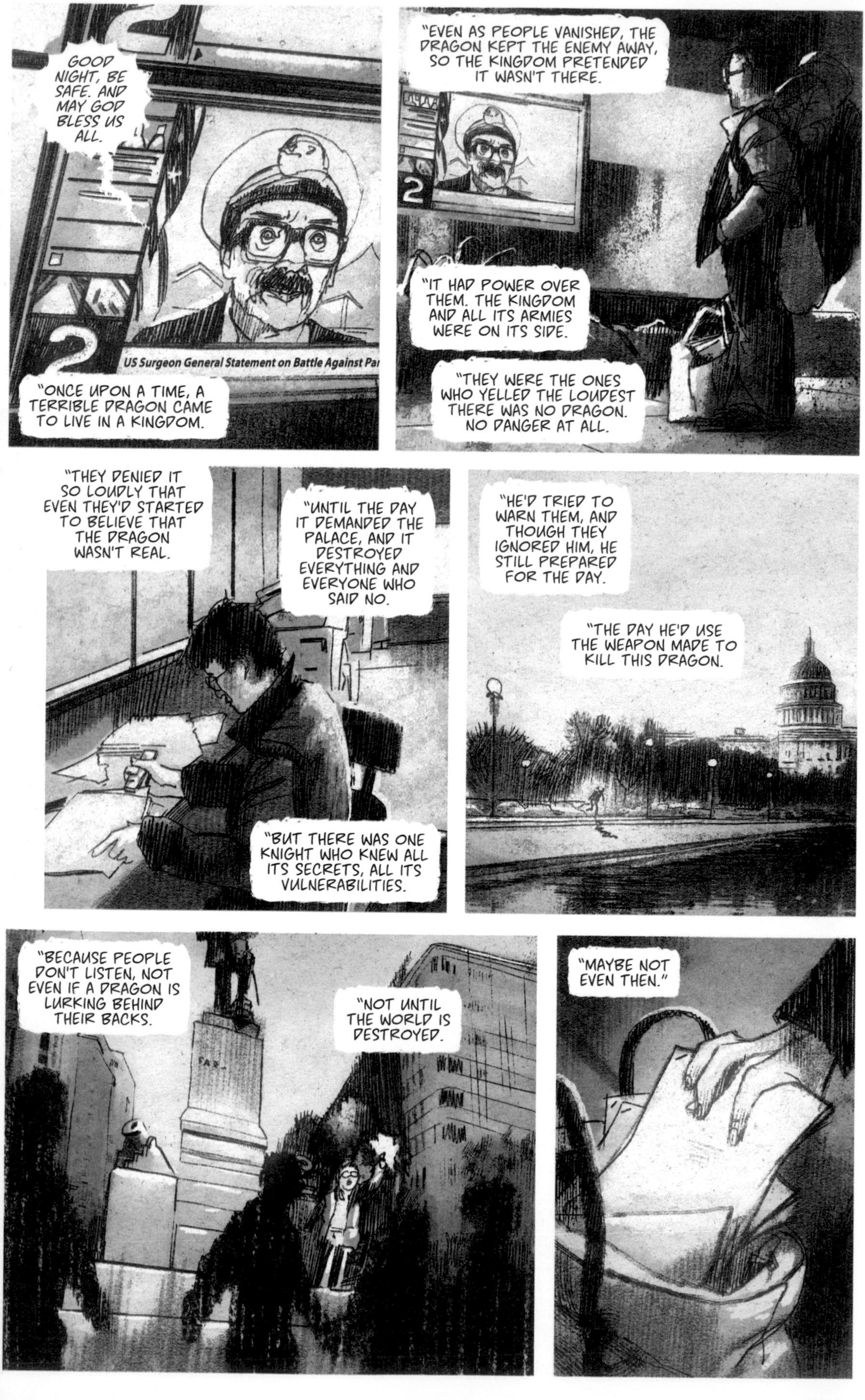
GOOD NIGHT, BE SAFE. AND MAY GOD BLESS US ALL.
US Surgeon General Statement on Battle Against Par
"ONCE UPON A TIME, A TERRIBLE DRAGON CAME TO LIVE IN A KINGDOM.
"EVEN AS PEOPLE VANISHED, THE DRAGON KEPT THE ENEMY AWAY, SO THE KINGDOM PRETENDED IT WASN'T THERE.
"IT HAD POWER OVER THEM. THE KINGDOM AND ALL ITS ARMIES WERE ON ITS SIDE.
"THEY WERE THE ONES WHO YELLED THE LOUDEST THERE WAS NO DRAGON. NO DANGER AT ALL.
"THEY DENIED IT SO LOUDLY THAT EVEN THEY'D STARTED TO BELIEVE THAT THE DRAGON WASN'T REAL.
"UNTIL THE DAY IT DEMANDED THE PALACE, AND IT DESTROYED EVERYTHING AND EVERYONE WHO SAID NO.
"BUT THERE WAS ONE KNIGHT WHO KNEW ALL ITS SECRETS, ALL ITS VULNERABILITIES.
"HE'D TRIED TO WARN THEM, AND THOUGH THEY IGNORED HIM, HE STILL PREPARED FOR THE DAY.
"THE DAY HE'D USE THE WEAPON MADE TO KILL THIS DRAGON.
"BECAUSE PEOPLE DON'T LISTEN, NOT EVEN IF A DRAGON IS LURKING BEHIND THEIR BACKS.
"NOT UNTIL THE WORLD IS DESTROYED.
"MAYBE NOT EVEN THEN."

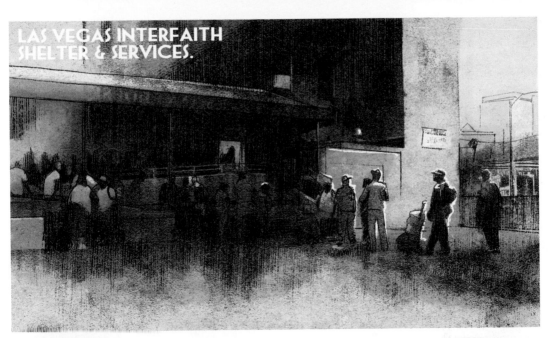

LAS VEGAS INTERFAITH SHELTER & SERVICES.

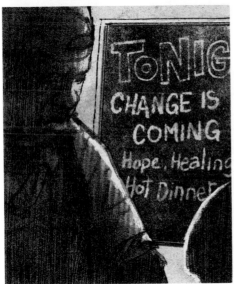

TONIG...
CHANGE IS COMING
Hope, Healing
Hot Dinner

ALRIGHT. WELCOME!

I REALLY AM PLEASED TO SEE SUCH A GOOD TURNOUT FOR SUCH A SPECIAL *GUEST*.

SISTER HANNAH HAS BEEN TRAVELING *ALL* AROUND THE COUNTRY THESE LAST FEW MONTHS TO PLACES LIKE OURS, AND FROM WHAT I'M HEARING, SHE'S BEEN TRANSFORMING A LOT OF LIVES.

WELL, THAT'S VERY KIND OF YOU TO SAY, BUT ONE THING I KNOW TO BE TRUE IS--

REAL TRANSFORMATION STARTS *INSIDE YOU.*

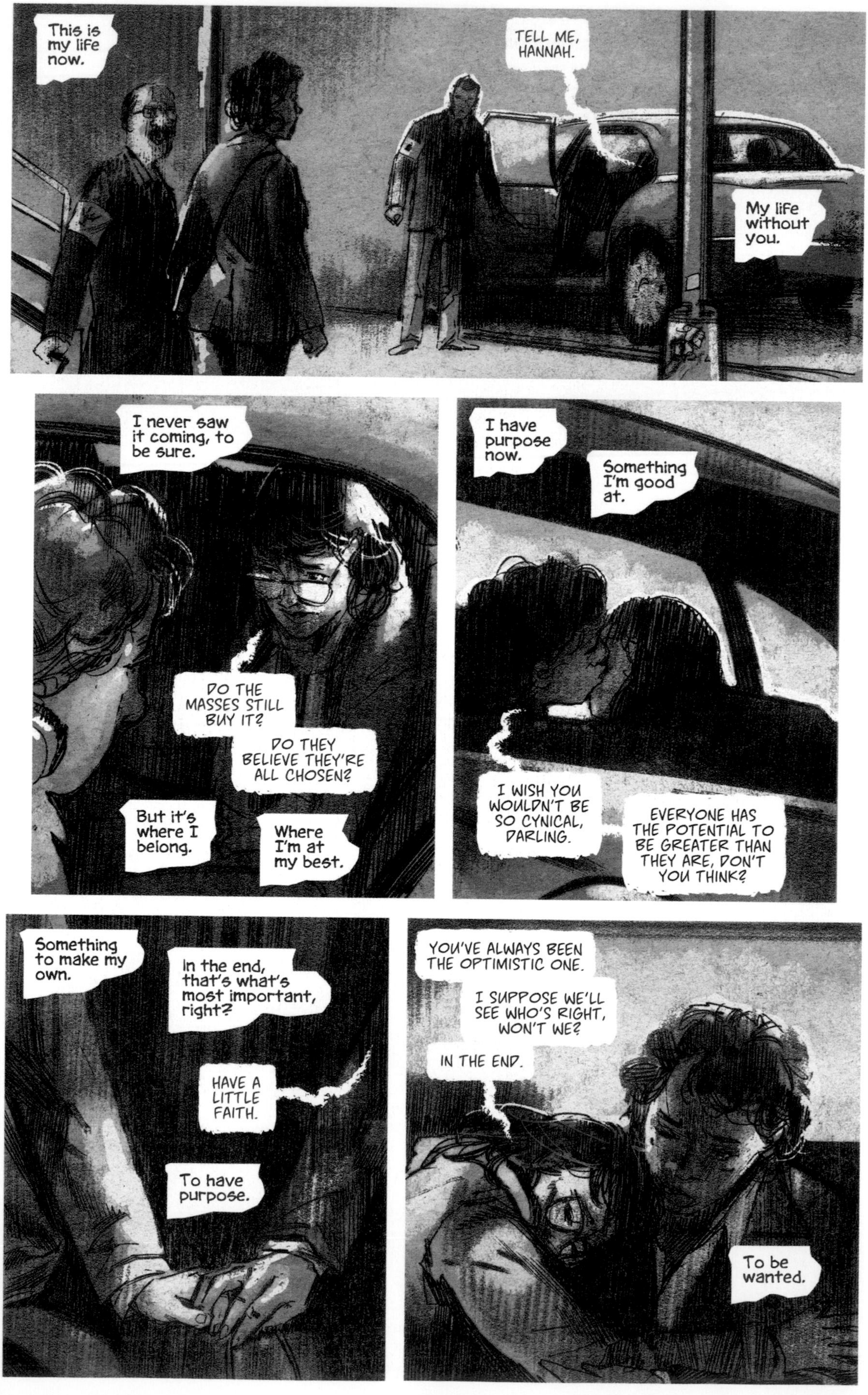
This is my life now.
TELL ME, HANNAH.
My life without you.
I never saw it coming, to be sure.
DO THE MASSES STILL BUY IT?
DO THEY BELIEVE THEY'RE ALL CHOSEN?
But it's where I belong.
Where I'm at my best.
I have purpose now.
Something I'm good at.
I WISH YOU WOULDN'T BE SO CYNICAL, DARLING.
EVERYONE HAS THE POTENTIAL TO BE GREATER THAN THEY ARE, DON'T YOU THINK?
Something to make my own.
In the end, that's what's most important, right?
HAVE A LITTLE FAITH.
To have purpose.
YOU'VE ALWAYS BEEN THE OPTIMISTIC ONE.
I SUPPOSE WE'LL SEE WHO'S RIGHT, WON'T WE?
IN THE END.
To be wanted.

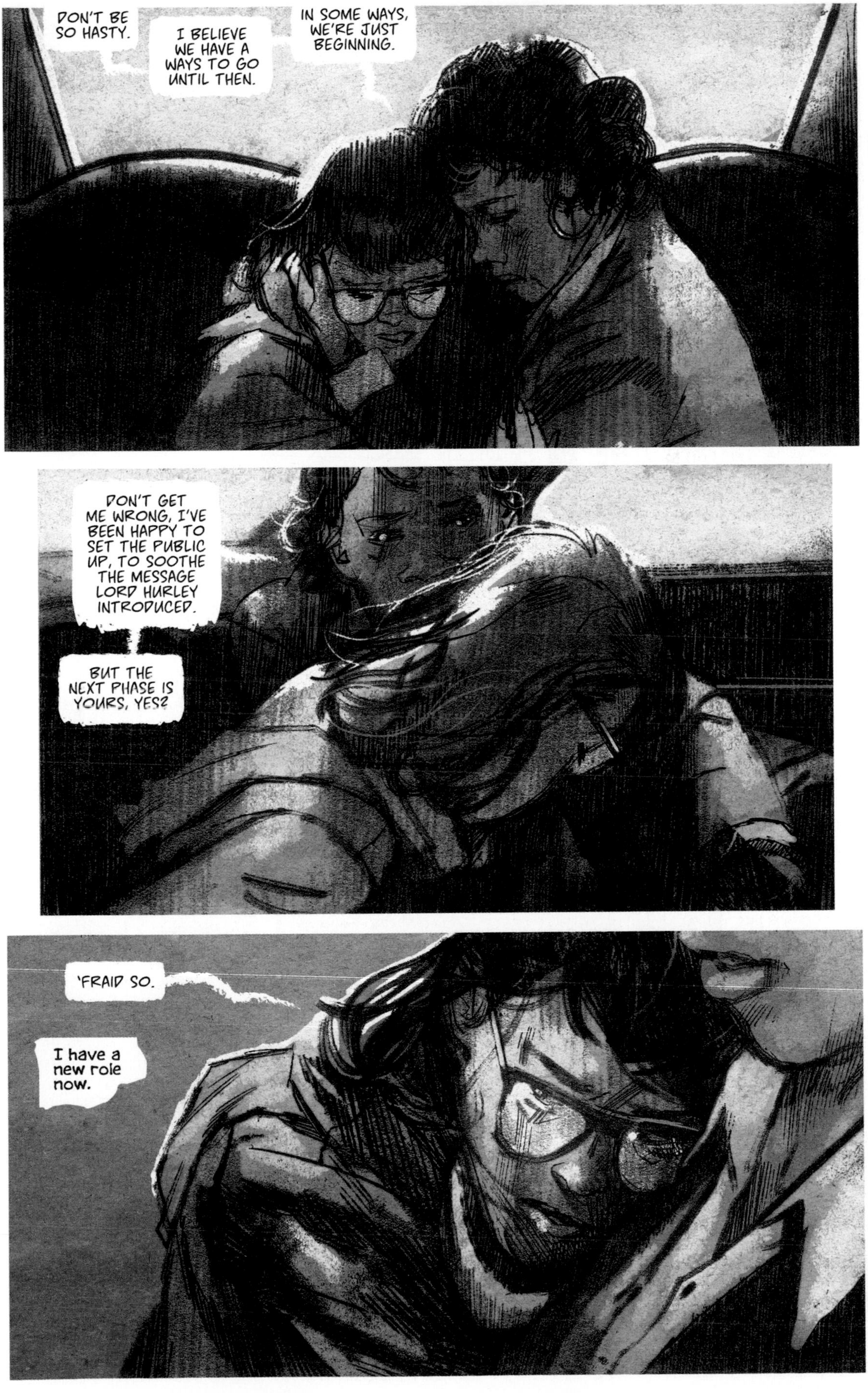
DON'T BE SO HASTY.
I BELIEVE WE HAVE A WAYS TO GO UNTIL THEN.
IN SOME WAYS, WE'RE JUST BEGINNING.
DON'T GET ME WRONG, I'VE BEEN HAPPY TO SET THE PUBLIC UP, TO SOOTHE THE MESSAGE LORD HURLEY INTRODUCED.
BUT THE NEXT PHASE IS YOURS, YES?
'FRAID SO.
I have a new role now.

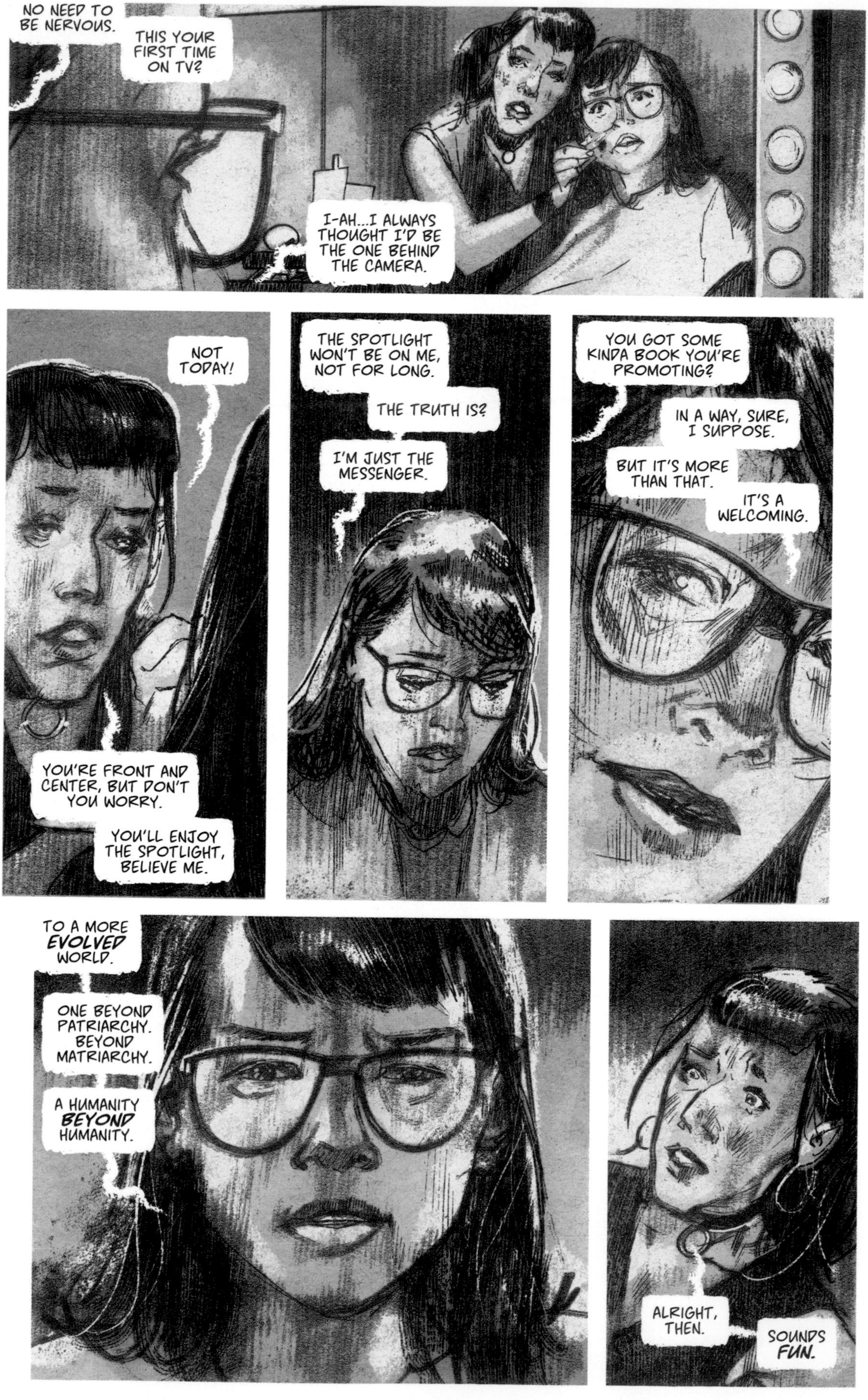
NO NEED TO BE NERVOUS.
THIS YOUR FIRST TIME ON TV?
I-AH...I ALWAYS THOUGHT I'D BE THE ONE BEHIND THE CAMERA.
NOT TODAY!
YOU'RE FRONT AND CENTER, BUT DON'T YOU WORRY.
YOU'LL ENJOY THE SPOTLIGHT, BELIEVE ME.
THE SPOTLIGHT WON'T BE ON ME, NOT FOR LONG.
THE TRUTH IS?
I'M JUST THE MESSENGER.
YOU GOT SOME KINDA BOOK YOU'RE PROMOTING?
IN A WAY, SURE, I SUPPOSE.
BUT IT'S MORE THAN THAT.
IT'S A WELCOMING.
TO A MORE EVOLVED WORLD.
ONE BEYOND PATRIARCHY. BEYOND MATRIARCHY.
A HUMANITY BEYOND HUMANITY.
ALRIGHT, THEN.
SOUNDS FUN.

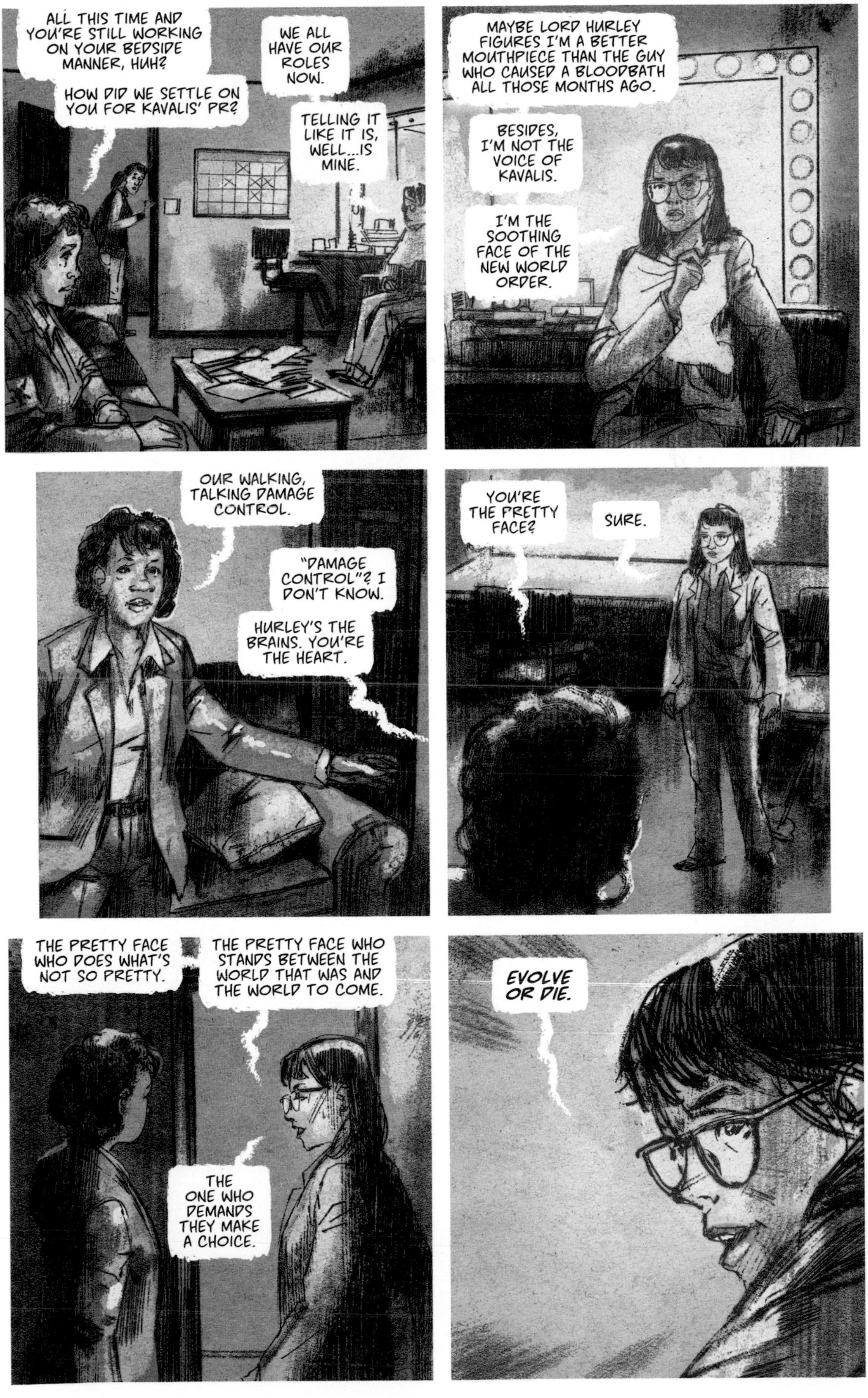
ALL THIS TIME AND YOU'RE STILL WORKING ON YOUR BEDSIDE MANNER, HUH?
HOW DID WE SETTLE ON YOU FOR KAVALIS' PR?
WE ALL HAVE OUR ROLES NOW.
TELLING IT LIKE IT IS, WELL...IS MINE.
MAYBE LORD HURLEY FIGURES I'M A BETTER MOUTHPIECE THAN THE GUY WHO CAUSED A BLOODBATH ALL THOSE MONTHS AGO.
BESIDES, I'M NOT THE VOICE OF KAVALIS.
I'M THE SOOTHING FACE OF THE NEW WORLD ORDER.
OUR WALKING, TALKING DAMAGE CONTROL.
"DAMAGE CONTROL"? I DON'T KNOW.
HURLEY'S THE BRAINS. YOU'RE THE HEART.
YOU'RE THE PRETTY FACE?
SURE.
THE PRETTY FACE WHO DOES WHAT'S NOT SO PRETTY.
THE PRETTY FACE WHO STANDS BETWEEN THE WORLD THAT WAS AND THE WORLD TO COME.
THE ONE WHO DEMANDS THEY MAKE A CHOICE.
EVOLVE OR DIE.

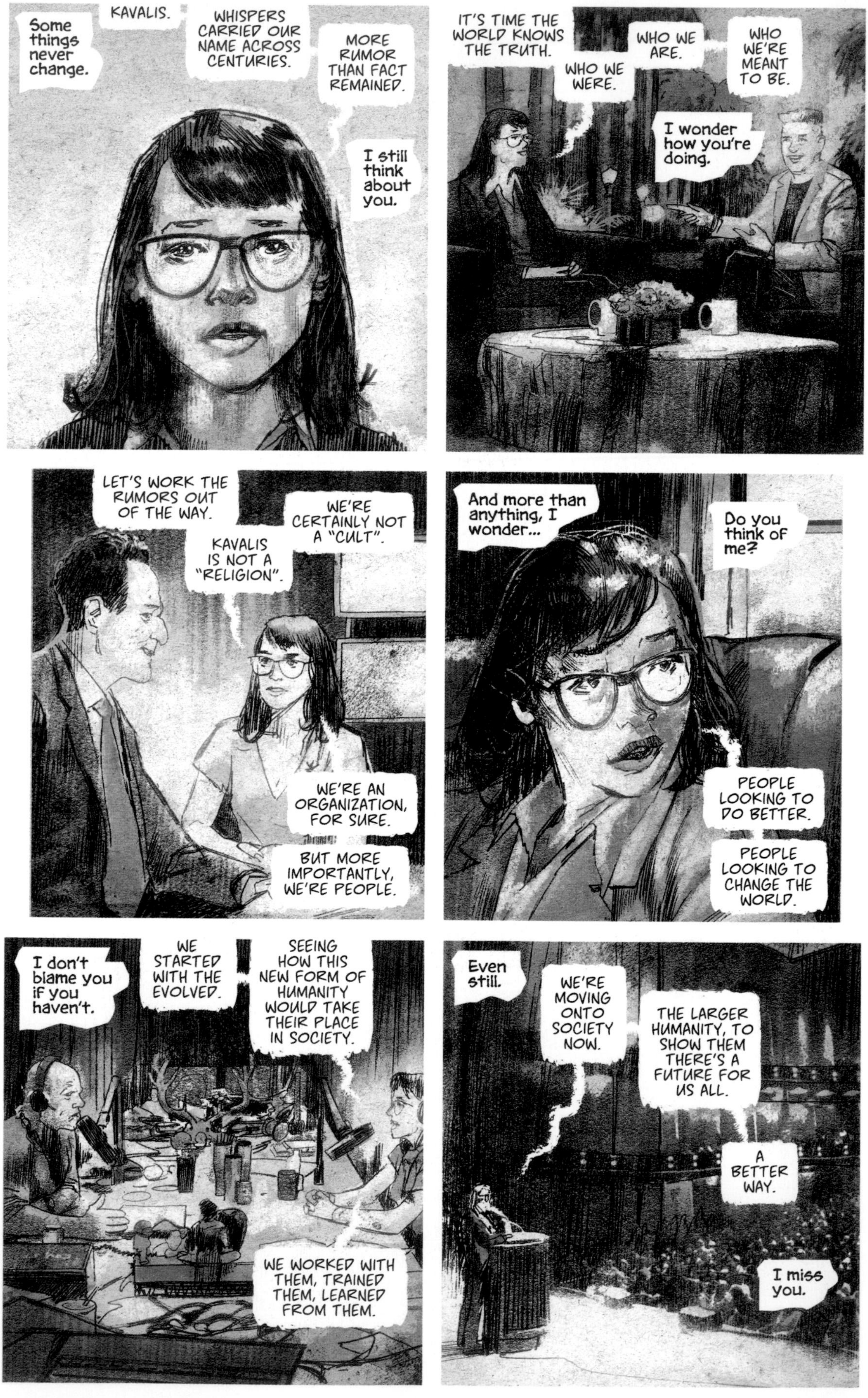
Some things never change.
KAVALIS.
WHISPERS CARRIED OUR NAME ACROSS CENTURIES.
MORE RUMOR THAN FACT REMAINED.
I still think about you.
IT'S TIME THE WORLD KNOWS THE TRUTH.
WHO WE WERE.
WHO WE ARE.
WHO WE'RE MEANT TO BE.
I wonder how you're doing.
LET'S WORK THE RUMORS OUT OF THE WAY.
KAVALIS IS NOT A "RELIGION".
WE'RE CERTAINLY NOT A "CULT".
WE'RE AN ORGANIZATION, FOR SURE.
BUT MORE IMPORTANTLY, WE'RE PEOPLE.
And more than anything, I wonder...
Do you think of me?
PEOPLE LOOKING TO DO BETTER.
PEOPLE LOOKING TO CHANGE THE WORLD.
I don't blame you if you haven't.
WE STARTED WITH THE EVOLVED.
SEEING HOW THIS NEW FORM OF HUMANITY WOULD TAKE THEIR PLACE IN SOCIETY.
WE WORKED WITH THEM, TRAINED THEM, LEARNED FROM THEM.
Even still.
WE'RE MOVING ONTO SOCIETY NOW.
THE LARGER HUMANITY, TO SHOW THEM THERE'S A FUTURE FOR US ALL.
A BETTER WAY.
I miss you.

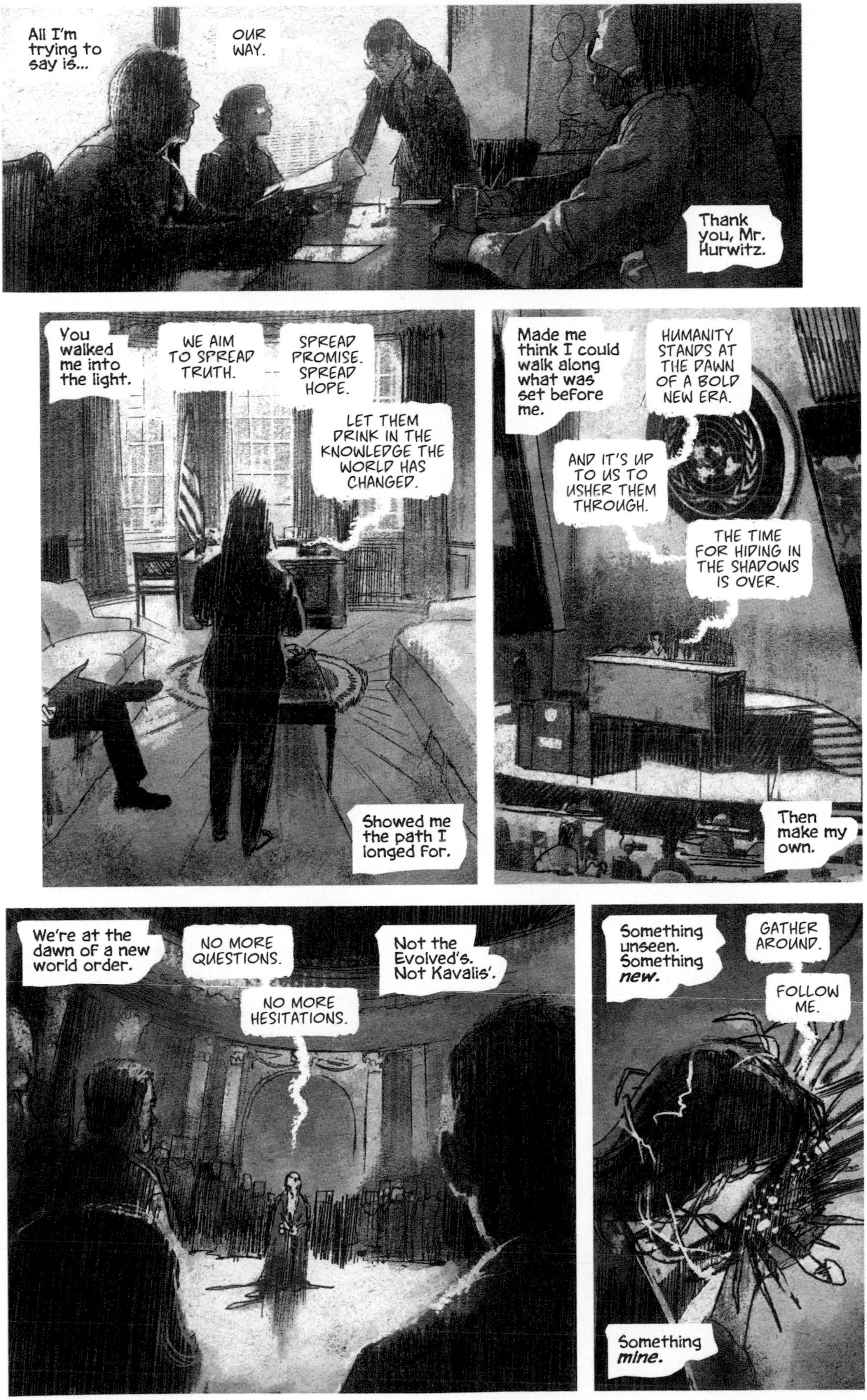
All I'm trying to say is...
OUR WAY.
Thank you, Mr. Hurwitz.
You walked me into the light.
WE AIM TO SPREAD TRUTH.
SPREAD PROMISE. SPREAD HOPE.
LET THEM DRINK IN THE KNOWLEDGE THE WORLD HAS CHANGED.
Showed me the path I longed for.
Made me think I could walk along what was set before me.
HUMANITY STANDS AT THE DAWN OF A BOLD NEW ERA.
AND IT'S UP TO US TO USHER THEM THROUGH.
THE TIME FOR HIDING IN THE SHADOWS IS OVER.
Then make my own.
We're at the dawn of a new world order.
NO MORE QUESTIONS.
NO MORE HESITATIONS.
Not the Evolved's. Not Kavalis'.
Something unseen. Something *new.*
GATHER AROUND.
FOLLOW ME.
Something *mine.*

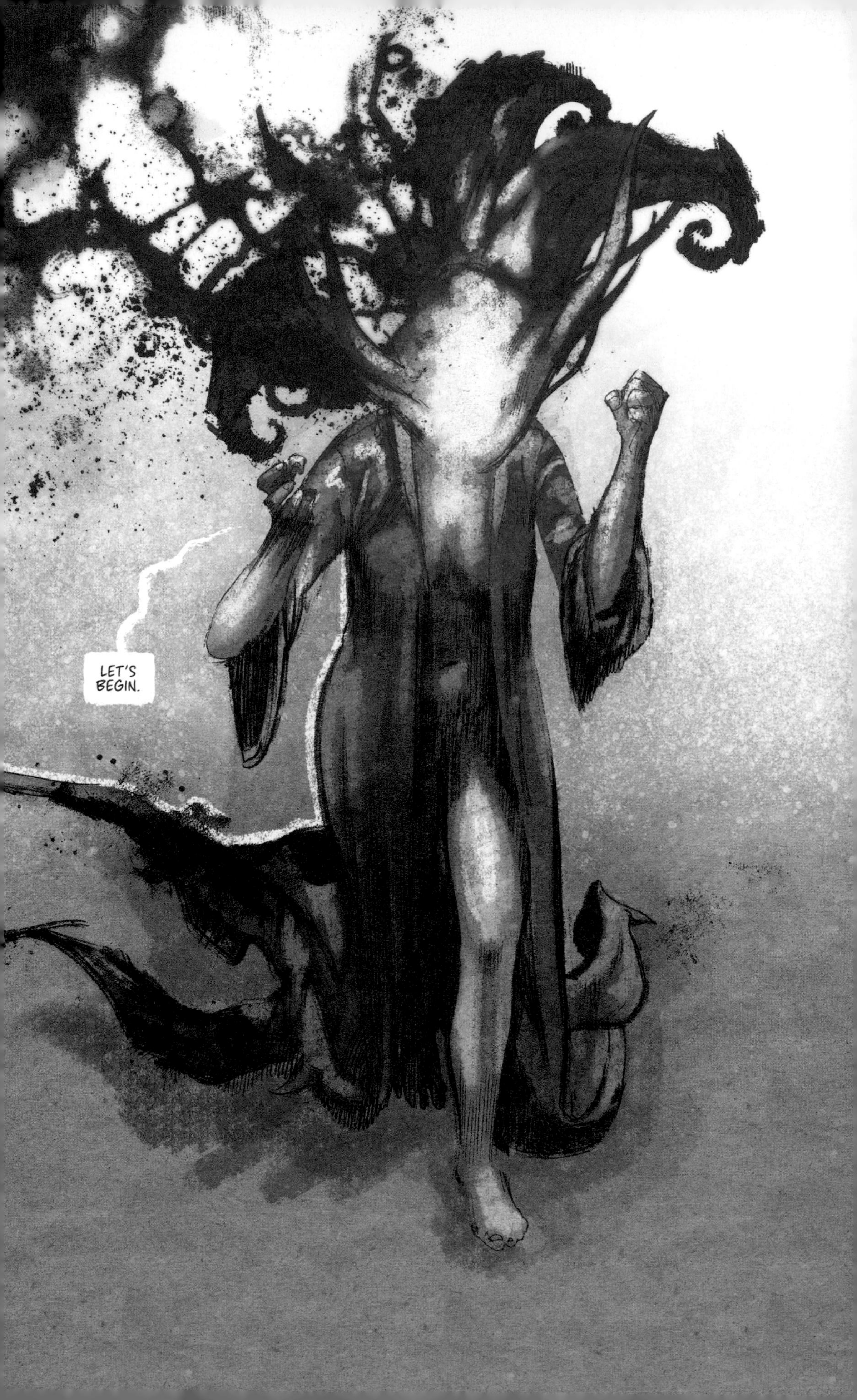
LET'S BEGIN.

The End

"Going forward?

Your world is ours."

For more tales from ROBERT KIRKMAN and SKYBOUND

OUTER DARKNESS
JOHN LAYMAN
AFU CHAN
EACH OTHER'S THROATS

VOL. 1: EACH OTHER'S THROATS TP
ISBN: 978-1-5343-1210-4
$16.99

REDNECK
Donny CATES Lisandro ESTHERREN Dee CUNNIFFE
VOLUME THREE
Longhorns

VOL. 1: DEEP IN THE HEART TP
ISBN: 978-1-5343-0331-7
$16.99

VOL. 2: THE EYES UPON YOU TP
ISBN: 978-1-5343-0665-3
$16.99

VOL. 3: LONGHORNS TP
ISBN: 978-1-5343-1050-6
$16.99

BIRTHRIGHT
WILLIAMSON BRESSAN LUCAS
BLOOD BROTHERS

VOL. 1: HOMECOMING TP
ISBN: 978-1-63215-231-2
$9.99

VOL. 2: CALL TO ADVENTURE TP
ISBN: 978-1-63215-446-0
$12.99

VOL. 3: ALLIES AND ENEMIES TP
ISBN: 978-1-63215-683-9
$12.99

VOL. 4: FAMILY HISTORY TP
ISBN: 978-1-63215-871-0
$12.99

VOL. 5: BELLY OF THE BEAST TP
ISBN: 978-1-53430-218-1
$12.99

VOL. 6: FATHERHOOD TP
ISBN: 978-1-53430-498-7
$14.99

VOL. 7: BLOOD BROTHERS TP
ISBN: 978-1-5343-1053-7
$14.99

ROBERT KIRKMAN
LORENZO DE FELICI
ANNALISA LEONI
OBLIVION SONG
CHAPTER THREE

CHAPTER ONE
ISBN: 978-1-5343-0642-4
$9.99

CHAPTER TWO
ISBN: 978-1-5343-1057-5
$16.99

CHAPTER THREE
ISBN: 978-1-5343-1326-2
$16.99

MANIFEST DESTINY
VOLUME 6 - FORTIS & INVISIBILIA

VOL. 1: FLORA & FAUNA TP
ISBN: 978-1-60706-982-9
$9.99

VOL. 2: AMPHIBIA & INSECTA TP
ISBN: 978-1-63215-052-3
$14.99

VOL. 3: CHIROPTERA & CARNIFORMAVES TP
ISBN: 978-1-63215-397-5
$14.99

VOL. 4: SASQUATCH TP
ISBN: 978-1-63215-890-1
$14.99

VOL. 5: MNEMOPHOBIA & CHRONOPHOBIA TP
ISBN: 978-1-5343-0230-3
$16.99

VOL. 6: FORTIS & INVISIBILIA TP
ISBN: 978-1-5343-0513-7
$16.99

VOLUME 7 THE DARKNESS GROWS
KIRKMAN
AZACETA
OUTCAST

VOL. 1: A DARKNESS SURROUNDS HIM TP
ISBN: 978-1-63215-053-0
$9.99

VOL. 2: A VAST AND UNENDING RUIN TP
ISBN: 978-1-63215-448-4
$14.99

VOL. 3: THIS LITTLE LIGHT TP
ISBN: 978-1-63215-693-8
$14.99

VOL. 4: UNDER DEVIL'S WING TP
ISBN: 978-1-5343-0050-7
$14.99

VOL. 5: THE NEW PATH TP
ISBN: 978-1-5343-0249-5
$16.99

VOL. 6: INVASION TP
ISBN: 978-1-5343-0751-3
$16.99

VOL. 7: THE DARKNESS GROWS TP
ISBN: 978-1-5343-1239-5
$16.99

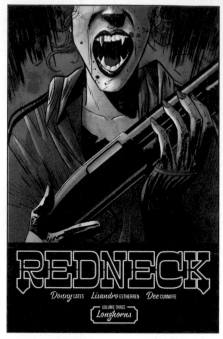